I0653302

Diary of the Lost Teen Age

a novel

by

Tony Gaines

GainsMedia Books

Diary of the Lost Teen Age
by Tony Gaines

© 2012 Tony Gaines

Published by Gainsmedia Books

Original Pencil Illustrations: Joseph Kerezsi, Andre Williams
Cover and Interior Design: Nick Zelinger, NZGraphics.com
Editors: April Hunziker, Craig Toogood
Consulting: Dr. Judith Briles (The Book Shepherd)

ISBN: 978-0-9859045-0-0

Library of Congress Control Number: 2012951272

First Edition

Printed in the United States of America

A sincere dedication to my sister Gail,
who taught everyone around her
the value of family, friendship and love.

CONTENTS

Part I
AT THIRTEEN
Growing Pains ... 11

Part II
AT FOURTEEN
The Wonder Years ... 105

Part III
AT FIFTEEN
All in the Family ... 163

Part IV
AT SIXTEEN
The Young and the Restless ... 281

Part V
AT SEVENTEEN
Valley of the Dolls ... 323

Part VI
AT EIGHTEEN
Days of Our Lives ... 383

Part VII
AT NINETEEN
One Life to Live ... 427

Dear Tom,

I want to thank you for letting me be the first person allowed to read your personal thoughts and observations about what went on in your life as you matured from adolescence to adulthood. While many cultures throughout the Chronicles of the time have considered diary updating to be more often a female pastime, it was both refreshing and enlightening to read about the thoughts, feelings, and emotions coming from the male gender perspective.

Having also grown up in the 1970's, I was naive to the fact that the term "teenager" wasn't always around to describe this fun loving, television watching, sports playing period of adolescent life.

History reveals to us that before the 1850's there was no such thing as "teenagers" as we define the term. Kids either went to work in factories or on family farms, usually before their tenth birthday, and often had children of their own by their teen years. Most people died before they turned thirty-five; the boys often died in the horrors of war, and the girls died giving birth to children.

My many thanks go out to you, Tom, for the gift of gracing my eyes with the pages in your diary as we came into contact with one another, and for the gift you so freely shared with me, which was revealed later in the pages to come in your diary; the gift that keeps on giving.

Love Always, Gina

Part I
AT THIRTEEN
Growing Pains

Saturday, June 10th, 1972

Dear Diary,

I'll never forget my thirteenth birthday. I hadn't had a birthday party since my mother became a Jehovah's Witness when I was five, and I wouldn't have had one this time if not for my Aunt Frances.

Aunt Frances is visiting us from New York, and she gave me a surprise party. She also gave me a new AM-FM portable radio and you, my fancy chocolate-colored diary equipped with a photo of some famous teenage person named James Dean who died young.

"Since you enjoy scribbling all over stuff, I thought it would be a good idea for you to start keeping a diary. James Dean was a hero in my teenage years and he was known for being a rebel without a cause," said Aunt Frances, which sounded okay to me, but, unfortunately, she didn't stop there. "By the way, you'd better share the radio with your brother and sisters."

There are five kids in my family—Mike, Gayle, Carol, Kim and me—and I didn't relish the idea of having to share my first birthday present in years.

Mama was out conducting a Bible study, so we didn't expect any trouble, but she came home early. Her face was red with anger as she walked in on the party. You see, our religion doesn't believe in celebrating birthdays or holidays or in dancing for that matter. James Smith, our next-door neighbor, said his church doesn't mind dancing. They even play bingo. Now that's the kind of church I wish we went to—a church where you have a chance to win money instead of always having to give money away.

Anyway, when Mama came home, all the neighborhood kids split. We had only lived in the neighborhood two years, but that's long enough for them to know that parties are not typical at our house. Mama saw what was going on immediately. She didn't give any of us a chance to explain. Mike and my sisters were afraid they would be punished, so when I ran off to my room, they also beat a hasty retreat. Mama followed her usual pattern. I could hear her winding up and starting in with one of her rages. Aunt Frances knows the rules, but she figured it would all be over before Mama got home.

"What do you think you're doing, involving my children in the devil's business?" Mama screamed. "You know the rules around here."

"I just thought someone ought to celebrate Tom becoming a teenager; he shouldn't be punished for your new religion," Aunt Frances retorted, slamming the door of the freezer where she had put the ice cream.

"I've been a baptized Jehovah's Witness for eight years. When are you going to accept that? And how I raise my children is my business, Frances," Mama said tersely, but a little more calmly.

"Okay, Louise, you're right, but that boy needs to know that someone is glad he was born, and if I want to give him a present to show him I care about him, that's my business," Frances said in a conciliatory tone. "I wasn't trying to sell his soul to the devil, and you know it. Just let him keep the presents, let me take the blame, and let's try to get along for the next week, okay, dear?"

"All right, Frances, I know you didn't mean any harm, but I expect to have my rules respected and followed in my own house. It's hard enough for me to raise these kids with Larry halfway around the world in Vietnam. Can't you try to help out around here, instead of under-mining my authority at every turn?"

"Sure, honey. You know I love you and the kids, and I'll do what I can to help you while I'm here."

Aunt Frances is actually the second oldest sister of 17 kids. Her mother died young, at 49 years old. Aunt Frances was the most mature of the children and assumed the role of family caretaker after her mother's death. She traveled a lot and visited her brothers and sisters frequently after they grew up and left the family home in the back woods of North Carolina. My aunt is tall, sturdy, and lean with a big voice. She never had any children of her own, but everyone calls her "aunty." Her husband was the first person in his family to graduate from college and an engineer on a major ship, but he died in a car crash on their 20th anniversary.

Aunt Frances seems to understand mama's emotional problems, even though she and my mother are so differ-ent that they don't really seem like sisters. Aunt Frances is a feisty, street-smart woman with long, shiny black hair.

Mama's sort of short and dumpy. She's a study in curves, from her Fifties-style bouffant hair to her bulging hourglass figure. My aunt doesn't think religion is the answer to mama's problems but she plays along because it seems to keep mama stable. I must admit that mama is less moody than she used to be, and the more time she spends doing church ministry, the less often she goes into one of her rages.

Mama didn't miss the chance to give us kids some harsh words of warning, though:

"The next time someone throws a party or some kind of worldly function of that nature and I'm not around, you kids had better not even think about joining in! You all know the rules. Shaking your hips to that kind of music is the devil's doing! Unless you all are sure you have another place to live, you'd better mind what I say!"

Just between you and me, Diary, I think she was serious. In fact, all of the Jehovah's Witness parents use the same threat—behave or get out. It sure works on us—any home is better than no home at all.

Well, I've written past the space they gave me under the 10th of June, clear into the 13th, so I guess I'd better call it a night.

Friday, June 16th, 1972

Dear Diary,

Well, there are several empty pages here, but who says a person has to write in their diary every day? I'm just too busy for that kind of routine, so I'll just write whenever I can find the time.

Let me explain a little bit about my history. The kids at school call me an "Air-Force brat," because my father is in the Air Force, and Air Force kids think they've traveled a lot and know it all. I was born in Boston. We lived there six months and then moved to Japan for five years. Then we moved to Hawaii, and mama converted. Since then, our lives have been much different and much busier. It seems like we're at Kingdom Hall every minute we're not in school. We lived in Hawaii another five years before we moved to Texas. We've lived in Abilene, in this nice middle-class neighborhood for a little over two years now.

Mama's been wandering through the house in a daze since we dropped Aunt Frances off at Andersen Regional Airport a couple of days ago. Before she got on the plane, Aunt Frances warned mama to keep taking her medicine.

I know one thing: We've had a much freer lifestyle since Aunt Frances came to visit. For the last week, we've been able to go outdoors without asking permission, play my new radio, and keep up with events in the world without mama scolding us or saying, "Bad associations spoil useful habits."

Then this morning, mama came thundering into the living room, where three of us were listening to the radio and watching television. I could see the resentment in her face when she appeared in the doorway. The veins in her neck popped out, and her face turned bright red. In one fluid motion, she ran over, snatched the radio out of Mike's hand, and threw it into the kitchen trash bin.

"That's where that devil's toy is going to stay!" she shouted. "Ever since we got that radio in this house, that's all I've seen you kids doing with your time! There will be no more tuning your minds to foolish worldly pleasures by listening to that radio all day. And turn that dumb TV set off! Between that radio and the TV set, you kids are either going to go deaf or blind! And, Tom, put your glasses back on. We didn't pay for them to sit around on the coffee table. From here on, I want to see you kids studying your Bible. No more worshipping those foolish devil's instruments."

We all had first-hand knowledge of what Mama can be like when she's not taking her medicine. The room became deathly silent but not for long. Mama barely took a breath before she started in hollering again.

"Where is Carol?" she demanded as she entered the room again. "Why isn't the kitchen clean?"

By the time I turned to respond, she had disappeared. Mike and I share a rebellious streak, and it seemed to us that our short-lived freedom was worth fighting to keep. Mike looked at me.

"She's just on the warpath again. She'll cool down."

"She's just missing dad again," Gayle added.

"Don't just sit there staring at a blank television screen!" she bellowed. "Go outside and find your sister, and then get this living room picked up!"

We were somewhat slow to move, but when objects started sailing out of mama's hands, we picked up speed.

My headphones had landed under the sofa, and as soon as mama left the room, I stooped down to pick them up. Then, I took the radio out of the trashcan. Mike thinks mama's rage is tied directly to the fact that she hasn't received a letter from my father, but I think she doesn't like what she's seeing in us kids nowadays. Ever since Aunt Frances came, something's been brewing with mama. We kids learned a few secrets from Aunt Frances on how to handle her. I think she knows we've been using a little psychology on her, and she resents it. No, mama's not upset over not receiving some dumb letter. Heck, I know for a fact the old man sent a message through his commanding officer to let her know that he'll be coming home soon.

I thought it over some more, and the answer just sort of popped into my mind. No one really expected it to happen, but that harmless little radio is changing our entire family. Never before in our home have children had control of a worldly device. Sure, we're a modern family. We've got a TV set and a record player in our living room, but with all the rules that govern it, such as the "boob tube" is only on about 30 minutes a day. No one in his right mind would ever say that we have "control" over it, though. As for the record player, we're only allowed to play Jehovah's Witness records on it. The radio, though—now that's different. It's small, portable, and easier for us to control. As a result, we're learning more about the outside world, and there's a lot going on. Between the war, the Civil Rights movement, and the changing roles of women in society, everything seems to be in flux.

I bounce back and forth between KRCC and KSEL, the two stations I can pick up. My new friend, Reggie, tells me that if we lived in Dallas, we would be able to hear lots of stations playing soul, jazz, and hippie stuff. Mama's worried that we're going to replace our Bibles with the radio. I don't understand her logic, because the way I see it, you listen to one and you read the other, so why would we replace one with the other?

The afternoon was filled with screaming around our house.

"Mama, I do not need a haircut," Mike said. "This is the style now. Jesus had long hair didn't he? Leave me alone."

Luckily, Mama was too distracted by my sisters shaking their hips to Diana Ross and The Supremes to give him the slap he normally would have had coming. She came completely unglued.

"You girls stop that! What's wrong with you? Are you trying to tempt the devil or anger God? Either way, if I catch you listening to that garbage again, I'll take that radio and paddle those butts you're so proud of," she yelled as she grabbed the radio and held it threateningly over her head.

Then she sent us all to our rooms and made us read Proverbs 22:15 over and over again—*Foolishness is tied up with the heart of a child; the rod of discipline is what will remove it far from them.* She got her belt out of the closet but put it away after we assured her that we understood the consequences of worldly behavior. My mother must have been born in the Dark Ages, when all kids did was sit around reading their Bibles by candlelight before bed. I don't think she understands that it's normal for kids today to dance and grow long hair.

Anyway, all is quiet now. Mama thinks I'm reading my Bible in my room, but I'm really sitting in the corner, listening to the radio while I write.

Friday, June 30th, 1972

Dear Diary,

Monday, my father came home, and boy, did we have a party! We all cried when he got off the C141. All of our neighbors are bragging about President Nixon bringing "the boys" home. He's a real hero around here. With dad back home, we seem to be having another welcome break from mama's rules. Our neighbors were so happy for us that they threw a party.

"This kind of party is okay," mama said, "since there's none of that rock and roll music or dancing going on."

Mama is trying hard to pretend that everything is back to normal, but I have a gnawing feeling in the pit of my stomach that nothing is right. I keep hearing the Beatles sing about revolution, and no matter how hard mama tries, she just cannot seem to keep the worldly revolution out of our home.

My father seems a bit strange since he came back from Vietnam. I can't actually put my finger on the difference, but he's jumpy and silent and runs hot and cold—one minute relaxed, the next working in a frantic, almost panicked way around the house and yard. He was usually so laid back and calm before the war, but now he takes nerve pills every four hours just to make him normal. Sometimes, he drinks with them. Mama gets upset and says he could die from mixing them.

Dad and Mama spend a lot of time in their room these days. My best friend, Charles, says that they're "making up for lost time"—whatever that means. Charles has lots of experience with adult-type matters, so he's probably right. He says he used to slip around and watch his parents in their bedroom all the time, and that's how he knows so much about adult situations. I kind of like it when my parents lock themselves up in their room. It's like a holiday for us kids; we can stay up late or raid the refrigerator without having to look over our shoulders. For the last couple of nights, my brother and I have watched the movies they show on Channel 9.

As a result, I'm getting way ahead of Charles in my knowledge of adult matters. I suspect what our parents are doing is tame compared to the shenanigans on television. Now, I probably have some idea of what's going on in my parents' bedroom, but it's not something I like to think about much.

Friday, July 21st, 1972

Dear Diary,

I'm twenty days short of being thirteen years old and two months. Hair is sprouting down below, and my underarm hair is multiplying rapidly. If that wasn't enough to convince me that I'm getting older, check this out: Mike and I got to go to the Westwood Theater all by ourselves today. As we piled in my parents' brown Ford station wagon, some of the neighborhood kids playing football in the street asked us what movie we were going to see. They recommended *Dirty Harry*.

"Oh, no, you don't," Mama said when we got to the theater and started walking to get tickets for *Dirty Harry*. "You two go see *Ben*. I don't want you watching all that violence. That's not how God meant us to live, and watching movies full of sin is just as bad as forming worldly associations."

Only a parent would make you see a movie about a bunch of rats when you could have seen a movie with real shooting scenes! One time, I asked Aunt Frances if they ever watched shoot'em up movies when they were kids. She said they did, but that it was different; when Roy Rogers and the Lone Ranger shot at someone, they usually missed, or if they didn't, you could tell the person wasn't really hurt, because there was no blood.

My sisters are pretty teed off that Mike and I have more freedom than they do. Those dumb girls don't realize that they're gonna ruin it for us all if they don't stop nagging mama. Sisters, what are they good for? Like the song says, "Absolutely nothing!" Girls should stay home. There's more trouble for them to get into than there is for guys. Our local newspaper, *Abilene Star Reporter*, has stuff on the front page nearly every day about girls being kidnapped. For once, mama knows best. When you think about it, who'd want to kidnap a boy? I bet a kidnapper could get a lot more money for a girl.

I have something else private to write about tonight. I got into my father's cigarettes this week and almost got caught! I found a pack my old man left open on the coffee table and some matches in the bathroom (Who does he think he's fooling in the morning, anyway?). After I'd smoked half a cigarette, I couldn't take any more. I felt nauseous and dizzy; it took over an hour for my head to stop spinning. I can't see how anyone enjoys smoking. If you get that dizzy from smoking just half a cigarette, I can't imagine smoking a whole one. Just then, I heard my parents pulling into the driveway. Talk about some fast thinking. I sprayed about half a can of air freshener around the house. Luckily, Mama thought I'd been cleaning up the house. Gotta go! Gotta find a secret hiding place for you, diary. If Mama ever gets wind that I've been smoking my father's cigarettes, I'll probably be grounded until I'm at least sixteen.

Wednesday, July 26th, 1972

Dear Diary,

Well, here we go again, and luckily, no one has found you so far. Some neat stuff happened this week. I finished reading my third romance novel called *We Live in Secret* by Dorothy Rivers. I've also read *Nobody's Child* by Catherine Airlie and *Where Is Love* by Norrey Ford. Diary, I'm only telling you where I get these books, and hopefully no one else will ever discover that I'm a dumpster diver. I wait for my neighbor, Miss Billie, to throw her trash out on Mondays. Then, I rummage through her garbage before the trash man comes on Tuesdays, and there I find all the romance a boy can read. Miss Billie must have hundreds of novels in her house, because she throws one away almost every week.

It's been one of those weeks when the Kool-Aid flows and the sweat pours.

Football is king in Texas, and about half the boys in Abilene dream of becoming the next great quarterback for the Dallas Cowboys. The guys in our neighborhood play street football every day during the summer, but it's been so hot lately that they haven't been able to finish their games. I always sit by the front porch window, watching their games and wishing I were out there with them. Some of the fellows think I'm a sissy because I won't come out and play, and because I've always got my head in a book, but others know that our religion forbids us from associating with "worldly" children. "Bad associations spoil useful habits."

I hate being a Jehovah's Witness, and I hate having to study the Bible for hours every day. Even though I'm smaller than everyone else, I know I could compete with the guys if given a chance. I may still be under 100 pounds and only 5'3" tall, but I'll catch up one day. Then my long gangly legs will turn into steel, and I'll run that ball faster than anyone's ever seen. I sure would like to know what it feels like to score a touchdown, but, knowing my mother, I probably never will, even if the world does last past 1975.

Boy, that was a narrow escape. I almost got caught writing instead of reading my Bible. I put you under my bed just as Mama came into my room to check to see if I was finished preparing for my Bible talk. Yes, here I am, pouring over the Bible again, but at least I'm studying for a reason this time. I have to give what the Jehovah's Witnesses call "a talk." The overseers only make teenage boys give these dumb talks. Most of us hate it when our turn comes up, but you'd have to be dead before they'd let you slide. They assign you a set of scriptures and make you summarize information from the *Watchtower* to explain the meaning of the verses. You have to give the presentation in front of the entire congregation. According to Charles, the whole thing is just one big brainwashing ploy: the man is just trying to brainwash us kids into believing that God is watching every move we make, even though it's really the man who is watching our every move (God only knows what Charles is talking about half of the time!).

Charles and his sister, Lois, have been at our house for the last two nights. Charles is asleep in my bed right now, wearing my pajamas. I had to lend him some of my clothes because he and Lois arrived at my house in a bit of a hurry. It's all mama's fault. When she converted Charles' mother, she also transformed two reasonably happy teenagers into utterly miserable human beings! It's not enough that Jehovah's Witnesses won't let their children participate in after-school activities; they have all this other stuff up their sleeves, too. Now, they've decided to integrate the two churches in town. Last week, Lois kept interrupting the sermon.

"Integration never works!" she shouted.

"Hold your tongue, child," Pastor Slowley said, but she kept chanting that phrase until the whole congregation was in an uproar. "Ma'am, get control of your child, or I will. This is the result of the kind of lax upbringing these children have had outside of the true faith. The only salvation for your children is the rod and diligent study of our scriptures."

The congregation joined in the pastor's condemnation of their lack of discipline until Mrs. Stevens was in tears, struggling to get a good hold on Lois and simultaneously swatting at her. Finally, the three of them left the sanctuary, Charles and Lois still cursing and spitting. But the argument continued.

Someone in the crowd yelled, "This integration stuff is coming from the top. Why don't we have a say? It's our church, too."

Another angry voice exclaimed, "Who here really believes that it's God's will that we be integrated? The Bible says, 'You shall not sow your field with mixed seed.'"

"Why should we be separated from our Christian brothers when we are forced by necessity to associate with this world of sin?"

People think I'm smart, because they see me reading all the time, and I guess I am sort of smart, but I have to admit that I'm a bit confused about the integration issue. All I know is that when Charles and I were introduced to the new pastor's daughter, I felt like my feet weren't touching the floor. Charles said he felt the same way. Lisa Slowley is a dream. She has creamy skin, bashful green eyes, and a shy, seductive smile. Her father will probably be the head pastor after the two churches integrate. One good thing about it: when I give my talk this week, Lisa will be in attendance. Believe me: Mama won't have to worry about me mispronouncing any of those long Biblical words.

Friday, July 28th, 1972

Dear Diary,

My Bible talk went wonderfully well tonight. Applause thundered from the new congregation.

Also, Charles and I were assigned to help clean up the parking lot before the service, and we found a real diamond ring. Guess who's wearing that diamond ring now? Lisa Slowley! Charles and I gave it to her as a special gift from both of us.

Charles and Lois went back home today. They will try to work things out with their mother about how often they have to go to Kingdom Hall.

I can't write very much tonight because I have to get up early for field service, which is when Jehovah's Witnesses go from house to house selling the *Watchtower* on Saturday mornings. I have no idea why it's called "field service," but Charles says it should be called "shame service." It's humiliating when we knock on a door and a classmate answers. Sometimes, people spit in our faces, or slam their doors on us. But, Mama says not to think about it, just to go on to the next door. According to her, when people spit in our faces or slam doors on us, that's a sure sign that we're preaching the true religion, and the people who don't listen to us are wicked and will be destroyed by God at the end of the world. The idea of Jesus arriving in all his fiery glory used to scare me, but now I can hardly wait; 1975 is fast approaching, so he could come any day now. I hope he comes tonight, so I won't have to go out selling magazines that hardly anyone buys.

Thursday, August 3rd, 1972

Dear Diary,

It's early morning and, as dawn breaks, I'm already wide awake. I've never exactly been asleep. I just lay here all night, dreaming about the day when I'll have all the answers. They took Charles away last night. A chubby welfare lady came and got him. Charles and Lois had a nasty brawl with their mother after they went back home. They roughed her up so bad that she has been in Hendricks Hospital for the past few days. The whole mess happened because of religion. Charles and Lois refused to go to church, and got into a fight with their mother. I can understand their reluctance after the scene last time, but they carried it a bit too far.

Even the police officers were in shock over the incident. They didn't know where to take them, so they drove around Abilene for nearly an hour before they came to our house. The officers said it was the first incident of its kind in Abilene. When the police first dropped them off here, I sort of wished they hadn't. I could hardly stand to listen to Charles boasting about how he hit and kicked his mother. I hate going to the church meetings as much as anybody, but I've never considered punching my mother over it.

When my mother walked past and saw them behaving like that, she jerked the plug right out of the wall, saying, "Television is a bad influence."

While Charles and Lois stayed with us, we got to watch more than our usual one television show every day. Diary, we got to watch a real movie on television—*License to Kill.* The movie was about some good guys roughing up several bad guys. Every time they got to a fight scene in the movie, Charles and Lois would stand up and re-enact how they did that same Kung Fu chop on their mother. When my mother walked past and saw them behaving like that, she jerked the plug right out of the wall, saying, "Television is a bad influence." She may be right, too. Thank God, so far, she hasn't noticed how many fight scenes there are in each episode of *The Three Stooges.* If she ever does, we'll be limited to watching the Dallas Cowboys with my dad on Sundays.

I know I shouldn't be writing curse words, but, brother, it's been hell around here the last two days. Of course, this is not really surprising, since the world in general seems to be going to pot. Kids are going crazy these days, and it's not just American teenagers, either.

Just yesterday, I read about some kids who helped their parents hijack a plane. It boggles the imagination to think that kids my age were actually involved in a hijacking! The world situation makes it look like, maybe, Mama and those church ladies are right about these being the last days.

While we're on the subject of bad news, I have some more to write about. Sunday at church, Lisa Slowley gave the ring back. Her face turned red and tears streamed down her face.

"Lisa, what's wrong? Don't you like the ring?" I asked.

"It's not that. It's my father. He said I had to return it," she sobbed. "I heard him talking to my mother. He said he never would have let me keep it if he'd known that 'black boys' had given it to me. I couldn't believe it, especially after I heard him rehearsing his sermon for today on brotherly love and racial integration. I'm so sorry, Tom."

"It's not your fault, Lisa. I'm not used to the racial rules here in Texas. We never had any problems like this in Japan or Hawaii. I just don't understand, I guess. I never would have guessed your father would object. I'm sorry you got into trouble over it."

I was crushed. I've never felt so humiliated in my entire life. I just stood in the hallway, hugging Lisa, while her father preached about how Christian brothers of all races "are going to have to start showing more love for one another." It hardly even felt real to me. Even now, it seems like a bad dream. It's all so confusing—I thought the idea was to integrate into one society. Instead, it seems like we are becoming more and more separate.

But know this, that in the last days, critical times hard to deal with will be here. For men will be lovers of themselves, lovers of money, self-assuming, haughty, blasphemers, children will be disobedient to parents, unthankful, disloyal headstrong, lovers of pleasure rather than lovers of God.

1 Timothy 3:1-3.

This was the scripture for Sunday's sermon, and from all that I see going on around me, it seems that these really are last days.

I think I'll go out, find a vacant house, and throw rocks at the windows. I hope I break out every one of them. Maybe that will make me feel better.

Thursday, August 10th, 1972

Dear Diary,

After all of last week's problems, I find it a lot simpler to write about this week. Nothing special really happened; I just kept my head tuned in to the radio all week. Bill Wither has a new song on the radio called *Lean on Me*. I must have waited three hours for that corny DJ to get around to playing my request. It's too bad KRBC is the only station in this town playing the latest sounds. Rumor has it that we may get an FM station in March, but I'll believe it when I hear it. You'd have to live in this town to know just how rumors spread.

Some of my friends tell me I'm overreacting to what happened with Charles and Lisa. I guess they may be right. Mr. Decker, my P.E. teacher from last year, said it was "sissy" for boys to get upset. He said God made boys out of "snakes and snails and puppy dog tails," but you know how people like to tell fibs on God's behalf.

Well, Charles won't be coming around anymore. His mom sent him and Lois to live with their grandmother three hundred miles away. I sure hope his grandma isn't one of those mean old ladies who won't let him play football, and makes him go to church with her all the time. Charles really hates that. He's really a smart guy— if he'd only learn you have to go along with grown-ups some of the time in order to get what you want the rest of the time.

I did some more dumpster diving again Tuesday and hit the romance jackpot. I found five books in Miss Billie's trash, and I've already read three of them. I hope to read the other two by the end of the week. I wonder why only women buy romance novels. Are they the only ones who know about love, and is that why men aren't supposed to have yucky feelings?

Tuesday, August 15th, 1972

Dear Diary,

For the last four days, my family and I have been away attending an assembly, which is an event where a lot of people travel from all over to hear different speakers. Jehovah's Witnesses call it an "assembly," but I hear it's similar to what is called a "revival" by other churches. The neat thing about assemblies is that, when the talks are over for the day, you can go back to your motel room and watch cable TV. Jehovah's Witnesses usually have assemblies three times a year. The biggest one is in the summer, and mama considers it our summer vacation. Phooey! That's no way to spend a summer vacation.

I have to admit, though, I did have fun on this trip. I worked in the cafeteria. My job was to deliver French fries with another guy. I can't begin to tell you how many French fries I swiped. There was a long stretch of open space to cross between the kitchen and the dining room. About half way across, we'd take a pit stop and pig out on the trays of hot fries. After four days of that, it wouldn't have bothered me if I never saw another French fry! I could just hear Charles saying, "The white man's got you doing slave labor," as I ran from the kitchen to the cafeteria. I had gotten so used to hearing Charles' voice ringing in my ear, and it seemed odd not to have him around.

I ended up hanging around with some new boys I met from Sweetwater, Texas. Their last name is Medlock, and they come from a big family—seven kids altogether, four girls and three boys. Two of the boys have the same names as my brother and I. Strange, huh? Howard is the oldest and is by far my favorite. Our families have a lot in common, and so do Howard and I. We both enjoy swiping French fries, playing street football, and listening to the radio. Howard knows the words to more songs on the radio than any person I've ever known. He says listening to the radio is his escape when he's frustrated by all of our religious restrictions. By the way, Howard's family might move to Abilene before school starts.

This year's convention focused on integration. I now know more about separation, segregation, integration and race relations in general than anybody needs to know. Howard said it was strange having so many white people at the convention. Because I grew up on an Air Force base, I never noticed all these colors until people around me started pointing them out. Dad drove us to the revival, but he stayed in the room watching cable TV the entire time. Lucky him. At one point, I heard Howard's stepfather, Leonard, try to convert my old man, but Dad just said, "I believe in God, but I lost my religion years ago." Howard's stepfather looked somewhat confused. I didn't quite understand, either.

Howard and I overheard them talking about "white flight" the other day. I'm not so sure exactly what that means, but I'm not as naïve as I once was, either. Vacant houses are springing up in our neighborhood, and when people around here start using words about the color of things, it can only mean something bad is about to happen.

I pray every night that Howard's family will move to our neighborhood. Since Mama will only let me hang out with other Jehovah's Witness kids, and there are three boys in Howard's family, and Charles left his football at our house when the welfare lady took him away, I've started thinking, "I could kill three birds with one stone."

Saturday, August 26th, 1972

Dear Diary,

"...*And the Lord said, let them believe, and they believed.*" I prayed every night for two weeks that Howard and his family would move into our neighborhood, and it happened. No kidding, God works fast! I'm the happiest kid in the whole world, and now mama won't have any worries about me associating with non-Christian kids. God only knows I needed a new Christian-type friend since Charles went away, so Howard will be my new best friend.

I spent this whole week helping Howard's family move in. He and I went together to register for school, and we've had a lot of fun, which I guess we both needed. I know it gave me a new lease on life. Now I can kind of put all the memories of Charles, and all the fun we had, somewhere in the back of my mind. Charles is just words on a page now. I'll probably never even get a letter from him. I know how he hates to write.

I guess this whole experience is part of growing up. Kids seem to learn about life so much earlier than my parents did. My oldest sister, Carol, said, "It's all about change, and if you don't adjust to the changes right away, then the other kids will leave you behind." I don't know where Carol gets all this stuff, but I have to admit she's smart. (We won't tell her though; it might go to her head!)

Next Thursday we get to pick our classes at Mann Junior High, which makes Howard and I feel very grown up. I glanced over the list of classes, and I've never heard of some of the classes they offer. If I can get away with it, I'll choose all P.E. classes and two lunch periods.

I wonder if junior high teachers are mean. I've heard that they're a lot stricter than the elementary school teachers are and they grade harder. The one thing I know for sure is that they make sure your parents see your report cards; they send report cards home through the mail, so you can't change your grades on the way home. Last year, mama found out my brother was flunking out in two subjects just by checking the mailbox. Of course, she didn't much care. "After all," she reminded him, "the world is going to end soon, and you won't need schooling when Jesus comes back." I'm beginning to see how this religion stuff just might work in my favor.

I hope Howard and I get all the same classes. I'm not sure if Howard is my best friend or not. It would seem a little queer to ask him, but it's important to have a best friend, so we'll see.

There's good news and bad news today. First, I saw Howard's sister, Vicky, in the nude yesterday. It wasn't my fault though. I swear to God, it was an accident. Vicky is two years older than Howard and fine as wine. Her body always has some man's eyes on her. She has a high-yellow skin tone with big bright eyes and silky weave hair. Sometimes, she wears her hair in an afro like a radical. She has a sharp tongue, but not a foul mouth, except when she is riled up. Music is her passion, and her hips are always moving. Anyway, I went over to their house, and Howard's younger sister let me in.

On the way to Howard's room, I got mixed up and opened the wrong door—the bathroom door, and there was Vicky, standing in front of the sink without a stitch on! She was washing her hair, and her eyes were covered in shampoo, so she couldn't see me. She thought it was her little sister and said, "Shut the door behind you." Even though it wasn't my fault, I feel guilty about it. I hope God will forgive me. It wouldn't be fair to punish me for sinning by accident.

The other deep, dark secret I have hanging over my head, concerns my brother, Mike. I was poking around in the closet today, looking for my birth certificate to take to school, and found his instead. I started reading, just curious about what time of day he was born, and stuff like that. According to the birth certificate, he was born on Monday, March 14th, 1957, at 11:35 a.m. The next paper I pulled out of the pile was my parents' marriage license, which said they were married on December 21, 1956. It didn't take one of those fancy new calculators to figure out that mama must have been pregnant when she and my father got married.

This piece of information solved a puzzle for me. When Aunt Frances was here this past summer, I over-heard her teasing mama about having known my father for two only months before they got married. People

---

My parents got married in December
of 1956, my brother arrived in March of 1957,
and my parents met in October of 1956.
Sounds like a deep, dark, family mystery to me!

---

might think I'm only a dumb kid, but I do know that it takes nine months to hatch a baby. However, lately, it seems like every time I learn something new, I end up losing, so I'm definitely going to hide you under my mattress from now on. But, one of these days, I'm going to muster the courage to bring up the subject of my brother's birth certificate to my parents. I'll probably have to trick them into telling me the truth about what exactly happened. It'll be worth the trouble, though, just to satisfy my curiosity.

Even with today's modern math tools, I can't quite figure out how it all happened. My parents got married in December of 1956, my brother arrived in March of 1957, and my parents met in October of 1956. Sounds like a deep, dark, family mystery to me!

Saturday, September 2nd, 1972

Dear Diary,

There's something in the air today— a special feeling that's hard to define. Maybe it's because the season is changing and the crisp fall air is doing battle with the remnants of summer heat. Maybe it's the change in routine with school starting up again. Whatever the reason, the normal Saturday routine does not seem half as bad, now that Howard lives in the neighborhood. We still had to go from house to house selling magazines this morning, though. Howard's brother, Thomas, doesn't like field service at all. In fact, there was a shouting match over it between Thomas and their stepfather.

"Why should we introduce ourselves to the neighborhood as freaks right away? School hasn't even started yet, and you're already ruining any chance I have of fitting in at my new school. For crying out loud, Dad, can't it wait until we get settled?", Thomas whined.

My brother saw Thomas' rebellion and took the same attitude.

"Mama, I think I'm old enough now to choose for myself. When are you going to start treating me like a man?" Mike shouted.

"When you start acting like one, boy!" Mama shouted, while the neighbors stood gawking from their yards. "You don't pay for this house or contribute money for bills. All you do is loaf around, listening to the devil's music. You can't even keep your room clean or do your own laundry. If you think you're ready for a man's responsibilities, why don't you spend this morning looking for a new place to live, young man? Now, get in that car before I give you a real reason to complain!"

Thomas and Mike climbed sheepishly into the cars, and not a word was heard from either of them for the rest of the afternoon.

In other news, I got my class schedule: math, science, health, modern history, P.E., lunch—all the usual school subjects. Mrs. Perkins, the scheduling counselor, said they couldn't let us have all P.E. classes and two lunch periods in the same semester, because we wouldn't have any P.E. or lunch periods left for the remainder of the year. I guess she has a point.

Wednesday, September 6th, 1972

Dear Diary,

It is the first week of school and, so far, I've loved every minute of it. It's the first year for me at a middle school, and it's all so different. The only thing bothering me right now is the integration thing. First, it was the churches; now, it's the public schools. Let me give a little background here. Abilene is about 200 miles west of Dallas, in Taylor County. The whole county has a population of about 100,000 people. Dyess Air Force Base is located to the west of the city. The racial makeup of the city is 71.74% White, 8.81% African American, and 19.45% Hispanic.

I've attended Air Force schools on base all my life and we never had any integration problems. They just put all of us in one school and said, "Now go learn something!" I don't see what the big deal is now. All the base kids had to switch over to the newly integrated public schools this year.

Being at this new school makes me feel all grown up. If you don't want to eat in the cafeteria, the teachers don't make you. If you want to munch on hamburgers and hot dogs everyday for lunch, nobody cares. And if you throw in the foxy girls walking around the halls every time the bell rings—well, it just makes a fellow never want to go home.

Some of the girls that I know from last year changed a lot over the summer break. At least three of them grew breasts as big as my mama's. Can you just imagine what their chests will look like after next summer?

It took a great amount of self discipline, but I waited until Tuesday evening to ask Mama why she was only married three months before she had my brother. I thought she was going to keel over and die right there on the kitchen floor.

"That's none of your _____ business. You're getting too _____ smart for my own good. I will not be interrogated by my own son. You just wait until your father gets home. I'm sure he'll know how to deal with you," she yelled, leaning over the dinner table and clutching me by the collar so that I could feel her breath on my face. I have to admit, I enjoyed aggravating her, but I didn't think about how Mike might feel. As it turned out, the situation really put a damper on his spirits.

As soon as Mama started to clear the table, the girls started teasing Mike.

"Maybe you were adopted," Carol taunted.

"Yeah, you sure don't look like daddy," Gayle chimed in.

Then, they both started chanting, "Mikey was adopted! Mikey was adopted!" until Mama walked back in and smacked Carol on the back of the head.

Then she grabbed Gayle by the chin and said, "You girls ought to know better. That is your brother. Apologize and go to your rooms. You, too, Tom. No dessert tonight, and no TV for the rest of the week."

Mike got so peeved that he wouldn't even go to church tonight. Mama didn't push the issue, as she normally would have. I have a feeling that trouble will continue brewing over the subject now that I've opened my big fat mouth. It's a good thing my father's away on a special duty assignment. Can you imagine what would have happened if I'd popped that question in front of both of them? Our parents and teachers preach this crap about how "honesty is the best policy," when all of the time they're hiding behind a wall of lies of their own.

The Hispanic dudes have claimed their own private restroom at school. Howard and I passed by it yesterday, and he dared me to go in, but I'm nobody's fool. Rumor has it that it's so rough in that restroom that not even the teachers go in. Besides, there was smoke billowing out every time the door opened, and I learned that where there's smoke, there's fire.

I saw a fight today between two Hispanic dudes in front of the Hispanic boys' restroom. It was my first time to see a real fight. Rumor around school is that all Hispanic dudes carry switchblades. During the fight, someone in the crowd screamed, "He's got a knife!" and everyone started to scatter. But, to tell you the truth, Diary, I saw the whole fight, and there wasn't very much blood. You know how the rumor mill goes around Mann Junior High; by tomorrow, the story will be that someone went to the hospital or died.

I am awfully glad Howard is huge for his age, a grade ahead of me, and has the biggest hands I've ever seen. Those hands are the first thing anyone notices. Coach Hayes stopped him and me in the hall the other day and asked Howard if he would like to play tight end for the Falcons. Howard was embarrassed to death, but he had to turn down the offer and explain about the religious situation at home.

Thursday, September 7th, 1972

I woke up this morning worrying about what's going to happen. When I was younger, I only worried about what would happen on that particular day. Now, I worry about the future in general. One thing I still don't understand is why grown-ups look like they'd like to smack you when you ask them a simple question.

I did some more fishing in Miss Billie's trash and recovered four more novels. *Believe in Tomorrow* by Nan Saquith, *Eve's Own Eden* by Karen Mutch, and *O Kiss Me, Kate* by Valerie Thian were all great reads. But the best one was *Romeo and Juliet* by William Shakespeare. It was really mind blowing at the end when the two main characters took their own lives, reuniting their feuding families. I was in tears. I learned a lot about romance from reading that novel, and can hardly wait for Miss Billie to take her trash out again.

Friday, September 8th, 1972

Que Paso! I'm learning a new language at school—Spanish. "Que Paso?" means "What's happening?" Lou Sosa and Robert Jimenez, two cool Mexican guys in my art class, taught me some other words, but I don't think they're appropriate to write down on good paper.

This week something terrible happened in the Olympics. The headlines in the paper read, "Eleven Israeli Athletes Killed." This morning, my father left the newspaper in the bathroom, which he calls his "library." I always get second dibs on the newspaper, and it does provide great entertainment for a fellow when he's doing No. 2. From what I could gather, the Israeli athletes were gunned down at the Munich Olympics by a group of Palestinians because of their religion. John Lennon said, "Imagine no religion," in one of his songs, and I finally understand what he meant.

The newspaper said the police killed all the bad guys, but the way my teacher explains it, they don't know who the good guys are—the Israelis or the Palestinians. You know it's a confusing world when your own teacher doesn't know who the bad guys are! If everybody would just believe in God, I bet the devil wouldn't ever make people do things like that.

This week was more like real school. The teachers started right in, making us get out text books for classes and handing out lists on how much money each subject's supplies would probably cost. Some poor kids couldn't afford the school supplies, so the school is just going to fork over the money for them. Mama was hot under the collar when I gave her mine. "When I was in school, all we ever needed was a pencil and paper," she complained, "and I certainly don't have any money to be donating to the school for all this extra stuff."

Mama is always complaining about money. She says she prays every day that Armageddon will come today. I hope not, though. I haven't had the chance to do all the things I want to do before I see Jesus. Mama needs to learn that money is not "the root of most evil" and that this is the Seventies, not the Forties—today's students need more than just a pencil and paper. Personally, I get sick and tired of hearing all the parents around here in our neighborhood complain about money being too tight. My solution is to let the schools provide every student with what they need. Our school has plenty of money – it charges 45 cents for a hamburger, and that hamburger line always stretches plumb around the building.

Howard's coming over to study the *Watchtower* with me, but we're really going to listen to the radio and just pretend that we're studying.

Saturday, September 9th, 1972

Today was a hot day but not weather-wise. I scoped out this gorgeous girl, Susan, who seems to be giving me that "Lisa Slowley" smile in my modern history class. I know that smile led to trouble for me last time, but there won't be any rings involved this time. I figure, maybe, by next Saturday, I might have enough money saved to buy two lunches. It'll take some guts, but I have the guts of John Wayne. I'll ask Susan to sit beside me at lunch, and then I'll offer to buy her lunch. I know this plan sounds bold, but that's what I see the upperclassmen doing.

Maybe I'd better think it over some more, though. I might just be imagining that Susan is smiling at me. I'd hate to be crushed by a girl this soon after school started. I'd be so embarrassed if she said, "No!" If she told me to get lost, I'd probably have to quit school.

Sunday, September 10th, 1972

Howard was sure I would chicken out about asking Susan for a lunch date, but I did it. Our modern history teacher had brought his World War II medals to class with him. Just a few minutes before lunchtime, I saw Susan standing alone, looking at his Purple Heart. At first, as I walked toward her, a scary voice in my head kept singing, "It's just my imagination running away with me." Then, right as I got close to her, the class bell sounded, startling me and causing me to shout her name. She jumped back a little in surprise. Talk about being totally embarrassed—she must have thought I'd lost my mind. My tongue stuck to the top of my mouth and when I pried it loose, words gushed out garbled and stuttering.

"Would you like to have lunch with me?" I said.

"Sure," she replied, but then she said, "Not today, though. I've already promised another girl I'd sit with her. Ask me again tomorrow."

There are three voices in my head these days, and I've named them "Spooky," "Smoothy," and "Swagger."

"A heavenly angel—that's what she is," I thought to myself, as she turned her beautiful, smiling eyes away and floated down the hall toward our modern history class, leaving her books behind her. It felt like I stood there transfixed for nearly five minutes before I ran after her with her books.

There are three voices in my head these days, and I've named them "Spooky," "Smoothy," and "Swagger." Spooky seems to rent the most space in my head these days. Thursday morning, as I jogged down the hall, they all spoke at once. Swagger jumped into my head, confident Susan would accept. Then, Spooky arrived out of nowhere, making me feel that I'd never be brave enough to ask her a second time, and even if I did, she would reject me. Smoothy reminded me that it's not the best-looking dude in the school who gets the girl, it's the dude in school who asks the girls that actually gets the girls.

Friday, the lunch hour belonged to Susan. I lost my appetite, knowing this glorious creature was sitting beside me. But she disappeared at the sound of the bell, leaving me with an empty lunch tray. The memory of her parting words still makes my heart skip a beat, as I repeat it in my head over and over. "We'll have to do this again," was all she said. In fact, those were the only words she spoke during our entire lunch date. However, those words continue to burn in my mind.

Tuesday, September 12th, 1972

I awoke Monday morning, and still everything seemed so incomplete. I thought to myself, "What about love, and where does it fit into the picture?" I couldn't just let her say, "We'll have to do this again," and never know when. Spooky was talking all day—"Is this love, and is it really worth getting all worked up about?" Swagger's answer was a resounding "Yes," and he soon convinced me that, in spite of our silent lunch date, I had indeed impressed her, and would probably see her again soon.

At the beginning of third-period math, I slipped the newspaper off of Mrs. Wells' desk. We had been studying the results of the polls in this year's presidential election in Mr. Moore's history class, so I read everything on the front page that dealt with the election results. I've never concentrated so hard in my life.

Later, Mr. Moore asked a question about the election results. I raised my hand, stood up, and totally blew his socks off. "Mr. Nixon had a strong hold on the country because of his effort to withdraw the American troops from Vietnam." I knew I had made an impression. This time I didn't have to ask Susan to lunch; she was waiting for me by the door when the bell rang. Now, I know the secret to keeping her interest. From now on, I'll study, study, study! I only wish that I had Susan in every class together, instead of my daydreaming through my other classes. I'd probably be an A student. I used to make straight A's, but ever since we became Jehovah's Witnesses and found out that the world will end by 1975, I've lost my interest in school.

Thursday, September 14th, 1972

Mike says only sissies keep diaries. I asked my English teacher, Miss Weaver, about it, and she advised me not to pay any attention to what he said. Miss Weaver also taught me a new word—"deception." She said it's all around us, and we have to be aware of when we're being deceived. She kept trying to explain how President Nixon is deceiving the country with Watergate. Then she grabbed the newspaper from her desk and pointed to an article about three large steel companies that were indicted for price fixing.

Miss Weaver must have needed someone to talk to, because she went on and on about deception and the lack of trust in our society. All I really wanted to know was whether or not I was a sissy for keeping a diary! Just before I approached her about the diary issue, she was talking to another teacher about how close she is to a pension. Miss Weaver wears her hair pinned up in a bun, and her glasses were made in the Fifties. She said she still loves teaching, but that she doesn't know how to deal with the pregnant students, disrespectful behavior, or stoned teens in her classroom.

Miss Weaver thought it was a swell idea for me to keep a diary. She even gave me names of all kinds of people who kept diaries before, who lived hundreds of years ago, and people still like to read them. Just think, Diary, maybe a hundred years from now, someone might read my words. I only hope I'm dead and gone by that time, so that I won't be embarrassed.

Friday, September 15th, 1972

Susan and I are doing great. She even lets me walk her to class after lunch. Boy, it seems I finally have a real girl-friend. Still, I don't dare put my arms around her or do any of the funny stuff I see older boys doing. Susan might think I'm weird if I try something funny with her.

Howard has found a group of guys his size to eat lunch with. Those punks always seem to eat close to where Susan and I sit. When Susan isn't looking, they make goo-goo eyes behind her back. They're so childish—kids in grown-up bodies, my father would say. Although I now consider

Susan my girlfriend, I've never officially asked her to "go with me." The fact is, I don't really know what it means to "go with" someone, but it sounds too serious for me. Besides, my parents would kill me if they knew I was sharing my allowance and lunch money with Susan.

Saturday, September 16th, 1972

I've been too distracted lately in class. We finished studying about that election stuff yesterday in modern history and moved on to busing today. I have never noticed before just how deeply our neighborhood is involved in the busing debate. I took my eyes and mind off of Susan, for a change, and paid close attention to Mr. Moore's entire lecture.

I was up early today. On Saturdays, I don't usually see the sun until seven o'clock, when Mama makes us get up, so we can be the first people out selling magazines. But today was different; my eyes popped open at about five o'clock. First, I heard my father getting his gear together for a fishing trip with Mr. Harrison. Then, I heard Mike and Mama shouting at the top of their lungs over whether or not Mike had to go out for field service. That cowardly old man of mine wouldn't take up for my brother, and Mama forced Mike to go. I just lay there in bed wishing it was some other day.

Like me, most of the kids at school don't feel like they know their parents anymore. In our neighborhood now, it seems like the adults are making the subject of how we get to school a major issue. If they knew what takes place after we get to school, they would have a real reason to be concerned. Even President Nixon is involved in this busing mess. Mr. Moore says that he doesn't have school-age kids, so he doesn't really understand. He also said, "The president should tend to his Watergate mess." I don't think Mr. Moore likes Nixon very much. Mr. Moore thinks "President Nixon has lost touch with the American people."

Monday, September 18th, 1972

We took a vote in modern history, and over 90 percent of the class said busing was alright with them. Mr. Moore commented that most of us have been in integrated classes already, anyway. It's funny how no one ever mentions brown students; it's always black or white. I guess people don't really care what school brown students attend. The subject of busing has me thinking more about race than before. Just like that song, "Black and White," by Three Dog Night: "The ink is black and the pages are white, and put them together and we learn to read and write."

Tuesday, September 19th, 1972

I'm grounded. I just had one hellish scrap with Gayle. Mama sent both of us to our rooms, though it's only half past seven. The feud started brewing early this morning and finally boiled over this evening. I don't know why, but I always feel sort of bad after I have a scrap with a girl, and being grounded doesn't help matters. Since my father had cable TV installed earlier this week, we get 10 channels instead of three boring network channels. We turned on the television set to watch cartoons and were just changing the channel when Gayle piped up.

"Hey, I'm watching *The Flintstones*. Hands off! I was here first," Gayle whined.

"We watched that yesterday," Carol said. "Besides, this is a repeat. Let's watch something else."

"Yeah, let's watch *Fat Albert*," Mike chimed in.

"No! I was here first; I get to decide what we watch. Those are the rules of the television," Gayle retorted.

"That's ridiculous!" I shouted. "You've already seen this one, and there are three of us who want to watch something else. You aren't the boss of the TV."

"The TV rule is first come, first serve. I woke up first, so I get to choose the station."

Everyone else was going to let her get away with it, but not me! As soon as she went into the kitchen to get a bowl of cereal, I changed the channel to *Fat Albert*. Boy, was she pissed! Tough cookie! I'm bigger than she is, and like Mr. Moore says, "In our society, might makes right." When Gayle saw what I had done, she made a swipe to change the channel back, but she knew I wasn't fooling around when I flung her away from the television set. When Mama walked in, I had my feet propped up on the coffee table, and Gayle was sobbing red-faced on the floor. Mama turned the TV off and swung around with her face in a scowl.

"You two get out of my living room! I told you this was the devil's instrument! Look at you two, fighting like savages! Go clean your rooms and be thankful that your punishment's not worse!" she screamed, her chest heaving.

Mike had tried to warn us that we ought to be thankful to be able to watch television before field service, but we didn't listen. I think our punishment would have been worse, but Mama didn't trust herself not to go too far.

Then, tonight after supper, Gayle pulled the same stunt. Channel 9 was advertising a new movie for tomorrow called *Love Story*. When I suggested it for family viewing hour, Gayle jumped up and claimed she'd already picked some other movie for the same time. That was a spiteful lie! That's when I got even with her. When no one was looking, I reached over and kicked her, but not very hard. So, she hit me across the face with the TV guide. If the old man hadn't warned me never to hit a girl, Gayle would have gotten a bloody nose for sure. But, there's no rule against kicking them, so I kicked her harder the next time. Mama gave us another long lecture and sent us to our rooms, grounding both of us, and no television for life.

I just hope she forgets about our punishment by tomorrow; I just have to see *Love Story*. I don't know anything about love. I tried asking Mike about love, and he laughed at me. Howard actually spit on me for asking him.

"Watch that movie, *Love Story*, from the way Channel 9 has been advertising it all day, we're bound to learn something," was my father's response.

Susan will be so impressed on Monday, once she finds out how much I know all about romance. You can only learn so much from reading novels, but once I actually know how it's played out on the screen, I'm sure I'll know how it's all supposed to go.

Sunday, October 1st, 1972

I just got done washing the supper dishes. Sundays are considered special days—I think because the Dallas Cowboys play—so we always have a big dinner. My old man never misses a Cowboys game, and I'm right there with him for every play. It was my turn to do the dishes, so I stayed longer at the table and ate two extra helpings of everything. Still, I can't be accused of overeating, because I still had room in my stomach for a little more. I just found out that overeating is considered a sin today, when the preacher recited a long list of sins. There are a lot of sins a person can commit without even knowing it. Who'd ever have guessed that overeating is a sin?

The big news in the *Abilene Reporter* and on all of the TV stations is that President Nixon has been lying—another sin. Every time you turn on the TV, the news is talking about Watergate. In my opinion, they should give the president a break. Channel 9 has the only female TV anchor, Barbara Walters. She said that Nixon's done such a horrible job that a lot of the people in the country don't like him anymore. My dad says the whole damn world is going to hell, and Pastor Slowley agrees, though he thinks our church will be saved. It scares me to think about the fact that my father doesn't attend our church. Does that mean he's going to die? I wonder whether this Armageddon thing will kill Susan, too; she doesn't go to our church, either.

My dad is okay most of the time. He's always been quiet, but he never talks about Vietnam. He takes a pill now and then, but it's become rare. He smokes around the house and in the car, but nothing ever really seems to get to him. You'd think he'd be too smart to smoke, since he was valedictorian of his class. He has two older brothers, Uncle Frank, who is in the Air Force, and Uncle Walter (Jr.), who still lives with their parents in South Carolina. My mother says Uncle Walter and his parents are "alcoholics," but it doesn't seem to bother my old man, or if it does, he never lets on to her about it. I don't think he worries much about things like the end of the world, sins, or meeting St. Peter; he only worries about whether Dallas will beat the Washington Redskins.

Mike, too, has missed church three out of the past four Sundays. He's also missed field service, lately. Once he found out about all the trickery with the dates on the birth certificate, he sort of quit on church all together. I think he's pissed off at my parents for lying to him. Mike said no one knows what's going on down here on earth, so no one can possibly tell him what it's like in heaven. My parents think he's become a radical, but I know the truth— Mike got a part-time job and works on the weekends.

Just to be on the safe side, I've decided to watch my sins a little more closely. I wouldn't want this Armageddon thing to catch me off-guard. Let's see: Two Saturdays ago, I know I committed three sins. First, I swiped a beer out of the refrigerator while Dad and his co-workers were playing dominos. It was the first time I ever drank a beer, and it'll probably be the last time; beer tastes yucky and has a nasty aftertaste. I don't know my father and his friends like it so much. Then, I took two allowances out of my father's wallet. And third, I switched price tags on the winter gloves at Kmart, so I'd have enough money for all the other junk I wanted to buy. Maybe I'll be okay if I can keep my sins under three a day. That will be hard, though, now that I know that overeating and listening to worldly music are sins.

The wages of sin are death, from Romans chapter 6, verse 23 was the topic of Pastor Slowley's sermon this Sunday. It was as if he was reading my mind as he looked around the church, seeming to single me out as words of warning came from his lips.

Sunday, October 8th, 1972

I made a 98% on Friday's math test, which is the best grade I've made on one since I've been at this school. I usually average around 90% on math tests. I could hardly believe it when Mrs. Fields handed my test back to me, and she was pleased with how excited I was. She just kept saying, "Very good, Tom, very good. I told you, you're a gifted student, and you can do anything if you try." Studying really works! Howard made a 64 on his math test, but he was reluctant to show it to me after he'd seen mine. I bet he'll study next time.

On Monday, Mike received his first paycheck from his dishwashing job at Sambo's Restaurant. He made a whopping $46 in two weeks, and he doesn't even wash the dishes by hand. They've got this machine that does all the work. He went out and bought all kinds of groovy new albums with the money. Some of the music he brought home is by people I've never heard of, like Sly and the Family Stones, Gilbert O'Sullivan, and Earth, Wind, and Fire. He bought one album by a guy who has a girl's name, Alice Cooper.

As for school these days, things are getting a little frightening. I think the older black students are collecting weapons to start a fight with the white students, and both sides are trying to recruit the brown students. They call it a "race riot," and if you ask me, it's the stupidest idea I've ever heard. When I asked one of the black upperclassmen why they want to have a race riot, he replied, "I don't actually know, it's just a school tradition, I guess." That's the dumbest answer I've ever heard.

Thursday, November 9th, 1972

There was quite a scene on the bus home today. It all started in school with some scuffling in the hallways between the black and white upperclassmen. It was pretty tame really—just some pushing and shoving and cruising the restrooms. It all came to a boil on the ride home from school. Bruce Smith said the wrong word too many times, and that's when Ray Sneed surprised him with a quick sucker-punch to the nose. There was so much blood coming from Bruce's nose that the driver, Mr. Sosa, stopped to put Bruce off the bus so he wouldn't bleed on everyone.

During lunch, some of the older blacks tried to convince me to participate in their race riot. They kept telling me about how white people used to keep black people in chains and whip us. They almost had me talked into it, but David, a white friend of mine, persuaded me that we should be fighting on the same side. He's also an Air Force brat. The older boys started laughing at us and told us to get lost until we were real men.

Susan was absent today, so we went to our fifth-period study hall early. Before class started, we sat in our desks discussing how stupid the upperclassmen were with their stupid riots. Surely we won't be so stupid when we get older. It's ridiculous that the upperclassmen play football on the same team for a whole season, and then, right after the season ends, they started this race riot business. Maybe if these guys hadn't used their heads as battering rams, they would know that race riots are not a tradition in Abilene at all. In fact, Abilene was mostly protest-free up until recently.

Friday, November 17th, 1972

I finally saw *Love Story*. It's very romantic but sort of sad. It's about a young couple, played by Ryan O'Neil and Ali McGraw, but mostly about this 25 year-old girl who dies at the end. She is very pretty and smart and loves music. Oliver, a student from Harvard Law School, meets Jennifer, and they fall in love. They get married but have to be very poor because Oliver's father doesn't like Jennifer and takes Oliver out of his will. At the end, Oliver says, "Love means never having to say you're sorry." I think I'm too young for this love stuff, because I always find myself having to say I'm sorry for something stupid that I've done.

It's a school day, but the principal cut school short because of all the racial strife and also because of the energy crisis. There were three fights at school today before the lunch bell even rang. Two of the fights were between blacks and whites, and the other one involved a black and a brown. I think the brown and the black fight is an indication that the browns are siding with the whites this year.

After watching that fight this morning, I didn't dare walk Susan, who, by the way, is Hispanic, to any of her classes. The color of her skin never mattered to me, but I think she's pretty upset with me for avoiding her. She has to understand that the rioting has me a little intimidated.

Early this afternoon while our parents were out shopping at the commissary, Mike and I played the album he bought, by the group Sly and the Family Stones, on the family stereo. One song, *Everyday People*, really got my attention. Here are some of the words:

There is a yellow one that won't
Accept the black one
That won't accept the red one
That won't accept the white one
Different strokes for different folks
And so on and so on and
Scooby dooby dooby
We got to live together

It doesn't sound like devil music to me. Mama's wrong, and so is Pastor Slowley. They just don't want us listening to that music because it tells us something they don't want us to know.

People are getting more suspicious of the President. At the press conference he made a remark to the press today that made a lot of people shake their heads. This Watergate is in the news a lot these days. No one seems to know a lot about watergate but they sure sound like they think it's going to get bigger by the way the press keeps hounding round.

The way Mr. Moore explains it is that in politics, just like in football, you want to win, but you still have to play by the rules, and it's against the rules to take unfair advantage of the competition. Nixon was afraid the Democrats would win the next election if he played fair, so he had some people break in to the Democratic campaign offices and steal some papers, but they got caught. They didn't fink on Nixon, though, at least not at first. I'll definitely have to keep an eye on this story.

Saturday, November 18th, 1972

Susan broke up with me yesterday. She was angry that I haven't been eating with her or walking with her in the halls. I got her phone number off of the class roster and called her this evening, but I couldn't convince her to take me back.

She said, "I want a guy who isn't afraid to stand up for what he believes in."

"I'll be dying for what I believe in, if I'm seen with you right now, and so will you," I responded.

"If you're not talking to me, eating with me, or walking me to class anyway, I don't know how you'll notice that we're broken up at all. *What's the point?*", she said, and hung up the phone before I could reply.

I guess we're finished. I couldn't make her the promise she most desperately wanted to hear, especially after I saw the two black college students on the evening news that got killed during riots in Baton Rouge.

Monday, November 20th, 1972

Abilene's famous these days on the national news. Some newscasters are even suggesting that the rioting in Abilene is far worse than the riots in other Southern areas. Most of the kids at school find it amusing that we're on the news, but I'm not laughing. I'd rather forget this gloomy episode ever happened.

Susan's sparkling brown eyes were filled with tears on Monday, as we came face to face for the first time, realizing what we'd lost. It seems that peer pressure has forced us to take opposite sides in a game we never wanted to play.

On Wednesday, the principal announced that two groups of National Guardsmen would be sent in to control the students if the fighting doesn't stop. The younger students aren't really involved, but we have to play along with the older kids. Fortunately for us, most of the violence is in the high schools. Losing Susan is enough to serve as a constant reminder of what racial hatred causes.

I can't get her out of my head. Donny Osmond may call it "puppy love," but that's too cute a name for what I'm feeling. I just sit around listening to the wind swirling against my window and wishing it would carry Susan and me away with it. I really miss Susan and her habits, like the way she always ordered a Coke, medium fries, and hamburger with no lettuce. She taught me compassion, but that goes out the window every time I catch the sight of her fingers clasped in some other guy's hand. How can society tear us apart like this?

Thursday, November 23th, 1972

The wind is blowing, giving West Texas notice of an early winter. As if the cold front weren't enough, the "cheer" of the holiday season is upon us, but it doesn't seem very cheerful to me. I usually hate November because everyone celebrates Thanksgiving except us. But this year I'm relieved that I don't have to be cheerful or thankful. There isn't much for me to be thankful for, except having an extra day off from school and the chance to watch the Cowboys on TV. Dallas lost, which put my father in a foul mood.

Still, there's something magical about this season that encourages peace among Americans of all ethnicities. Even the conflicts at school have largely subsided. In fact, there hasn't been any violence at school for over a week. It's little solace for me, though; Susan still refuses to cast her brown eyes in my direction.

If I could do it all again, the pressure wouldn't have gotten to me so easily, and I'd wake up each morning knowing I had a dream of my own waiting for me in the school yard. I haven't had a decent night's sleep for nearly a week. Instead, each night I call the local DJ and request a song from Mike's new album, "Alone Again, Naturally." It's uncanny how the song agrees with my situation these days. When Mike first brought the album home, I said, "Who the heck is Gilbert O'Sullivan?" Now, he's the guy singing me to sleep each night.

The people of our generation relate to music differently than our parents did. Our scruples, morals, and principles are reflected in our music, just as theirs were, but our attitudes toward everything have changed—sex, authority, education, and even the government. Times are changing fast, and musicians stress the need to "be who you want to be." Everyone is reaching for a new understanding, and that understanding is long overdue. God only knows that the old traditions planted in us have only caused stagnation and stunted our growth.

This week lacked excitement, at least until about two hours ago. My dad was so depressed by Dallas' loss that he mixed his nerve pills with booze. He could hardly stand up by the time Mama got home from Bible Study. The way he staggered around the room and slurred his words was hilarious. Those pills must be strong stuff. My folks had a terrible argument. Dad staggered and hit his head on the bedpost as he passed out. Mama started to call an ambulance, but once she saw that he was alright, she hung up the phone and walked away. The whole scene ruined my entire evening, so I decided to escape to my room and write. I think that fight has been brewing for a while. They're always arguing over money and religion. It seems that money, race, and religion are capable of destroying any relationship.

Monday, December 11th, 1972

I'm still not over losing Susan. I never thought this would hurt so long, but fortunately there are signs that I am starting to recover.

Report cards are due to arrive any day now. I've already figured out what my grades will be: five A's, one B, and one D. The D is in study hall. Yes, a D in study hall. I've been busy thinking up excuses to tell my dad before he gives me the third degree and a serious punishment. I can already hear it: "How on earth did you get a D in study hall?" This is one time when I wish he was a Jehovah's Witness and believed that the world will end before 1975. I can't tell him the truth.

Study hall is the easiest class there is. Unfortunately, study hall follows lunch, so I'm tired—Strike one. And, before Susan dumped me, I was usually too busy daydreaming to study—Strike two. Also, David talks to me during study hall—Strike three. Napping, daydreaming, and talking in study hall are considered serious sins by Mrs. Hamlet, so she gave me a D.

Saturday, December 16th, 1972

Friday the 13th is usually considered unlucky, but Friday the 15th was my day of doom. It seemed like bad luck haunted me from the moment I placed my feet on the floor. First, my left shoelace snapped. Then, I missed breakfast. Not ten minutes later, I got involved in watching TV and missed the bus. I was so mad at myself; I couldn't believe I had it in me to do something so childish. I've never even lost my lunch money! The worst part was mama having to call the old man home from work just to take me to school. Boy, was he pissed!

The morning was just the tip of the iceberg. I arrived at school with only 20 minutes remaining before first period ended, so I decided to wait outside until the bell rang. Just my luck—I was looking at the football trophies, when our 300-pound principal, Mr. Jenkins, walked up and asked, "Why aren't you in class, son?"

The words stuck in my throat, and before I knew it, he was hauling me into his office on a charge of cutting class. Luckily, the school has a new policy of notifying the parents before they can paddle you, or I'd have been spanked just for being curious. Fortunately, my mother confirmed my alibi.

Boy, you should have seen the surprised expressions of the students in my first-period class when they thought I'd managed to get away with cutting. Instantly, my luck changed. I went from being a delinquent to a hero. But my claim to fame ended as swiftly as it came. Lou (Susan's new, older, Mexican boyfriend) and one of his mean amigos showed up at my locker as I was getting my books for second period.

"*Bam!*", I heard, as Lou grabbed the collar of my blue-jean jacket and slammed my head up against my locker. I was petrified.

"All I've heard about from Susan since I took her as my girlfriend is you. If you don't come up with some way to get your name off her lips, I'll figure out a way to cut you out—literally. Do you understand?" Lou hollered, not six inches from my face.

I nodded as he eased his stranglehold. I saw Susan shaking behind him. Her usually beautiful tan complexion was ashy and pale. The terrified expression on her face set off a spark in me. Lou grabbed her hand, and the trio walked down the hall.

The steam in my head caused my feet to follow them. Susan and her two chaperones stopped in front of the Hispanic boys' restroom. They gave her the "stay-and-wait" signal as they entered the smoke-filled bathroom. It was at that moment that the spark inside me grew into a raging fire. Love, honor and respect, all of the traits Susan had once revealed in me, swelled to the surface and gave me courage.

I wanted to use some of these convictions to defend the girl that had originally given them to me. I thundered into the smoke-filled room with righteousness on my side. By the time the air cleared, Lou's nose was bloody and he lay curled up on the floor. I don't know how many times I hit him or how I managed to get him on the floor—he's nearly twice my size, but I was still hitting him when Mr. Jenkins pulled me off. This time, in his office, Mr. Jenkins didn't want to hear my story, nor did he offer to call my parents. He simply expelled me for three days.

I came home to an empty house, thank God. Mama had already left for a full day of field service. It's just past one o'clock and the jury is still out on what kind of punishment I'll receive once my parents find out I've been expelled. Mike came home a few minutes ago.

"The news about the fight is all over the high school," he said. "They've declared you a hero, little brother. I didn't know you cared for race riots." I tried to explain to him what really happened, but he just went on and on about me being the next Malcolm X. Finally, I'm a hero, but no one understands that I was fighting for love, not hate. I just wish everybody else would see it the way it really happened.

Tuesday, December 19th, 1972

Today, I served out the final day of my sentence. At first it was unclear whether I'd won the battle or lost the war, or both. I didn't receive the typical punishment of being grounded in my room or no TV for a week. Instead, on Monday morning mama said she wasn't about to give up her full-time ministry status to stay home and babysit me. However, the thought of me watching the tube all day during my punishment didn't sit too well with her, either. So, after *The Little Rascals* was over and all the other kids had left for school, I noticed her pacing around the kitchen. Suddenly, the pacing stopped. She walked over and stood between me and the screen.

Then, she launched into one of her tirades. Suddenly, she grabbed the remote control.

"There's no pardon for you, Mister. I knew this cable TV would eventually turn into a blessing in disguise," she said sarcastically, changing the channel to Jimmy Swaggert's station. She continued with mock-politeness, "Tom, for your punishment, I want you to watch and report to me each day on what mistakes Jimmy Swaggert makes in his sermons."

I was in shock. I had planned on having three fun-filled days of watching all the game shows that I'd heard about but never seen, but instead I was being forced to listen to a TV preacher and find errors in his sermons. His first sermon was on the evils of modern music and its secret agenda to cause teens to take drugs and have unholy sex.

The sound of a horn tooted outside. Mama's friends had arrived to pick her up. Before she left, though, she handed me a pen, a notepad, and the Bible.

"Take notes," she commanded. "I'll have questions for you later." Then, she took the key out of the cable box and locked the channels. Still puzzled, I delved into my assignment. Soon, the injustice of the situation began to distract me from my assignment, and I began to think about escape. Spooky vetoed the votes of Smoothy and Swagger, though, and I threw myself back into my note-taking. Just when I was about to muster my nerve and do something radical, a sound at the front door provided me with a good reason to get up. To my surprise and delight, it was Susan. She had skipped school in order to comfort her hero through his time in exile. "Yes," I said out loud, "Thank you, God!"

Susan came over every day of my suspension. From the time Mama left until two o'clock, we took over the house. She helped me take notes in the morning, and then we fixed lunch together. We couldn't wait for Thursday to arrive. It would be great to go back to school and order burgers and fries. Our own cooking left a lot to be desired. After lunch we would close out our afternoons by standing guard behind the front window, holding hands and listening to the radio.

As for today, my hatred for Mama's harsh religious ways have eased. It must be the joy of feeling so connected to another human being. I once heard a song on the radio that said that some people can't love right; for me, Susan can't love wrong. It's almost Christmas, and I thought it would be a pleasant surprise for Susan to come to church with me on Sunday.

Saturday, December 24th, 1972

The white flag Susan and I waved pitifully in the wind on Thursday was torn down today. Susan's mom brought her by our house for church, and what was to be the start of a new era of peace between us and our parents turned into renewed conflict. Once Susan's mother saw that I was black, and once my mama found out that Susan is Catholic, their shouting rattled the windows like machine gun fire. I was in the bathroom giving my attire the final touch up when I heard shouting on the front porch. By the time I arrived, our mothers were engaged in a bitter argument.

"But, baby, he's not our kind. Tell him you can't see him anymore. Honey, you know what Father O'Malley says about mixed relationships," Susan's mother was saying as I walked in. Susan was crying and my mother stood in the open doorway, blocking them from entering.

"That's right! We're not your kind!" Mama ranted. "We're members of the one true church, unlike you Catholics with your pagan ceremonies and blasphemous idolatry. I wouldn't let my son associate with your daughter if they were the only two people left on the planet. Our church has been engaged in battle with you people to save the lost souls of this world for eons."

"Mama!" I shouted. "What are you doing?"

"I'm saving you from the tentacles of the whore of Babylon, son. Go to your room. And you," she said, pointing out the door, "get off of our property!"

How can our own parents preach the Golden Rule to us, but instead be at each other's throats?

Monday, December 25th, 1972

The wise one prepares for the battle before the war begins;
Preparation's impossible though, when you're born into sin.

Our thirteen-year earthly stay has become filled
with fright;
Now that we realize Satan's become victor of
this fight.
We've surrendered now, but the conflict rages beyond
our control.
Yes indeed, Satan's become captor of lost souls
Jehovah, please spare us judgment in the end
Remember, it was us who knew,
It's impossible to win when the war's within!

The meaning of "deception" is clearer to me now, and isn't it ironic that it ends this way? The clock on the wall in the vacant house where Susan and I are hiding just struck twelve; it's Christmas.

Susan and I aren't going to be deceived any longer. Burgers, fries, and cold Cokes are all we'll remember. A few hours ago, I swiped a bottle of the old man's nerve pills. Susan and I downed the whole bottle of pills and drank a bottle of his wine. This will surely be my last entry, and not just because it's the only page left, Diary. "Vincent" by Don McLean is playing on the radio, and Susan's lying next to me on the blanket, watching me write and smiling dreamily.

Diary of the Lost Teen Age

Susan Marie Herrera, born August 29th, 1959,
died December 26th, 1972.
Apparent cause of death: suicide by
drug overdose.

Thursday, January 25th, 1973

Today, I overheard the doctors saying that my father's nerve pills caused Susan's death. I woke up in the Dyess Air Force Base Hospital two days ago. I've been in a coma for a month. Mama bought me a new diary for 1973, but the early pages will have to remain blank, because I don't know what was going on while I was unconscious. I guess I could have written this: *Thomas Leroy Jones, 13, remains in a coma.* But I couldn't; after all, I was in a coma.

In the days since I woke up, I have almost managed to convince myself that the way it happened was all a dream. What do you think, was it a dream? I remember feeling like I had to look down, and I saw myself lying on the bed, but how could that be? I couldn't be in two places at once, could I? I felt that I had a difficult decision to make. Something happened as I was about to emerge from my lengthy sleep that was so strange, like waking up from a dream, only I couldn't see anything. Then, the room came into focus, and I was floating above everything. It was the most peaceful feeling I've ever had.

Next, it was like I heard someone say, "Don't look down, don't look down," but before I could make up my

---

**How does a person come to grips with
the consequences of their actions when they
had no idea what the consequences would be?**

---

mind whether I wanted to stay in that delicious place floating so peacefully or return to my miserable self lying on the bed, I heard mama call my name and say, "I love you." Let me tell you, I could count on one hand the number of times in my life she has ever said those words to me. And then, the decision was out of my hands. Her words and my re-entry to this miserable world were simultaneous.

Why hadn't it worked like in *Romeo and Juliet*? That play changed my whole life. How could I ever face the kids at school again after being so stupid? I'm not at all sure that I'm happy to be back, and now they say I have to see a psychiatrist.

Monday, January 29th, 1973

How does a person come to grips with the consequences of their actions when they had no idea what the consequences would be? Our parents told us that when we died, we'd go to heaven, where St. Peter would be waiting to greet us with all the pleasures not granted on earth. Why shouldn't Susan and I have taken our own way out, when everything around us indicates that everyone ends up dead, anyway?

I remember that night, though the details are fuzzy.

"Tom, are you starting to feel as woozy as I am?" Susan said after she'd swallowed the tenth pill. We'd agreed to split my dad's pills and the wine fifty-fifty.

"It may be the wine that's causing my head to suddenly spin out of control. I tried alcohol once before, and felt a bit dizzy."

"I guess we'll be seeing the pearly gates soon," she said.

The doctors here keep saying I'm "depressed." If I had to describe it, I'd say it's just plain hopelessness. Lately, Spooky completely dominates my thoughts.

The food here is terrible, but I love having my own television. *The Flip Wilson Show* is my favorite show. I just love to hear him say, "The devil made me do it."

Tuesday, February 13th, 1973

The reality of my actions came flooding in on me today when I had to face my family. "Teenagers can really be so cruel!"

"I bet you thought you'd never have to take the trash out again, Mr. Failed Suicide Boy," Mike said, as I hauled two bags out to the dumpster. In the alley, I heard an angelic voice speaking that seemed to come from heaven. A cloud of smoke rose from the community tree house next door that overlooks the alley.

"Hey! Aren't you that crazy kid who tried to commit suicide?" the voice said. As the smoke dispersed, I noticed a blonde, blue-eyed girl, looking down on me with a cigarette dangling from her lips. "Hi, I'm Laurie," she said, tossing a pack of Marlboro cigarettes down at my feet. "Do you smoke? I bet you can't wait to get back to all the homework awaiting you at school. How long has it been since you've been to classes? I bet those Mexican boys at school can't wait to see you after what you did to that girl," she continued, without pausing to let me answer her questions.

It hit me like a ton of bricks; my past had become the present. I had been away from the anarchy of Mann Junior High for over a month, and now I'd have to return to that place and face the music. Laurie started my mind whirling. Smoke! Mexican Boys! Suicide! Yes, this is the real world now, and the comfort of hospital beds and sympathetic nurses is over. Susan would never have to hear the whispers of our peers, but our suicide pact had only netted one of us. Laurie's voice alerted me to the bottomless pit of tortures that await me at school. I'll go back to school on Tuesday, since Monday the 19th is President's Day. But first I have to be cleared by the psychiatrist, Dr. Scott. Laurie talked to me for nearly half an hour about what to expect when I return to school. Diary, I didn't ask to be born into this world. All I ever wanted was to go quietly. Now that I've missed my opportunity, you can't imagine how Spooky dominates the dialogue in my mind.

Wednesday, February 14th, 1973

There are moments when I wish my family would stop being so nice to me. I just want things to be like they were before all this happened. Mike just stares at me with his tiny black eyes, waiting to see if I'll try it again. My sisters act as if touching me will somehow cause them to attempt suicide, too—as if I have a disease. I just want to scream, "I'm not a freak! I'm not a freak! I'm not a freak!"

Saturday, February 17th, 1973

Guess what? It's Saturday morning, and I'm home. Guess where my brother and sisters are? You bet—out doing field service in the cold. I'm milking it for all it's worth, in hopes that I won't have to go ever again.

Smoothy paid me a visit today. After the meltdowns I've had with Spooky over the previous few days, Smoothy is a welcome change. Yesterday, Dr. Scott said it's to be expected that a person in my condition would have dramatic mood swings. They want to read my last diary to determine my treatment. It's the first time an adult has asked my permission, and the first time I've had a choice in a matter that's important to me. To be honest, Diary, I can't even go back and read that stuff myself, so why would I let anyone else read it?

By the way, Dr. Scott said I wasn't ready to be back in school, yet. He's really cool! He said he needs to evaluate my behavior more before he can determine whether I should be around my peers. Dr. Scott's office has the greatest collection of magazines I've ever read. My parents said I started reading *Reader's Digest* when I was three years old. I could stay in Dr. Scott's office all day, looking through the *National Geographic* magazines in his waiting room. If that cool doctor says I'm not ready to be around normal school kids, then I'll just stay home and watch TV. I love watching *The Little Rascals* each morning while I wave good-bye to my father and siblings. Then Mom leaves for field service, and the television's all mine.

Saturday, February 24th, 1973

My once-accommodating siblings turned on me like a pack of wild animals today.

"Why doesn't Tom have to go out for field service today?" Carol bellowed, as they all prepared to go door-to-door on a chilly Saturday morning. It was around 8 o'clock, and I was enjoying a bowl of frosted flakes, intently watching the television.

"Mama, Tom's feeling a lot better. He should go with us," Gayle added. Diary, don't think for a moment Mike joined forces with them. He just happened to have the day off, and Mama seized the opportunity to employee him in her scheme to save every soul in Abilene.

"Tom's not stable enough to face the heated pressure of this intense soul-saving campaign. The book of

Matthew says, 'This gospel shall be preached in all the land and then the end will come.' We have plenty of people spreading the gospel today," mama said, leaving the room. The minute she was out of earshot, my siblings started in on me:

"Hey, Romeo, you killed Juliet."

"I wish you'd never come out of that coma."

"I hope they take you back to the nut house and never let you out again."

"Why should you get to watch TV while we pass out magazines all day?"

I would never have predicted the barrage of insults coming from what previously had been a very supportive cast a few days ago.

Later, mama read this passage of Scripture to me over and over again: *While I did not hold back from telling you any of the things that were profitable nor from teaching you publicly and from house to house. Acts 20:* 20. I'm pretty sure she wants me to start witnessing again—another church requirement for all members.

Monday, February 26th, 1973

Today, Carol brought me two months of back home-work. My blank-et-y-blank sister handed me a surprise bundle of gradable trash tied together with a red bow, smirking with satisfaction.

"Your teachers want this homework turned back in before spring break," she said sarcastically.

So, my phony vacation is history; it'll take every ounce of energy to catch up on my homework by spring break.

See you.

Monday, March 5th, 1973

"As our nation welcomes soldiers home from Vietnam, it also examines what appears to be a series of unlawful acts and abuses of power by various departments of the federal government." This caught my eye first thing this morning in the family bathroom. Mama calls the family bathroom the "library," because my father leaves the newspaper scattered about on the bathroom floor each morning after he's read it. I'm still not attending school these days, but I keep up with the outside world by glancing at the headlines while I'm in the bathroom each morning.

Diary, you wouldn't think so, but it's true: This long absence from school gets boring. I wake up in the morning, sneak in television cartoons while mama's out on field service, and then make a peanut-butter-and-jelly sandwich for lunch. Then, in the afternoons, I go to the back alley and listen to the radio while I pretend to be a star quarterback for the Cowboys. I see Laurie in the tree house almost every day. She's a year older than I am, but she's actually in my grade. Laurie looks like she could be Joni Mitchell's sister; they look almost identical. Laurie's parents know she smokes cigarettes, and she's allowed to watch any television show or movie on TV. She no longer refers to me as "the dumb freak they've been talking about at school." Now, she just calls me the "hooky freak." Everybody's some kind of freak in Laurie's eyes. I always know when she's up in the community tree house by the cloud of smoke coming out the top. She and I discuss all kinds of stuff about the world. Sometimes, I think she must be smarter than God.

I get to see Dr. Scott again this week. I enjoy going to Dr. Scott's office. Last week, I tried to take home old issues of *National Geographic*, but the receptionist wouldn't let me (Why shouldn't they let me take home an issue that's two years old?). I find reading National Geographic a lot more interesting than reading *Watchtower*. I found out all kinds of stuff that I've always wondered about. Marvin Gaye has a song about the environment being destroyed, and from what I read in *National Geographic*, it's true. What's going on?

Friday, March 9th, 1973

Around here, the news is gloomy. On the evening news, all you hear about is the oil shortage, on the radio Marvin Gaye sings about wasted oil on the ocean floor, and in the newspaper all is gloom and doom. One picture in the paper showed an Israeli teenager pointing a gun at the head of a Palestinian teenager. Like mama repeats daily, "Thank God, these are the last days."

When am I ever going to learn? You know the old saying, "There's no such thing as a dumb question"?

Well, I got thrown out of Dr. Scott's office today for asking a question. Pointing to an African lady in *National Geographic*, I asked Dr. Scott why in Africa it's okay for a lady to show her bare breasts but in America it's illegal. Mama's jaw dropped, and Dr. Scott's glasses fell from his face. The way the two of them reacted made me feel like a criminal.

"That's it, buster! You've been in my office on three different occasions, and the more I see you, the less I believe there's anything wrong with you," Dr. Scott said.

Mother stood up to add her two cents, and I pointed out that dad's boobs are larger than hers, so it shouldn't be a big deal. She put her hands over her chest, turning red with rage and embarrassment.

So, what was so bad about asking a question about boobs? I posed the same question to Laurie this evening, and she said, "Africans just have a different culture than we do here in America." Now, why couldn't those two adults just give me a straight answer, like Laurie? Never believe grown-ups when they say, "There's no such thing as a dumb question." Believe me, there are questions they don't want to answer.

Anyhow, I won't be seeing Dr. Scott again. He released me to go back to school on Monday. I could have told them I wasn't crazy. Laurie thinks its mama who's crazy.

"Who in their right mind would think the world's coming to an end by the year 1975?" she asked.

Laurie has made some interesting points recently. She said that if the world is going to be destroyed and

Jehovah's Witnesses are going to be living in a new world, what are we going to use for transportation? What will we eat in this paradise? Boy! There are more questions than answers. Sometimes, Laurie seems smarter than God. God wrote the Bible, but never thought about transportation issues in this new paradise on Earth.

Sunday, March 11th, 1973

Spooky, Swagger and Smoothy all paid me a visit over the weekend. I know I'm making progress in my journey back to normality—whatever that is. Saturday, Spooky played a dominant role in my thinking. I haven't been out in the field service for what seems like forever, and Saturday was my first day back. Howard came over early on Saturday to give me some encouragement and to help me with my presentation. We practiced over and over again. By 10 a.m., Smoothy had taken over in my head, and I'd sold magazines at seven out of eight doors. This is a big deal. Normally, three out of four people decline. And on occasion, they slam the door in your face. I've even seen people turn their dogs loose on us or spit in our faces. By 1 p.m., I'd sold over 15 copies. By three, I'd sold over 27, and Swagger had taken over. I actually didn't want to come home from field service for the first time I can remember. God must be looking down from heaven at me with a huge smile on his face. Saving 27 souls in one day is more than pretty good. Howard and his two brothers only sold 12 magazines altogether.

Mama was so pleased that she let me have a slumber party with Howard and his brothers that night. James, Reggie, and some of the other neighborhood boys wanted to join our slumber party, but mama drew the line at inviting worldly kids. The boys and I played hide-and-seek with my sisters and a new black convert, Michelle. Later in the evening, we listened to some of my brother's new albums. Howard says he doesn't like white people's music, but he was grooving to the solid sounds of Elton John all night long, not realizing that Elton John is white. That Howard is a trip sometimes, with his white-boy-this-black-brother-that routine.

On Sunday, Spooky hijacked my head, big time. Since the football season is over and Sundays are a bore, I spend most of my time talking to Laurie in the tree house after we come home from church. She smokes her Marlboros, and I listen to her rants. She's pissed off at her father, Fred, about his drinking on Saturday night. She says he's been way over the line lately, and calls him an alcoholic. It was Laurie's rant that set Spooky off in my head. She reminded me about the fact that I have to face the heat at school. Tomorrow! Her advice to me is as follows:

"When a kid at school asks you why you tried to commit suicide, just say, 'Fuck you.' When a classmate says, 'What happened to Susan?' say, 'Fuck you.' Tom, if someone continues to bug you about it, just say, 'Fuck you and your mama, too.' You've been sheltered much too long, but hang with me, freak, and I'll show you how to get by in this world." Then we left the tree house.

Tuesday, March 13th, 1973

"We have nothing to fear but fear itself," Franklin Roosevelt once said, and I'm living proof that he's right. The past two days haven't been as bad as I expected. I only had to use Laurie's advice once, and it surprised the person I used it on so much that I don't think they'll ever speak to me again. Yeah, I said it, and now I'm a bad dude. Swagger outmaneuvered Spooky in my head, and before you knew it the F-word popped out.

Today was career day at school, and people from the community came to school to convince us to join their profession when we graduate from high school. I think I'd love to be a fireman. Man, the uniform is worth all the trouble of rescuing some dame from a burning building. Wow! Or being a policeman would be cool. I could be like Lincoln Hays from *The Mod Squad*. How groovy would it be to grow an afro and work undercover, busting thugs for smoking marijuana?

Laurie thinks I should become a journalist because I'm always writing. My neighbor, James, probably will be a professional basketball player. He won a trophy for being the best player in the city tournament this year. I guess all that extra practice his father makes him do in their driveway is paying off. Reggie, my other neighbor, is considered to be the next Roger Staubach.

I got so excited about the possibilities of growing up and being somebody that I lost sight of the real world.

Howard busted my bubble this afternoon when he called to remind me that the end is near.

Confused? You bet! Is Armageddon really
going to happen? Or should I plan a future?

I have some interesting classes this semester. Sometimes, it seems like I'm learning so much so fast my head will pop open! I'm taking algebra, sociology and culture, American history, and technology. They keep telling us about this thing called a computer that's supposed to do everything for us in the future. Technology class is a new class being offered.

Confused? You bet! Is Armageddon really going to happen? Or should I plan a future?

Tuesday, March 20th, 1973

My journey home after school has changed forever. Riding home from school these past few days, flying my bike past the laundry hanging out on the various clotheslines throughout the different neighborhoods, has given me a totally different perspective. Yes, Diary, I did say "riding my bike." There's an unbelievable freedom you experience when you're on a bicycle riding home from school, while the other kids have to take the bus home. Howard and I were selling *The Watchtower* in a rich white neighborhood a couple of days ago when we spotted the bikes in the trash. There wasn't much wrong with them, so we took them home and gathered scrap parts from other junk bikes to fix them up. Howard's so good with his hands. We've been riding our bikes to school for the past few days.

Seeing how different the neighborhoods are from area to area has given me a completely different perspective. We live in the Air Force base neighborhood. Then, as you head toward my middle school, there's a short cut through the white neighborhood, where Howard and I found the bikes. Then there's "The Fanning Neighborhood," which is poor and mostly Mexican. My dad said we're lucky that we found the bikes since gas has risen above 30 cents a gallon. Soon everyone will be riding bicycles, he said.

Dad said he's thinking about quitting smoking, because he "can't afford luxuries anymore." That means money must really be tight, because he loves his Pall Mall reds. I overheard my parents arguing about the money spent on my therapy. My father is supporting a family of seven on a sergeant's pay at a time when the energy crisis is driving up fuel costs, and inflation is sky high.

Well, Diary, I guess this is enough information about what's going on around here. I'd better get back to updating my tons of homework before my father catches me updating you, Diary. I hate homework!

Wednesday, March 21st, 1973

These days my mind soaks up every drop of every new piece of information like a sponge. I read an article in the *Abilene Lone Star* that said the average age at death of a soldier in the Vietnam War is nineteen years old. I would have never imagined that. It's suddenly obvious to me why all the protest songs on the radio are by young people.

I'm finally caught up on my homework. Thinking about Susan still brings tears to my eyes, even though it seems like it happened years ago. So much has changed in my life since that night.

I hardly see Mike in the evenings anymore, since he started working evenings as well as weekends, and Carol constantly talks back to my parents. I'm finally beginning to branch out and enjoy the world again, noticing little stuff like the morning dew that settles on the grass each morning, and exploring new routes to school every morning.

Of course, I miss Susan, but these days it lifts my spirits when I hang out in the tree house talking to Laurie. There is such freedom up there. We say whatever we want about whomever we want without regret. Honestly, Diary, I get more out of talking to Laurie than I ever got from chatting with Dr. Scott. If I told my dad that, though, it might cause him to start smoking again, after what he spent on the sessions and all of the arguments with mama.

Yesterday, I was waiting for Laurie after school, because I'd beaten the bus home by half an hour, since I discovered an even shorter route home on my bike. I was perched in the tree house, doing nothing, when I saw Laurie's mother,

Lynn, sitting cross-legged, the palms of her hands together, and her eyes closed in front of a statue in their back yard. She sat motionless for what seemed like hours. Wow! And I thought I had a weird mother.

Thursday, March 22nd, 1973

Lynn was out again when Laurie finally made her way up the stairs to the tree house. Laurie's got her ritual, too, so I waited patiently for her to tap her cigarettes against the tree house windowsill, before introducing the subject of the day. But today, I beat her to the punch by asking what's up with her mom.

"Laurie, don't you find it strange that your mother stares at a statue in your back yard?" I said, pointing at Lynn in their back yard.

"It looks stupid, but my mother's a Buddhist, and she meditates like that once a day. Lynn!" she shouted as her mother ended her meditation, "come up here and explain to Tom what a Buddhist is."

Pure panic set in at first! This devil woman was coming right at me, and I was stuck in the tree house, the only exit being the stairs Lynn was lumbering up. I thought about jumping out of the window, but decided against it.

Our conversation was bizarre. It was as if Lynn and I both were talking a foreign language to one another. She tried to explain reincarnation to me, and I witnessed to her about what the verse of Revelations predicts about the great tribulations. Laurie just sat in the corner, laughing at us. I can't really say who won the debate. I still think Lynn's strange, but I kind of like her. Somehow, it's groovy to have a mother who gives you a choice about smoking and whenever you want to come home at night at Laurie's age. Heck, if my mother even knew Laurie had matches, she'd probably ban me from the tree house altogether.

Monday, March 26th, 1973

As you can see, Diary, I've been away at another assembly for few days. I couldn't wait to get back home and catch you up on what's been going on. We left on Friday morning and stayed until Sunday evening. It was held in Sweetwater, which is only 70 miles away, but we still stayed at the Ramada Inn instead of driving back each night, like Howard's family did. As usual, dad stayed at the motel, while the rest of us were at the convention all day. They introduced a new book at the convention called *Paradise Lost, Paradise Gained.* We're going to study it at Kingdom Hall until Armageddon gets here, which won't be long. Some of the speakers at the convention prophesied that the world may end before the year is up. I hope they're right so I won't have to start high school in September. Mike stayed home because he had to work. My parents even gave him his own front door key! He's still at work, and the only reason I'm up this late is that we have spring break this week.

I spent most of the day just bumming around. Dad made me cut the grass, but other than that, it was like a real spring break day. Normally, when we come home from these conventions, we have to go out to do field service right away and spread the good news of the Kingdom to come to the wicked people of Abilene.

For some reason today, Mama didn't make us do field service. My dad thinks it's because she forgot about it being spring break. Howard's coming over to spend the night, so I'd better put you away.

Tuesday, March 27th, 1973

Spring break didn't last long. Today, Howard and I and all of our siblings went out in full force, spreading the good news to the wicked. A lot of people are interested in the new book. Out of sixty or so doors, I'd say half seemed genuinely interested. Most people in Abilene don't even know the end is near. Like mama said, "There are a lot of souls to be saved between now and the end."

I saw Lynn today. She was in her regular meditation spot, looking at that statue of the Buddha. When she finished, I called her over.

"Mrs. Lane," I shouted from high in the tree house. "I've got something my mother wants you to read."

As she came through the gate that divides our yards, I came down to meet her with a copy of our latest book. I told her it was a gift from my mother, and I felt so proud of myself for saving another sinner.

Saturday, March 31st, 1973

It's been raining on and off since Thursday night. Abilene hardly ever floods, but the creek near the Bootry Shoe Store swelled its banks and flooded most of the north side of town. The paper said it's the worst flood since the great flood of the 1940s. The newspaper failed to mention the Noah's Ark flood in the article on great floods. Maybe they forgot, or it was too long ago.

I got a chance to see Laurie again this evening. I'd been wondering why she hadn't been to the tree house all week. It turns out that she'd been out of town at her grandparents' house. We didn't get to chat much, but I see Laurie's got a new hairdo with beads and flowers.

I hate to admit it, but my father's a coward! Yeah, he fought in the war and all, and everyone's real proud of him, but he won't even stand up to my mother. Carol wants to celebrate her 13th birthday on Thursday, and my father caved when mama forbade it. Then Carol asked my father if she could just have the cake, and after a long argument with mama, he caved in. My old man isn't even a Jehovah's Witness; why couldn't Carol at least have a cake on her birthday?

The argument between my parents was quite loud. James heard it from across the street. He told me about it this afternoon when I saw him shooting hoops in his driveway.

"What's all the fuss about?" he asked.

When I told him about the birthday celebration denial, he made an interesting comment. James said that in their Bible at their church he doesn't recall hearing anything about not celebrating birthdays. Sometimes, I wish I was born into James' family, or any family but this one.

Monday, April 2nd, 1973

"Eat everything on your plate. There are kids in China who are starving." These words rang out over the cafeteria PA system at lunchtime. I've heard this reasoning repeated by my parents, but never before in school. Everywhere you turn, people are talking about hard times.

"You've never seen hard times like you're going to see soon," dad said Sunday.

They interrupted *The Flip Wilson Show* the other night so that President Nixon could talk about the energy crisis. "Bad news on every doorstep" is how my dad refers to the morning paper these days.

Mike and Dad are arguing about money in the living room as I write. Mike doesn't want to share his paycheck with the rest of the family, and Dad thinks he should start forking over a few dollars for food. I'll tell you how it turns out, Diary.

Wednesday, April 4th, 1973

"He's got some nerve telling me what I should be doing on a Wednesday night on my day off," I heard Mike saying a couple of hours ago. This argument between my dad and brother never seems to cease. Mike's got a point. My dad never sets foot in Kingdom Hall, but he insists that Mike go with us on his evening off.

"You can't spend every dime you make on those rock and soul albums!" Dad shouted.

They both have a point, and for me, the point is this: I can't wait to grow up and get out of this house. There's too much noise, and I don't mean the radio or the television. My consolation tonight is that I got to stay home and watch *The Mod Squad*. Mama took off for the church meeting with the girls. I hope Dad and Mike get into an argument every Wednesday; I love watching *The Mod Squad*.

Friday, April 6th, 1973

"Tom, you must have been put on earth to learn patience," Lynn said softly, returning the copy of *Paradise Lost, Paradise Gained*, which I'd given her about a week ago. She came in the tree house unexpectedly today, while Laurie and I were chatting. "Tom, tell your mother that her religion is a cult, just like the Moonies. Does your mother honestly believe everything in this book you gave me?"

"Yes, Mrs. Lane, we do," I replied.

"And I thought the Catholics had some strange beliefs," Mrs. Lane mumbled, sighing as she left.

I don't know what the heck she meant by saying I'm supposed to be on earth to learn about patience. She's the one who's nuts! Does she honestly believe people have lived before in different bodies? Or that staring at a statue makes any sense? And what's a Moonie?

Monday, April 9th, 1973

"The Catholics are causing problems in the world because the Pope forbids birth control, and most of the world is Catholic, so the world is becoming overpopulated," Laurie said Saturday afternoon, when we were sitting on the lawn. Now I understand! Laurie made sense of it all. Two weeks ago, all I worried about was Carol not having a cake for her thirteenth birthday. Now, I'm too worried about the Catholic birthrate to care about cake. It's no wonder there's no food in China, no gas in America, and no money left over from my dad's paycheck. Mike said it's a good thing, too. Mike looks at it this way: No food, no gas, and no money will eventually lead to no school.

Mike brought the new Stevie Wonder album home this weekend. It's hands-down the best album I've ever heard. "Superstition," "You are the Sunshine of My Life," and "Higher Ground" are just a few of the songs we played on his new record player. Mike is hot stuff with the neighborhood fellas these days. He's the first one on the Bowie block to own a stereo system with an 8-track player and AM-FM radio.

Howard and I stared at the new stereo all weekend. Mike told us not to touch it while he was at work, but we did anyway, and I accidentally scratched his Stevie Wonder album. Hopefully, he won't play "Higher Ground," or I might have to find a job to pay for it.

Thursday, April 12th, 1973

I'm so darn glad he let me try it again
'Cause my last time on earth I lived a whole
world of sin
I'm so glad a that I know more than I knew then
Gonna keep on trying
Till I reach higher ground

That song is sinking into my head more each day. The lyrics are from Stevie Wonder's new hit song, "Higher Ground." Examine them a little closer. What did he mean by "my last time on earth?" Is he a Buddhist?

Something magical happened over these past few days. It all started on Tuesday after school. I was up in the tree house waiting for Laurie. I had my eyes focused on Lynn and the devil worshiping she does in front of that statue. Suddenly, it occurred to me where I'd seen that statue before—in Hawaii and Japan. Mystical and magical is the only way to describe what happened. Laurie appeared out of the blue in the tree house, and I told her about my realization. Then she tried to convince me that there were indications all around us that human beings are on a recurring mystical journey.

"Believing in reincarnation is no more ridiculous than believing that the world is going to end next year," Laurie said. "Besides, Buddhism has been around a lot longer than Christianity."

"So what's with worshiping statues?" I asked.

"Lynn's not worshiping the statue; she's meditating. That means she's thinking about the qualities and teachings of the Buddha in hopes of freeing herself from the cycle of suffering and rebirth, like the Buddha did," she replied.

"I don't think I understand. Is she praying?"

"No, Buddhists don't believe that Buddha is a god who goes around granting wishes like a fairy," Laurie giggled. "And they don't believe in heaven and hell. They believe that this world is a world of suffering, and that we must end our attachment to the world in order to avoid having to come back and do it again."

"What? Like having to repeat a grade in school?" I said, laughing. "So, does she believe in God?"

"Yes and no. She believes that we are all equally divine—that the entire universe is a part of God, that there is a divine hum of energy present in everything, and once we realize our unity with everything, we can let go of our egos and..." She took another puff. "What was I just saying?" she said, chuckling.

Her laughter was infectious, and we both burst into loud, breathless giggling. Our lengthy exchange about this life and the afterlife brought us to a place I'd never been before. We were so caught up in the moment that she passed me her cigarette. That was the first time I'd seen her roll her own cigarettes. She used strawberry-colored rolling papers. Laurie knows I don't smoke, but she kept trying to pass me the cigarette anyway. The smoke cleared from the tree house, and Laurie mentioned something about me having a contact high as she adjusted the beads in her beautiful blonde hair.

"A contact high?! What's that?" I said. She didn't clarify, but I think she was referring to the cigarette she was smoking. All I know is that I felt a strong connection to her and a tremendous desire to kiss her. It happened again yesterday afternoon, as we discussed other people from school. I took the match off the deck floor of the tree house to give Laurie a light, and the magic began again. I heard my mother's voice calling me home for the Wednesday meeting, but my mind could only focus on the body in front of me.

Here I sit, filling out the empty pages in my diary, trying to understand. If only Smoothy had entered my mind a little quicker on Wednesday night, by this time, I might have been sharing a sweet secret about Laurie and me between these pages. Swagger kept telling me that she wanted to touch my lips just as much as I wanted to touch hers.

Thank God, the tree house remained empty today. Laurie had band practice, and I knew she wouldn't be home until late, though it didn't stop me from going out in our back yard to stare up at the tree house. Sensational is the only word for the way I feel. Did the past few afternoons really happen? Have we lived before? Is thinking about Laurie this way a sin?

Thursday, April 26th, 1973

Shock! Disbelief! Despair! Diary, I'm most certain this is our last entry. First, I've got to clear the record with God before I pack you away for good. We got a phone call on the 23rd during the CBS movie of the week, *FireHouse.*

The operator came on the line and asked, "Will you accept a long distance call from Frank Jones in California?" Dad took the phone from Gayle, and all hell broke loose. It was Uncle Frank calling to tell us my grandmother, grandfather, and Uncle Walter all died in a house fire! Isn't it strange how we were watching a movie about people getting burned up in a fire, and at the same time it happened to my dad's family?

I take full responsibility for the tragic event. If I hadn't read about reincarnation and started reading horoscopes in the newspaper lately, this wouldn't have happened. God, I wish I'd never seen Laurie's face! It's her that convinced me to explore other spiritual avenues. Now I know how Adam must have felt when Eve gave him that rotten apple to eat. That devil, he's doing it to me again.

Another thing: I swear I'll never call my dad a coward again. He didn't even cry when he got the news about his family. Now, that's a real man. The funerals are on Saturday, and Dad took the Greyhound bus yesterday. The rest of us can't afford to go. I've only visited my father's parents twice. They lived in South Carolina, and I guess I'll always remember them sitting on the dusty porch, watching the cars drive up and down the dirt road. Mama said that it's a shame they were all too drunk to escape a burning house. Supposedly, they all died in their beds.

Diary, I'm closing you for good. *Paradise Lost, Paradise Gained* is over on my headboard. From now on, there will be no more reading horoscopes or any other material not authorized by the Jehovah's Witnesses. My *Watchtower* magazine, *Awake* magazine, and Bible are all I need until Jesus arrives.

Wednesday, May 30th, 1973

I tried hard not to write again, Diary, but I just couldn't restrain myself any longer. There's nobody I can talk to, so I write. It gets lonely out here by myself. Mike works all the time, and Laurie doesn't seem to have time to spend in the tree house anymore.

It's read the newspaper or write. The headline says Thomas Bradley was elected mayor of Los Angeles, making him the first black mayor of a major city in the United States. Black folks sure are moving on up. Since the church integrated last year, Howard said white folks in the congregation can't continue to hold us down. I've been diligent in keeping to the headlines and not glancing at the horoscopes. It may be superstitious, but I've heard that horoscopes sometimes come true, so I don't read them, hoping they won't.

Part II
AT FOURTEEN
The Wonder Years

Sunday, June 10th, 1973

When the moon is in the seventh house,
And Jupiter aligns with Mars,
then peace will guide the planets
and love will steer the stars.
This is the dawning of the Age of Aquarius

The lines above are lyrics from a song, "Aquarius," by the Fifth Dimension, which Laurie and I recently discussed. The lyrics clearly reference astrology. I am finally learning what horoscopes are all about. A horoscope is a prediction based on a chart of the universe, which gives the positions of the sun and moon for the exact moment, place, and date of your birth. I found out today that not only am I a Gemini, but Reggie from across the street is a Gemini, too.

I didn't dare read my horoscope again,
so Reggie read it to me.

I didn't dare read my horoscope again, so Reggie read it to me. Reggie's mother can't afford the newspaper, so he reads his horoscope from our paper. As soon as the newspaper lands on our front porch stoop, Reggie strolls over to our house to see if he's made the print news. Reggie's been featured in the news twice in the past

10 days. Today, there was even a picture of Reggie in his football jersey with a caption that read, "The future looks bright." There was Reggie, grinning as if he'd just won the Heisman trophy. Although we're both freshmen this year, Reggie turned 16 in May. It didn't take a calculator to figure out that Reggie's failed one or two grades in his academic career. I don't just look at the pictures in the paper; I read the articles. The stories about Reggie suggest that he's going to be the next Bobby Lane.

Life's not fair! It's my 14th birthday, and there's no fanfare from anyone, while Reggie's in the newspaper for the second time in 10 days. Reggie reads the horoscope and nothing bad happens, but when I do it most of my father's family dies.

Gosh, I wish someone besides Reggie would acknowledge that it's my birthday today.

Tuesday, June 12th, 1973

Summer vacation might not be so bad after all. It is evening time, the air is still, the sun has just left the sky for the night, and you can hear the Bowie kids' laughter in the distance way past 9 p.m. I wish I could have stayed outdoors and played with the group, but I should just be thankful for the time I spent with them this morning.

The overseers don't make us kids go out for field service on Tuesday mornings, because on Tuesdays grownups conduct in-home Bible studies with the new members they've converted. Mother's newest convert is Michelle's mother, Pat. Michelle is sixteen, as is Howard, and has dark, chocolate-colored skin. Howard and I both want her, but I'm not giving up just because she's older and is in his class. Like they say, age is only a number.

Today, Howard and I played street football with the Bowie Bombers while our mothers were away. It's really Reggie's team, but since we all live on Bowie Street, we decided to name ourselves after our street. We played the Crockett Rockets today. Crockett is the street Laurie lives on. I don't know why the boys on that street call themselves the Rockets; Gayle could outrun most of the dudes on that team. The game wasn't even close. Bowie 49, Crockett 14!

Laurie was born under Scorpio, and Reggie is a Gemini. They met one another for the first time today, and it's plain that Scorpios and Geminis aren't compatible. The two of them fought like cats and dogs. What I don't understand is, if Scorpios and Geminis don't get along, why do Laurie and I get along so well? Oh, well.

Earth signs blend in easily with water signs, but air signs require some tolerance to blend with fire signs, and Reggie doesn't have any tolerance, so he and Laurie don't mix well. At least, that's how Mike explained what's going on between Reggie, Laurie and me.

"You and Reggie are air signs, and Laurie's a water sign, and since Reggie's birthday is on the edge of Taurus, an Earth sign, there's friction between the three of you."

Frankly, you'd have to be a fool to believe all this horoscope crap. The only air and fire I want to hear about is Earth, Wind, and Fire. Mike let Howard and I listen to his new album on his new stereo system, and it sounded groovy.

By the way, guess who was my partner today in field service? Michelle. Howard was so jealous.

People around here refer to me as the book worm because I read everything from books to magazines to every other printed materials in a effort to get some kind of understanding about what it all means. After reading more bits and pieces of the newspaper I think I finally understand what happened with this Watergate thing. I guess most people are sick and tired of hearing about it, and so am I, but I understand more about it now. The Watergate scandal began last year, when five men from the Committee to Re-elect the President broke into the Democratic headquarters at the Watergate Apartments in Washington D.C. and got caught going through the Democrats' files. Nixon's dudes were also installing electronic listening devices so they could eavesdrop.

Now if I could only find out how to get one of those eavesdropping devices I wouldn't have to read so much about earth signs, water signs, and Watergate.

Tuesday, June 19th, 1973

"This boy grew up a bit today," echoed within the confines of my brain for most of the day. My dad caught the tail end of our game against the Robert Lee Warriors while he was home on his lunch break.

"Boy, that was a beautiful play you designed for the winning touchdown," he said.

I think it was the first time he's ever complimented me, and I have been grinning ever since.

Dad's been talking to Uncle Frank, who lives in California, on the phone more often since his parents' funeral. What a strong man! I've never seen him shed a single tear since their deaths six weeks ago, but I'll never forget the look on his face when he hung up the telephone that night; his whole face seemed to sag, like he'd just aged ten years. I keep listening for him to say something profound, but maybe I've missed it already.

Tuesday, June 26th, 1973

If you're picking a team to play against the Cowboys, you're better off choosing Reggie, but, if you need someone to help you fight Muhammad Ali, you'd better choose Howard.

"Howard, your brother Mike catches a football like a punk! And your sissy brother, Tom, shouldn't even be allowed to play! He runs and throws like a girl, and he practically cries if you so much as touch him!" Reggie shouted at our Tuesday morning practice.

Howard sprang toward Reggie, thrusting his right fist under Reggie's ribs and pulling Reggie's head into his shoulder with his left. Then Howard let Reggie drop like a sack of potatoes to the ground, his head landing on the hard asphalt. Reggie stayed down! Reggie has got the feet but Howard definitely has the hands. James said, "If we had purchased tickets to this fight, they'd have to give us our money back."

Thursday, June 28th, 1973

Reggie hates Laurie, Laurie hates Reggie, and James hates Reggie's younger brother, Derrick. Michelle hates Laurie, Laurie likes James, Howard hates Reggie, Reggie hates Michelle, and Howard and I both love Michelle. It's like *As the World Turns* around here these days.

Sweet Dark Chocolate, a.k.a. Michelle, is a refreshing change after all of my recent relationship troubles. First of all, she's black—no race issues to complicate things, like with Lisa. Second, her mother just joined our church, so religion isn't a problem, like with Susan. After my last two heartbreaks, the prospect of a simple relationship is a relief. Thank you, God!

By the way, Tuesday's football scores: Bowie Bombers 42, LaSalle Hornets 21.

Thursday, July 19th, 1973:
Bowie Bombers 48, Congress Rebels 14!

Monday, July 30th, 1973

"After months of preliminary research, the Senate investigating committee began public hearings on Watergate in the full glare of the TV lights and cameras."

"The dollar is steadily dropping in value on the European markets, and the stock market steadily drops to new lows."

"The rock music festival at Watkins Glen, New York, was attended by 600,000—the largest crowd ever to gather for an entertainment festival."

"Dallas Cowboys open preseason with extremely high expectations."

Those are the first sentences of each section in Sunday's paper. You'd think they could find something to write about besides Watergate. Spare us the details already; it's been three months, and Sgt. Schultz on *Hogan's Heroes* knows more than they do. And we all know he knows nothing. The financial news section speaks for itself. My mother reacted to the entertainment news by quoting 2 Timothy 3:4, which says, "In the last days, people would be lovers of pleasure rather than lovers of God." Thank God for the sports section. The Cowboys' coach is already talking Super Bowl in the preseason. We sure needed a bit of good news around here.

There's something suspicious going on in church these days. Yesterday, the elders met behind closed doors after services for the third Sunday in a row. I don't know all the details, but I know they're talking about Howard's stepfather, Leonard. I'll keep you posted, Diary.

Thursday, August 9th, 1973

A week ago, James's family got the news that his 19-year-old brother was coming home in a body bag. Evidence of the toll the war is taking is hitting close to home. All this time, I've been under the delusion that the war was over. I can only hope that Nixon ends this war or goes to jail for Watergate before I'm eligible for the draft. If it's not one thing, it's another; if I don't die in Armageddon, I'll probably die in Vietnam, especially when I consider the fact that I don't even know how to shoot a gun.

A week ago, "body bag" wasn't even in my vocabulary, but it seems like that word pops up everywhere recently. The Tuesday before the huge playoff game we won against the Congress Cardinals, I was sitting in the "library" and happened to glance at the newspaper on the floor when I saw a story that mentioned body bags and a bombing accident in Cambodia that the U.S. was alleged to be involved in. Then Barbara Walters led off the evening news tonight with a story about a multiple murder case in Houston in which 27 homosexuals were taken away in body bags. I heard it was the largest case in U.S. criminal history. So there you have it, Diary! In a short span of time, literally hundreds of people ended up in body bags all over the world, and my main concern is whether Reggie will have the arm strength to throw Howard the ball on the fly pattern that we diagrammed for the championship game against the North Nine Forty-Niners on August 25th.

Monday, August 27th, 1973

"Bad news always comes in threes." I think about this quote often as I read in the "library"each morning. My old man complains that I take longer than a woman in there, but he lacks foresight. If he wouldn't leave the newspaper on the floor, I wouldn't take half as long.

The headlines last week said that the Secret Service uncovered a conspiracy to assassinate President Nixon, which caused the cancellation of a motorcade, and that seven prominent Republicans were indicted for a conspiracy to conceal contributions to the 1972 presidential campaign. Today, the headlines said that three steel companies have been indicted for conspiring to fix prices. What do all these articles have in common? Conspiracy, that's what. I looked it up in the dictionary and found out it refers to a secret plan involving multiple people or organizations. Not only are there conspirators all over the country, there are conspirators living right under my own roof.

The championship game was planned for last Saturday. All of the other games have been on a Tuesday, but since this was the championship, the boys decided to play on a Saturday in Lee Park. Four out of our eleven players happen to be Jehovah's Witnesses, and you know what we do on Saturday mornings. There was no getting around it. The game was a forfeit. The Bowie Bombers didn't have enough players to take to the field. I should have known this was coming. Two days before the big game, I hinted to my old man about the game being on a Saturday morning, and his eyes reassured me that we'd be able to play. Friday night came, and the boys were all excited. Howard and his brothers spent the night at my house.

When we awoke Saturday morning, Dad had already left for a fishing trip, and Mama woke us up saying, "Do not be misled. Bad associations spoil useful habits."

Dad had sold us out! That's why he'd left so early.

James couldn't attend either, leaving the team with only five players, so we had to forfeit the biggest game in our history. I heard that Reggie was pissed off at everyone who didn't show. At least James had a legitimate excuse—his brother's funeral. Howard and I wanted to go to the funeral, but our mothers said we can't set foot in churches that teach false religion. I did get a chance to meet some of James' relatives from Utah. Jamess' uncle, Alex, is a Mormon and has three wives. One of them is only 15, and the other two are 19 years old. My Dad says Alex is a "polygamist," which means he's allowed to have more than one wife.

Laurie was smoking a cigarette up in the tree house today when she saw me taking out the trash and yelled down, "Hey, Tom, I just read that Diana Ross and the Supremes have broken up." What's next?! Nothing stays the same anymore.

Monday, September 3rd, 1973

"The country's two highest officials are under investigation, and with major companies being charged in antitrust suits, how can American youth be expected to trust or show respect for authority?" The front page of the *Abilene Reporter* headline asked.

It's Labor Day, and I've got nothing better to do than watch the news. ABC has been promoting their new anchorwoman, Barbara Walters. Dad says he's sick of seeing her already, and that the only reason why she's on TV is that the networks have to start giving women equal rights.

Things are so stupid around here. Check this out! We started school on Thursday. Now, it's Monday, and we're already on holiday. Why not just start school tomorrow instead of wasting our time with two meaningless days of school?

Here's another thing! Disfellowship! It was announced yesterday after church that Howard's stepfather has been disfellowshipped for "conduct unbecoming a Christian."

"During his disfellowship, Leonard is not allowed to sit in Christian fellowship with the other members of this congregation. Although he is expected to attend services and fulfill all of his Christian duties, no one, including his family is allowed to speak to him or otherwise acknowledge his presence in any way for one year. He will sit alone on the back pew, where he can reflect on his sins and fervently pray for reunion with God and His true church of Christ. Anyone who disobeys the rules of disfellowship will be duly punished. Let no one be misled into believing that Leonard will in any way benefit from companionship; his sentence is for one full year and will be extended to ensure he has a solid year of contemplation from the time that any member speaks to him," Pastor Slowley explained. "After a year, he will go before the elders, who will vote on his reinstatement."

Imagine not being able to speak to your own father for a year. Howard says he's bummed out about it. At least Leonard can't order Howard to cut the lawn for the next year. Howard should be grateful.

Sunday, September 16th, 1973

Did you write the book of love and do you have faith in God above.
If the Bible tells you so.
Now do you believe in Rock 'n' roll and can music save your mortal soul
Bye, Bye, Miss American Pie I drove my Chevy to the levee but the levee was dry and good old boys

were drinkin' whiskey and rye
Singing this'll be the day that I die.

Don MacLean's lyrics express how I felt when I read the headline in the *Abilene Reporter* —"Nine teens die in car accident—One survivor." The paper says it was the worst two-car accident in U.S. history, and it happened right here in Abilene on Labor Day. Four white teens and five black teens died in a head-on collision on their way home from Fort Freedom Lake. Michelle is related to the black kids, and two of the white kids attended my school. Jeff, one of the white kids, was in my Spanish class.

Don MacLean sang, "I met a girl who sang the blues, and I asked her for some happy news, but she just smiled and turned away," which perfectly fit Michelle's reaction to our pastor's argument with the black pastor from Woodson Baptist Church over who should perform the eulogy for her cousins.

And in the streets the children screamed,
the lovers cried, and the poets dreamed.
Not a word was spoken
The church bells all were broken.

I only catch glimpses of what these lyrics mean. This town is eerily silent since the accident. The dead are all buried now, but the newspaper continues to run stories about them on page two. Laurie and I shared a moment in the tree house the other day and came to the conclusion that this tragedy touched everyone deeply. Not only does it feel like the music died, it feels like the soul of Abilene died, too.

Friday, September 21st, 1973

"You've come a long way baby," Barbara Waters commented as she concluded a story about Billie Jean King's smashing tennis defeat of Bobby Riggs in Houston. The game was advertised as the "Battle of the Sexes." They say 100,000 people came to the Astrodome to watch the match. I wasn't one of them, but my dad let us watch it on TV. As usual, the girls cheered when the woman scored, and the boys cheered for the man. Bobby Riggs can't show his face since losing to a woman on national television. Still, it was great to be able to cheer about something again, after all the sadness of the Labor Day weekend events. It seemed like even the normally gloomy voice of Barbara Walters had some sparkle when she announced Billie Jean's victory.

Thursday, September 27th, 1973

Mother would kill me if she found out that I lied this morning about staying after school to study. Instead, I rode my bike over to the junior high to see Reggie quarterback the Falcons. His team is on a 42-game winning streak over the past three seasons, and the whole town is buzzing about how impressive Reggie's record is. He hasn't lost a game in his entire junior high school football career. Howard thinks it's unfair that Reggie is 16 and playing against 14 year olds, but I think Howard's jealous that Reggie's mentioned in the sports pages nearly every other day.

Howard says, "Just wait until Reggie has to face players his own age when he's a freshman next year."

He says that Thursday after-school games can't compare with "Friday nights under the lights." How would he know? We aren't even allowed to watch after-school games, let alone play.

What an impressive talent that Reggie is! He scored four touchdowns on the ground and three touchdowns throwing in today's game.

Thursday, October 4th, 1973

"Tom, you spend a lot of time talking to that white girl in the tree house," Michelle whispers every time she's at our house with her mother. Pat is now a baptized member of our church, but she still comes over to study *Watchtowers* with my mother, so I see Michelle at least three times a week. Without fail, she comes to our back door to look for me, sees me up in the tree house, frowns, and then gets my sister to call me down. As soon as we're alone, she complains that I spend too much time in the tree house with Laurie. I tried to convince her that Laurie and I are just friends, but she won't listen. Dad says women want equal rights, but they couldn't fight if the government loaded their rifles and pulled the trigger for them—whatever that means. Anyway, trying to convince Michelle that Laurie is only teaching me things that I would never learn in school is like trying to convince my mother something isn't quite right with our religious beliefs.

I learn about Nixon and Watergate, the stock market, and the Cowboys from the newspaper, but Laurie knows interesting stuff about life, like that Easter rabbits don't really lay eggs and that the world might not end by 1975, like Mama says our Bible says. Laurie thinks that I need to think about finding a career just in case the world doesn't end.

If I could just convince Michelle to trust me, I might even persuade her to kiss me.

Thursday, October 11th, 1973

He did it again, and I was there to witness it. Reggie scored seven times—this time four passing and three ground! Reggie was having a hard time reading what to do against the 5-3 defenses, so on Wednesday I worked with him after school in his backyard. It certainly paid off. Although Reggie's sixteen, he's not really all that bright. I had to go over the plays three or four times before he got it. It's as if Reggie sees the plays backwards. But once he finally gets it, he's got it. I loved helping

Reggie with the plays. It was so rewarding—more satisfying even than the fact that I got to second base with Michelle the other day.

Michelle and her mother arrived at our house yesterday, just like every Wednesday. When Michelle couldn't find me in the tree house, Carol told me she had a fit about not knowing my whereabouts. When I saw Michelle as our families piled into Mom's station wagon before church, I became frustrated, trying to explain about teaching Reggie the playbook. Michelle wouldn't believe a word of it. Instead, she thinks I disappeared somewhere with Laurie, so, during the service, Michelle tried to make me jealous by hanging out with Howard. The nerve of her! I caught a glimpse of her with her arm around his shoulder during intermission. I could care less that Howard is her age; I asked her to go with me first, and she accepted with a ring on her finger. I talked to her on the way home, and we made out in the backyard, while our mothers talked inside. Now, if I could only get past second base with her….

Thursday, October 18th, 1973

Who could script this stuff? The score was 49-3, but I didn't get to see Reggie's semi-finals game because I ran out of alibis, so I had to wait for him to come home and tell me about the game. It was close to 9 p.m., and we'd just gotten back from church when Reggie saw our car pull into the driveway. He rushed over to my side of the car with the great news. Reggie scored all but one touchdown for his team.

I'm so excited, I can hardly contain myself as I write about it in the pages of this diary. Next Thursday is the final game. I know Reggie will be up for it, and the Falcons will win. Gosh, I wish I had another excuse to use. I just have to see Reggie's final game as a junior high school player. From what Reggie says, the whole town's planning to be there, even the newspaper people.

Thursday, October 25th, 1973

"Alert for U.S. military forces throughout the world ordered by President Nixon" was the headline this morning. I purposely got up early to look at the sports page before dad got it, only to find that he had hurried off to work because of the President's order. What blindsided me was the picture on the front page. It showed an Arab teenager and an Israeli teenager with machine guns pointed at each other's heads. Suddenly, finding out the score of Reggie's game seemed unimportant. Kids shooting at kids with machine guns? Why? Reading further, I found out that the Arabs and Israelis are at war, and both sides use their children to further their cause. What a pity! How barbaric!

By the way, the Falcons won. Reggie scored five times and won the Most Valuable Player award for the third time (a record in this town, even with all the great football players that have come from here). Jack Clark, the

> This is like an episode from *The Twilight Zone*. It all happened so fast, and it just kept building momentum as the facts unfolded.

sportswriter, wrote, "Going into his first high-school game this fall with a 45-game winning streak ain't bad. Reggie Thomas might just be the next football superstar."

Wednesday, November 28th, 1973

This is like an episode from *The Twilight Zone*. It all happened so fast, and it just kept building momentum as the facts unfolded. If I told you this was the first time in a month that I've had time to write, you'd think I was exaggerating, but I'm completely serious. Let me tell you what's gone down. It all revolves around someone's interpretation of the Scriptures. Howard got caught hitting a home run with Michelle at the end of October, and now the church elders, with the consent of their mothers, are forcing them to get married. It all happened so fast that I still don't quite understand the details, but I thank God that I only got to second base with Michelle.

To the best of my recollection, it went like this: Howard and Michelle were caught having sex by one of the elders. Minutes later, another member of the congregation read them the riot act, quoting them a Scripture that says something about a woman only having one husband. The next thing I know, the entire congregation is being fitted for wedding attire. That fast, Diary, no joke. Tomorrow, while the rest of the world is celebrating Thanksgiving, we'll be having a wedding feast for Mr. and Mrs. Howard Medlock.

For the first time in my life, I'm beginning to realize my parents don't have a clue, and neither do any of the other adults at our church. Laurie and I agree wholeheartedly that making teenagers get married over having sex is crazy. Not only did I lose a girlfriend, but I've lost a great buddy, too. Howard's expression during the rehearsal ceremony said it all.

Pastor Slowley asked, "Do you take this woman to be your lawfully wedded wife?"

Howard's eyes were dull, his body sagged toward the floor, as he said, "I do."

It was like watching a man being sentenced to life imprisonment. Three weeks ago, Howard had to quit school and start working nights at the new Church's Chicken. Howard says he doesn't mind working nights, because at least he won't have to spend as much time with Michelle's mother. He and Michelle are staying with her mother until they can afford their own place, or until Armageddon, whichever comes first.

Friday, November 30th, 1973

Q: You describe marriage as an institution created to regulate reproduction. Has it outlived today's liberated woman?

A: Once society figured out that the endgame of sex wasn't ejaculation but conception, something had to be done. The concern was to avoid confusion over paternity, no easy matter given the universal assumption sustained until around the 1800s—that all women are nymphomaniacs by nature.

Q: In your new book you say that women and horrible marriages collided in the 1800s. What made you conclude that women had horrible marriages in the 1800s?

A: There were double standards for women and men in marriage up until the 1800s, and it still goes on today in some sectors of our society. A woman could have only one sexual partner at a time—her husband—while a man could marry or fuck any woman who didn't belong to another man.

Q: Your new book is causing quite a stir in many parts of our society. What would you say to all the people in the conservative movements who want your book banned?

A: Marriage is still the foundation of the family, and, thanks to secular culture, the choice of when, how and whether to separate is left to the individuals concerned, and the double standard has become, theoretically, a single one.

Q: You address several issues associated with marriage and the newly liberated women of the 1970s. What would you say to those women who read your book and follow the blueprint you give them on how to escape unwanted marriages?

A: We've come a long way, baby, and the last hundred years are proof that we can overcome the cruel morality that religion and man have forced upon us. The score will never be even until every woman in the world is free to choose her marital state for herself.

"Tom, you don't just look at the pictures; you actually read the words," Reggie said, after we discovered a *Playboy* in the dumpster and I started reading the interview above to Reggie, as he lusted over the cum-stained pictures.

I love history, but I don't know what happened in the 1800s that led up to the women's movement. We never learned anything about it in school.

Saturday, December 1st, 1973

He placed a ring on her finger, they waved good-bye, and the happy couple was gone. I've kept a souvenir bulletin with the date of their wedding date scrawled on it, so I'll never forget how fast things can change in this fast-paced world. One week, you're riding your bike to school with your best friend, and the next thing you know you're looking at a photo of him on his new driver's license. Howard got his license the Monday before he and Michelle were married. The two of them drove off in Michelle's mother's car for a one-night stay at the Holiday Inn in Sweetwater. He's lucky to have gotten his driver's license so quickly, since as of next year Abilene will require all teens to take driver's education before getting their license because of the accident last Labor Day.

Laurie, James, Reggie and a few other teens from the neighborhood all came to the wedding in James' father's car. Since the start of the Arab-Israeli war, the energy shortage has reached crisis levels in Texas, so everyone's doing their part to save fuel. I'm glad I didn't have to ride with them. Laurie says James' father won't even allow them to turn on the radio.

"Is she pregnant?" Laurie whispered as Pastor Slowley said, "You may kiss the bride." The idea had never occurred to me. Over these past few weeks I've been living in a trance of sorts. I have a recurring nightmare that Pastor Slowley asks me if I've had sex with someone in the church and then forces me up to the altar to say, "I do."

Diary, I haven't been holding back on you; I haven't had sex, yet. But I have been waking up lately with a "Teepee." God only knows why this happens so often. Why does it get so hard, if I'm not supposed to be using it already?

Reggie thinks I should be mad at Howard and Michelle for what happened, but to be honest, I've been so concerned about Howard not having a chance to play wide receiver that I forgot that Michelle was supposed to be my girlfriend. Heck, Howard hit a home run with Michelle and got stuck at home plate with her for the rest of his life. I only got to second, so I'm still free to roam the outfield. Yeah, I guess it's better to suck at some games, especially "the players game."

Tuesday, December 11th, 1973

Guess Who's Coming to Dinner is a funny movie, and I'd like to see it again if I ever get back in a funny mood. Asking what's got me in a foul mood? "Guess who's pregnant?" You guessed it! Michelle. And we all know it takes more than two weeks to find out you're pregnant. *That bitch!* That means she lied to me three weeks ago when I confronted her about getting caught having sex. She swore up and down that it was the first time. Reggie's right; you can't trust dark-skinned girls.

Reggie said, "Tom, you got to get you one of them white girls or a high-yellow—them high-yellow black chicks are the kind that won't lead you wrong, and most white girls have money, if you know what I mean."

My heart fell into my hands when I got the news from Carol about that. All this time, Michelle's been pulling that shit on me about my being too close to Laurie, and the whole time she was on her back behind my back. How did it get this far?! I can't understand the way some girls are!

Monday, December 31st, 1973

And one of the seven angels that had the seven bowls came and spoke with me, saying: 'Come, I will show you the judgment upon the great harlot who sits on many waters. With whom the kings of the earth committed fornication whereas those who inhabit the earth were made drunk with the wine of her fornication. And I caught sight of a woman sitting upon a scarlet-colored wild beast that was full of blasphemous names, and the woman was full of disgusting things.' Well, on catching sight of her I wondered with great wonderment. And Jesus said, 'Why is it you wonder? I will tell you the mystery of the woman and of the wild beast that is carrying her.' Rev: 17

Pastor Slowley preached on this passage yesterday. From what I understood, Satan and his followers revolted against God and were cast down upon the earth to lead the pagan world against the Jehovah's Witnesses. The pagan world is the anti-Christ with all of its worldly Christmas celebrations. It won't be long before Jehovah God destroys the entire wicked system and brings about a new heaven on earth where those of the true religion will live in. While Pastor Slowley preached on Revelations, I substituted Michelle for the great harlot in my mind. I hate that girl, and I hope she's destroyed with the rest of the wicked at Armageddon. She was supposed to be my girlfriend, and I was supposed to have her, not Howard.

It's all so stupid anyhow. Who can interpret Revelations? Wild beasts, seven angels, and seven bowls—it all seems so foreign to me at times. All I know is that Pastor Slowley promises us this will be our last year on earth.

I'm not the only one in a foul mood tonight. Everyone in Texas shares in my disappointment because the Cowboys lost to the Vikings, 27-10, in the playoffs yesterday. I hate the Minnesota Vikings! I hate Michelle! I hate everybody, except Reggie!

Sunday, January 6th, 1974

Boy, the way Glen Miller played
Songs that made the hit parade

Don't know which show I enjoy more, *All in the Family* or *Sanford and Son*. They grabbed the top two spots in TV ratings this year. I love Archie Bunker, even if he is a prejudiced dummy. I love the way he has of speaking the truth about a controversial subject and making the audience laugh about it at the same time. I'm glad Dad's been more lenient with the television lately. Mama only lets us watch the evening news, the same tragic news every day. Wednesday, President Nixon lowered the speed limit to 55 mph in order to save 200,000 barrels of fuel a day, and today they pushed all the clocks ahead an hour to save even more fuel. Obviously the President hasn't been reading *The Watchtower*; if he had, he wouldn't worry, because the end is near. The President made a pretty smart move pushing the clocks ahead, but for a teenager it only means one thing—school starts an hour earlier tomorrow, and we got screwed out of an hour of sleep. Teenagers might look dumb, but some of us aren't.

Sunday, January 13th, 1974

Dad and I watched the Super Bowl together, and both roared our approval of the 24-7 Miami victory over the Vikings! I love the Miami Dolphins! And so does everyone else in Texas. Minnesota finally got what they deserved. Now that the Super Bowl is over, there's no more football until next season on TV. I miss Sunday football with my dad already!

Saturday, January 19th, 1974

"We interrupt this program to bring you this special message"—then President Nixon announced to the nation that voluntarily saving energy can prevent home-heating hardship and gasoline rationing. It wasn't the President's message that upset me so much; it was that he interrupted *Sanford and Son* just as Fred and Lamont were having one of their classic arguments. That big dummy should know by now that everybody already knows that we're running out of fuel and that people in the Middle East are responsible for it. Heck! You can't turn on the evening news without hearing "today in Iran," "today in Lebanon," or "today in Syria" something or other happened. According to the *Abilene Reporter*, the Arabs are ruining the world. I just think they're ruining Friday night TV in America.

Sunday, January 20th, 1974

The Apocalypse (hidden things revealed), the coming of the kingdom of God, will be preceded by Satan and the heyday of evil. Satan and his followers who revolt against God are defeated by Jesus and his angels. Satan and his satanic host are cast down to the world to lead a satanic world against the true Christians, us Jehovah's Witnesses.

The punishments that will fall upon the earth will be plagues of locust for five months that will torture all that inhabit the earth except for those with the mark of the 144,000 stamped on their foreheads. Other angels will empty God's wrath upon the earth, affecting men with terrible sores and turning the sea into blood so every living thing in the sea will die. Another angel will let loose the full heat of the sun upon all unrepentant men. Another angel will cover the earth with darkness. Four angels will lead twice 10,000 times 10,000 knights to slaughter a third of mankind.

Four horsemen will ride forth to kill the people with swords, famine and the wild beasts of the earth. A great earthquake will tumble the planet into ruin. Huge hills with stones will fall upon the surviving infidels and the earth will be destroyed.

The Kings of the earth will come together on the plains of Armageddon for one last conflict with

God, but they will be defeated. Satan and his cohorts everywhere, after they are defeated, will be plunged into hell. Only true Christians will be saved from these disasters. And those of us who have suffered for Christ's sake and are washed in the blood of the lamb will have the bountiful reward that awaits us.

After a thousand years, Satan will be released again to prey upon mankind. Sin will mount again in an unbelieving world. The forces of evil will mount again to try and undo the work of God. They will be defeated again and this time they will be cast into the lake of fire forever. Then will come the last judgment when all the dead will be raised from the graves and the drowned will be raised from the seas. On that day all the names that aren't found in the book of life will be cast in the lake of fire and brimstone forever with Satan.

A new heaven and earth will be formed from the hand of God for a paradise on earth for all of us that have heeded the call of Christ Jesus.

Book of Revelation

Pastor Slowley recited this passage today at church. After hearing it, Spooky wondered, "Why is the President of the United States only worried about the energy shortage? It seems to me that there are a lot of other, more important, things to worry about these days." Oh, well, who am I to wonder about what the President has on his mind? Between Spooky, Smoothy, and Swagger, I've got plenty in my own head to sort out.

Monday, January 28th, 1974

It was an unusual weekend. First, I found Reggie asleep on my bedroom floor Saturday morning. Actually, it was Mama who discovered him when she came in to wake me for Saturday field service. He dropped by Friday night after making his neighborhood rounds, and we talked until the both of us ran out of words.

Mother offered to take Reggie with us Saturday morning to spread the gospel, but Reggie refused the invitation after eating an entire box of Frosted Flakes. Tony the Tiger says, "They're great!"—and I think Reggie agrees with him.

I caught up with Reggie again after church on Sunday. He came by to let me know how well James did in his basketball game on Saturday. James is becoming a real stud. I guess the extra practice is paying off.

Reggie also taught me a phrase I've heard before among my peers. He used "brainwashed" to describe what the Jehovah's Witnesses have done to me. Charles used that word before he went to live with his granny, and Laurie also used that word to describe our religion's method of conversion. Sometimes, I wonder if they're onto something, but other times I feel certain that I'm lucky to be part of the true faith.

Monday, February 4th, 1974

"Patricia Hearst, 19-year-old granddaughter of publisher William Randolph Hearst, was taken from her apartment in Berkeley today." It's about time Barbara Walters led off with something besides the fuel shortage. I feel sorry for the chick, but I am sick and tired of hearing about long gasoline lines.

Friday, February 22nd, 1974

"The attempted hijacking of a Delta flight was prevented when the hijacker was shot to death after killing a policeman and the plane's copilot," a TV newsman said today. It happened at the Baltimore-Washington Airport, and it was neat to watch the dead being pulled off the airplane right there on the boob tube. And yesterday, there was another kidnapping. This time, it was an *Atlanta Constitution* editor by the name of J. Reginald Murphy. The kidnappers made off with about $700,000. Not bad for a day's work. By the way, I found out who Patty Hearst is. She's the granddaughter of one of the richest men in the world. I bet the kidnappers who snatched her get a lot more than $700,000. With all this terrible stuff going on in the world these days, Pastor Slowley must be right: The end is near.

Friday, March 1st, 1974

Frantically I searched, but I couldn't find them! I spent hours in the "library" each morning searching for articles that were assigned by my modern history teacher, Mr. Moore, but it was just a cruel joke. Our assignment Monday morning was: "Class, I want you to find these articles from the *Abilene Reporter* in February. All I'm giving you is the headline, and you're responsible for finding the articles. You can search the archives in the school library, if needed. Your assignment is due by Friday. Here are the three headlines: 'Mother kills her five kids, says they're better off in heaven,' 'Hundreds shaken by San Francisco earthquake,' and 'Officers search for men who blew up the post office.'"

I didn't think I would have to use the school library, since my dad keeps about a month of back issues on hand. But when I looked through them Monday night, I couldn't find a thing. By Wednesday, after rummaging through nearly 21 days of back issues, it was plain that my search was in vain. I showed up in class on Friday morning empty-handed, and so did nearly all of the class. Holly Winter, Annabel Hudson, and Laurie were the only three who completed the assignment. It turns out that all of the events happened between 50 and 100 years ago in the month of February.

Who knew that the world was just as out of control 100 years ago as it is now? The way people talk these days, you'd think that times have never been this bad.

"Spooky" is starting to wonder if I'm being frightened by prophesies of catastrophe, demons and Armageddon for nothing. "Swagger" says I should listen to Reggie and Laurie; they're starting to make more sense than my mother does.

Saturday, March 2nd, 1974

Gemini: *Your family life will be in chaos today, but you rise above it all. In the evening, write a letter to a dear friend.*

I've been listening to "Swagger." I'm feeling cocky, and, yeah, I know I'm bad! I read my horoscope today, and it was right on. You want to talk about chaos in a family? It started as soon as my eyes popped open.

I could hear yelling coming from the kitchen. Mama and Carol were having a fight about "the bloody mess." I later found out that Carol started her first period this morning at the age of 13, something Mother had not anticipated. The sound of slamming doors brought me to my feet. I took a quick peek at the clock on Mike's side of the room, saw it wasn't even 7 a.m., and Mike wasn't in his bed. Slamming doors on Saturday mornings are becoming a habit. I walked into the kitchen to find Mike and Dad engaged in one of their biweekly payday disputes. Mike spends his paychecks on new albums on Friday, after he gets paid. Then, Saturday morning, Dad always asks him for money to help out with household expenses.

"Get back here, young man," dad said. "If you think you don't have responsibilities around here, you are sadly mistaken. There is a price to pay for not being around to help with household chores. Just because you get paid for your work now doesn't mean that you don't have to help out around here. You either start pulling your own weight by doing chores like everyone else, or you pay your part of the bills."

"Just because you can't pay for all of the children you fathered doesn't mean that I'm responsible for them. I already pay for my own clothes, and I gave up my allowance when I started working, so I figure we're about even," Mike said, walking out the screen door and letting it slam behind him.

"That kind of thinking is going to figure you right out of this house, Michael! You'd better consider that before you spend your next paycheck!" Dad shouted after him, slamming the storm door.

By nine, I was delighted to go do field service and escape the ruckus at home. As I knocked on my first door, I was more at peace than I had been all morning. I had a pretty good day, too. I sold 13 magazines in three-and-a-half hours.

It's evening, and the final proof of my horoscope's accuracy is that I am indeed finishing off my day by writing a letter to a dear friend. Thanks for listening, Diary.

Sunday, March 3rd, 1974

Gemini: *Learn to listen to others when important events baffle you. You hear from distant relatives concerning their whereabouts.*

Today's horoscope has been equally accurate.

The headline sprawled on the bathroom floor caught my attention—"Worst air disaster in history kills 346." Normally, when I read something like that, "Spooky" takes control of my thoughts, and I think about last days. But today was different. I met up with Howard after church and casually mentioned yesterday's air disaster to him, but he just shrugged it off as the cost of flying in an airplane.

Later in the afternoon, I purposely ran into Reggie to see if he had written a letter to an old friend on Saturday night, since he's a Gemini, too. He said he hadn't written to an old friend, but he did write a note to his math teacher, apologizing for falling asleep in her class for the third time. Wow, those horoscopes are amazing; for Reggie to write anything is a miracle.

I happened to mention yesterday's air disaster to Reggie, too, but, as usual, he was unaware of anything to do with current events, except for the scores of the three NBA games on Saturday.

The climax of this evening came by way of a telephone call.

"Hello, Frank. How are you doing?"

"_____"

"Yeah, I know you just retired, why?"

"_____"

"Well, I can see how you don't want to raise your kids out in California with all of those crazies, but I thought you wanted to move back to South Carolina."

"_____"

"Yeah, things are different now."

"_____"

"We really like it. Abilene is pretty quiet, and this neighborhood has some pretty good deals on housing right now."

"_____"

"Well, if you're serious about coming out here, you'd better do it before school starts. How soon can you get here?"

"_____"

"Mid-March? That soon, huh? Well, I'm not sure about the kids missing so much school, but I know you have to get out of the base housing pretty soon, and there's no sense in moving twice."

"_____"

"Sure. You guys can all stay here until you find a place. We'll make room. Call me back when you know what day you'll arrive. Bye. Give my love to your family."

Diary, I know it's rude to eavesdrop on conversations, but it was just my dad. That accounts for the distant relatives and their whereabouts.

Tuesday, March 5th, 1974

"Hey, Tom, what did our horoscope in the newspaper predict for us today?" Reggie asked eagerly as he walked in our front door.

My mama heard him from the kitchen and frowned in disapproval. Reggie has a way of knocking and entering before he's invited inside. He had no idea of the jeopardy he placed me in with my mother. If only he'd waited a millisecond before blurting that out, I could have warned him, and I wouldn't be in so much trouble.

After Reggie left, Mom came over to me and asked me sarcastically, "Tom, have you been reading the horoscopes in the paper? Your punishment for such sinful behavior is that you can no longer have that boy over here. Do I make myself clear? Reggie is part of this demon-possessed world, and you've been warned about worldly associations. Besides, Tom, Reggie looks too much older than you."

Before I could tell her that Reggie is only 376 days older, I found him banned from my life. According to Bible chronology, these are the last days, but it feels as if my life is over already. It's terrible to lose another best friend, again in the name of religion—first Charles, then Howard, and now Reggie. I just don't get it!

Gemini: *Watch what you say to others; it just might cause you more pain than previously thought.*

Diary, this was yesterday's horoscope. After reading it and going through what happened between Reggie and me during the past 24 hours, I'm starting to believe in astrology.

Sunday, March 10th, 1974

Picture this: "A harlot is sitting on the back of a fearsome beast with seven heads and ten horns." (Revelation 17: 1-4) Whom does the harlot represent? She exerts influence "over the kings of the earth," "dresses in purple," "uses incense," and is "exceedingly wealthy." In addition, by means of her spiritual practice, "all the nations are misled." Pastor Slowley says that this harlot is worldwide religion—not any one religion, but all the false religions in the world. His sermon today focused on the idea that Jehovah's Witnesses are the only true Christians. Sunday sermons have intensified lately, and all the members in the congregation are eager for Armageddon to arrive. Sister Franklin has already sold her house-cleaning business, and most of the congregation have sold their homes.

What must you do if you do not want to share in the fate of false religion? "Get out of here, my people," urges God's messenger. If this is fire and brimstone preaching, I can do without it, but I guess you've got to go through hell before you get to heaven. I hate the book of Revelation; it frightens the devil out of me to hear about the fate of all the worldly people, especially since that includes Reggie and Laurie.

My dad's not buying into Mama's doomsday prophesies. He told us this week that Frank and his family are moving to Texas soon; they'll be here by the end of spring break. He jokes that if all of Mama's crazy friends want to sell their homes, that just means there will be plenty for Frank to choose from when they arrive.

Thursday, March 14th, 1974

"Hey, Tom! That shit your mama is raising you in is a cult!" Reggie said when I picked up the phone. Then the phone went silent. When it rang again, I heard, "You're being brainwashed, partner."

Word had gotten to Reggie somehow that he's not allowed in our home any longer. It's the age of communication, and teenagers always find a way to communicate no matter how hard their parents try to stop them. I have my suspicions about who told him, but I can't prove it. Around our house secrets leak out in two ways—by telephone or by tell-a-Carol.

It's a cult?! Laurie had said the same thing a year and a half ago. I'll never forget the way she extinguished her cigarette and looked at me with her emerald eyes as if

---

"Hey, Tom! That shit your mama is raising you in is a cult!" Reggie said when I picked up the phone. Then the phone went silent. When it rang again, I heard, "You're being brainwashed, partner."

---

she could see right through me as she said, "Tom, it's a cult."

I looked up "cult" in the dictionary, and the definition is: "a system or community of religious worship and ritual, usually with a charismatic leader and unorthodox or extremist views." I still don't understand. It seems like the simple things are the hardest to comprehend. Are Laurie and Reggie right, or are they just devils, bent on undermining my salvation?

Saturday, March 16th, 1974

One o'clock in the morning, and guess who is sitting up with his bedside-table light on? Mike is working the graveyard shift, and I'm here alone, pondering the latest twist of events around here. First, I had six hours of field service today, and then we had a special three-hour Bible study at Kingdom Hall about how to greet the resurrected after Armageddon. Who would have thought that I will soon be talking to people who were once dead? Pastor Slowley read 1 Thessalonians 4:16 and said it means that those of us who are saved will have to preach the gospel to them. That should cure my boredom with ministry.

Diary, I was so burned out this evening that I fell asleep around eight, only to be wide awake again now. It was the first time I can remember falling asleep without saying my prayers, which is what woke me from my dream. I sat up in bed and started thinking about the 346 people who died two weeks ago, and wondered if they had all died because they forgot to pray before boarding the plane.

It's bizarre what thoughts will come and go in my head, and sometimes I wonder if I'm crazy. Questions float through my mind while I'm trying to sleep: Where does a thought come from? Why am I scared when all the lights are out? When is my brother coming home from work? I try hard to get back to sleep so that these disturbing thoughts will stop, but the harder I try the less sleepy I feel. I wonder what the astrological prediction was on the day all those people died in that airline disaster? Hopefully, when I wake up, I'll find I've only been dreaming all this stuff.

Wednesday, March 20th, 1974

"Curious George" is what Pastor Slowley called me when I asked about the plane crash and the victims' prayers. Curious George is a cartoon monkey.

"All you need to know, Tom, is that we Jehovah's Witnesses know the truth. We're the only religion preaching the true gospel of Jesus Christ, and to be saved you just need to continue spreading the good news." He was going to leave it at that, but then he looked into my eyes and saw that I wasn't really satisfied with his response. "Tom, when Jesus was on earth, he spoke extensively about the kingdom of God. People who heard him wanted to know when his marvelous kingdom would come.

Three days before he was crucified, his disciples asked him: "What will be the sign?" Jesus told them that only Jehovah God knew the precise time when the kingdom would take full control of the earth. However, Tom, Jesus did foretell certain events that would serve as proof that he was ruling. Before I explain the visible evidence that we are living in the last days, let us briefly consider an event that happened in the spirit realm. Jesus became the King of heaven in 1914. Immediately after receiving kingdom power, Jesus took action. Revelation twelve tells us: 'War broke out in heaven: Michael and his angels battled with the dragon, and the dragon and his angels battled.' Michael is Jesus and the dragon is Satan, and the devil's fury has brought woe, suffering, and affliction to those dwelling on earth. Tom, the Devil is causing all this unrest and bad things to happen."

So there you have it, Diary. According to Pastor Slowley, the Devil caused that plane to crash. He's running loose on earth for a short time creating chaos. The pastor's explanation sounded logical to me, but today, when I was sitting on the toilet, I saw in the *Abilene Reporter* that some FAA guy said the crash was caused by a mechanical failure.

I only have one thing to say: "Thank God I wasn't on that flight."

Sunday, March 24th, 1974

The problem with children is not that they are childish, for that is excusable: "When I was a child,

I spoke as a child; I understood as a child, I thought as a child." Rather, the problem with children is that they are foolish, bound in the folly of sin. (1 Corinthians 13:11)

The Devil made me do it! If Flip Wilson can use this line, so can I. Flip Wilson is this famous, black comedian my dad watches on Saturday nights. He says, "The devil made me do it," whenever he does bad things on the show. Today was the first time I didn't put my offering in the plate at church. The Devil made me do it! The way I see it, God doesn't need another dollar. I had to do a little sleight of hand to fool my mother. I saw this trick in a movie called *Cool Hand Luke* a month ago, and I figure, if I do it 10 times, I can stash away $10 in three weeks, since we go to church three times a week. Not bad thinking, considering only yesterday I couldn't figure out how I was ever going to save enough money for a Johnny Unitas leather football.

Sunday, March 31st, 1974

March was the wettest month on record in West Texas, according to an article last Tuesday. The paper said that Abilene got more rain this month than Seattle did. Dad loves the extra water, because the fishing ponds and lakes he and his buddies frequent in the spring will have loads of Texas black bass.

My afternoons lately have been spent in the high school library, working on an assignment—not a school project, a church project. Mama, I suspect with a little prodding from Pastor Slowley, gave me the task of finding out where the pagan Easter celebration originated. We don't celebrate Easter. Pastor Slowley says that the Bible clearly says it's a sin to put any day above another, so we don't even celebrate birthdays. Most kids at school ridicule us for our beliefs, but some feel sorry for us sitting on the sidelines during holiday or birthday celebrations at school. I've grown accustomed to being left out and ridiculed. Anyway, the assignment turned out to be an eye-opening experience. Guess what I discovered? Got to run! I hear Mama coming, and I'm supposed to be studying my *Watchtower*.

Monday, April 1st, 1974

No April fooling—it rained again today! This is about the 10th day of rain in a row, and the forecast for tomorrow calls for more. The meteorologist said Abilene set a new March precipitation record. Mama says it's a sign of the end, but Dad says she's nuts to believe that. Dad also said that the entire city is on suicide alert, because of the gloomy days. Now, I find that hard to believe!

Diary, this is a bit off the subject but it does correlate with what's going on with me these days. Wet dreams! Do I need to say anymore? Another wet dream! For the second time in five days, I've had a wet dream and can't figure out why. I swear I haven't looked at any nude girls since that time I saw Vicky. But at one o'clock this morning I was up cleaning the off-white-colored stains on my underwear. If these dreams continue, I may have to ask Mike about them. The only reason I know it's called a "wet dream" is that Reggie mentioned it in a remark to Laurie last summer when we were playing football.

He said, "I had a wet dream about you last night, sweetheart." Laurie got really angry, gave him the finger, and stalked away.

Speaking of dreams, I wonder whether I have control over my wet dreams or if this is just another trick by the Devil. I don't know what to believe anymore. Whatever the case, Diary, just between us, a wet dream feels pretty darn good when you're in the middle of one. Of course, it's a nuisance to have to get up and clean your underwear before your mother sees them in the laundry.

Friday, April 5th, 1974

Foolishness is found in the heart of a child! It is such an integral part of his nature that he cannot escape from it. As surely as Israel's thoughts and actions were to be governed by Jehovah's laws, bound to their foreheads and hands, so surely are a child's thoughts and actions governed by the foolishness bound in his heart.
Deuteronomy 6:8

Mother Nature continues to produce her little surprises and pushes you to do things you'd never dream you'd do. For me, this meant finally getting up enough nerve to ask my older brother about these inconvenient dreams. I had another wet dream Monday night—three times in less than two weeks! But the anticipated nightmare didn't turn out the way I thought it would.

Mike said, "Tom, subconsciously you're probably wanting to get a piece of ass off one of those hot, high school chicks, but consciously you know you'll never get it, and that our old man would kill you if he found out you hooked up before you got married."

Mike's got a way with words. He left me with these parting words as he drifted away from our bedroom. "Tom," he shouted, "if you don't like my explanation of what causes wet dreams, you could always go ask our old man to explain it!" Then, he laughed sarcastically. No teenage boy in his right mind would ever ask his dad where wet dreams come from!

By the way, Diary, I turned in my research assignment. Pastor Slowley and Mama were very pleased with my attention to detail. When I was reading up on Easter, I found out that there are thousands of different religions and philosophies around the world. Some of their beliefs will astound you! Check this out. Hindus believe in reincarnation and a supreme being of many forms and natures, so they think that when we eat meat we could be eating one of their ancestors. How funny! Buddhists, like Laurie's mom, believe that inward extinction of the self and the senses culminates in a state of illumination beyond both suffering and existence. They also believe they've been on earth before, and they keep coming back until they're perfect. Imagine me being a Buddhist; I'd have to come back to earth a million times. People will believe anything! Some people even believe we've descended from monkeys. Ridiculous!

Monday, April 15th, 1974

Crash! I heard the plate chattered against the kitchen wall. It barely missed Mike's head as he ducked out the back door. Luckily, Mama has never had the greatest aim.

"Louise, those damn taxes have to be postmarked today," I heard my dad say just before she threw the dish at my brother.

"Tom has been in the bathroom three minutes longer than his allotted time this morning," Carol whined.

"Yeah, well, we're always rushing to school because you have to have your cereal toasted before you'll eat it."

Diary, this is what it's like every morning around here in this house. Like my brother says, "It's a zoo around here before school." But I always think that this havoc is just a prelude to the real circus at Abilene High School. Lions fighting with tigers and bears swapping barbs with hyenas—all this animosity makes you want to stay in bed and keep dreaming, but you always awaken to the nightmare of another school day.

I haven't had any wet dreams for almost two weeks. I'm also happy to report that I did some research on dreams at school. I found out that once upon a time dreams were considered visions of the highest order by tribal rulers. It seems ancient man was more in touch with his inner self and the workings of the soul than we are today, and believed dreams were messages from the gods. But, more recently, psychologists have suggested that dreams come from the subconscious, not from God. So my brother's analysis of the situation wasn't completely wrong. Freud asserted that our dreams put us in touch with our dark sides, the subconscious, un-recognized aspects of our personality and so on.

Some of their beliefs will astound you! At school, the principal and faculty decided to introduce a new security measure to the campus. They hired a new secu-rity person whose only job is to make sure every person on campus has a genuine reason for being there. The guard is 6'4" and has an arrogant attitude toward the students. They call him Cowboy John, and he's the first real black cowboy I've even seen. He has ropes tied to the side of his Ford truck and dried cow manure in the truck bed. He announced that he is around to make sure that our campus remains free of unwanted guests, referring to the teens that hang around our school but don't belong there. Why would anyone come to school if he didn't have to?

The evening hours caught me comforting Laurie in the tree house. Her eyes were full of tears when I arrived, but she never really explained why she'd been crying. From what little I could gather it had something to do with her father. She mentioned him a few times while we were talking, but if she doesn't want to confide all of her deepest secrets to me, I guess I'll remain in the dark.

I want her to consider me her closest ally, but for some reason she still refers to me as a "little punk," and thinks I'm "a cross between Einstein and Frankenstein."

While we're on the subject of secrets, Diary, something secret is also going on at church. I gathered bits and pieces of the story yesterday at the church picnic, and I'm left with the impression that the elders are in the middle of another disfellowship discussion. "Molestation" kept popping up in adult conversations. That word is probably serious, like other "ation" words: segregation, integration, interrogation and globalization. But when adults say "molestation," it's as if they're embarrassed. Mr. Sonny mentioned it, and the entire table came to a hush.

Friday, April 26th, 1974

Who in the heck is looking out for us? Diary, when I say "us," I'm talking about the teenagers. I looked up "molestation," and it means to make annoying sexual advances upon another persona, usually a child or a weaker person. A rumor circulated around church that an elder had gotten his hands on Lisa Slowley. Sister Booker says the entire mess should be swept under the rug for the sake of preserving order. Is he guilty? Yes, according to Lisa. She confided with me that Brother Herman had touched her inappropriately several times. The elders had a three-hour meeting, and then the top elder announced that Jehovah God's will was to leave Brother Herman's punishment to God's discretion. Lisa said it's because Brother Herman is rich, and no one wanted to see his money leave the church.

So there you have it, Diary. "Money talks and bullshit walks," as Reggie likes to say, and now I know what he means. Brother Herman's only punishment is that he can't be alone with teenage girls any longer. Mother said two of the black elders alleged racism, because of the discrepancy between Leonard's and Brother Herman's sentences. Others in the congregation remained rather tight-lipped after the decision was handed down, and some even questioned the authority of the Watchtower Bible and Tract Society, which is the headquarters in New York City, that sets the rules for our church. I'm not totally sure if Jehovah God lives there, too, but they say they get messages straight from Jehovah God himself at the headquarters and put this information into our publications.

The priest! The pastor! The polygamist! Diary, I wonder at times whether God really gave these people their authority. If religious authorities can defend child molesters, create racial hatred, and force teenage girls into marriage with polygamists in the name of God, I wonder what kind of a god I'm supposed to believe in.

Tuesday, April 30th, 1974

Crash! Another plate chattered against the kitchen wall, barely missing Mike. Mama's justification for this repeat performance came out when I got to school.

"Yo, your brother is a real radical! I didn't know he was so cool!" said a couple of teenagers as I arrived.

It didn't take long for me to discover what had made Mike an overnight sensation. He was standing in the middle of the hall wearing a white T-shirt with "Fuck you" in bold black lettering. Cowboy John also saw the shirt, and, as of today, Mike is expelled from school. No wonder Mama was ranting. I would have thrown the kitchen sink at him if I had seen his fashion creation. But, on the other hand, I wouldn't have been so suddenly popular, except for his antics. Girls who wouldn't give me the time of day suddenly wanted to talk to me about Mike's shirt.

Monday, May 20th, 1974

I've been talking to myself and feeling not quite as bold as I have in the past. Some days, I'd like to just quit living. Nothing in life seems to fit, and it's true that rainy days and Mondays have a way of bringing you down. Diary, it's funny how I always end up here with you when I feel this way. It's so nice that I can always vent my inner feelings with pen and paper.

You ask, "How are you feeling, Tom?"

Well, I don't actually know; I can't really put my finger on it, so I'm sitting here with a pen in one hand and my dad's pistol in the other.

Spooky says to me, "Pull the trigger, Tom; no one would ever miss you."

Swagger says, "Tom, you're a little chicken. I double-dog dare you to pull the trigger; you haven't got the guts."

Thank God for Smoothy, who says, "Tom, these uneasy feelings will pass, too, and tomorrow will look a lot brighter than today."

Dr. Scott once told me that a suicide attempt is likely to lead to another attempt. Is it too late for me? Has my mind crossed over the fine line separating insanity from sanity? I've been sitting nearly catatonic, contemplating suicide for the past 45 minutes. Diary, I think I'll slip the gun back under Dad's mattress, before he discovers it's missing. I can always decide later.

Friday, May 31st, 1974

The long and winding road always leads me back to these blank pages! Diary, a maze of events changed the shape of my world in May. If April showers are supposed to bring May flowers, then God's got things all screwed up with the weather. It's still raining.

I stayed after school today at the library to do some more research on dreams, but after several hours I had to close the books because there's just too much to ponder. Are your dreams composed from your reality, or just events lost in your head from previous lives? I've come to the conclusion that I'll never know, so I'm not going to bother reading anymore about them. The what-ifs could go on indefinitely.

I started seeing Dr. Scott again. I landed back in his office as the result of a bizarre series of events. I started accompanying my mother to her appointments with him after her miscarriage. Yes, you heard me right. Our family spent several sleepless nights and restless days since her miscarriage near the beginning of the month. Nothing could have prepared us for such an uncanny event. This episode is difficult to write about, but my emotions are way off the charts on this one.

So I've got to keep writing about it, or I'll go crazy. It's not just me having a rough time; I can see the anguish painted on the faces of my sisters and my dad. When the news of the miscarriage first surfaced, Carol had to explain to me what happened. After she did, my brain went into overload. Questions exploded in my head, like, "Why were Mama and Dad trying to have another baby?" and "Why would Mama want to bring another child into a world that was on the edge of destruction?" Other voices in my head started to cloud my thinking, too—not Spooky, Smoothy or Swagger, but new voices sending signals of distress and doubt about everything that I'd ever believed. I'd never heard so much confusion in my head at the same time.

My dad's voice echoed in my head loud and clear: "Louise, we don't have enough money for any extras this month, so watch your spending when you go to the commissary." I couldn't help wondering why he would be making more children, if his budget was too tight to support the children he already has. This is the litany of questioning that had me sitting on the verge of suicide a couple of weeks ago. I'd like to forget how close I came to pulling the trigger, and am thankful that Smoothy convinced me not to.

Looking back on this month, I realize that it all came together for me around the 23rd. For the first time in my life, I realized that the teenagers in our house are smarter than the grown-ups. Over the past month, I've come to pity my mother, because I finally realize how lost she must be to believe the predictions of our church leaders.

My brother nailed it when he said, "Mama's hormones are out of balance; that's why she's thrown a couple of plates at my head recently. We learned about it in health class."

Diary, it seems that Mama had no idea what was going on in her own body until she saw blood on the toilet seat one morning before we left for school.

During the past several visits to Dr. Scott's office, he gave me an I.Q. test. I got the results back today, and scored a 148 on the testing. I don't know what the fuss is about, but everyone in the office was blown away by the results. It seems a score of 148 is in the top 1% of all the people who have taken the test. For me, the score means little, because it takes Mike, Carol, Reggie, and Laurie to help me understand even the simplest things about life.

Monday, June 3rd, 1974

Just for a moment, imagine that it's pouring rain as you ride to Sunday church services, when you see Howard's stepfather dressed in his seersucker suit, changing a flat tire on the side of the road. As you pull alongside him, Leonard looks first relieved and then horrified as he realizes that the occupants of the vehicle stopping to help him are members of his congregation. They start to roll down the window to offer assistance, but quickly roll it back up and speed away once they see Leonard's face. This is exactly what happened yesterday. The entire situation was crazy, because later that morning, Leonard arrived at church soaking wet and shivering. He took his seat on the back pew, and no one offered him anything for warmth. I tried to explain to Howard how I'd tried to force Leonard into our car, but Mama sped away, yelling to us that we couldn't speak to him. Howard explained to me that Leonard has to take a separate car to church and that no one in his family had spoken to him since he was disfellowshipped several months ago.

Even with a 148 I.Q., I'm not clever enough to understand how a religious organization can prevent a man from associating with his own family. "Cult" really does seem to fit our church sometimes. Why would a man walk to church in the pouring rain just because another man told him that it was the only way to return to God's grace? It must be that he believes that our church is the only true way to God, and that makes me think he may be right. Job, Jonah, Isaiah, and Ezekiel, please, hear me now, because I can't make sense of the fact that Leonard is out in the cold rain, even though Brother Herman is still warm inside. Please, tell me that I'm not losing my mind!

Friday, June 7th, 1974

I sent a letter through the mail to my mother, stating that I no longer think it best for me to continue going to the Jehovah's Witness meetings, and I laid out my reasons for this decision.

"Boy, as long as you live under my roof, you will do as I tell you, and you're going to attend those church meetings," my dad yelled, as I walked in the house this evening.

He doesn't go to those church meetings, so why should I go? Am I not old enough to make up my own mind? Is it all a cult of brainwashing, or is the world really going to end in 1975?

Part III
AT FIFTEEN
All in the Family

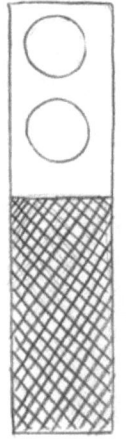

Thursday, July 25th, 1974

The picture is changing, and I'm now part of the crowd; they're all laughing at something, and the music is playing loud.

I said, "Laurie, let me introduce you to my cousin Joe. This is his brother, Derrick, and his sisters, Ann, Mallory and Sheila."

"Nice to meet you all," she replied with a smile.

Diary, our nation celebrated its 198th year of independence three weeks ago, and today Tom is celebrating his 16th day of independence from parental rules. I haven't attended a single Jehovah's Witness meeting since my proclamation that I was taking charge of my own life. It's not that I dislike being one of Jehovah's Witnesses; it's just that I don't like being forced to do something I don't fully understand.

I keep hearing the elders say, "Repent before it's too late! The end is at hand!"

But my eyes see the world saying something entirely different. Who doesn't want to avoid dying in Armageddon? Unlike America's bullet-ridden fight for freedom from British rule two centuries ago, my battle for independence was won without firing a single shot. It all seems a little too easy.

A few weeks ago, I overheard Dad talking to Uncle Frank about his family's arrival in Abilene.

"What day are you arriving? And there are seven of you, right? So we'll need at least two cars, maybe more, since you'll have a lot of luggage," Dad said, scribbling notes on a legal pad. As soon as he hung up the phone, he was bombarded with questions.

"Are Uncle Frank and his family really moving to Abilene next week?" Gayle shouted.

"How many kids are in Uncle Frank's family?" Carol asked.

"Where are they going to stay, Larry?" Mama said, already looking displeased.

"Louise, I told Frank that we'd put them up here until they can find a place of their own. With all the foreclosures on the market now, you know it won't take long for them to find a place."

"I know it won't be easy either," she retorted. "You know how devilish Frank can be, given his history."

The question of where they are going to stay has turned out to be the answer to my prayers. Uncle Frank, Aunt Trudy, and their five teenagers have left their mark on our quiet household over the past two weeks. If their arrival hadn't interfered, I'm fairly certain my declaration would have resulted in a war between my parents and me. I was prepared for a fight with my parents, but when two taxis appeared in our driveway and luggage began to clutter our halls, the war between the generations swiftly culminated in a landslide victory for the teenagers.

"Frank, will you, please, tell Joe not to smoke in our house?" "Ann, will you please turn down that music?!"

"Trudy, will you please tell Mallory that her skirt is too short to wear in public?"

The "pleases" continued coming from my parents' lips, but by the second day, it was clear they didn't have the stomach to fight. The day before they arrived, my mother made us stand at attention while she lectured us about how to conduct ourselves while Frank's family stayed with us. Forty-eight hours later, the teenage occupation had begun.

Rules! What rules? How can our parents enforce them? Even a blind man could see that with seven teenagers living under one roof it's only a matter of time before they have total control of the house. My fight for freedom was won, and there's not one bit of collateral damage.

Tuesday, August 6th, 1974

With fourteen people sharing one bathroom, the "family library" just isn't the same. The past few days, my butt hardly touches the toilet seat before someone's knocking at the bathroom door, accusing me of taking too long. Reading the newspaper in there is history.

"It won't be long before Frank gets the approval from the Veteran's Administration to purchase the foreclosed home they looked at last week," Dad said today.

"I don't know about that, Larry. The real estate agent said Frank's credit history isn't good," Mama said sullenly.

With the arrival of my cousins came a smorgasbord of music. Our family stereo has been playing Al Wilson, Hues Corporation, Roberta Flack, Billy Preston, The Spinners, and Carl Douglas to the chagrin of my mother, who just sighs and walks away.

When I first heard that they might move to Texas, I assumed that my cousins would be devout Baptists, challenging me to Biblical debates on a regular basis. Innocent Baptists, indeed! Brother, when I say far from innocent, I mean 180 degrees from it. People say that I've got a lot of book-sense, but no amount of reading library books could have prepared me for the kind of education I've gotten from my cousins. I never fully understood the term "worldly" before. Mom often used it to describe my older brother and his music albums. Well, the picture around our house has certainly changed. My cousins smoke, have three-inch afros, and listen to 45s and LPs whenever they want. Even God couldn't have predicted this change under our JW household roof.

Thursday, August 15th, 1974

"Eat all your food. There are starving people in China." "Don't masturbate or you'll go blind." "When I was a kid we had to walk to school in the snow uphill both ways." "People in hell want ice water." Diary, I'm beginning to think the kids in our house have heard just about every cliché, and, frankly, I have my doubts about whether any of them are true.

Although my cousins have only been living with us for a little over three weeks, my mother says she can already see their worldly influence rubbing off on Mike and me. All I did wrong was leave the house without Mom's permission, and I only went to Kmart. I was with my cousin, Joe, so what's the big deal? Mike, on the other hand, spent his entire paycheck on new albums, which really pissed off my father.

Diary, I seriously thought about leaving you to collect dust on a shelf in my room after my cousins arrived, since I have people my own age to chat with, but even they can't replace you. For one thing, I find that, at times like this, I really need another outlet to express what's going on inside of me, rather than talking to a person, no matter how closely we're related. Diary, how do I begin to tell you what's gone down over the past week around here?

Tuesday was a typical sweaty 99-degree day in Texas, and every creature under the sun was looking for shade to escape the heat. Joe, Reggie and I found a cool shady spot in Reggie's mom's room. Reggie's mom, Shirley, is tough, 6'2", stocky, and a single mother of four. She was at work, so the three of us had her air-conditioned room to ourselves for a few hours while we watched *The Summer of '42* on TV. The movie is a coming-of-age story about a teenage boy on summer vacation on Nantucket Island in 1942 who begins a one-sided romance with an older woman whose husband is overseas fighting in the war. Their relationship ends after the depressed and drunk woman makes love to him after receiving news of her husband's death.

"Get the fuck out of my bedroom!" Shirley yelled from her bedroom door. We were so engrossed in the movie that we hadn't heard her come in the front door. "Who the hell told you niggers that you could put your sweaty asses on my clean sheets? Reggie, who said you could run my damned air conditioner for these hoodlums without paying one cent towards the electric bill?"

"Chill out, Mama," he said, his bright smile lighting up the dark room. Then, suddenly, the three of us found ourselves outside running away from various hurling objects.

"I masturbate at least twice a day," Joe said to Reggie and me as we stood under the shade tree in my yard.

"I masturbate three times a day," Reggie boasted. Then the two of them looked my way.

"I masturbate four times a day," I lied with a confident stare.

"Damn, Tom, you're a bad mother fucker," Reggie said, as he and Joe broke out laughing.

I don't know if they believed me then, but as of today, I'm telling the truth. I was under the impression that boys were only supposed to masturbate every once in a while, but after hearing how much Reggie and Joe masturbate, I decided to give my pecker a few more yanks. Reggie also told me that black guys have bigger dicks than other races, and the reason is that we masturbate more often.

So, first thing yesterday morning, I started in. I brought my mind back to a Henry Miller novel I'd read in a single day, *Tropic of Cancer*. That novel gave me ideas about girls I'd never imagined before. I had awakened with the teepee already, so it was no big deal to get started. Later, I masturbated in the shower, and then again while I was in the tree house waiting for Laurie. She never did show up. To my surprise, the darn thing got hard again at night when I was in the shower. Count them, Diary. Four times in one day. Before yesterday, I thought it was impossible to masturbate four times in one day. And I'm not so sure I believe my parents about masturbation leading to blindness, but I'll keep an eye on it. Get it?! I'll keep an eye on it! Ha ha. Later!

Saturday, August 17th, 1974

Yes, the picture around our home has certainly changed. Diary, for the first time, I feel part of the worldly crowd and not the spectator I've been for so many years.

My mother left for field service without me this Saturday. All three of my sisters still had to go, and Mike always makes sure he's scheduled to work Saturday mornings. For some reason, though, Mother hasn't pushed me to come for the past three Saturdays. My cousins and I watched cartoons first thing Saturday morning—*The Flintstones*, then *Scooby-Doo*, then *Fat Albert*, and then *The Jetsons*.

"It's so nice to be at home on a Saturday. I've never seen any of these shows before. We always have to leave before they start," I said, munching on my second bowl of cereal.

"What do you usually do?" Mallory asked.

"Up until a few weeks ago, I had to go out to do field service with my mother and sisters, but I wrote my mother a letter before you arrived and said I wouldn't do it anymore. Luckily, she hasn't made a big deal over it, since the crowd in the house has distracted her."

"What's field service?" Mallory asked.

"Well, Jehovah's Witnesses are commanded by God to witness their faith to non-believers. That's why we're called Witnesses. So, every Saturday, we all go door to door selling *Watchtower* magazines in an effort to spread God's word about his true church," I said.

"So how much do you make off of each magazine?" she asked.

"We buy the magazine from the elders for 10 cents apiece with our own money, and then we sell the magazines for 10 cents apiece. We don't salute the flag or pledge allegiance to the government or anything like that, either. It's all in the Bible."

"So, let me get this straight," Mallory said. "You buy the magazines for 10 cents and then you sell them for the same price. Where's the profit in that?"

"We don't sell them for profit; we sell them to save souls," I said. "We believe the world will end within the next year, so we're running out of time to save the non-believers from Armageddon."

Laughter exploded from my cousins. "Tom, your dad is in the military, so don't you think it's strange that you won't pledge allegiance or salute the American flag?" Mallory asked.

"Wow, that's a question no one's ever asked me," I said in confusion.

"Where does it say in the Bible that the world won't last past the year 1975?" asked my older cousin, Sheila.

"I don't remember where exactly, but I do know that the latest Watchtower says, 'Millions living today will never die,' and the world will end by the year 1975. It says God will set up a paradise on earth for us after He destroys the wicked people of the earth."

"How do you know that you're not knocking on a Christian's door?" Mallory demanded, skeptically.

"We know all of the Jehovah's Witnesses in town, and we believe that only our church members will really be saved. Most other Christians don't know about the end of the world that's coming or about how their worldly activities are jeopardizing their souls."

Mallory couldn't get over the fact that I'd never seen *The Jetsons* before, and she wasn't buying the fact that God had ordained field service or that other Christians aren't saved.

"That's the most arrogant thing I've ever heard," Mallory exclaimed. "So, you're saying that your mother believes that we're all going to hell?"

"Well, yeah. It's not that she wants you to go to hell; she'd love to save your souls, but, unless you convert to Christ's true church, there's nothing she can do to help you."

"That's the most ridiculous load of crap I've ever heard," she said, stomping away.

As Saturday rolled on, we Bowie boys went out in the hot street to throw the pigskin around. Howard came down with his brothers to join us.

"Why weren't you out for field service this morning?" Howard asked, throwing the football over my head.

"Howard, meet my cousins, Joe and Derrick. They moved here from California a few weeks ago," I said, ignoring his question. I thought to myself, "No need to bring that up again."

"Where are you guys staying?" Howard asked Derrick.

"Brother Man, we're Joneses, and Joneses can pile up in one house and think nothing of it," Derrick replied, pointing at our small three-bedroom house. "I've got three sisters that moved down with us, and we're all staying at Tom's house."

"You mean to tell me that there are fourteen people living in Tom's house, all sharing one bathroom?!" Howard said. "Tom, I've been wondering why we haven't seen you around the Kingdom Hall lately."

"Howard and his family are Jehovah's Witnesses, too," I told my cousins, who were staring at Howard's huge hands.

"With hands that big, I bet a ball would catch hell!" Joe remarked, as we all laughed.

"I've seen people like you before in California—those guys who sell magazines door to door," Derrick said to Howard.

"The Bible tells us not to associate with outside children, because they're a bad influence, but I guess that, since you're Thomas' cousins, it's alright," Howard said.

"Come on, man, you're kidding us," Joe said, looking at me. "Are you telling me you're only allowed to play with other Jehovah's Witnesses?"

"Yes, 1 Corinthians 15:33 says that bad associations spoil useful habits," I replied.

"Throw me the goddamn football," a voice echoed, as Reggie Thomas came striding up to join the game. I was thankful for the interruption in the conversation after my dispute with Mallory this morning.

"Joe, Derrick, you remember Reggie," I said, noticing that Derrick was busy talking to Howard.

"Another Mike and Thomas?" Derrick asked. "Howard, do you mean to tell me that your brothers' names are Mike and Thomas, too?"

"Yeah, I guess it worked out that way," Howard replied, "but we've always called your cousin, 'Tom,' so it's never been confusing."

"It's not a Jehovah's Witness thing, though, right?" Derrick teased, ducking the football that came crashing into the crowd.

"Enough of that Jehovah's Witness bullshit—Tom, go long for a pass," Reggie ordered.

With that, I found myself playing on the Bowie team against some boys who live the next block over, the San Jose Sharks. I'd always imagined what it must feel like to play as I watched out our living room window with one eye on a Watchtower magazine, pretending to study. Today, I was laughing and playing football for the very first time with my neighbors. And Howard and his brothers played out a dream years in the making, as they, too, had never truly lived until that day.

Our block team goes by the name "the Bowie Bombers," and Reggie's our quarterback. Near the end of the game, we were so far ahead that we gave the Sharks 12 points per touchdown, but they still never got within three touchdowns of taking the lead.

Reggie's a darn good quarterback. James used to say that Reggie is special. I have to agree; Reggie Thomas is something special with a football in his hands. Reggie said he might be the starting quarterback for the Abilene Eagles in September, if all goes well. He admitted that it's a long shot, though, because no freshman has ever been chosen to quarterback a high school football team in a Texas 5A-level school. Diary, it's only my opinion, but I've never seen a quarterback play as well as Reggie did on Saturday. The moves, the speed, and the throwing action while he was on the run were things you'd have to see to believe. He has all the necessary qualities in one big package. It's no wonder he never lost a game as the quarterback during his junior high career.

Diary, Aunt Trudy is calling us to supper now. She and my mother are splitting supper duties while both families live under the same roof. Whatever she's cooking tonight sure smells good! I could write on and on about the wonderful days I've had lately, hanging out with my cousins and neighborhood friends, but we'll have to continue this conversation later.

Saturday, August 24th, 1974

It's just past one in the morning on Saturday night, so to be technical, it's actually Sunday the 25th. It's changing around here at breakneck speed. Around midnight, I climbed out of my once single bed that I now share with two cousins to go to the bathroom after all the red Kool-Aid I drank today. To my surprise, the bathroom was occupied when I knocked.

"Hey, I'm next—I've been waiting a long time," a voice whispered from the shadows. My cousin, Ann, was quietly awaiting her turn behind Carol, who had just gone in. I barely made it out to the tree house to relieve myself in an empty mayo jar, but on the way out, I hastily grabbed a candle and you, Diary.

Maybe it's my recent lack of sleep, or maybe it's the Texas heat, but whatever the reason, something inside of my soul has started beating to the sound of a different drum. A math teacher I once had told me I have no excuse for ever making less than a 98% on a test. She said I was born blessed with a natural gift for figuring out mathematical problems, but, Diary, I can't seem to figure out what's going on inside my head.

On Monday, I finally realized how silly it is to believe that placing my head under my desk would save me from a nuclear missile. Don't laugh, but out of all the drills at school, this head-under-the-desk drill is the one I've always paid the most attention to, and now I discover it's useless. A 5000-pound nuclear bomb would wipe out an entire city, including my desk.

Since Mallory mentioned that it's odd that my father is in the military and the rest of us won't salute the flag on religious principle, I've seriously wrestled with our peculiar family situation. Is my father going to die at the battle of Armageddon? Jehovah's Witnesses believe that if you're not one of us, you won't survive Armageddon, and he's not one of us. If I had to describe his belief system, I would have to say that football would be his God, and the Dallas Cowboys his denomination.

> Gemini: Tuesday, August 20th 1974: *You may make use of some new means of communication today, although smoke signals are almost certainly out. Fire up other modern means of communications and you're sure to get results.*

Early Tuesday morning, Reggie came over with my father's newspaper under his arm. We shared a box of Frosted Flakes as we glanced at the horoscopes. My mother came into the kitchen shortly after Reggie read me our horoscope. He quietly folded the horoscopes under the sports section and started reading sports news while my mother made coffee.

"Damn, Tom, that was close!" Reggie said when my mother left the kitchen with a cup of coffee for my father. I made eye contact with Reggie, as I saw her coming back, and he seemed to be making a signal of some kind. It suddenly dawned on me what he was trying to say. The horoscope thing! That was the whole reason why Reggie and I hadn't seen one another for several months. Now, with our house so full, Reggie is back and the horoscope is back on the kitchen table. Reggie quietly left our house that morning, but later we talked for hours on the telephone, a conversation that our horoscope had predicted would take place.

> Gemini: Thursday, August 22nd, 1974:
> *Circumstances beyond your control are affecting how the people in your immediate family see you, for better or worse. It's a good time to let your reputation take care of itself. An old friend has come back into your life. Stay connected with him.*

Then, Thursday, guess who came home from basketball camp? Reggie and I welcomed James, confirming that day's horoscope as well. James' parents sent him to an expensive basketball camp in Philly over the summer. I think James is Reggie's athletic rival. Both will be freshmen at Abilene High School this year. James has grown at least another four inches since he's been away, making him even lankier than before.

"James, I'd like for you to meet my cousins, Joe and Derrick," I said. "They moved here from California while you were away."

"Hey, blood, who are the sistas sneaking a glimpse of me from your house?" James asked.

"Oh, they are their sisters, Mallory, Sheila and Ann," I said.

"How in the world do fourteen people split one pot in y'all's crib?" James asked Joe.

"Yo, the bathroom does resemble a Chinese fire drill after evening chow, but we're Joneses, and Joneses know how to make do," Joe replied as they exchanged soul handshakes. "James, you're the coolest white boy I've ever met."

> Gemini: Saturday, August 24th, 1974: *There is a strong possibility you will find yourself involved in a peculiar situation earlier in the day, and by nightfall you may speak about it with a lover who will gladly listen.*

Case in point: This afternoon after field service, Howard couldn't join the Bowie Bombers for football because Michelle wanted him at home. They still live with her parents, even though it's been nearly a year since their marriage. It was unlucky for his brother, Thomas, that Howard didn't show up today.

"You're a fucking punk, Thomas Medlock," Reggie said before the game against the LaSalle Lions, and smacked him to the ground for no apparent reason. The fight between them didn't last very long, but it shouldn't have happened in the first place.

"Reggie Thomas, you're the most homophobic son of a bitch I've ever known," Laurie shouted, helping Thomas to his feet.

"Thomas is a faggot who likes to play with dolls and has to have his big brother around to protect him. Just look at the way he's got this white bitch sticking up for him," Reggie shouted, walking swiftly away. Thomas covered his bloody nose and slunk away with Laurie's arm around his shoulder. His brother, Mike, stayed to play, but I don't think the Bowie Bombers will ever see Thomas again, unless Howard comes back around. These are strange days, indeed—me not going out on field service, JW kids playing football with worldly kids, and our parents not severely protesting.

The game ended with an astonishing 54 to 12 Bombers victory over the Lions. The boys were sitting under the shade tree in my yard, sipping Kool-Aid and celebrating, when Joe spoke up.

"I'll be eighteen on my birthday in October. I've played football for eleven years in three states, and I'm here to tell you, brother man, that the boys in Texas are by far the best players I've ever seen. You, soul brother, are the best damn quarterback I've ever seen," Joe said, pointing at Reggie. "Didn't you score all our points today? Where did you get all those slick moves? You must be able to throw 65 yards. How old did you say you are?"

"Brother man, I'm only sixteen, but every coach I've ever had has referred to me as a 'man-child,'" Reggie boasted.

"How much do you weigh now?" Joe asked.

"The last time I checked, I tipped the scales at 188 pounds," Reggie said.

"And how tall are you?" Joe asked.

"I think I'm a bit taller than my mother now, so I must be about six-foot-two-and-a-half or six-three."

Joe reached into the tobacco-stained pocket of his T-shirt and pulled out a Kool from an open pack. Placing the cigarette in the left side of his month, he lit it up and looked Reggie up and down.

"Blood, you got National Football League written all over you."

"I know, man. I'm going to be just like Joe Gilman of the Pittsburgh Steelers—a starting black quarterback in the N.F.L.!" Reggie exclaimed without a pause.

"Reggie, you were right to call out that fag, Thomas Medlock, earlier today," Joe said.

"Piss off! Both of you mother-fuckers! Pick on someone else," Laurie shouted, striding across the lawn toward us. "Joe Jones, you sound as homophobic as that dumb-ass, Reggie. Hey, let me bum one of your Kools," she said, reaching out her hand. "How do y'all know Thomas isn't a hermaphrodite?"

Diary, I spent the better part of my evening with Laurie in the tree house discussing what a hermaphrodite is and where they come from. The horoscope said I'd be spending my evening chatting with a possible lover. Laurie may not be my lover now, but she did sit and listen all evening to every word I said. I may have scored well on my I.Q. test, but Laurie is far smarter than I'll ever be. I think I love her! Wow! Did I just write that?! Anyway, we were discussing Thomas, and Laurie just might be right about the possibility of him being a hermaphrodite. Diary, it seems that hermaphrodites were born with both a dick and a pussy. No kidding! I wonder how Thomas would masturbate, and if he would be considered gay or lesbian. Now that's a question for Laurie on another evening. Good night.

Thursday, August 29th, 1974

Sometimes I'm right and I can be wrong
My own beliefs are in my song
I am everyday people, yeah yeah
There is a blue one who can't accept the green one
For living with a fat one trying to be a skinny one
And different strokes for different folks
And so on and so on and Scooby doobie doo-bee
Oh sha sha - we got to live together
I am no better and neither are you
We are the same whatever we do
You love me you hate me you know me and then
You can't figure out the bag I'm in
I am everyday people, yeah yeah
There is a long hair that doesn't like the short hair
For bein' such a rich one that will not help the poor one
And different strokes for different folks
And so on and so on and scooby dooby doo-bee

Oh sha sha-we got to live together
There is a yellow one that won't accept the black one
That won't accept the red one that won't accept the
white one
And different strokes for different folks

Diary, these lyrics are from a song by Sly and The Family Stone. We listen to a transistor radio in the tree house on summer evenings, and KRBC, the local station, played this song. The radio signal was just starting to fade as Laurie extinguished her last cigarette on the floor of the tree house.

"Joe, could you bring back a new nine-volt battery for the radio when you go to 7-11 to score a pack of smokes?" Laurie shouted down as Joe disappeared in the distance.

Laurie and I were alone for the first time all evening, and I wanted so badly to sneak a kiss from her, but I never got up enough nerve. Laurie and I started talking about the voices I have in my head. I think everyone has some kind of voice in his head, especially during times of conflict and confusion. Laurie says I'm not crazy to suggest that theory. She added that she thinks the difference between insanity and sanity is whether we think others can hear what's being said in our own minds—like, when we start talking to ourselves without realizing it. While we were alone in the tree house, Spooky kept saying, "Tell Laurie you think you love her." Just when I was about ready to say it, Swagger would chant: "First comes love, then comes marriage, and then comes Laurie with a baby carriage." Instead, I had to settle for listening to Laurie's smooth voice as we huddled together around the fading radio signal, listening to that new song "Me and Miss Jones."

Seeing Joe come up the tree house steps, Laurie lamented, "Damn, Joe, I wish you didn't smoke menthol cigs; I'm not so crazy about the taste."

"Kool cigs are the black folks' brand. Those wimpy Marlboros and Winstons are for you white folks," Joe said handing her a cigarette from his pack. "A dollar, my darling, barely leaves you with a nickel left in your pocket after you buy smokes and a nine-volt battery. I remember a time when I could squeeze the shit out of a Buffalo nickel. I'm holding on to two quarters in my pocket hoping to spend them on Mary Jane. Hey, Laurie, do you know where I could find her?"

"I didn't know you knew Mary Jane," Laurie said, pulling a strawberry-colored cigarette from under one of the floor boards. "Do you want your sister, Mallory, to meet Mary Jane, too?"

"Sure, that would be groovy, Laurie. Does Tom know Mary Jane?" Joe asked.

"No, Tom is still too green to know her," Laurie replied, giggling behind her hand.

They sent me to fetch Mallory, and then made me go inside to watch *The Flip Wilson Show* with the rest of the family. I'm not quite sure who this Mary Jane is and why I couldn't meet her, but I know Laurie and Joe were talking in code. Maybe Joe was bragging about getting Mary Jane's phone number when he said something about finding out where they could spark up another number.

Diary, all this code language among the teen set I now associate with is a bit hard to keep up with at times. I certainly know now that Kool cigarettes contain menthol, and menthol cigarettes were made for black folks, and the white folks are supposed to stick to Marlboro and Winston. I guess the lyrics in that song should be updated to, "Different *smokes* for different folks."

Catch you on the flip-side!

Saturday, August 31st, 1974

The teenage learning curve continues at a rapid pace. Spooky reminded me that I must've been stupid to think that Laurie and my cousins were talking about a girl named "Mary Jane" last Saturday. I quickly discovered that it's another word for "marijuana."

"Mary Jane, rolling papers, potang"—the list of new words and phrases goes on and on, and none of them were in my vocabulary a week ago. I'm more familiar with words like: "Satan," "Armageddon," "heavenly paradise," and "sin." I've also found out that "Kool" is not just a brand of cigarettes, but a word for being a hip person as well. Also, to my astonishment, I've recently learned that "coke" doesn't always mean a beverage that comes in a bottle.

"Mrs. Robinson, are you trying to seduce me?"

The steamy Texas day saw Joe, Reggie and I tucked away in Reggie's mother's room again, running her a/c unit on full blast Tuesday afternoon. The weatherman that evening said it had been the hottest day of the year. The fellows and I escaped the blistering heat with another mid-afternoon movie, lounging on Shirley's clean bedspread.

"Mrs. Robinson, are you trying to seduce me?" Dustin Hoffman asked in *The Graduate*, as we watched it on the HBO channel. He played the role of Benjamin Braddock, a 21-year-old boy who just earned his bachelor's degree at a college in the Northeast. His parents throw a party for him after graduation, and Mrs. Robinson, the wife of his father's business partner, asks Benjamin to drive her home, which he reluctantly does. Once there, Mrs. Robinson begs him to come inside, then forces a drink upon him, undresses, and offers to sleep with him. Reggie said he must have been a coward not to take her up on it right then and there. Later, Benjamin does have an affair with her, but not until a few days later.

Joe said he's been seduced by an older woman and that getting pussy from an older woman is better, because they have more bedroom experience than younger girls. Reggie also said he's been with an older woman and that often older women will pay a younger guy to have sex with them.

Diary, it's hard to imagine really getting laid—for now, I'll have to settle for masturbation four times a day. Oh, by the way, Diary, Reggie told me on Monday that I don't have to masturbate four times a day, like I thought.

"Tom, it's not how many times a day a dude masturbates; it's how long you can keep it hard that counts. Longer masturbation is what makes our dicks longer than the white dudes," Reggie said. There is a lot to learn, but I know I can trust Reggie, because he's the kind of guy who tells it like it is.

Tuesday after supper, Reggie, Joe, and I went up in the tree house.

"I know you're my cousin, Tom, but you're the whitest black guy I've ever known. Don't you know anything about sex?" Joe said, lighting another Kool from the pack in the pocket of his bell-bottoms. Combing his four-inch afro with a pick, he winked at Reggie, and I got the feeling they knew something more about sex than they've been telling me. "Cuz, my dad can get a motorcycle for my birthday. Have you ever ridden a motorcycle before?"

"No, man, my mother would kill me if she ever saw me on one of those things."

"Come October, little cousin, me and you are going for a ride on the new Suzuki GT 750 I plan on buying."

Then, Laurie, Mallory and James joined us in the tree house.

"Has anybody seen Mary Jane around today?" Laurie said, winking one blue eye at Joe.

"Not everyone in this tree house is cool enough to meet her," Mallory said.

"Don't light that shit up in here," Reggie said angrily.

"Ok, Mr. Jock, we'll take our stuff around the block. Mary Jane isn't very fond of jocks like you anyway," Laurie said snidely.

"Hey, baby, you wish you could fondle this," Reggie retorted with his right hand over his crotch.

"Your mama wishes," Laurie replied, shooting him the finger. "Let's boogie," she said to Joe and Mallory, and then they all climbed down from the tree house steps and disappeared into the distance.

"I'm an athlete," Reggie boldly proclaimed to James and me.

Pointing after Laurie, Joe and Mallory, James looked me in the eyes and said, "Yo, bro, let me give you the skinny—marijuana makes you get mellow and gives you the munchies. I'm an athlete, too, and I ain't got time for that shit myself."

I never will let on to the other three that I know what they've been up to. I know they went to smoke marijuana. Reggie's been my "hip teacher," but lately James' insight has also proved invaluable to me. Teenagers know more than I ever thought they did.

Before the night was over, Reggie, James, and I found ourselves down at the local YMCA with a basketball in our hands, playing a game called 21. James won all three games.

"Your cousin, Joe, was right; you really are the whitest black dude on the planet," James said, chuckling. "I'm a white boy and I'm hipper than he will ever be," he said to Reggie as the two of them had a royal laugh at my expense. "Tom, do you live in the stone ages? You've got to get out of your mama's house more often. Isn't this the first night you've been out since your family moved to the neighborhood?"

James was right. It took the right set of circumstances, but I was indeed out at night for the first time, hanging out with my peers. And I loved it!

Wednesday, September 4th, 1974

School started on Monday, and the start of my sophomore year saw me more comfortable than ever in school. First of all, my cousins are enrolled in the same school. When you've been an Air Force brat all your life, it's hard to fathom how good it feels having kin living close for the first time. Mike passes me in the hall and Carol waves her hand in my direction once in a while on her way to classes, but nothing beats getting a high five from your seventeen-year-old cousin as he passes you with a Kool tucked behind his ear. I feel so cool.

Mallory is a sophomore, too, Derrick is a freshman, and Joe is a senior. Mike should be a senior, too, but he's technically a junior because he didn't attend enough of his classes last year. My mother doesn't mind that much because she thinks education will be unnecessary when Christ returns.

It blows my mind to think of how much writing has

come to mean to me. I would have never thought that an empty book I can fill with my thoughts would provide me such comfort and company. Being a Jehovah's Witness has a way of distancing you from your peers, but now that Reggie and James are freshmen, I feel more connected than ever.

I was standing in the hallway at school yesterday, chatting with Reggie, and someone actually asked him my name. It's kind of strange, my being a sophomore and younger than Reggie, but he failed the fourth grade twice, so Reggie is a year older than I am, but I'm a year ahead of him in school.

It seems like just yesterday I was a child. Then, one day I woke up beside beautiful, dead Susan. Spooky recently made me suspect that, maybe, she never existed at all. He kept trying to convince me that Susan was only someone in a passing dream that I dreamt years ago. Then Smoothy, or was it Swagger, or perhaps both of them, came to the forefront of my mind and asked, "Am I just a dream that Susan had two years ago? Am I just imagining that I'm Tom, who died beside Susan, and she's about to wake up?" When you think about it, dreams are creepy, aren't they?! Some days I awaken after a long nap and wonder who the people that I talked to in the dream were. Other times I awaken and wonder why we dream at all. Perhaps the people I dreamt about are real, or I'm just a participant in their dreams. Anyhow, it's so strange how one voice in my head overshadows the others, like Spooky has done recently, overshadowing Smoothy and Swagger.

One reason that Spooky dominates my mind these days is that the end of the world is less than three months away, according to the *Watchtower*:

> *And in the end times there will be critical times hard to deal with. Nation will rise against nation and kingdoms will rise against kingdoms. This good news of the gospel will be preached in all the lands of the earth for a witness to me. And then the end would come. – Matthew 24.*

Our latest issue pointed out that the good news of the kingdom is now heard by every land and nation. The article also focused on the Vietnam War, pointing out the fact that over 55,000 U.S. soldiers have lost their lives is evidence that the end times are only months away.

The school library has become my second home. I spend the better part of my free time there, the most wonderful place on earth. *For Whom the Bell Tolls* by Earnest Hemingway is my favorite novel ever. I also recently read his *The Old Man and the Sea*, but *For Whom the Bell Tolls* was even better. I also liked *Gone with the Wind*, too. Reading all of these war novels, I see that there's always been some kind of war going on throughout the history of the world, and that all of the authors glorify it in their novels.

There is so much to read about, so much to learn, and so little time to do it all in. I glanced through a book called *The Story of the Civilization* by Will Durant. I was surprised to find that the Bible was written over a

700-year period. It really turned on a light in my mind. If that's true, and some of the books were left out because a woman wrote them, for instance, then the Bible really isn't inspired by God as they say. God wouldn't discriminate against women, would he? Will Durant also wrote about Pompeii, which is one of the most famous cities in world history, yet recently discovered ruins show that a new city was built right over the top of the old Pompeii. It's mind-boggling to think that such a famous city is buried under another, and no one bothers to mention it.

I really miss the privacy of having the family "library" to myself. Since Uncle Frank's family moved in, it seems like I haven't had a moment to myself to keep up with current events. Now there's only time to get in, do your business, and get out. And, people won't even leave you in peace for the necessities without knocking and complaining.

I've got to run now because it's time for *The Waltons*. I wish I could spend my last days on earth reading, but time goes by so fast, and the TV is the instrument that brings us up to speed the fastest. It seems that all my schoolmates who catch what's on the evening news are rapidly becoming the smartest kids in class. Miss Wiseman once said, "Why read the paper when you can catch the news on the run by glancing at the tube?"

The Waltons is the show I look forward to the most. I just love the way the show ends each week.

"Good night, John-Boy."

Friday, September 13th, 1974

Gemini: *Unexpected changes are coming and will affect your outlook on life. Just when you think things are looking up, situations could turn around or be short-lived.*

Carol told me that the Elders pulled my mother aside after church Wednesday night.

"Louise, why haven't we seen Mike or Tom at church in over a month?" Carol said they asked her. "You know that Ephesians 6:1 says that children must be obedient to their parents. As a faithful member, you know all too well how short the times are. Scripture says that in the last days, many will come, but few will remain until the last day. These are the last days. Your sons' lives are at stake, and their blood is on your hands."

Diary, that chastening ends my carefree days with my friends. Starting tomorrow, she says, I'll have to start going back to the Kingdom Hall three times a week, and I will be selling magazines again, starting this Saturday. But field service won't be the hardest thing to adjust to. Frankly, I've spent more than half my life attending Jehovah's Witness church meetings. I have to admit that I was deluded about having a choice; I thought I'd made a decision not to attend Kingdom Hall meetings any longer. Here's the real dilemma: missing *The Waltons* on Thurday nights.

The Waltons remind me of my family situation with so many people living under one roof. The Walton family has nine people—John and Olivia Walton, the parents, and their seven children. John Boy, the eldest son, is a writer, and he's the narrator. At the close of every episode, the family house is dark except for one light in an upstairs window. A few family members have a brief conversation at the end, and then they all say good-night. The last to say good-night at the end of the show is John Boy, which is why I sometimes end my entries with, "Good-night, John-Boy."

Reggie and I checked our horoscope for
Saturday in the Friday evening paper.
The words, "unexpected changes," echoed
in my mind, as Reggie and I sat staring
out at the horizon by candlelight in
the dark tree house.

With such a crowd, it seems natural to want to escape and find some peace and quiet during the evening. Reggie and I did just that this evening in the tree house. Reggie was upset at his mother for not coming home Thursday night, as she'd promised. "It won't be long, Tom, before I won't have to play daddy to my brothers and sisters while Mama runs around all night. No more standing in line for that fucking government cheese and no more powdered milk after I sign my pro football deal."

Reggie and I checked our horoscope for Saturday in the Friday evening paper. The words, "unexpected changes," echoed in my mind, as Reggie and I sat staring out at the horizon by candlelight in the dark tree house.

It was the first time I'd ever heard Reggie say "Daddy." He told me in a low voice how his father had left them.

"Tom, what little living my old man made, he left in cheap motel rooms," Reggie explained. "Mama caught him in bed with another man in Oklahoma City in one of those rooms. She had her pistol with her when she caught him with that punk, but she just turned around and left them. That was seven years ago, and the rest of my family hasn't seen that bastard since. My father—six-foot-seven and 270 pounds—turned out to be a homo of all things."

I didn't know how to respond to Reggie's sudden revelation, so we just sat in silence for a while.

"Hey, Joe, is that you up there?" a loud voice cried from below. "You got a cigarette you can spare?"

Laurie was coming up the stairs, relieving our awkward silence.

"You ought to give those damn cigs up if you can't afford to buy your own," Reggie said.

"Hey, Mr. Jock, the rumor at school is that you did very well in the first week of practice, and Coach Hayes might start you as quarterback in the first game of the season," Laurie said to a now-smiling Reggie.

"News travel fast. It's not a rumor anymore; I am the starter, and I will be the first freshman to start as quarterback in a Texas 5A school," Reggie responded. "You want to start on this?" Reggie said, whipping out his penis from his football pants and wiggling it at her.

Pow! Laurie suddenly smacked Reggie's face hard, catching him off guard.

"You nasty-ass pervert!" she shouted. "Reggie, I hope your fucking mother knows you can't keep your dick in your pants!" She quickly turned and ran back down the steps. It all happened so fast—just like everything happens around here lately.

"Good-night, John-Boy."

Saturday, September 21st, 1974

It's all so stupid! Spooky has taken up full-time residence in my head for the majority of the week. For the second Saturday in a row, I spent the bulk of my time doing field service. With end times getting ever closer, our congregation has intensified its religious activities.

The Elders briefly spoke to the small group of congregation brothers and sisters who had gotten up at six and dressed in suits and ties in preparation for the long day of service. Then the Elders read Acts 20:20, which stated that we must go and preach publicly and from house to house. We said a long prayer asking God to open the hearts and minds of the wicked so that they may receive God's spiritual blessings.

My cousins from California teased me about having to dispense magazines on a Saturday morning.

"Yo, Tom, you're going to miss *The Jetsons* this morning."

"Yo, Tom, you look like a real preacher dressed in that suit and tie."

"Yo, Tom, how much money you got in that briefcase you're carrying?"

"Yo, Tom, is that overloaded briefcase very heavy?"

The jokes went on and on, but Mama said just to ignore their remarks—that it's only Satan's ploy to keep us from doing God's work.

Here's a new word: atheist. I'd heard it on many occasions in the Kingdom Hall, but when Joe said his entire family is atheist, it came as a shock to me. An atheist doesn't believe in God. Imagine a whole family of atheists living right here under our roof, sharing meals with us, and hogging up our bathroom.

"Tom, no one in our family has seen the inside of a church since our grandparents died," Mallory said. "Oh, we celebrate Christmas, Easter, and all that jazz, but we haven't gone to church services for years."

My cousins are atheists, yet they celebrate the two biggest days on the Christian calendar. And Jehovah's Witnesses totally believe in God, but it's against our religious beliefs to celebrate either. Strange, very strange!

Although it's only been a week since my privileges of hanging out in the tree house with Reggie were yanked by the Elders, I dearly miss him.

I was washing the sleep from my eyes this morning in the bathroom, preparing for field service, when I caught sight of the newspaper on the bathroom floor. A quick glance at the sports section in the *Abilene Reporter* revealed that the final score in the first Eagles game of the season was Eagles 28-14 over the Big Springs Steers. Reggie had a pretty good debut as quarterback, throwing for three touchdowns and running over a hundred yards. I would've done anything in that moment to cross the street and congratulate Reggie, but the Elders were serious when they told my mother I couldn't associate with worldly kids any longer. The way they harp on that one verse makes me wonder if they've read the rest of the Bible. We can preach the gospel to our worldly peers, but we aren't supposed to have any fun with them.

It was hard to tell Reggie that I'm not allowed to hang out with him anymore, especially since my cousins, who are also "worldly" children, live with us and are still allowed to associate with him. None of it makes any sense—not to me and not to Reggie.

Today I was back in the groove of going from house to house preaching the good news to the lost. But it was nice to see Howard and Michelle. They must have forgotten how close the end is, because she's pregnant again.

Diary, Sunday mornings come quickly, so I've got to say goodnight. I've got to study my *Watchtower* to prepare for the church service.

"Good-night, John-Boy."

Friday, September 27th, 1974

From "What I Did on my Summer Vacation"
by Laurie Lane

While rambling through my dying grandma's hope chest, I found and discovered the items that Scott, my MIA 19-year-old brother, had left behind at her house.

Laurie Lane is in my modern history class. After the countless hours we have spent chatting in the tree house, you'd think I would know just about everything there is to know about her, but it looks as if I'm totally in the dark once again. Miss Wiseman, my modern history teacher, assigned an essay about what we did over the summer break. It blows me away to think that all the time she was at her granny's house this summer, Laurie was doing this closure stuff. She never mentioned that her grandma had died or that she has a brother who's been MIA for years.

"Tom, I haven't seen you in the tree house lately," she said as we left class.

"My mother and the church Elders had a conference and decided I can't associate with worldly teens or hang out in the tree house anymore," I told her.

"Oh, well, like the old proverb says, 'To each his own.' So, I bet you're back to selling salvation again, too, huh?"

"Yeah, they're really clamping down. So, why haven't you ever mentioned this long lost brother of yours?" I inquired.

"Scott's disappearance is a sore subject with me, and he's been MIA for several years. I will always think of Scott as a nineteen-year-old boy whose youth was cut short by the Man's war. He's officially listed as missing, but God only knows if he's a POW, if he's alive or dead, or even if he's now a North Vietnamese citizen, married to a Vietnamese woman and living happily somewhere over the rainbow. It kills you inside not to know, and that's why I never mention him," Laurie responded in a tone of voice I've never heard before. "The last my family heard of Scott was that he was involved in the North Vietnam carpet bombing that nobody wants to talk about, including me at this moment, so fuck off," Laurie said, suddenly icy. Then, she stormed off toward "the potheads."

I've read a lot about the Vietnam War in the paper. You read all these acronyms, like MIA and POW, but you never think twice about them until the girl you're secretly in love with has a missing brother. The summer of 1974 taught me more about the outside world than I could have ever imagined. There are times when I'm half asleep in bed, feeling as if the rest of the world is fast asleep, but the questions still linger on.

For instance, I'm just beginning to understand why Reggie called his dad a homo. I'd heard of homosexuals before from the Bible, but I'd never heard the term "homo" used to describe a homosexual person. So, Reggie's dad is a homo, Howard's brother is a hermaphrodite, Joe is an atheist, Laurie's brother is MIA, and, I know this must sound insane, but I still can't figure out who am I in the scheme of things.

"Good-night, John-Boy."

Saturday, October 12th, 1974

"We're counting them down, until we get to the number one song in America—and the hits just keep rolling on," says Casey Kasem, a disc jockey on the weekly radio countdown show, *American Top 40*, which plays the 40 most listened-to songs in America for the past week. It's the second Saturday in a row that I escaped to the backyard with my old transistor radio to listen. Here I sit, listening and writing in my diary, while just above me in the next yard, Joe, Derrick, and Mallory laugh in the tree house with Laurie and James. To an outsider, it must look peculiar.

"Hey, Tom," Laurie shouted, "why don't you bring your radio up, so we can hear the number one song, too?"

"He's not allowed up here. It's a bad association thing," Joe said sarcastically.

"Yeah, I've heard," Laurie said, with a twisted smile of delight on her lips. "Don't you guys find it bizarre for Tom to have to live that way? Joe, your family is sharing the same house with Tom, but he's not allowed to come out and play with you all in the tree house."

I could hear the bitterness in their voices, but what can I do? I know it must seem to them that the Elders are saying that Jehovah's Witnesses are better than everyone else. I guess that's exactly what the Elders are saying, but it's not my fault. It's not what I think. But the church rules must be obeyed, so here I sit, alone with my radio.

Frankly, I think the Elders know that my cousins live with us in the same house. So what's the point of not letting us play together? We all sleep together, right? Mother should clarify this whole thing. It's driving me nuts.

By the way, I got a brief chance to see Reggie this week.

"Hey, blood, I want you to meet Kelly and Rhonda!" he yelled out, spotting me in a crowded hallway between classes as I was passing his locker on Wednesday. The girls were nice to me, and Rhonda, one of Reggie's new friends, even asked me how long I had known Reggie.

"Hey, Tom, did you read about the game in the newspaper?" he asked.

"I've been meaning to sneak by your house, but, you know," I said. "Reggie, you're too good. The sports editor of the paper put your game stats on the same page with Frank Robinson, the new manager of the Cleveland Indians. Being on the same sports page with Frank Robinson, the first black manager in major league baseball, is quite an accomplishment."

"Hey, don't sweat it, Tom! I know your mom's tripping with the JW bullshit, so you've got no explaining to do to me. You know Geminis always find a way to communicate. Bro, we'll always be solid," Reggie reassured me, giving me a soul handshake. "The world's not going to end by 1975—trust me. You get my drift?" Reggie said, moving off toward the practice fields with the two girls close behind him.

Casey Kasem announced that "Bennie and the Jets", by Elton John, had been the No. 1 song in America months ago, making it a historical trivia song. "That song made history by becoming the first song to be No. 1 on the pop charts and No. 1 on the soul charts at the same time. But for now Billy Preston owns the top spot this week with his smash hit Nothing from Nothing." He said.

Saturday, October 19th, 1974

The *Watchtower* for this week said, "Human existence will not last long enough for young people to grow old; the worldly system will end in a few months." Young Jehovah's Witnesses are not encouraged to pursue tertiary education for this reason.

"Hey, what's cracking, Tom? What are you going to wear to the homecoming dance on Saturday?" James asked as we bumped into each other in the cafeteria.

"James, you know I'm not allowed to attend dances," I replied.

"But the dance is sponsored by our high school. Can't your mother make just one exception?" he asked.

"The Elders don't care about things like that. The latest magazine warns us that the end could come at any moment now," I said.

"Suit yourself, green boy. I'll see you on the hip side," James said, hurrying after another buddy.

The faces of the kids around me clue me in to the fact that they all think I'm crazy for believing the end of the world is near. But I read again tonight where Matthew chapter 24 tells us that these are the last days. No matter how often I read that chapter, Smoothy still thinks I should be at the homecoming dance—that it's only natural to want to dance with the other kids my age. Spooky countered that it's sinful to dance or even to want to. So there you have it: home alone again on a Saturday night, while Joe is at the dance with the girl I'm secretly in love with.

Monday, November 4th, 1974

The arrival of a new month brings a whole different meaning to the phrase "My, have times ever changed!" The last time I wrote to you, Diary, I was bummed out about not being able to go to the homecoming dance. The next Saturday night, I decided to stand up for myself.

Two weeks ago, I was in the living room, studying for Sunday services, when Joe and Laurie came in the back door from the tree house, where they spend most of their time.

"Tom, we're headed to the 7-11 for smokes. Do you want us to bring you anything from the store?" Joe asked as he and Laurie collected loose coins for their purchase.

"No, I'll go with y'all this time," I replied, suddenly feeling brave and invincible.

It was time for some changes. After all the nights of secretly crying inside and longing to be with my peers, I decided that rebellion might be hard, but it was harder to just ignore my loneliness. I'm fifteen; I should be able to go around the corner without permission. What's the worst my parents could do to me just for walking a few blocks away with my cousin?! Diary, the rest is history. As Kris Kristofferson wrote, "Freedom's just another word for nothin' left to lose," and I've been free to do as I please, ever since I realized that I have nothing to lose by asserting my independence.

"Tom, I think it's time for your weekly haircut," my father said a few days later.

"Dad, I think I want to grow an afro, like Cousin Joe," I told him.

"Wow! Where did that come from?" Smoothy said as father walked away without a word of protest.

This new awakening has Laurie, Cousin Joe, and me cutting a path to the 7-11 for cigarettes almost daily. We call ourselves "The Mod Squad", after the TV show which is a police drama featuring three young, hip, crime fighters—one black, one blonde, and one white. I've only watched the show a few times, but I know the characters well enough to figure out that Joe is the black guy, Clarence Williams III. Clarence and Joe both have huge afros. Laurie is Peggy Lipton, the blonde, and I got stuck with the role of Michael Cole, the white guy.

"Tom, I want to apologize to you for my father's behavior last night. He was drunker than a barrel of monkeys, and my mother has just about given up on him," Laurie said as we took our daily stroll to the 7-11. A look of concern accompanied her facial features as words came from her cherry red lips once more. "I suspect my father's and your Uncle Frank's brains both fell into the bottom of their whiskey glasses. I suspect that they're both alcoholics."

My mother calls Uncle Frank a "bigamist" under her breath, and I heard Aunt Trudy call him an alcoholic to his face a few weeks ago, but it's hard to keep up with all these new terms and with nuances surrounding our living situation. Mom says that kind of stuff about anybody she disapproves of, and I just thought that Aunt Trudy was angry and exaggerating. Now, Lynn has made the same accusation about her husband, and Laurie thinks both of them are alcoholics.

Diary, Laurie's grubby father, Fred, is hard to describe on clean paper. To be brutally honest, he looks as if he drove the Mac truck that hit him. Yeah, that rough!

It was Sunday, October 26th, and for the third night in a row, Fred and Uncle Frank were out on our back porch until well after midnight. My mother woke my father and sent him to break up their raucous tea party.

"Fellows, I don't want to have to warn y'all again about this excessive noise," he told them.

"Larry, sit down and join us," Uncle Frank said, staggering around the back yard.

"I'm not retired yet, like you flyboys are," dad joked, bending over to pick up two empty bottles.

The next thing I know, Diary, I heard my mother come out and start preaching to the two drunkards out of her Bible about the Promised Land. I swear, it sounded just like an episode of *Laugh In*. An alcoholic is "a person who drinks alcoholic liquor habitually and to excess," which summarizes Uncle Frank's and Fred's behavior of late. The three-day drunk-fest ended late Sunday night with Mama's sermonizing driving the men grudgingly off the porch to get some sleep.

That brings us to last weekend. Fred's sudden friendship with Uncle Frank is odd to begin with. If you didn't know either of them, and you took the dark skin color away from my uncle, you would think they were brothers. Outside of looks, they're more alike than my father and Uncle Frank are. Fred passed out in our back yard last night and slept there 'til morning. The drinking started on Friday night, and I don't think the two of them stopped drinking the entire weekend. Fred and Frank act like long lost brothers, which isn't a bad thing, except that they celebrate their reunion every night.

Up until two weeks ago, I'd only seen a few glimpses of Fred, even though he's been living here as long as we have. Since his meeting Uncle Frank, we've seen him for two consecutive three-day weekends. Fred showed up with bags full of vodka bottles Friday night and planted his butt in one of my father's broken-down, faded green and white, aluminum lawn chairs on the back porch, and he didn't leave until Lynn came to get him early Monday morning. Over the weekend, I overheard the drunkards' discussions of everything from President Nixon's war stance to Fred's son, Scott.

War may be hell, but Fred and Uncle Frank both seem to enjoy telling stories from their war days. I sat perched atop the tree house, observing the changes taking place around the Bowie block. Laurie and my older cousins still run me out of the tree house when they want to smoke marijuana, but that's OK with me, because hanging around with them some of the time is better than nothing.

My mother still gives me the evil eye when she sees me headed towards the tree house, but as long as I keep attending church meetings three evenings a week and passing out my share of magazines on Saturdays, I don't foresee her making a real fuss. Besides, what choice does she have?

I won't end this entry with the Walton's sign-off. Since I started coming to the tree house again, I have a different perspective. I no longer look at our backyard as a fairy-tale Walton's paradise—"Dream On."

Monday, November 11th, 1974

Uncle Frank can't get financing for a foreclosed home, but he still manages to buy televisions. My mother is on the verge of another nervous breakdown over the two new television sets that have been installed in our home over the past week. They'll probably drive her right back into Dr. Scott's office. Thursday night, Fred and Uncle Frank pulled up in Fred's Mercury four-door and started unloading a 13-inch black and white, and a 19-inch color television. They plugged the black and white into an outlet on our back porch and put the color television in Uncle Frank's room. It was immediately obvious that the two new media outlets bothered my mother. She was practically twitching with irritation.

"The Bible says Satan will use any means to distract God's people from reading his word, and more television sets are just what we don't need in this house," she said to the two half-intoxicated men as they unloaded their bounty.

The heavy drinking began Thursday, immediately after Uncle Frank and Fred hooked up the rabbit ears to the black and white television on the porch. They were in their usual form: one laughing, the other swearing loudly at the television, which stayed on until the end-of-broadcast national anthem at midnight.

I'm rapidly becoming aware of my lack of street smarts, but it doesn't take a genius to figure out that it's alcohol that bonds those two. I spied on them from my bird's-eye view in the tree house as they drank and watched everything from sports to war movies. I'm no TV smart guy like Maxwell Smart of *Get Smart* or Dr. Scott, but I can tell you from my short observation of Fred and Frank over this weekend that I learned a lot about them, and have noticed that they are two completely different types of alcoholics.

Grown-ups are oblivious as to how closely their kids watch them, and Frank and Fred were both too drunk to notice that I was watching them. At first, I felt like a peeping Tom spying on them, but then it became interesting as the same pattern replayed itself over and over as the weekend unfolded. First, Uncle Frank: he gets drunk and is the most apologetic, slap-happy human being on the face of the planet. After he's intoxicated, he actually looks for someone to apologize to—his brother, his wife, my mother. Once, Uncle Frank spotted my mother and went out of his way to apologize to her for leaving his liquor bottles hidden underneath her living room sofa and other places around the house.

My mother's response to him was more Scripture. "Frank, the Bible says, 'Alcohol is the devil's poison,' she reminded him compassionately. "You know, you can't hide your bottles from Jesus. Christ Jesus sees your hidden whiskey bottles, whether they are underneath the couch, stashed in the dirty laundry hamper, or in the back of the bathroom cabinets. Jesus sees everything."

Then there's Fred, who's a real Dr. Jekyll and Mr. Hyde when he drinks. After he's had the fourth or fifth gulp from the bottle, you'd better watch out for him. Once he's drunk, every other word out of his mouth is "motherfucker."

Diary, we'll have to continue this explanation of alcoholics later. It's late, I'm exhausted, and I think I'm going to crash. By the way, the term, "crash," is a new word I picked up recently, and it means "go to bed."

Thursday, November 14th, 1974

"Keep on stepping, jive turkey," Joe said to me a few moments ago, when I tried to enter the tree house after dinner. He stood blocking the doorway as I climbed the steps. A mild cold front has drifted into West Texas, and the temperature in Abilene has dipped 20 degrees from what it was four days ago, so I was just looking for a warmer spot to write and relax after dinner, and thought I'd hang out with the gang I saw heading up to the tree house.

"We're going to spark up a doobie in here, so Mr. Shakespeare, you've got to take that pen you've got tucked behind your ear and the diary in your hand and

---

Kids are figuring out what's going on younger and younger, and Joe may not realize it yet, but Carol already knows what the words "doobie," "number," and "joint" mean.

---

go elsewhere to scribble. Tom, look behind you. Carol is following you, and we wouldn't want her to know about the gang sparking up in the tree house," Joe whispered, winking out of Carol's view. "Why don't the both of you go watch *The Brady Bunch*, and I'll let you know when it's cool to come back around." Joe pointed toward the house and the television set that was playing in the background.

Kids are figuring out what's going on younger and younger, and Joe may not realize it yet, but Carol already knows what the words "doobie," "number," and "joint" mean. Carol asked, so I told her. Why shouldn't she know?

"Tom, what do y'all be doing up in the tree house on the weekend?" she asked me, looking at me with suspicion.

"I like to take my diary up there and write about what's going on in the neighborhood, while I look down on our back yard," I told her.

"But I see smoke coming from the tree house windows sometimes," Carol probed.

"They're smoking cigarettes up there."

"But why do our cousins laugh so loudly after they come back down, and why are their eyes all red?" Carol asked innocently.

"Grasshopper," I said, imitating a Kung-Fu master, "they also smoke marijuana up there." Then, I explained to her some of the slang terms for marijuana I've learned, and then our brief pop culture history lesson was over.

Carol's acute observations got my attention. It looks as if I'm not the only adolescent around here playing detective.

Catch you on the flip side.

Sunday, November 17th, 1974

"What it is, Diary? You catch my drift?"

Diary, you can now count me among the hip and cool teenagers that the *Abilene Reporter* calls the product of '70s pop culture. I'm starting to pick up on today's lingo very fast.

The weather has warmed back up nicely, but I can't say the same for those cruel teenagers who won't let me in the tree house again this evening. It's close to 6 p.m., and I'm sitting alone, watching the sun go down while sharing my most intimate thoughts with myself in a diary. Before Joe's family moved here, it was just Laurie and me chatting up there for hours on end. Now I've been supplanted and exiled. They all barred me from climbing the stairs after dinner again, even though Carol wasn't following me this time.

"Tom, you know the drill. No squares allowed in the tree house after dinner—it's our time," Mallory proclaimed.

The nerve of her—calling me "square!" I might own the label of "Mr. Nerd," but I'm certainly not a square. It's not as if I don't know what they're doing up there, so why can't I just watch?

Yesterday morning, I was awakened by the foul odor of Derrick's feet. Then I couldn't fall back to sleep, so I stumbled out of the crowded bed and made my way to the kitchen to pour myself a large bowl of frosted flakes. Glancing out the window, I was spooked by the discovery of Fred and Uncle Frank sitting in the lawn chairs on our back porch, chatting to one another about the Vietnam War. I glanced at the clock on the kitchen wall and saw that it was only 6:35 a.m. Fred and Uncle Frank had been drinking on our porch all night long, after popping the first top early yesterday afternoon.

"How can those stupid men drink so much and have so little to say?" I heard my mama say to Dad as he closed the station wagon door.

"Have a good time with field service," Dad happily replied as we were backing out of the driveway. "Louise, just remember that Frank is family, and I'm sure it won't be long before something comes through with the VA financing so they can get their own place. That twenty-dollar bill on the dash is for new winter coats for Carol and Gayle."

My mother placed the bill in her purse and said, "I'm not buying the girls winter coats. They won't need them for more than a few months before Armageddon comes. They can wear last year's."

When we arrived at Kingdom Hall, the Elders read several Scriptures, and said the customary prayer. Everyone headed for the cars, and we started morning field service. By 8:30, I was knocking on my first door in my suit and tie.

"Hi, I'm Tom Jones of the Jehovah's Witness field service ministry, and I'd like to talk to you about the soon-to-be coming of Jesus."

"Do you know what time of the morning it is?" the man shouted, slamming the door in my face before I could even finish.

Knock, knock on the next door.

"Hi, I'm Tom Jones of the JW field service ministry, and I'd like to talk to you about the second coming of Jesus Christ," I told the lady in front of me.

"Son, I'm not interested in what your magazine has to say about Jesus," she said politely, motioning for me to step out of her doorway.

"Madam, you don't want to die in the upcoming battle of Armageddon, do you?" I asked aggressively, following the strategy I was taught by the Elders for situations like this.

"Sonny, I'm a Baptist, so please go on to the next house," she said.

"Madam, I can leave you this *Watchtower* magazine for a small contribution," I said, sticking to the script.

"Get your foot out of my door before I slam the door on it!" she said tersely, and I hurried away with the magazine still in my hand.

Diary, my entire Saturday spiraled downhill, just as the morning ministry had. I didn't sell a single magazine during the entire seven hours, and that was only the beginning of an even worse Saturday afternoon.

Pastor Slowley said not to be discouraged about not selling any magazines, because it's a sign of the end times that the wicked won't listen to God's true prophets. He quoted verses to reassure me and the other members that we are the only true believers and that the rest of the world will soon be destroyed.

When we came home, I was bored so I went looking for Joe. I stopped at the tree house first, but he wasn't there; nor was anyone else. There was, though, half of a poem on the window ledge with a crushed Marlboro butt lying neatly beside it. When I found Laurie's half-written poem, I thought I was reading about me. The words she'd written caught me totally by surprise, because I'd never seen those feelings in her eyes. The poem said she thought she'd found the love she's been waiting for. Wouldn't you know it, Laurie never ever showed it. As I read on, a smile came over my face. But then, the words revealed that she was referring to Joe. "Crushed" isn't a strong enough word to describe how disappointed I felt, learning that Laurie had a crush on Joe and not me. The way I read it, Laurie was saying that she and Joe have a special connection because of their fathers' drinking, as if she and Joe were somehow glued together, body and soul, because both of their fathers were alcoholics.

Diary, just between you and me, I now hate Cousin Joe, and I hate that his family lives in our house. There's never enough hot water for showers since they moved in with us. I also hate that I never have any time or privacy to masturbate anymore. I feel just like my mother feels; we both wish Uncle Frank's family had never come to Abilene. I don't want to share Laurie with Joe. Why does she love him and not me? I'm the one who's listened to her problems and had deep conversations with her for the last year and a half. I wish my father was an alcoholic; maybe then Laurie would think I'm the secret love she's been waiting for.

Monday, November 18th, 1974

Times are changing, now the poor get fat
But the fever's gonna catch you
when the bitch gets back
– Elton John

KRBC is in hot water, according to Monday's evening edition of the *Abilene Reporter*, for playing Elton John's new song, "The Bitch is Back." I think Elton wrote that song for Laurie, because she's a bitch. I hate girls! KRBC should play "The Bitch is Back" more, but the song's being taken off the playlist. Elton John was sure that he's justified for raising cane and that the times are changing. Laurie's a bitch; she's a bitch, and she's not better than me. Besides, what is the big deal about the word "bitch"? It's only a word, and what good are words when nobody listens anymore anyway? The article also said that the City of Abilene might ban the KRBC radio station from the airways. That would be just my luck. First I lose Laurie to talk to, and now it looks as if I'll be losing the only radio station in Abilene that plays *American Top 40*.

Saturday, November 23rd, 1974

It was supposed to be the most glorious time in the life of an African-American family. A loan officer from Citizens National Bank called Uncle Frank yesterday to announce that the bank had decided to let him take over the payments on one of the bank's hundreds of foreclosed houses, so his family is moving into a house on our block just down Bowie Street on Monday. This unexpected call was cause for celebration in our neighborhood, and Uncle Frank and Fred began drinking

---

The party lasted until about three hours ago, when Gayle called the police. "Abiline Police Department. What's your emergency?"

---

whiskey soon after Frank and Aunt Trudy signed the loan documents at the bank Friday morning. The party lasted until about three hours ago, when Gayle called the police.

"Abiline Police Department. What's your emergency?"

"My cousin just split this white man's skull with a whiskey bottle, and there's blood everywhere," Gayle said, panicked.

"Slow down, dear, and repeat what you just said," the dispatcher said.

"They're all fighting in the backyard, and there's blood everywhere. Mama said to call the police. Come quickly!" Gayle yelled.

"Calm down. I can't understand you. Start from the beginning."

"There's a fight and a guy bleeding on the porch. Bring the police quick!"

"What's your address?"

"Um, uh, 2099 Bowie Street! It's my fault. I shouldn't have told Fred—it's my fault—I shouldn't have told 'em."

"All right, it's going to be all right, now. The police are on their way."

It's all quiet and clear around here now, but three hours ago the spark from a joint ignited what's sure to become the most dramatic event in the history of the Bowie block. Diary, it's about ten past midnight, and my hands were still shaking as I struck a match to light a candle in the tree house before starting to write. Spooky tried to tell me that the entire incident never took place, but I will always remember the fiery landscape, yelling and chaos. I witnessed just how quickly a few small sparks can ignite into an out-of-control blaze. What started out as a typical Saturday evening (if one wants to consider the past month of Saturdays typical), turned out to be a spectacular light show of fire and smoke, red and blue police lights, red ambulance and fire truck lights, and sirens.

Supper had just ended, and Fred and Uncle Frank were sitting in the aluminum lawn chairs on the back porch, watching television. Fred mentioned something to my uncle about being a carpet bomber in Vietnam. I saw Joe, Mallory, Sheila and Laurie heading up to the tree house for an after dinner smoke, so, like an abandoned dog, I tried again to follow them.

"Go away, Mr. Square," Joe said, as Laurie and the other girls giggled.

I was so focused on my envy of Joe's relationship with Laurie that I didn't notice that the conversation between Uncle Frank and Fred was beginning to boil over. All I noticed was them taking the top off of another bottle of Jack Daniel's to my left. The teenagers to my right, up in the tree house, were carelessly blowing smoke down from the window. I could hear Fred and Uncle Frank carrying on a senseless argument about something that happened years ago in the war. Both men were drunk, and their conversation had become a harsh exchange of curses directed at one another. Then my mother came outside to break up their argument. Carrying her Bible in one hand and holding my sister Gayle's hand with her other, she started yelling.

"The Bible says alcohol is Satan's playground! You two grown men are acting like children in an evil playground! You're a fine example for your children, with your carrying on and fighting!" She struggled to get their attention over the haze of their intoxication, and the volume of the TV, and their slurred shouting.

The two men momentarily stopped their intoxicated skirmish to look at my mother standing there with Gayle. The hip teenagers in the tree house were in a trance-like state at first but then started laughing hysterically.

"The last place my son was seen was just outside of Saigon in 1970, and now I find out that I'm sharing a bottle with a nigger that may have killed him!" Fred shouted, grabbing at Frank. "Frank, you could have been responsible for Scott's MIA!"

The two men went flying over the television set, and I heard a faint scream from my sister. Suddenly, I was hypnotized, watching Fred stagger to his feet and look at Gayle.

"I'm never coming back over here again. Where's my daughter? I'm going home!"

"Laurie's up in the tree house smoking Mary Jane with Joe," Gayle stammered, pointing at the tree house.

Bash! A whiskey bottle crashed over Fred's head, as I caught sight of Joe wielding the bottle.

"That's my fucking father you're choking!" Laurie exclaimed.

From there, all hell broke loose, and comedy turned into tragedy in a blink of an eye.

Reggie came by to ask what happened about an hour after the police left with Joe in custody.

When Mike got home, he saw me writing and asked, "There's blood all over the back porch, and what's with that yellow police tape?"

I just shrugged. Presently, I'm too traumatized to stop writing, but sooner or later Mike will know every sordid detail about this evening, because a reporter from the *Abilene Reporter* showed up to cover the story and said it will be the lead story in the Sunday edition. My brother was working while the mayhem took place.

Three police cars and one ambulance responded to Gayle's call. We hadn't had the police at our home since Charles and Louise were dropped off a couple of years ago. Those same officers also came tonight. I heard one of them say, "Every generation of teenagers is worse than the one before." Another said, "Thank God the end is near." A third said, "Smoking that marijuana stuff makes these teenagers go crazy." And I think all three of them are probably right.

Sunday, December 15th, 1974

While he was sitting upon the Mount of Olives, the disciples approached him privately, saying: "Tell us, When will these things be, and what will be the sign of your presence and of the conclusion of the system of things? And in answer, Jesus said to them: "Look out that nobody misleads you. You are going to hear of wars, and reports of wars; see that you are not terrified for these things must take place, but the end is not yet. For nation will rise against nation, and kingdom will rise against kingdom, and there will be food shortages and earthquakes in one place after another. All these things are a beginning of pangs of distress. Then, people will deliver you up to tribulation and will persecute you, and you will be objects of hatred by all the nations on account of my name. Then, also many will stumble and will betray one another

and will hate one another. And many false
prophets will arise and mislead many, and because
of the increasing lawlessness, the love of the greater
number will cool off. But he that has endured to
the end is the one that will be saved. And this good
news of the kingdom will be preached in all the
inhabited earth for a witness to all the nations:
and then the end will come." – Matthew 24

The entire congregation gave Pastor Slowley a stand-ing ovation as he ended his sermon today. He read from *The Watchtower* article, "Millions Living Today Will Never Die," referencing the fact that only Jehovah's Witnesses will be among those on earth who won't die at Armageddon. Over one-third of our congregation has sold their homes and businesses in anticipation of Armageddon. The President of the Watchtower Society in New York told all congregation youth not to return to school and to pursue full-time field service ministry until Armageddon arrives.

Some kids wanted to return to school, but Pastor Slowley read two Scriptures justifying the Watchtower Society's position. The first passage he read said, "Fool-ishness is found in the heart of a child." The other was Ephesians 6:1, which says that children must obey their parents. I've upheld the order not to go back to school, and, for nineteen of the past twenty-one days, I haven't missed a single day of field service.

It's been three weeks since the tree house fiasco, and since that time, Pastor Slowley has read Scripture after

Scripture showing that we are living in the last days. The apostles Matthew and Timothy must have foreseen what would happen in the 1970s. All the events predicted are taking place right before our eyes in the 1970s. Thankfully, my mother is a Christian and she has steered me in the direction of salvation so I won't be one of those who lose their lives at Armageddon. Other Elders cited further evidence that we are in the final days. Howard's step-father pointed out that the foreclosure rate hit record highs and the stock market has fallen to a record low in the United States. Then, he read 1 Timothy 6:10 which states that "the love of money is the root of all evil," and the entire congregation applauded.

Although the Bowie block is notorious since the brawl in our backyard, I haven't been back to school to face the reaction of my peers. There was a shot of our infamous community tree house on the front page of the Sunday edition with a caption that read: "Smoked out!" The reporter quoted a policeman who said that the brawl should be blamed on marijuana users and that our community tree house was facilitating American youth in destroying their lives. He was also quoted in yesterday's paper, saying that the district attorney will charge Joe as an adult in the case, even though he was only seventeen at the time of the offense. Joe turned eighteen on December 1st, while he was in the Taylor County Jail awaiting trial.

I read in today's editorial that District Attorney Wilkins is known for his successful prosecution of two teenagers that he put behind bars for possessing a single marijuana seed. Mr. Wilkins is charging Joe with attempted second-degree murder, and he has a 99% conviction rate.

Since I haven't been to school, I haven't seen Laurie, either, since that night. After reading about my cousin's fate yesterday, I wanted to speak to her about his case, so I walked out to our backyard and stared up at the tree house hoping to catch a glimpse of her. No such luck. Since Uncle Frank and his family moved into their new home down the street, our once-popular tree house resembles a ghost town.

Yesterday, while I sat alone in our backyard, staring up at the vast Texas sky, I happened to look up and see a single sheet of paper dangling from the window of the tree house. I climbed the stairs toward the mysterious article, which turned out to be a half-written poem by Laurie. It started with the words, "Our Mod Squad has seen its last episode." Using the names of the characters in the show to represent us, she went on to explain how she'd fallen in love with Joe. She also wrote about how affectionate she felt toward me, the brilliant white guy who is always the brains of the operation. So what if the love of my life sees me as a smart-ass white boy, when I'm actually a scholarly black kid who wants to be as cool as his cousin Joe. I was more than pleased with the words Laurie had written about me. And for that reason alone, I wish for Laurie all the sweet things she'll find in hell, because hell is where she's headed, since she's certainly not a Christian.

The drink and the smoke came to carry us all away, but was it the adults that got too drunk, then went too far, or us that got too stoned and never realized just how blown away we were? Who'd have thought the drink and the smoke would come one day and carry us all away. I can't remember if I smoked the last joint or if Fred drank the last swallow from the bottle. These are the days when neighborhood friends have replaced families. Usually, I know the whereabouts of neighborhood friends, but rarely do I hear where my brother, Scott, has been. The drink and the smoke came to carry us all away, and I still can't figure out if it was them that got too drunk, then went too far, or us that got too stoned and never realized just how far blown away we were.

– Laurie Lane

Sunday, January 12th, 1975

"Hey, Tee, I know you're glad all them niggers have moved into their own crib," Reggie said to me, as I looked over the Kmart cash register in search of the familiar voice I'd just heard.

"Yeah, Uncle Frank and his family had begun to wear out their welcome at our house," I said, and we both smiled at the unexpected sight of each other.

I was at Kmart, purchasing a new diary for 1975, and

Reggie was buying the old X-mas candies that hadn't sold during the holiday for his four siblings.

"Hey, Tom, are you and your old man going to watch the Super Bowl tomorrow?" Reggie asked me in a pleading voice.

"You know, brother man, I hadn't even thought about it—who's playing?"

"Homey, it's the Steel Curtain against the Purple People Eaters."

"You mean the Steelers made it to the Super Bowl?" I asked, astonished.

"Yeah, man, they're playing the Vikings on Channel 9 tomorrow," Reggie replied as the cashier waved us off to the side so she could wait on another customer.

"What time does the game start?" I asked.

"Kickoff is at 4 o'clock," Reggie said.

"Reggie, why don't you stop by my house about three something? My father would love to see you again, and I'm sure I'll be home from church by then."

"Later, Homey," Reggie said, and with that a new chapter began in my diary.

What prompted me to buy a new diary was the headline I'd read in the newspaper on Friday, January 10th. The headline read: *Mother kills her five kids—thinks they're better off in heaven.* I was sitting in the family library when my eyes caught sight of the headline. The article was about a crazy Houston woman who'd drowned her kids, all less than eight years old, in their family bathtub, while her husband was away on a business trip in San Antonio. The woman told the police that her husband had gotten her pregnant again against her wishes, and she thought that her other children would be better off in heaven, so she drowned them.

And seeing the multitudes, he went up onto a mountain: and when he was set, his disciples came unto him:

And he opened his mouth, and taught them, saying, Blessed are the poor in spirit: for theirs is the kingdom of heaven.

Blessed are they that mourn: for they shall be comforted.

Blessed are the meek: for they shall inherit the earth.

Blessed are they which do hunger and thirst after righteousness: for they shall be filled.

Blessed are the merciful: for they shall obtain mercy.

Blessed are the pure in heart: for they shall see God.

Blessed are the peacemakers: for they shall be called the children of God.

Blessed are they which are persecuted for righteousness sake: for theirs is the kingdom of heaven.

Blessed are ye, when men shall revile you, and persecute you, and shall say all manner of evil against you falsely, for my sake.

Rejoice, and be exceedingly glad: for great is your reward in heaven: for so persecuted they the prophets which were before you.

I've read over this famous passage 20 or 30 times over the past 24 hours, and nothing makes sense. I am so freaking lost! Just weeks ago, I was wondering if John-Boy of *The Waltons* would be among the saved in the new paradise on earth. Now, I'm sitting here, writing about a Super Bowl game that I never imagined watching with Reggie. The article about the woman in Houston has got me even more confused. Spooky dominates my thoughts, constantly telling me that the suicidal ledge is starting to look inviting again.

If this new diary is discovered with empty pages, people will know that I decided to throw myself off the ledge. I am embarrassed and shattered by the fact that I have been living a lie for more than half of my life. I've preached up and down the streets of my neighborhood, proclaiming this lie, predicting the certain destruction of my schoolmates if they didn't repent. Now it's 1975, and I find myself dumfounded and humiliated over how stupid I was to have believed that the world was ending.

I waited until the last possible minute before I realized that it wasn't going to happen. On New Year's Eve around 10:59 p.m., I was on my knees praying to Jehovah God, like I'd been doing for the past six hours, begging Him not to destroy me, when I heard the sound of the national anthem playing on TV. Dick Clark was in Times Square, wishing the thousands of people in Times Square and the millions around the world a happy new year. Suddenly, it dawned on me that it was already 1975 in the Eastern

Time zone, and the world hadn't been destroyed. I got off my knees and went out to the 19-inch color television set Uncle Frank had left us as a gift for our hospitality, just in time to see the New Year's Eve ball dropping.

"Ladies and gentlemen, welcome to the year 1975."

"Tom, go get me that bottle of champagne that Captain Johnson gave me yesterday from the refrigerator," Dad said as I came into his room to look at the television.

After my father had a glass of champagne, he said, "Tom, put this away for me—I don't think I'll be able to stay up until midnight, so I'm headed for bed."

"What's wrong with you, little brother?" Mike asked, discarding his Sambo's shirt on his bed when he came home around 12:30. I just sat watching TV, sad about the world not ending.

"It's 1975, and the world didn't end," I muttered.

"Cheer up, little brother. I knew all the time those crazy Jehovah Witnesses were just trying to scare us with their absurd predictions. They just wanted to keep us coming back to their church—that's all. You didn't see me sweating and praying all day today. I went to work sure that life would go on the same as always after midnight. You and those knobble-headed Jehovah's Witnesses were lying around on floors, praying to some God who doesn't even know your name, for forgiveness of sins that are just part of human nature. It must be one hell of a relief to see that it's all a huge hoax. Tom, when are you gonna realize that all churches tell you pretty little lies? It's all designed to convince people that they need a certain brand of religion to save them from themselves. I haven't been to a church in over a year, and God ain't destroyed me."

"But the Bible said these were the last days!" I cried. "What about Armageddon?"

"Preachers make the Scriptures say what they want them to say," Mike said. "Well, I've worked a double shift tonight, and I'm thirsty as all hell. What's there to drink in the refrigerator?"

Mike found the open bottle of champagne and downed about a fourth of it; I killed the remainder. I felt like I was spinning on a merry-go-round, lying in my twin-sized bed. No one ever told me that something that tastes so fruity and sparkleberry in your mouth could make you feel so stupid and drowsy in your head. This was the first time I'd ever been drunk before.

Sunday, Dad moved the color television from my parents' room to the living room for the Super-Bowl kickoff. The Pittsburgh Steelers hammered the Minnesota Vikings 16-6, and I'll always remember that game for the atmosphere in our living room, rather than the defensive game that it turned out to be. Uncle Frank came over with his son, Derrick. Uncle Frank's not much of a football guy, but after he'd had a few drinks, he thought he knew everything about every player on both teams. After a few more drinks, he started crying, because Joe is still in jail.

My dad's boss and friend, Captain Johnson, came by our house to watch the game, too. You could tell Mr.

Johnson was a Steelers fan. He's originally from Philadelphia, and said people on the East Coast are a lot faster than people in the South. I can see why my dad likes him; Captain Johnson has to be one of the coolest people I've ever met. My dad, on the other hand, rooted for the Vikings because they're in the National Football Conference, like the Cowboys. Of course, our Super Bowl Sunday festivities were capped off by the presence of Reggie, who came over for the evening.

"Hey, Tom, that Mr. Johnson is a pretty cool cat. How long has your father known him?" Reggie asked as we were walking after the game ended.

"Yes, I agree with you, Reggie," I said as we stood talking underneath Reggie's porch light. "Mr. Johnson has an infectious personality. I've heard my father mention his name a time or two to my mother, but I don't really know how or when he met him. All I know is that he's a huge sports fan, and he doesn't like the Cowboys, because he's an Eagles fan, and they're in the same division as Dallas."

"Hey, Tom, when are you gonna bring your ass back to school?" Reggie suddenly asked. It dawned on me that I hadn't been back to school since the backyard fiasco two months ago. "I haven't seen a nigger in the halls of the high school since I don't know when," Reggie said in a silly, concerned tone of voice. "Nigger, Christmas break ended last Monday, and everybody else got their asses back in class, and yo ass ain't been anywhere to be seen."

"Wow, has it really been that long since I was at school?" I said aloud to nobody in particular.

"Listen, Pee, I know that the whole 'end-of-the-world' thing didn't happen for you, but you better get yo' shit back together and get on with the fucking program," Reggie said as I looked back blankly.

Diary, it was the first time in my life that anyone— let alone Reggie Thomas—had called me his "Pee." Diary, when your buddy calls you his "Pee," he means "partner," and "partner" has more affection among buddies than any other term on the planet.

"Hey, Pee, I'll see you at school tomorrow," I promised, giving him the soul handshake as we parted in the cool night air.

Saturday, January 18th, 1975

How do you explain being absent from your high school classes for over 40 days? You don't.

"Tom, did you enjoy your extended winter break?" Miss Wiseman asked me on my first Monday back.

"Well, I don't know where to begin, Miss Wiseman. You see there was this big fight in our back yard right before Thanksgiving. Then, there was this whole Armageddon, 'end-of-the-world' thing that occupied my time during December, and now I'm back."

She looked at me and shook her head as if she truly understood.

"Tom, I read about the failed Jehovah's Witnesses pre- diction in the local paper. Doomsday prophesies have circulated many times in the history of the world. You should do some history research before you jump on the doomsday bandwagon again," Miss Wiseman said, handing me about a thousand make-up assignments. "Have these done before the end of the semester, and I won't have to fail you."

I looked at the forty pound stack of paper and watched her tiny butt walk toward her desk.

After I came home from field service today, Reggie came over to greet me. "Hey, Pee, look who's in the latest *Sports Illustrated!*"

There it was on page 78—Reggie Thomas' name in bold black lettering. With shared excitement, Reggie and I read the half-page article titled "The Lone Star." The editor wrote, "Abilene High Eagles' freshman quarterback, Reggie Thomas, enjoyed one of the best statistical starts of any quarterback in Texas, leading the Eagles in an impressive 10-1 record. Thomas, who completed more than 72 percent of his passes and ran for over 1400 yards this season, is the latest Texas sensation with three more seasons ahead of him. Not only did this freshman quarterback break every freshman record for the state of Texas, but the college coaches I've spoken with say that his speed is his greatest strength."

"You're a star, Reggie!" I kept saying as we hugged one another and jumped around my mother's coffee table.

Monday, February 3rd, 1975

The Elders have been meeting behind closed doors for the past two Sundays. Pastor Slowley advised some disgruntled members that he has the power to disfellowship any and all members who aren't pleased by the direction the Watchtower Society has recently taken. A disfellowshipped member cannot be reinstated for at least one year; Leonard wasn't reinstated for nearly two years. Some of our members are angry over the Watchtower Society's false prophesy. Pastor Slowley assured us yesterday that the world is still going to end soon, but that the calculations were off by just a few months.

"Don't appease this group of heathens," I overheard him say to an elder, as I passed by them in the men's room. He's also been saying "Get Satan behind you!" to members who question the church's predictions.

Then later today:

"So what's been happening with you, Pee?" Reggie said, as we crossed paths between classes.

"Hanging out in the library, trying to catch up on all this extra homework that I got tangled up in," I said.

"Yo, Pee, are you going to the basketball game tomorrow?" Reggie said. "James has his first start as the forward position, and we should be there to back him."

Suddenly, a stunning brunette walked between us and distracted Reggie.

"Yo, Pee, I'll catch up with you later," Reggie said with

a hasty grin, following her closely as she smiled slyly at him over her shoulder.

Diary, it's always something!

Catch you up later.

Friday, February 14th, 1975

"Hundreds of Jehovah's Witnesses staged a protest outside of their Brooklyn headquarters to protest the Watchtower Society's refusal to acknowledge that their 1975 end-of-the-world prediction didn't materialize."

I read this in the evening edition of yesterday's paper. Here I sit, unable to figure out what to write. Spooky berates me with his continual drone: "Tom, the JW's played you!" I don't want to listen to him, but I think he's right. When your own mind keeps telling you that you've been played, it's not easy to tell yourself that people don't play when it comes to religious issues. I'm never sure anymore which voice I should listen to.

When Reggie and I were at James' basketball game, I heard a voice come over the PA system.

"Tom, what's the name of the game?"

I was at my first high school basketball game, but in body only; my mind was miles away. "Tom, what's the name of the game?" echoed louder and louder in my head. Had the press box announcer somehow gotten into my head, or was it Swagger, finally registering the truth locked inside my own mind?

Then, Smoothy said without warning, "Wake up, Tom, no more living in your head—no time for dreaming—time is for thinking ahead."

"Tom, your world has changed so much from what you were told it would be!" Reggie said, the sound of his voice breaking the chaotic hamster wheel that was running in my head. In a crowded gymnasium, with the excitement of my first high school sporting event, I felt alone with my thoughts. "Tom, you must be smarter than you seem to be. You're always reading, and you get good grades. How did you let yourself get fooled by those quacks?"

All those empty years of disassociation from my peers had ended, and I still couldn't live in the moment. Reggie was absolutely right; there was nothing wrong with enjoying myself for a change. The Elders had fed me a line, and I wasn't falling for it anymore. All those years of the Jehovah's Witnesses telling me over and over that sporting events are sponsored by Satan, and that "bad association spoils useful habits"—well, it's all over now. Mike is right; they took the Scriptures and interpreted them to say whatever they wanted them to say. Yes, I had been blinded, hypnotized, and perhaps most of all, just plain afraid. But why? What was the nature of their game?

When Reggie said, "Pee, don't let those adults fool you again," I knew from the tone of his voice that he meant more than some manipulated Biblical interpretations, and that there was a lot my Pee had in store to teach me.

Suddenly, I realized that more than a third of our congregation no longer had their homes, more than a third sold their family businesses, and that my mother had refused to buy winter coats. I'm starting to suspect that there's more to their game than saving souls. I just don't yet know what their real game is. As I sit here with a pen gripped in my hand, I realize that I know no other way to live. Tomorrow is Saturday, and all I know to do is go from house to house proclaiming the good news. So that's exactly what I intend to do until I figure things out.

Tuesday, February 25th, 1975

I'm sitting in the gymnasium next to Reggie, feeling much more present than last time.

"The final score is Abilene Eagles 67, Sweetwater Steers 43. Folks, be careful going home tonight, and to the Eagle student body, we'll see you in classes tomorrow. Good night," the announcer said as the game came to an end.

"Hey, Pee, it's early—I'm going to catch a ride home with Teri. You can ride home with us, but we plan on making a stop at the local Mickey Dee's to grab some grub before hitting the crib," Reggie said as we stood beside a shiny, red and white Ford Mustang that belonged to this white girl, Teri Hunt.

"I'll tag along," I replied. "I'm in no hurry to get home."

"O.K., Pee, get in the back seat. Teri's buying, so don't worry about a thing; you're with Reggie Thomas, and Reggie's looking out for you."

The engine started, and off we went.

"Teri, this is my neighbor, Tom Jones—Tom, this is Teri Hunt. She's a senior, and look what kind of cars seniors get to drive," Reggie said, pointing out the elegant features of Teri's new Mustang.

"Tom, you got pretty drunk last Saturday night; for an instant, it seemed like your mind was lost in space," Reggie said, smiling as our order of burgers came to the car window. "It's a new day. Forget the past. Snap out of that JW trance, and start living in the real world."

Reggie was right about my being drunk last weekend. Mr. Johnson came over with a couple of bottles of booze to watch the NCAA basketball tournament with my father. I vaguely remember Reggie stopping over during the game. The next thing I remember was Reggie telling me how drunk I was. I remember sipping some vodka from Captain Johnson's stash. After a few sips, I discovered that vodka wasn't harsh at all, so I downed about half of the bottle. Then, I wandered into the bathroom and found several of my father's pills in the medicine cabinet. After swallowing a few of the pills, I must have gone into a trance of some kind. The next thing I knew, it was 10 p.m. on a Tuesday night, and Reggie and I were being dropped off on Bowie Street by Teri.

Tuesday, March 4th, 1975

Déjà vu all over again!

It's a Tuesday night, and I'm coming to from another lost weekend. The slamming of Teri's car door as I got out brought me back to the present. "Damn, James is a pretty nice basketball player. What house does he live in?" Teri said to Reggie.

"The green and white house is James," he said.

"It was a damn good game tonight," Teri said.

"Damn good game," Reggie repeated as I started toward my house. Over my shoulder, I saw them kissing passionately as I closed the front door.

"Tom, whose car was that?" my father asked as I made my way to my bedroom.

"Oh, that's a girlfriend of Reggie's. She dropped us off after the game," I said, closing my door on my father's questions.

Mr. Johnson showed up again this weekend to watch the NCAA games, and again, I found my way into the grownups' unsecured alcohol. It was the same scenario, a bottle of vodka, nerve pills, and a complete loss of time for 48 hours. I know I went to school. I don't know why I didn't go out on field service, or why instead, I'm watching sports with my father on weekends. Who is this guy, and what has he done with Tom?

Reggie told me at school yesterday that I was pretty drunk after Mr. Johnson left and that he'd kept me from getting busted by my father. Diary, I have no recollection of what happened after the booze and pills hit me, but thank God Reggie's been around to cover my butt.

"Tom, what were you studying so intensely in the library on Monday?" Miss Wiseman said today as she passed out assignments for her class project. "I said hello to you, but you never acknowledged my presence." I was surprised to hear I had been in the library at all, but I just shrugged her off.

Usually when I walk into the high school library, I go immediately to the section about world history, sit and read. According to one book, there have been several end of the world predictions. Some guy named Zoroaster wandered the mountains of western Iran 3400 years ago, warning of a time when the sun would stand still overhead for 10 days and molten lava would sweep across the lands. In another account, Jesus Christ told his disciples that the stars would fall from the sky in their lifetime—"Flee to the mountains! Let no one on the roof of his house go down to take anything out of the house! Let no one in the fields go back to get his cloak!" (Matthew 24:16-18). I also read about an end-of-the-age story in the 14th century when Pope Clement VI led Christian cultists through town after town. They bloodied themselves with whips as penance to prepare for the arrival of God.

"Miss Wiseman, why don't all people commit suicide?" I asked, as she handed me my assignment. "Death is what awaits each and every one of us anyway—isn't it?"

"Tom, everyone has to answer that question for himself," she replied. "All I know are the facts, and the fact is, every moment we live brings us closer to the second we will die." Our eyes met. It was as if we saw each other for the first time, like a spark leapt between us at that moment, but then it was gone, and I'm not sure it ever really happened.

I don't have the answers to the many questions that rotate between my head, but I keep asking myself this one question about my mother's religious beliefs. That question is: What's the name of the game? I still can't understand why they've been lying to us, even though I'm pretty sure that they have.

Friday, March 7th, 1975

I heard this song on the radio, and the lyrics keep playing over and over in my head:

Hello, darkness, my old friend,

I've come to talk with you again,

Yesterday, I read in the obituaries section of the newspaper:

Scott Peter Lane, 20, of Abilene was officially pronounced dead on Wednesday, March 5th, 1975. Lane had been listed MIA in Vietnam for the past three years before his remains were discovered in Saigon and shipped to the United States. Services will be held at 3 p.m. Saturday at the First Church of the Nazarene in Abilene, with the Reverend Patterson officiating. Burial will be in Buffalo Gap Cemetery, directed by the Norman Funeral Home in Abilene. Visitation will be from 6 p.m. to 8 p.m. today at the funeral home.

Scott was born in Los Angeles on Peterson Air Force Base on March 5th, 1955. He enjoyed hunting, fishing, and cars. Survivors include his parents, Fred and Lynn Lane, and his sister, Laurie.

I killed Scott, didn't I? I should have never questioned God and the end-of-the-age stuff. Now, the entire block is grieving. Poor Laurie! I'm so blind. I should have seen how my doubts and disobedience could cause terrible events. I'm paralyzed by what I've done.

Wednesday, March 12th, 1975

"Mother-fucker, you ain't caused nobody to die," Reggie said sternly. "You'd better get yo' shit back together, boy. Life comes down to pussy or money, or both if you can get them at the same time."

My family didn't attend the funeral because of our religion. Pastor Slowley says that if we go into another church, Satan will have a foothold on our souls. Believe me, I sure wanted to go, but I also wanted to keep Satan from capturing my soul. I can tell Satan has already got his hooks in me. I got drunk again this weekend, and Reggie saved my butt again, this time by letting me sleep it off at his house in his mother's room. Shirley had gone off for the entire weekend with her boyfriend, Billy Bob, giving me the perfect cover to recuperate.

Diary, I don't know what's gotten into me lately—the more I don't want to drink alcohol, the more I find myself in front of a bottle. Tuesday after the game, I found myself with Reggie, Teri, and her younger sister, Wendy, parked in Wendy's junior high school parking lot. Wendy is twelve and came to the basketball game with Teri. After the game, Teri drove us all to the parking lot, where Reggie and Teri made out in the Mustang. Wendy and I kept watch while they did the nasty. Mostly, we listened to my transistor radio, so we wouldn't hear Teri moaning and groaning. That Simon and Garfunkel song came on the radio again while we were listening.

People talking without speaking,
People hearing without listening,

Although there was no silence between Reggie and Teri while they did the nasty, I couldn't help but reflect on how badly I wanted the silence to conquer my brain. I enjoy writing in you, Diary, and updating you on what is going on around here, but if only the voices in my head would stop.

Reggie is so lucky. Wendy told me that all the girls in her junior high class know who he is, and all the girls in her class would do anything just to touch him.

Miss Wiseman is right, every moment we live does bring us closer to death, and I am just a fool who doesn't know why people bow and pray to man-made neon gods. There is no god. Like the song said, silence is a cancer growing inside of me because I am still hung up on what the JW religion has taught me. I would give anything to be Reggie; it seems like he has all the answers to the questions that plague my mind.

Our Tuesday evening ended with Teri and I hopping into the Mustang for a quick trip to 7-11 to buy cigarettes. On our way back, the headlights bounced off the schoolyard walls. There, in the distance, I glimpsed Reggie with Wendy's pants pulled down around her ankles. When I realized what was going on, I thought quickly and beeped the horn just in the nick of time.

"Thanks, brother," Reggie said to me as the girls dropped us off. "I almost got into Wendy's potang. My motto is 'Eight to eighty, blind, crippled or crazy. Hey, Pee, I owe you one!" he shouted as his screen door closed behind him.

Tuesday, March 18th, 1975

I don't know what I'm doing anymore!

"Hey, Pee, look out for a brother," Reggie said to me as he handed me a week's worth of homework to do for him. I finished it while he and Teri did the nasty in her car after the final basketball game of the regular season.

James received the player of the year award after the game. Abilene High might be eligible for the 5A playoffs, but we won't know until the other teams in our district finish their games this weekend. It was so much fun watching James play this season. He's a 6'4", 211-pound freshman, and he averaged 23 points, 11 rebounds, and 5 assists per game.

A lot has happened this past weekend. Something new, called the "1975 NCAA Men's Division I Basketball Tournament," which involves 32 schools, started up on Saturday. Captain Johnson came over, and although I tried not to, I got drunk again and took some pills from my parents' medicine cabinet. I wound up sleeping at Reggie's again. The vodka isn't so bad, but those damn pills send me off to places in my mind that I wouldn't go otherwise. This time, Diary, I slept all night and into the Sunday morning hours. Saturday was Mike's seventeenth birthday, but, of course, no party. My mother refuses to let go of her religious beliefs, in spite of our continued existence.

"The Bible says, in Romans 14:5, 'No Jehovah Witness shall celebrate any birthdays or holidays,'" she said when Mike asked about possibly having a party.

Diary, I took the liberty of reading this passage and found that my brother is right. Verses 5 to 9 reads:

> *5 One [man] judges one day as above another; another [man] judges one day as all others; let each [man] be fully convinced in his own mind. 6 He who observes the day observes it to Jehovah. Also, he who eats, eats to Jehovah, for he gives thanks to God; and he who does not eat does not eat to Jehovah, and yet gives thanks to God. 7 None of us, in fact, lives with regard to himself only, and*

*no one dies with regard to himself only; **8** for both
if we live, we live to Jehovah, and if we die, we die
to Jehovah. Therefore both if we live and if we die,
we belong to Jehovah. **9** For to this end Christ died
and came to life again, that he might be Lord over
both the dead and the living.*

All this time I believed these verses and justified not
celebrating birthdays or holidays, but it's just a matter
of interpretation and taking things out of context. Over
half of my life, I've lived with no birthdays, no Christmas
celebrations, no Easter eggs, no Halloween decorations,
no Thanksgiving feasts, and a list of "thou-shalt-nots"
that goes on and on, based on someone's interpretation
of the Bible. Miss Wiseman was right to say that history
shows that contempt prior to investigation is one of
ancient man's most evil sins.

Diary, there's a song playing on the local radio stations
that sums up what's been going on in our teenage lifetime.
The song is by The Who, and some of the lyrics go as
follows:

*The change, it had to come
We knew it all along
We were liberated from the foe, that's all
And the world looks just the same
And history ain't changed
'Cause the banners, they all flown in the last war*

*I'll tip my hat to the new constitution
Take a bow for the new revolution*

Smile and grin at the change all around me
Pick up my guitar and play
Just like yesterday
Then I'll get on my knees and pray
We don't get fooled again
No, no!

Diary, I've come to the conclusion that teens know more than their parents, and this teenager will never be fooled again!

Sunday, March 23rd, 1975

It's the information age. Just pick up any newspaper or walk into your local library and you'll find out anything you've ever wanted to know about anybody or anything.

Yesterday was a repeat of the last several Saturdays—Captain Johnson came by with booze to watch basketball with my father, and you can guess most of the rest. I came in from field service and put my overloaded bag of tracts and magazines down next to the front door inside our home just before the door busted open. Reggie came in with an inscrutable look on his face and a sheet of newspaper tucked under his left arm.

"Guess what I have under my arm," Reggie said.

"Looks like the *Abilene Reporter*," I said as he walked toward me.

Reggie said, "My fucking father's in the obituary section."

Unbeknownst to me, at that very moment,
the shock of my life was still to come.
When I turned to hand the obituary back
to Reggie so he could keep it as a souvenir,
I noticed another bit of news: "Father O'Malley
arrested on two counts of child molestation."

He pointed to his father's name—it read: "Reggie J. Thomas, Sr., 34, died Thursday at Fisher County Hospital. Services will be at 2 p.m. Saturday at the Church of Christ under the direction of Weathers Funeral Home in Oklahoma City, OK."

I was stunned, and stumbled back over the coffee table when Reggie smoothly and deftly caught me before my head could hit the floor.

"Don't sweat it, Tom," Reggie said without expression. "The fucking man was a rolling stone, and now that the bastard's dead, all he's left our family is alone. Not much change there."

We nodded to Captain Johnson in my father's room as we headed for the refrigerator, where we quietly and indiscriminately opened the bottles Captain Johnson had brought. It was the first time I'd seen Reggie drink, but he drank as if he'd done it before.

"My mother must've known he was dead, but she didn't tell us," Reggie said as we stood in the backyard.

Even though Reggie's father died in Oklahoma, his obituary was in our local newspaper. I read it over again in the backyard after I'd chugged a few bottles of liquid courage. Unbeknownst to me, at that very moment, the shock of my life was still to come. When I turned to hand the obituary back to Reggie so he could keep it as a souvenir, I noticed another bit of news: "Father O'Malley arrested on two counts of child molestation."

"Reggie!" I said, stumbling to my feet. "Give me back that newspaper."

Father O'Malley of Saint Paul Parrish was arrested and charged with molesting two boys, ages 10 and 12. Bond was set at $10,000. O'Malley is expected to remain in the Taylor County Jail until at least Monday, when a judge will set a hearing date.

This priest was the same priest who had told Susan's mother that it was against God's will for Susan and I to remain together just days before our suicide. If by some chance there is a God, I would bet he never spoke to Father O'Malley. What a pervert!

"Reggie!" I shouted, but he was lost in his own thoughts. "Hey, Pee, you got any matches?"

Reggie fumbled dazedly in his pockets and said, "What do you need sparks for?"

"I'll show you," I said.

Ten minutes later, a bonfire blazed in my backyard, containing all the magazines and tracts I'd brought home from field service.

"I might as well throw this in, too, Tom. At least, I know from now on that no man's got his dick up my father's ass or vice versa," Reggie said, tossing the obituary on top of the flames.

I'll always remember us staring blankly and swaying as the fire consumed the wasted remnants of lives we'd never need again. In that moment, my attitude concerning figures of authority changed radically. Never again would I be blindly led down a path of ignorance—not with information at the tips of my fingers in every news report and library. From now on, I'd figure out the truth for myself. Smoothy made a tremendous power play in my shift of consciousness.

I said out loud to no one, "No more of this confusion. No more of the same old mistakes. Everybody's playing a game these days, and it's time you, Tom Jones, started playing a game of your own."

Then Spooky countered, "Tom, it's lonely and dangerous out there on your own. What will you do when they come creeping around again to fill you with their worn-out lies?"

Then, help came as Swagger took charge. "Tom Jones, you've got Reggie now, and he knows how to play their games. Just watch and learn."

Tuesday, April 1st, 1975

"Hey, Pee, it's about the fucking money," replayed in my head over and over again as I awoke remembering Reggie's words. "Hey, Pee, never bullshit yourself—it comes down to those who want it, those who have it, and those who are gonna get it."

When I opened my eyes, my mother was standing over me.

"Tom, do you need to go see Dr. Scott?" she said.

"What day is it?" I asked.

"Tuesday," she said, looking concerned.

"What happened to Monday?"

"You shouldn't worry about Monday," she said. "If I were you, I'd be worrying about what you did on Sunday and how you're going to apologize to all those people."

I started to retrace my steps, beginning with Monday and working my way back to Sunday, which was still very blurry but becoming clearer by the minute—certainly a day I wanted to forget. That left Saturday to remember, as my mother stood over me, trying to make me more coherent about what I'd done on Sunday.

Oh, yes, I remembered, Saturday was the final game of the new NCAA single-elimination tournament. I vaguely remember that the final score was UCLA 92, Kentucky 85. Or, was it Kentucky 92, UCLA 85?

"You've been passed out the entire day," she said.

"What day is it?" I asked her again.

"It's Tuesday, the 1st. You've been out for over 36 hours."

"Is this some kind of April Fool's joke?" I said, desperately trying to gain my balance as I stood up.

Smoothy echoed in my head, "No more confusion."

Reggie's voice repeated, "Hey, Pee, it's about the fucking money."

"Tom, how are you going to face those people again?" my mother asked.

Then it hit me as the fog began to clear from my brain. I remembered Captain Johnson arriving Saturday and that I had gone out to field service, and then seeing Reggie and I stand over a bonfire, but somehow I was rip-roaring drunk by half time. Captain Johnson said that Richard Washington of UCLA had received the most valuable player award.

"You mean the game's over?" I said.

"Tom, I think you've had a few sips out of the jug tonight. It's not like you to forget what quarter is being played," my father said, winking at me.

I heard Captain Johnson say, "Let him sleep it off. All teenage boys experiment with alcohol, Larry. Don't tell me you didn't do it."

Unbeknownst to Captain Johnson, I had taken several bottles of wine from the back seat of his Impala and had gotten an even earlier start with the booze than anyone had thought. I remembered the smell of the toothpaste I'd swished and swallowed to mask the smell of the wine. On Sunday morning, I don't remember waking up; I just came to, but I will always remember the Sunday morning service that day. There I was, full of booze, leading the procession with Pastor Slowley.

Reggie's voice kept repeating in my head, "Hey, Pee, it's all about the fucking money. The game goes like this: there are those who want it, those who've got it, and those who're gonna get it."

"The Jehovah's Witnesses are the 40th most profitable company in New York," I heard myself say from the microphone at the lectern. As the congregation stared in horror, I continued my tirade. "It's the age of information, and I, Tom Jones, went to the high school library, and guess what I found out! This organization is profiting off of your free labor. They're the 40th most profitable entity in New York because you people have made them that way."

"Get him off the pulpit!" someone shouted.

"Let him continue!" I heard one woman say.

Then I remember saying something that I don't remember reading: "This is not the first time the Jehovah's Witnesses have done this sort of thing. It happened in 1914; the Jehovah's Witnesses prophesied an end to the world, and hundreds of people sold their homes, only to find out it was a hoax. And again in 1925. Get up folks and walk out while you still can. People, it's the same game, just a different year. Don't get fooled again! Don't get fooled again!"

I hitchhiked home after the bizarre scene I'd instigated, but I can't tell you how I lost the last 36 hours. All I know is that the information age has stories to reveal as this Diary of the Lost Teen Age continues...

Tuesday, April 8th, 1975

More than a week has passed since I hijacked the pulpit last Sunday. I told Reggie about it, and he congratulated me and rewarded my bold move with a high-five. But it doesn't matter, now, does it? I'm not welcome in church any longer. They can look for other naive converts to do their dirty work. Homeboy, you'd expect me to be locked up in Dr. Scott's office at this point, but guess again. It's my mother who's crazy. She and the rest of the members who are willing to listen to Pastor Slowley preach about a mythical Christ to come are the ones who need to be in Dr. Scott's office.

I read this week in the school library that Jehovah's Witnesses, according to an Australian study, are "three times more likely to be diagnosed schizophrenic, and nearly four times more likely to suffer from paranoid schizophrenia than the rest of the population." The Jehovah's Witness Society has altered its doomsday calculations over the years on many occasions. Before the 1975 prediction of Christ's return, there were other predictions for 1874, 1914 and 1925. I'd suggest the organization spend its profits on new calendars or just get out of the prediction business altogether.

Homeboy, it's like an episode from "The Twilight Zone" at church. Many have abandoned their faith, but some congregation members who have spent more than half of their lives waiting for a mythical paradise are still walking around, reassuring one another that it will happen any day now. I, just like most of the teens from our congregation, have decided not to return. Jesus Christ is not coming! I repeat, Jesus Christ is not coming! All we have left is these living men, the Jehovah's Witness elders, who're trying to suck the last dime out of unsuspecting dupes.

Yesterday, my father unexpectedly said, "Son, I don't have more than a ninth-grade education, but there are PhDs that I feel smarter than. Our ancestors survived the legal rape of their women, slavery, sitting in the back of the bus, lynching, and still, we forgave the people responsible. If you think the white man was responsible, you'd better read your history. Black Africans sold each other both to foreign white men and to each other. Should I then be mad at the black man? I am the black man. Son, sometimes life comes down to letting go and letting up, which is what you should do with your anger over your mother's religion."

Monday, April 21st, 1975

A chance meeting brought several of the Bowie gang together in front of Church's Chicken. Howard still works there as the night cook.

"Tom, they shouldn't have done us like that," Howard said, while Reggie and I were ordering. Right away, Reggie picked up on Howard's meaning.

"You niggers need to let that shit go; slave days are over, brothers," Reggie said.

Beep, beep, came the sound of a horn from the drive-through lane. James appeared at the window driving his father's Chrysler.

"What in the world are you doing driving?" I yelled when I recognized his grin.

"James has his learner's permit," his father said, sticking his head out the passenger side.

"How long have you been driving?" Reggie asked as we all migrated toward the window.

"James will be getting plenty of practice over the next two weeks, since we're taking a road trip to Utah to see his cousins," Mr. Smith proudly said.

"Don't worry, Pop. I can handle it—8 hours, and you and mom won't have to drive a single mile."

"My brother, Scott, was driving when he was 14," Laurie chimed in from the back seat. "Yeah, I decided to see if James could really drive, so I tagged along. Howard, since you're the head cook at this chicken joint, why not give your neighborhood buddies a discount on an 8-piece box of chicken?" Laurie asked in a persuasive tone of voice.

Everyone was laughing and smiling, and I realized how fast time flies when I thought about James driving already.

"Why haven't you guys gotten your learner's permits?" Laurie asked as Howard handed bags of fried chicken out the window.

"Why haven't we applied for our permits?" I asked myself. Well, Howard and I had been so busy preparing for the end of the world that we never considered it.

"Tom, you should sign up for the next Driver's Ed class at school," Laurie said softly just before the Chrysler drove away. "I think the deadline is Wednesday."

Wednesday, April 23rd, 1975

Homeboy, I'm here to inform you that Tom Jones now has a learner's permit. No shit! I've got an official document in the back pocket of my Levis that says I can legally drive once I perform certain requirements. As luck would have it, Miss Wiseman is one of the two teachers in charge of the Driver's Ed program. I went to her class on Tuesday and mentioned something about wanting a learner's permit.

"Tom, I can issue you one, but it's a $15 charge to sign up, and I'm not sure if I have any more, but I'll check after class."

Homeboy, the stars must have lined up correctly for me, because there was one, only one, permit left.

"Tom, that'll be $15," Miss Wiseman said, tearing a receipt from the logbook.

"I didn't know that you were serious about that fee," I told her sadly.

"Tom, you can't register without the $15 fee," she said, putting the permit back in the envelope. But I've learned a lot about how to play the game from Reggie.

"Miss Wiseman, you'll have the $15 in your hands by the end of tomorrow. Just write my name on that last receipt and trust me." So here I sit, Homeboy, with a driver's permit in my pocket. If I hadn't fronted her, I wouldn't be able to drive until next year, because this is the last chance to sign up this year, and I officially turn

16 on June 10th—it's less than two months until I have a real license, if I pass the test on my birthday. I can't wait to tell Reggie. He'll be so proud of me.

Saturday, April 26th, 1975

It was so exciting to see James drive off, steering the Chrysler away to visit his cousins. I met his cousin, Janice, last year, before she got married. I guess all teenagers grow up faster these days, but it doesn't seem right to get married so young, especially to someone who's already married.

On Wednesday, I begged to borrow $15 from Reggie to solve the permit predicament, and on Thursday morning, as I was racing to modern history, Reggie stopped me just before I went in.

"Hey, Pee," he said, sliding the cash into my back pocket. "That's why I only fuck white girls; white girls have money. Remember, Pee, there are those who have it, those who want it, and those who are going to get it. I'll sprinkle in a high-yellow black girl every now and then, if she has some money, but white girls are where it's at."

After class, we strolled toward the track field.

"This brother," Reggie said, "has to get to the track field in ten minutes. I've got an important meet after school. Pee, did you finish my algebra homework from Monday? I think it's due today."

"Sure, partner. I'll get it from my locker," I told him.

"Sweet!"

"Pee, I know you made me an A on this. You must be the smartest brother on the planet." He jogged away, holding the paper like a baton.

The driver's handbook Miss Wiseman gave me Thursday is already read. She told me on Friday, handing it back to me with a perfect score, that she's never seen a student driver complete the written exam in one afternoon. My high I.Q. comes in handy these days, especially when I'm memorizing things for a test. Now all I have to do is find someone to teach me how to drive.

Monday, May 5th, 1975

I don't know what I was waiting for when I spent so much of my time thinking my time was running out. By now I should be living in paradise. Instead, over the past five months I have been watching the prison walls Spooky built up in my head slowly start to crumble. This world is five months into the calendar year 1975, and no heathen or devils, Jew or Gentile, have been annihilated.

So, do the adults deceive us? Why do they fill our heads with fairy stories of paradise and Santa Claus? Why do they teach us honesty and then lie? I can't quite see their motives, but grown-ups must think that kids are so naïve!

James came back home from Utah this weekend, and his first visit to the Mormon state will undoubtedly be his last. The howling stories my pale-skinned, hip neighbor told me about Utah caused him some deep pain. I didn't know what James expected to find when he left Texas for his cousin's wedding in Utah a week ago, but I did discover what he found there. Over and over, James spoke as if the arranged marriage of his 14-year-old female cousin to her 32-year-old polygamist husband wasn't something that he thought was in the normal.

James calls Utah "the Mormon State," and he talks about Mormonism as if it enslaved women. I didn't really understand why he felt so passionately about his cousin's situation from one short trip. Then I ended up at the Abilene Christian College library. Reggie and I borrowed Shirley's '69 Oldsmobile for the afternoon with the plan of finding some open space where I could learn how to drive.

"Reggie, you're almost 17. Why haven't you gotten a learner's permit?" I asked out of curiosity.

"Tom, I have dyslexia, so I have a hard time reading, and the doctor who diagnosed me said that's why I have a tendency to see letters juxtaposed or backward," Reggie said as we were looking for a place for me to practice driving. I really don't know much about dyslexia, so I was curious to find out just what it meant.

"I know," I said, "let's go to the parking lots of ACC; there's sure to be open space there."

"Great idea, Pee," Reggie said, pointing the car toward the campus across town. We got to the college, and sure enough there were plenty of wide open spaces, but Reggie was drawn to the track practice nearby, and I saw a sign for the ACC Library. Before long, Reggie was at the practice, and I was in the library reading up on everything from dyslexia to dementia. Since it's a Christian college, it has a huge section on religion— bigger than I'd ever thought possible. It was there that I discovered more about why James was so upset after his trip.

The Mormon religion is filled with doctrine that leads its members to be openly homophobic, racist and sexist. Some guy named Joseph Smith, Jr. started Mormonism and then was killed by a mob in 1844. Then various movements were spawned as the denominations vied for supremacy. The books I found suggested that federal legislators began passing laws designed to ban polygamy specifically to discourage Mormonism, but certain Mormon sects still practice this way of life.

I wrapped up my brief investigation and went to talk to James. He practically fell to his knees, and I could see in his eyes that he must feel the same thing I did—we had been deceived and betrayed by our leaders and parents. James, too, had caught a glimpse of the truth and turned away in disgust.

Information is so easy to find these days, but I'm starting to realize that I don't want to know any more. There are more than 1,400 Christian denominations in America, and I don't have time to investigate all of them to find out which is true. It seems I always find myself running into a dead end in my search for truth. My generation is smarter than my parents'—I bet they have no idea why they believe what they do. Six months ago my mother didn't even realize she was pregnant—simple biology. I bet biology wasn't even a subject when they were in school. I've only been around for almost sixteen years, and I know about hermaphrodites, marijuana, coke, bigamists, segregation, mutations, and so many other evils in the world, in spite of their efforts to keep me from knowing the truth. The evils of this world seem to be created by priests, pastors, polygamists, police, pedophiles and presidents.

Tuesday, May 13th, 1975

Last week, Homeboy, I finished my entry on a rather injured note, protesting what I referred to as the deceitful "P"s in my world (the priest, the police, the polygamist, the pastor and the president). This week, I'd like to start by adding two more. First, my parents—I tried unsuccessfully to get my mother to apologize for what she put me through with the Jehovah's Witness thing, but she refused, and then insinuated that I should be the one apologizing for my behavior at church. I still hear her talking to Howard's parents about what the world will look like when Jesus comes. Even after five months, the "faithful" JW members never admit that the church leaders were wrong; they only talk among themselves, as if no mistake was made. This entire mishap has taught me one thing: a person always hears what he wants to hear and disregards the rest.

Dr. Scott called last week to check up on me, since it's been a year or so since our last session. He said he was required by state regulation to contact me after a year to check on my state of mind. He's the other deceitful "P" I'd like to add—the psychiatrist. We talked briefly on the phone about how I'm feeling these days and what I've been up to lately. We talked about Susan and how lucky I am to be alive. I talked to him about my religious disillusionment, and he said to move on and make the most of my life. Then, I jokingly asked if he still had magazines with the nude photos of African women in his reception room.

"Tom," he chuckled, "you think too much. Still crazy after all these years. Call me if you ever need someone to guide you through the haze," he said before hanging up the phone.

This is not what I wanted to hear from that wacko. Dr. Scott isn't smart enough to answer a simple question about African culture, and he wants to guide me? No fucking way. Never take advice from a deceitful "P".

Reggie is away this week on his first college recruiting trip. Though he's only a freshman, Ohio State University is already calling. Reggie flew out this weekend to visit the campus in Columbus, with hopes that he'll sign on with the Buckeyes after he graduates. Next week, he's going to Austin to talk to the Longhorn coaches. His name was in the sports section today. The short clip said that he has the best statewide high-school running time in the 100-yard dash. That Reggie is absolutely amazing. I don't know how he does it. One night he's up all night banging a cheerleader in the back of her father's car, and the next afternoon he's running faster than anyone in the state. And to top that off, by evening, he's hopping on a plane en route to another university interview.

Something about Reggie brings a smile to my face. I always feel like it's okay to be myself around him, and when he's away, my days are empty. The newspapers write about him as if he'll be the next superstar. He's more than just a friend to me, because he always tells me the truth. He'll never know what that means to me— just know he's my Pee, and that means more than he'll ever know.

Check U Later.

Tuesday, May 20th, 1975

Here's the skinny on what's going on this week. Reggie went on another college recruiting trip, and I was feeling left out once more, so I decided to get on my bicycle and explore the unfamiliar areas of Abilene. I got a new battery for my old radio, tied it to my bike, and set out on a mission to nowhere in particular.

There is one thing glorious about the end of the world not coming to pass. Suddenly, I find myself with a very relaxed curfew, and after I've done both Reggie's and my own homework, there's plenty of down time to do whatever I feel like doing. I never realized just how much time those JW meetings took out of my life. Charles was absolutely right when he said that they keep you busy attending meetings in an effort to brainwash you into thinking that there's no other way to live.

My bicycle brought me to my brother's job at Sambo's. It was the first time I've seen him in action, busing dishes in the back room. The manager, Dave Cognomi, handed me a menu as I came to the counter.

"What will you have, young man?" he asked, pouring me a cup of coffee.

"Just coffee," I said, checking my pockets for change.

Dave placed a wooden nickel on the counter next to my cup and said, "These wooden nickels represent all the free coffee you can drink. It's Sambo's policy—the first cup of coffee is on you, but after that, it's on us," Dave said, capturing my attention with his exuberant, Italian hand gestures.

"But how do you stay in business if you give coffee away?" I asked.

"Son, that's a great question. In the restaurant industry, we call this a 'loss leader,'" he explained. "We start out losing money on the coffee, but coffee's cheap, and people drinking coffee stay here longer and order more food—maybe pie, maybe a meal."

"Tom, it's all about the money," I thought as Dave explained. "There are those who have it, those who want it, and those who are going to get it."

I drank my first cup of coffee, watching my surprised brother go back and forth with loads of dishes. I picked up a soiled copy of the evening paper from one of the bus tubs nearby. The headline read: "101 Churches and 101 Private Clubs." I was intrigued, so I read on. It turns out that Abilene is in the middle of a battle over whether or not alcohol can be sold within the city limits. The city is in a dry county, but the city council is considering a vote to make it wet. All of this wet and dry county business just puzzles the shit out of me. Dave sat down beside me with his full pot of coffee. I was reading so intently that I didn't notice when he refilled my cup.

"The town of Abilene is split virtually in half over this liquor sales business," he said. "I'm hoping the city votes to start selling alcohol. It would be good for business owners. The religious hicks have had a monopoly on morality in this town for its 100-year history, and it's time for that monopoly to end."

"I agree with you, boss man," I said. "I think it's time we took the power back."

Dave looked a bit stunned. "Son, you're pretty smart for your age," he said as he hurried away to greet the customers who had just come in.

Mike came over to chat while I sat sipping the second cup of coffee in my life, feeling very sophisticated and grown up.

"It's a mad house here tonight, and as usual we're short of help. Two dish-washers quit this week and one waitress is a no-show tonight, so Dave is helping with the tables until the night waitresses come in," Mike said. "I wish you were 16 and legal to work, little bro', because we could sure use another hand."

Dave sat back down beside me, looking through a stack of job applications he pulled out from under the bar.

"Son," Dave said, "it's like this: Impact, Texas, which is fifteen miles away, is the closest place, aside from the Air Force base, that sells alcohol. Impact is owned by the largest group of churches in Abilene, so they've had a 100-year monopoly on liquor sales. Rumor has it that Impact is the richest city in the state, due entirely to liquor sales. With the upcoming city council vote in August, that might all change."

"You're a busy man. What's with all the paper work?".

"Good help is a bitch to find. I lost two dishwashers this week, and one of my evening waitresses failed to show up again. These are job applications for the dishwasher positions, and this pile is for the waitress positions. I plan on hiring tomorrow." Dave hurried off again to greet customers.

Ten minutes later, coffee splashed into my empty cup, and a voice from behind me asked, "How old are you, son?"

"Sir, I'm sixteen—seventeen next month," I lied. "Boss man, I'm the best damn help in these parts, and I won't let you down. When do you want me to start?" I said, extending my shaky right hand.

"Son, I'm a master at reading body language, and I can see by the way you've managed to hang on to that lonely dime in your pocket for the past two hours while drinking away my 'loss leader' scheme that we've got a business venture in our future. Can you start this weekend?" Dave said, shaking my hand.

Before I could even respond, Spooky and Smoothy were already celebrating my first money-making venture. Swagger took over and before I knew it I'd replied, "Boss man, I'll start tomorrow. Just give Mike a clean apron for me, and I'll have him show me what to do."

I rode home in record time, listening to "Nothing from Nothing" by Billy Preston. So what if I'd lied. It was a little white lie, and like Billy Preston's song said, "nothing from nothing leaves nothing," and I had nothing to lose by lying about my age. Reggie's voice echoed in my mind as I pedaled onto our driveway, resting my bike against the garage door before going in to tell my parents about my new job. "Nothing from nothing leaves nothing," but I've got something; I've got a job.

Check U Later.

Sunday, May 25th, 1975

It all happened so fast, and it all keeps revolving at a breakneck pace for me. Captain Johnson came over to watch the NBA finals with my father. They both had a huge stake in the outcome because it's the first time in any major professional American sports league that a championship game featured two black head coaches pitted against one another. Al Attles coaches the Golden State Warriors, and KC Jones coaches the Washington Bullets. As I sat there with my Pee in the living room, watching the television and watching my father's and

Captain Johnson's reactions to each foul, I knew this was an important moment in black history.

"Larry, we've come a long way from Jim-Crow, haven't we?" Captain Johnson kept saying, but my father was too nervous to respond.

"You're a Captain in the United States Air Force, sir," my father finally answered during a commercial break.

"Yes, but there are only a handful of black officers," Captain Johnson said. "Larry, you've been in the Air Force for over eighteen years; I'm sure you saw your share of prejudice as you worked your way up."

"Captain Johnson, sir, I could have been an officer, too," my father said.

"You don't say," the captain said.

"Yeah, I was bumped up two grades in elementary school," my father said. "All my classmates thought I'd be very successful. I was valedictorian of my class, but then the Vietnam War got to my nerves."

"Now we've got two African-American coaches leading their teams in the NBA finals. It's got to give you goose bumps to know that a black coach will be crowned champion in the end," Captain Johnson exclaimed, raising his glass.

"I'm going to be the first black quarterback to lead a pro team to the Super Bowl," Reggie interjected into the happy, but premature celebration that was already reaching a fevered pitch.

"That's a pretty bold prediction," Captain Johnson said as Reggie nonchalantly dangled a toothpick out the side of his mouth. "Boy, you've got to lead your high-school team to the district championship first."

Reggie stood up to argue the point.

"Sit your black ass back down in that chair," Captain Johnson said, already tipsy.

"Don't call me a black ass! You just keep your eyes on the television set, and one day you'll see me stroll across the screen with a white wife hanging on my arm and doing a postgame interview for my winning Super Bowl team."

"A white wife, boy? Don't you let those peckerwoods hear you say that," Captain Johnson said. "What's wrong with a black wife?" Not getting an answer from Reggie, Captain Johnson looked my way and said, "The second half of the game is about to start. Tom, grab me a cold beer from the refrigerator."

Captain Johnson, who was a massive man, stood shoulder to shoulder with Reggie.

"Larry, these young whippersnappers don't know what we had to endure in our youth. They think that just because the newspapers hold them up as being the best thing since sliced bread, they'll live up to all the hype," Captain Johnson said as the conversation turned in a friendlier direction.

The underdogs, the Golden State Warriors, won the title game, sweeping the Bullets in the fourth game on Sunday as we watched history in the making.

Just as the game concluded, a bicycle crashed loudly into our garage. It was my Uncle Frank, who had ridden down to our house to join in the celebration.

"Did you niggers see the game?" he shouted, his booze-filled breath cluing us all in to his state of intoxication.

"Frank, you're drunk," my father said as Frank fumbled clumsily to put his bicycle upright.

"Frank, where's your car?" Captain Johnson asked.

"I don't need a car to get around."

"When Frank got his third DUI last month, the judge told him he couldn't drive for a year, and the base commander barred Frank from buying alcohol on the base," my father said.

"That county judge can't stop me from getting my booze. I rode this here bicycle all the way to Impact," my uncle bragged.

"Impact is fifteen miles away!" Captain Johnson exclaimed.

"Black power! Black power! Black power!" erupted from the group watching the postgame celebration on TV.

"Tom, I hear you've got a gig these days," Captain Johnson said.

"Yes sir, brother man. I managed to score a dishwashing gig at Sambo's about a week ago," I said proudly as Captain Johnson got up and began to gather his things to leave.

"I'll tell you what, Tom—when you get your first paycheck, I'll sell you my old yellow '65 Fairlane, if it's alright with Sergeant Major Jones; I never use it anymore," Captain Johnson offered. "Sergeant Major Jones, find a way to get your brother home."

With that, I knew my life was about to change. Not only did I have a job now; soon I would also have wheels.

"Reggie Thomas, you come to me when you've got your name printed on a college diploma. It's hard enough for a black man to earn a four-year degree, let alone take a team to the Super Bowl," Captain Johnson said, closing the door and heading out to his car.

Sunday, June 1st, 1975

Gemini: *You'll be receiving money from an event that happened last month. Spending wisely is not normally your thing. Make the best out of a losing love proposition.*

Reggie and I opened a new 28-ounce box of Frosted Flakes this morning as we viewed our horoscope in today's paper. Reggie ate most of it, leaving me with only a couple of bowls, but why complain? He does outweigh me by at least 50 pounds. At first it seemed rather odd to be sitting at home on a Sunday morning, reading my horoscope, as most of my Sundays have been spent listening to some preacher warn me against exactly this sort of thing.

That horoscope was just what Reggie and I needed; everything our horoscope predicted had come to pass. Reggie had indeed received unexpected money; his mother had handed him a check for $250 from his father's life insurance. And I had just received my first paycheck.

Reggie and I were rich as hell on Friday, though my earnings were a lot less than expected. I had worked 50 hours at $2.10 an hour—minimum wage these days, so I had estimated around $105 or so, but Friday, when Dave Cognomi handed me a check for $72, I thought he had cheated me.

"What are all of these deductions?" I asked.

"Well, Tom, Social Security is a program where the government sets money aside for your retirement," Dave answered.

"But that's not for another fifty years; I want my $9.62 back. What about the other stuff? FICA took $17.43."

"FICA is the Federal Insurance Contributions Act. It's an employment tax we both pay to fund Social Security and Medicare benefits."

"But, Dave, all these benefits are for old people," I cried.

"Tom, welcome to the real world," he said, laughing. "Sambo's has one of the best corporate retirement plans; that's what I have. I've been working for the company for eight years, and the company pays for my retirement after ten. Two more years and I can retire."

"That's awesome, Dave. You won't even be old."

"Son, I knew a great deal when I saw one," Dave said. "Eight years ago, when Sambo's introduced the plan for their managers, there were 812 managers in the program. Now, there are only twelve of us left."

"What happened to the others?" I asked.

"The upper management has found ways to get rid of them over the years. They realized after a few years that the retirement package they put together would cost the company millions, but it was too late to rescind the offer, so they started finding ways to get rid of us before we could collect our retirement. You're looking at a survivor. Money makes the world go around, so go out and spend the measly few dollars left of your check, and we'll see you in the morning. By the way, thanks for working so many extra hours lately. Now that school's out, I hope you'll still work all the hours I can give you," he said.

I looked down at my disappointing check. A series of thoughts flashed through my mind about the injustice of it all, and all of the ways money affects me, now that I'm working. Then a message sprang into my mind: "Tom, buy when you can, sell when you have to, and be who you must—it's all part of the plan. State your arrival, because life comes down to a matter of survival."

"Dave, I'm your man!" I said. "I'll see you bright and early tomorrow morning, and on any other day you need me to work a shift this summer."

Reggie borrowed his mother's Oldsmobile Cutlass that afternoon, and we spent the afternoon unloading every penny in our pockets at the mall. Then, yesterday, before I went to work, I made a deal to sell my old bicycle to James' nine-year-old brother. I saw them both in their front yard, putting suitcases in the trunk of the car, and rode up to them.

"Where the hell are you going?" I asked James.

"He's going back to that professional basketball camp in Philadelphia, just like last year," James' brother replied.

"He'll be gone for two months, and I'll have nobody to play with. Dad says that sending James to camp is an investment in the future."

Feeling a little sorry for him, I said, "Kid, I won't need this old bicycle in a few days. I'll let you have it at a great price. Get a job cutting lawns or something this summer, and when you earn enough money you can pay me. I'm buying Captain Johnson's old Fairlane," I said to him, pointing to my new vehicle across the street in our driveway. "I can't officially drive it until after my birthday next week, but after that I won't be needing this bike."

"Thanks," he said, waving as he climbed into the back seat of the car. James got behind the wheel and drove with his father and brother. It seems like only yesterday that I was bargaining with my parents about my hair, and now I'm negotiating the sale of my bicycle, and James is driving.

Reggie has spent many hours teaching me how to drive, and I'll be legal in less than ten days. Ask me why I prematurely sold my bike. Well, the way I see it, life does indeed come down to this: Buy when you can, sell when you have to and be who you must.

Sunday, June 8th, 1975

"Make the best out of a losing love proposition." Reggie did that indeed. He's black as night, and Teri is whiter than white, and it'll make for a dangerous combination if her father sees him with his big hands all over her body at the Friday night picture show. It was just a little teenage fun really. The three of us—Reggie, Teri and I—took Teri's Mustang to the Westgate Mall movie theater to see *One Flew Over the Cuckoo's Nest*. We were gathered around Teri's car, talking after the show—Teri and Reggie embracing on one side of the car when the sheriff's car pulled up.

"Boy, get your hands off my red Mustang," the sheriff said, getting out of his patrol car and walking toward me. Then he spotted his daughter with Reggie's hands under her shirt. "Boy, that's my daughter you've got your black hands on," he shouted.

"Daddy!" Teri cried.

"I thought this was Teri's car," Reggie said, looking down on the smaller man in front of him. I looked hard at Teri's father's badge.

"She's a high school senior. Where in the world did you think she got the money for a fancy ride like the one you've got your black ass pinned up against?" the sheriff asked in a voice that indicated he didn't expect a response. Anyone could see that it wasn't about the car; it was his daughter's taste for brown sugar that caused his sudden rage. "Teri, get in the car and take your ass home," he ordered as Teri sobbed. "Boy, I don't give a damn if you are the starting quarterback; some things will never be acceptable in my eyes."

The expression on Reggie's face said it all. Reggie knew excactly where he stood in Teri's father's eyes as he watched the lawman spit-polishing his badge. Reggie and I turned around and began walking toward Bowie Street without responding or looking back.

"'Bennie and the Jets' was the number one song on the soul charts and the pop charts about a year ago, and according to Casey Kasem, it was the first time that any song has ever been number one on both charts at the same time," I said to Reggie.

"So what?" he replied.

"So, Pee, our generation is changing the world," I said. "The integrated style of music we listen to is changing everything. The white kids are always listening to 'That's the Way of the World,' by Earth, Wind, and Fire, and black kids have made 'Bennie and the Jets' number one on the soul charts. Reggie, people are changing, so don't let Teri or her father keep you from getting what you want."

"Tom, Teri's father didn't scare me tonight," Reggie said to my surprise. "In 'One Flew Over the Cuckoo's Nest,' there was a huge Native American that nobody fucked with. You know why?" Reggie asked. "Because he's huge. Tom, people don't fuck with black men my size. And now I know that Teri's got no money! All this time I thought that was her Mustang. Her father couldn't fuck with me at his size, even with a badge and a pistol on his hip. There are bigger fish to catch. Romance is fairy tale stuff out of those books you've always got your nose in. But, out there in the real world, it's all a game. There are all kinds of games in life, but the two main games are the money game and the pussy game. Tom, when you find the girl with the most money and the prettiest pussy, that's the fish to snag," Reggie said coldly. "Take it from a guy who knows: for the love of money people will steal from their mothers and rob their own brothers. A woman will sell her body for a green piece of paper. The dollar carries a lot of weight. Some people have it, some people really need it, and some people, like me, are fixin' to get it," he said, winking at me.

"But, don't you see? This is the losing love proposition from your horoscope," I said.

"*A losing love proposition?* Tom, I told you, it's all about the fucking money, and the sooner you open your eyes to the facts of life, the sooner you'll understand that money makes the rules."

Part IV
AT SIXTEEN
The Young and
the Restless

Tuesday, June 10th, 1975

Gemini: *It's time to let go of a childhood friend—your energy would be better spent looking toward an older and wiser partner for life's new challenges. What awaits you may come as a shock, but this is the moment you've been waiting for your whole life.*

I worked the graveyard shift and awake with barely enough time to race down to the driver's license bureau for my license. I was standing in line, waiting for the next clerk to call me over, and glancing through the morning paper I'd found on the floor. Reading my birthday horoscope, I couldn't make heads or tails of it.

It's time to let go of a childhood friend. "Is that Reggie?" I asked myself.

"Next, please," I heard as a clerk nodded to me. "Well, I see you passed the road test, and—wow—you also aced the written test. That'll be $12 for the license."

Looking up at me, she pointed toward the camera in the corner.

"Sir, are you going to have your photo taken looking like that? You know this photo will be your official identification for the next four years, don't you?" she asked.

Looking into the camera, I suddenly realized what she meant. I had been in such a rush to get there before they closed today that I had forgotten that my hair was still pinned up in braids. Braids are the new style black guys use to make their hair grow faster. "Well, if you'll give me ten minutes, I can undo these braids and make myself more presentable," I responded.

"Son, we don't have ten minutes. The office is closing, so you'll have to either come back tomorrow or look like a thug in your photo," she said.

"Come back tomorrow?" I thought. "I've waited my entire life for the privilege of driving; it's now or never."

"Just take the photo," I told her, as she was putting the camera away.

"Hon, what's one more day?"

"Ma'am, I'm sixteen years old today—there's no such thing as tomorrow," I said, as the flashbulb exploded.

"Are you legal, Pee?" Reggie asked, as I hopped into the driver's side of his mom's car with a huge grin beaming from my face as the both of us looked back at the doors being locked of the building I had just exited.

"You're damn right, I'm legal," I said to Reggie, starting the engine.

Your energy would be better spent if you started to look toward an older and wiser partner for life's new challenges. This part of the horoscope replayed in my mind, as Reggie said, "Our shit is legit, Pee, so we can go drive wherever the fuck we want without the man saying a damn thing."

Now, I'm convinced that the "childhood friend" is you, Diary, and the "older, wiser partner" is Reggie. Who would be a better teacher than my Pee?

Reggie and I drove back to our neighborhood and parked in Reggie's driveway. We hopped in the Fairlane, and for once in my life, I spent a June afternoon having fun in the sun. I didn't get home until about an hour ago, just in time to see the evening edition land on our porch.

"Son, please bring the paper inside," my father said as I came in the front door. I glanced at the headlines: *"10,000-pound boulder kills six".* Wow! To satisfy my curiosity, I decided to read on:

> *A 10,000-pound boulder rolled down a mountain in Colorado Springs today, hitting a tour bus and killing six Japanese tourists. The tourists were on a sight-seeing tour of the United States and were crushed only three hours after their flight landed. The boulder has been on the side of Pikes Peak for at least 10 million years—since the range was formed. Witnesses say a pebble dropped from the mouth of an eagle and set the boulder in motion. But experts say that it would have been impossible for a pebble to have dislodged the boulder. A local geologist says that the most likely scenario is that water erosion combined with heavy rains in the area caused the freak chain of events. Interstate 25 from Colorado Springs to Denver will be closed for at least a week for a Federal investigation.*

I stopped right there. Wow! To have flown 21 hours just to be wiped off the face of the Earth! We really don't have tomorrow. Homeboy, I'm developing a new philosophy called "the pebble syndrome." I asked my dad to read the article and tell me what he thought. About an hour later, I saw him in the kitchen.

"Well, I guess it was God's will," he said, opening the ice box to get some ice cream.

God took them? Somebody has got to give me a better answer than that. Why in the hell would God let them fly 3000 miles just to kill them?

I look at my bumbling parents, and they seem so ignorant, focusing on silly pastimes—my mother with her crazy religion and my dad with his daft loyalty to the Cowboys. They've spent most of their lives in a sort of daze. Adults can't even run their own lives, so I'll be damned if they'll run mine. We teens are so much smarter than they think we are.

Homeboy, I won't be updating my diary regularly from now on. Who has the time for writing anymore? As my consciousness starts to awaken and I see all the mistakes grownups make and the lies they tell me and themselves, I see I've already wasted too much of my life. Confess to priests? Hell no! Rely on the police? Hell no. They lie to us, just like our parents do. I've got my buddy, Reggie, here to help me; he must be the "wise partner" from my horoscope. I'm done believing in the Garden of Eden and Heaven; it's time to start living in the present.

Reggie is going to take me places. I don't know how, but I know. It's the pebble syndrome with Reggie and me. If I hadn't moved to the Bowie block, I wouldn't have met Reggie or learned that life's about who has the money. Reggie and I are going to get our share. We're

> The crowd of 15,000 got exactly what
> they came to see, as the seventeen-year-old
> phenomenon displayed what some called
> 'the best quarterbacking skills ever seen.'

legit. We've got the Fairlane, we've got the legal papers, and now we're off to get the fucking money.

Friday, August 8th, 1975

"The season-opening football scrimmage between the Abilene Eagles and the Cooper Cougars ended in a five-touchdown lead for the Eagles, who were led by the sophomore sensation, Reggie Thomas. The crowd of 15,000 got exactly what they came to see, as the seventeen-year-old phenomenon displayed what some called 'the best quarterbacking skills ever seen.' The Eagles scored during every possession against a Cougars' defense that was thought to be the best in the Texas 5A division," the bubble-headed bleached blonde said, leading off the 10 p.m. Channel 9 newscast.

There we were, watching Reggie on the local news.

"Reggie, you're famous!" I shouted, though he was sitting right next to me on our couch. The sports anchor announced that there would be more game highlights during the sports report, and then the station went to a commercial. "Reggie, not only are you the biggest story on the sportscast, you led off the entire newscast."

Then the blonde anchor came back and said, "In other news, President Gerald Ford formally announced his candidacy for president. New York City laid off 40,000 policemen, firemen, and other city workers as a result of the current financial crisis." With a gleam in her eye, she turned to her co-anchor, who had the prettiest hair I've ever seen on a man and said, "Bob, back to our lead story of the day, Reggie Thomas, new Eagles quarterback, who looks to me to be the real deal. What do you think?"

"Well, Barbara, I was at the city scrimmage with the other 15,000 viewers, and I was just as overwhelmed with Thomas' skills as anyone at the stadium. I heard a rumor that there are a few sour City Council members from the Cooper-High side of town who now wish they'd voted in favor of the redistricting plan proposed last year so that Thomas would be a Cougar. I've been covering sports for over 13 years, and I think this guy's got what it takes to go pro."

The taped video of the scrimmage rolled as the sports anchor continued.

"Who is that tall, good-looking girl in the background holding the flash cards?" Reggie asked.

"Oh, that gorgeous chick? I saw her at the game today, while I was on the sidelines with the press credentials you gave me," I said nonchalantly. "She really wanted to meet you after the game, but with all the reporters standing around you, she finally gave up and decided to get her interview later."

Bob interrupted the sports highlight video feed of Reggie's incredible performance with more words of his own. "Barbara, teenage sports pros are becoming more and more common these days. There's Tracy Austin, who turned into a pro tennis sensation at thirteen years old. She's won a couple of professional tennis tournaments already. And then there's Moss Malone, who joined the NBA right out of high school, but Reggie Thomas just might become a household name before anyone hears of either of them."

"Bob, they're getting younger and younger every day. I bet the Cougars wish they'd found Reggie Thomas when he was in diapers," Barbara joked.

Reggie scratched his head, looking hard at the television. "Tom, I've got it!" he said. "That tall dame in the background was Jill Andersen."

"Jill who?" I replied.

"Jill Andersen, the heiress to the Andersen oil fortune," Reggie said. "She's a cheerleader for Cooper."

"That beauty queen is heir to a fortune?!" I cried. "Reggie, she passed herself off to me as a reporter. How old is she? I bet not more than seventeen or eighteen. How did she get her press credentials for the game?"

"Tom, when you've got money, you can get anything." Reggie said.

"Hey, Pee," I said, searching my jeans for a crumpled up piece of paper lodged in my front pocket, "that chick gave me this note for you before she left. I'm sure it's her telephone number. I thought she was just another reporter."

He looked over the crumpled note and broke into a dance. "Tom, this is it," he cried, hugging my neck, "that big fish I told you about! This is the break I've waited for all my life. You've heard of Andersen Airport. Guess whose last name that is? You're a fucking genius. I knew from the first day I met you that we were going to be great partners."

Homeboy, I don't quite know what it was all about, but when Reggie left my house that evening, I really felt appreciated.

Saturday, August 16th, 1975

With her photographs of Grace Slick of Jefferson Airplane and her pictures of the nineteen Learjets she'd flown in hanging on her walls, it was clear that Jill Andersen was born with a silver spoon in her mouth. I couldn't begin to tell you, Homeboy, how rich her family is, and I, Tom Jones, was in her house. Jill's parents were away in Saudi Arabia this week, so Reggie and I went to the movies with Jill Friday night to see *Jaws*.

If you had told me two weeks ago that there'd be a Jaguar parked in my driveway, I would have said you were crazy. But I've got the keys to Jill's Jaguar, which is parked in our driveway at this very moment.

Thursday night I was getting off work after a double shift, which started at six that morning and ended at the stroke of ten. Dave walked over to me and said, "Tom, you made a lot of money working so many hours this summer. I bet you'll miss all this money once school starts up on the 26th, won't you?"

"Yeah, I will," I said as he poured me a cup of coffee while I filled out my time card.

"Tom," Dave said, winking at a four-day-old headline: "Town finally goes wet after a hundred years." "We finally got over on them church-going bastards," he said. "I'm keeping a copy of that headline as a souvenir. Listen, Tom, I like you. You're the best damn worker I've ever had, and I don't plan on losing you. Even that brother of yours didn't last very long. I've had a dozen or so dish-washers quit or get fired since you came to work, and I really don't understand this new generation's work ethic. Even with the unemployment rate over 9 percent, I can't keep a good waiter. Tom, what I'm trying to say is: starting tomorrow, I'd like for you to be my new waiter. Now, I know the waiter shift is from 7 a.m. to 3 p.m. and 3 p.m. to 11 p.m., but, if you'll promise to be here by about 4 every day after school, I'll pay you for the full eight-hour shift."

"I'll take it."

"Great! Tom, I knew you would. I can read a person's body language, and I've studied you enough to know I've got a real winner. Go ahead and take Friday off, and start training for your new position Saturday morning," Dave said, walking away. "By the way, you're getting paid for a festive Friday night."

"What do you mean I'm getting paid for a festive Friday night?" I said, confused.

"Tom, go out and have a good time. I'm filling in your timecard as if you were working tomorrow," Dave said with a wink.

It was as if Reggie had been watching the front door of our house. "Tom, can you give me a ride over to Jill's house?" Reggie asked, as he stepped through the doorway right behind me. Sometimes, it seems as if my whole life consists of working double shifts and driving Reggie around, so why not one more errand? "Tom, I wish you were off on Friday. Jill wants to meet you."

"It just so happens, I am off tomorrow. Why?" I asked.

"Why don't the three of us go to see *Jaws*? I hear it's the best damn movie out right now," Reggie suggested.

And the rest is history.

Jill Andersen, with her China blue eyes, a veritable fairy-tale princess, showed Reggie and I around her castle as we looked with awe on how rich people live their lives. I never knew their side of Abilene harbored such manicured lawns and every imaginable nicety at their beck and call. Jill had this device called a garage-door opener that she pushed, and behind the massive garage door sat a new, black, 1976 Jaguar convertible.

"Tom, we'll take my car to the theater," she said, as she handed me the keys. "You don't mind driving, do you?" she said, with an impish grin on her painted pink lips.

There I was, chauffeuring the teen queen and king of the night to the premier movie in town. Every teenager on the strip knew the royal couple. Homeboy, I've got to admit, I've never felt as cool and important as I felt Friday night. I like Jill; she made me feel like I belonged in her elite world from the first moment she let me into "the castle." Throughout the evening, she always included me.

I pulled up in front of one of the five garages at "the castle."

"Tom, Reggie is spending the night here," Jill called out the door. "My parents' flight doesn't touch down until Sunday evening around six. Why don't you leave your car parked on the street and take my Jaguar?"

"Really? Sunday evening is 44 hours away," I responded to my new best friend.

"I guess I'm not the only one in this car passing math," Jill said sardonically as the three of us chuckled.

"But Reggie didn't bring any clothes for tomorrow," I pointed out.

"Tom, I like you," the blue-eyed princess said, giving me a hug from the back seat. "We'll get him some new stuff in the morning," she said, without blinking an eye. "My sister, Tracy, is in San Francisco at the Giants game this weekend, so I've got the keys to her Mercedes."

I parked the Jaguar next to Dave's Pontiac Grand Prix at Sambo's Saturday morning when I went in to start training for my new position.

"Son, you know the waiter's position only pays forty cents more an hour than the dishwashing position," Dave said wryly as I passed him at the coffee counter.

"Sir, you're not the only one who can read body language. For instance, I can tell by yours that you're jealous as hell right now," I said, half-jokingly.

"Damn, Tom, I like your style," Dave responded, handing me my new gear. "Suit yourself, but don't let the police arrest you while you're still on the clock."

Homeboy, this is the best moment of my life so far. I can't wait to see the look on my father's face when he sees a Jaguar parked in his driveway. But I have to remember to pick Reggie up from Jill's house before the Cinderella hour on Sunday. Gosh, I wonder what it was like to spend the night in a house like that. Reggie had better fill me in on every little detail.

Friday, September 12th, 1975

On the first full week back after Labor Day, it seems all hell has broken loose at schools across the country. First, President Ford warned the U.S.S.R. that the United States is stepping up development of nuclear weapons unless the Soviets drastically curb their atomic weapon production. As usual, the schools in Abilene overreacted to the speech, and we had to suffer through one more of those stupid bomb drills that anyone with a brain knows won't work. There we were, with our heads stuck under our school desks pretending to be safe from the strike of a 10,000 pound nuclear warhead.

Teachers in Boston, Chicago, and New York are all on strike, with roughly 1.5 million students left without classes to attend. Lucky them! As far as I'm concerned, school is the biggest joke known to mankind. After we receive a diploma, none of us will need to know anything about science or biology; all we need to know is how to count the money, right?

The high schools in town have "open campuses," which simply means that students can leave at lunch and eat wherever they want, as long as they make it back on time. So Jill and I have been shuffling back and forth between the ritzy Cooper campus and the Abilene High campus for lunch. I never thought I'd say this, but after a month, I almost feel as if I know her as well as I know Reggie. I like being around her; she always treats me like I matter. Sometimes, I think I could go anywhere with her and feel comfortable.

But there is hate brewing on both campuses because of Jill. The students at Abilene High think she's a spy from Cooper, trying to convince Reggie to play the next two years at Cooper. But when I eat with her at Cooper, it's clear that everyone knows she's the most popular girl on their campus. I don't know if it's simply because she's also the richest girl at school, or if it's just her infectious personality. Also, Jill is the most radical creature on earth, male or female, hands down. No schoolroom will ever keep her feet on the ground because she's always been able to escape into her own thoughts. Today I had lunch with her at Cooper. She was dressed in her cheerleading outfit after a school pep rally, and I couldn't help but overhear people talking about her.

"She's our main cheerleader. What's she doing fraternizing with the enemy?"

"Yeah, she should be true to her school."

Jill, in her polished way, simply said, "When you get to where I am, you too can make the rules instead of trying to find ways around them."

That's my girl! Right on, Jill!

A little over a week ago, Jill suggested I get my own phone line in my room. It had never occurred to me, although I had noticed that Jill had her own line when we toured her house. I examined my savings account and noticed I had more than $226, so without informing the folks, I had Ma Bell install a line in my room last week, and now I can communicate with the rest of the world. But the telephone hasn't rung once yet. My parents probably don't know about it yet. I gave Jill my number first. The private line is probably a good idea, since Jill's parents are cutting back on their travels and will be home a lot more on weekends. There go the secret rendezvous that Jill and Reggie have managed so successfully since August. Reggie practically lives at Jill's house on the weekends. Since I work so much on weekends, I generally don't miss my Pee. And, when I pick him up, he always fills me in on all the illicit details.

Friday, September 26th, 1975

Thank God for sports! Turn on the television set and there's nothing but bad news. This week, someone tried to kill President Ford in San Francisco. It was the second assassination attempt this month. Also, Patty Hearst was finally taken into custody by the FBI along with her kidnappers, the Symbionese Liberation Army. My dad said the only reason people care is that she's rich, and rich people have a way of making the news.

Bob, the local sportscaster on Channel 9, aired a sports update from the Eagles game just as I was getting home from work around 10:20. Boy, I wish I could have been there!

"As a freshman, Abilene got to know him. As a sophomore, the entire state is hearing about him. When Reggie Thomas becomes a junior next year, the whole world may know who he is. Tonight, Thomas had the best performance of any high-school player, scoring a record 11 touchdowns—five throwing and six running. The Eagles dominated the Brownwood Lions 77 – 10 at Abilene's Shotwell Stadium in front of 26,000 onlookers. Reggie amassed 1083 yards in a single game, surpassing the old record by a whopping 231 yards," Bob announced.

Television has begun to replace print formats, like newspapers, and thank God for that. Although I wasn't able to attend the game, I was able to see the game highlights, including all eleven touchdowns Reggie scored. Wow! Reggie really is a teenage phenomenon, just like they said. It's so cool that he's my best friend and neighbor. I can't wait to see him tomorrow and tell him I saw him on TV.

Thursday, October 16th, 1975

"The pebble syndrome" brought me to my knees this past week. October has been a downward spiral for me, and I don't see an end to it. Yesterday, a jet airliner in New York City crashed, killing all 144 people aboard. The PanAm flight 359's passenger list showed 145 passengers; the lone survivor turned out to be a man who had missed the flight, which contained four members of his family, because he was stuck in the bathroom at Kennedy Airport. Homeboy, it's the pebble syndrome all over again—here a man barely escapes death because he's stuck in the bathroom.

"Isn't it strange?" the man told reporters. "It would have been my first time to fly."

Again, one tiny event sets life-changing events in motion.

I've also seen a lot less of Reggie this month. Everyone wants a piece of him these days and that leaves me on the outside looking in. It's not that Reggie doesn't make time for me; it's that his life doesn't leave room for us to spend any time together. Jill, Reggie, and I tried to double date with Jill's friend, Melissa, from Cooper last Friday. It was Cooper's homecoming, and I was invited to take Melissa to the dance after the game. Jill set it up because she desperately wanted Reggie to come, and I was his ride again.

Reggie and I arrived at the Hilton Hotel for the dance. I was decked out in my Flagg Brothers shoes with Cuban heels and my imitation leather jacket, which had cost me a small fortune. "Get Down Tonight" by K.C. and the Sunshine Band was jamming on my car radio. Jill and this beautiful girl, Melissa, spotted us as we pulled into the hotel parking lot.

"Tom, thank you so much for bringing my baby," Jill exclaimed, opening the passenger door to let him out. Melissa came around to the driver's side to greet me.

"Tom, is this your car or your grandmother's?" she asked, frowning. I couldn't believe what I'd just heard from this stranger, so I turned the radio dial down a notch.

"Yes, this is my ride," I said, getting out to greet my blind date.

"Jill, I thought you said Tom was a football player at Abilene High," she said as Jill passionately locked lips with Reggie on the other side of the car.

"No, Melissa, you misunderstood. I said Tom is Abilene High's quarterback's best friend," Jill said, turning back to gaze into Reggie's eyes.

"Honey, this skinny, raggedy-car-driving S.O.B. is not my kind," Melissa said as a crowd of teenagers gathered around to witness my humiliation.

I could hear laughter behind me as I got back into my car and headed towards the parking lot exit.

"My gosh, that's rough—standing him up like that, but there's no point in him staying," I heard a compassionate girl's voice trail off as I left alone, crushed, humiliated, and traumatized by my inner shame.

I was positively shattered by her words—the girl who was to be my very first date. Who was I kidding to think I ever belonged in that world of high society and football heroes? I drove around Abilene, looking for the nearest cliff to jump off, until it dawned on me that Abilene is flat; there are no cliffs within a 200-mile radius. I drove home all alone, with Janis Ian's voice cutting me into little pieces: "And those of us with ravaged faces, lacking in the social graces, desperately remained at home, inventing lovers on the phone who called to say, 'Come out and dance with me' and murmured vague obscenities—it isn't all it seems at seventeen." I had thought Friday would be my coming-out party—Tom's chance to mingle with the popular crowd. I had that evening all planned out: I was going to do a little dancing, possibly make a little love, and get down. Instead, I left the dance with a heart badly broken and bruised.

I haven't seen Reggie or Jill since that night. Yesterday I watched the ball game on TV all by myself for the first time. The Cincinnati Reds beat the Boston Red Sox in Game 7 of the World Series. I figure I might as well get used to Friday nights alone. My name will never be called when choosing sides at basketball, and I now realize that my private line will only ring if Dave needs me to work an extra shift. It isn't all it seems at sixteen, and I've got dreary years ahead of me to ponder what it's like to be just another working stiff on a Friday night, all dressed up with no place to go.

Friday, October 31st, 1975

"We have come to the end of another broadcasting day" was the signal from my new 13-inch black-and-white television at midnight last night. I bought it a week ago to accompany the phone that never rings. I'm pretty sure it was the sixth straight night in a row that I'd fallen asleep with the television on, but for a teenager with no friends, it's a nice way to fall asleep. My telephone finally rang this morning. At first, I thought I was dreaming—that it was my alarm clock.

"Hello?" I said.

"Tom, I'm glad you're still home," a desperate voice said on the other end of the line. "Tom, I need your help. Do you happen to have $125 cash?"

"Yeah, I think so," I replied.

"Tom, can you pick me up in about an hour? I've got serious business to attend to in Dallas," Jill pleaded.

"Dallas? Dallas, Texas?!" I exclaimed.

"Yeah, Tom, Dallas Fucking Texas," Jill said. "Are you going to pick me up or not?"

"Well, yeah. Where?"

"Pick me up at the 7-11 around the corner from my house around 8:15, and I'll fill you in on all the details," Jill said before the line went dead.

It was the sight of a similar looking car as mine heading in the opposite direction that got my attention just before Jill spoke. "Take Interstate 20 to Fort Worth. Then take Interstate 30 to Market Street," Jill ordered as I drove down the highway en route to an unfamiliar destination. "Tom, you know I'm good for the money. You're a real life-saver. I lifted my sister's ID this morning; the clinic will never know I'm not 21. My pregnancy test turned up positive yesterday, and I freaked. Before I could think straight, I already had an appointment at a clinic in Dallas without figuring out how I would get there or pay for it without my nosy parents suspecting something. You know I love you for doing this for me."

The trip to Dallas took us a total of nine hours. Jill knew exactly what she was doing, because it went off without a hitch. She swore it was her first abortion and that she had a friend who told her about the clinic. On the way back to Abilene, I stopped at a pay phone to call Dave and tell him that I would be a couple of hours late. He gave me his blessings, and we were back on the road again. The ride home was awkward.

"Tom, if you were stuck on a desert island and could have only one album, which one would you take?" Jill said, breaking the silence.

"It would definitely be the new *Fire* album by the Ohio Players," I replied, thinking her question only made things seem more awkward. "How about you? What album would you bring?"

"*Fame* by David Bowie," Jill said quickly, as she stared down the highway.

Jill pulled out a joint about halfway through the 150-mile journey.

"Tom, you don't smoke do you?" she asked. "Boy, after the past 24 hours, I need this," she said, reaching for the cigarette lighter.

"I never knew you smoked pot," I said as she passed me the joint.

"Tom, there are a lot of things I do that you don't know about," Jill said.

Jill and I talked about how her family bought the airport 40 years ago and how J.R., her father, and his baby brother, Tony, had grown the family fortune through wise business practices. Airplanes, oil, and fuel mixtures have made her family rich beyond their wildest dreams. J.R. always gets what he wants; nobody says "no" to her father who is 6'6" and larger than life. Her mother, Scarlet, on the other hand, is just the opposite—a left-wing liberal—who never saw a cause she didn't like.

"I have a cousin, Kelly, who lives in Abilene, too," Jill said. "Kelly is Uncle Tony's daughter. She's my age but has private tutors. Our family likes to refer to Kelly and me as the Rockefellers."

I told Jill about the people I've known who'd flown from the airport, starting with Aunt Frances. I explained about my diary and told her that our journey would soon be printed in its pages.

"Tom," Jill suddenly shouted, "Reggie cannot ever know about what happened today. Agreed?" Her big blue eyes met my tiny pupils.

"Your secret's safe with me," I promised as she hugged my neck.

Saturday, December 13th, 1975

I was by Reggie's side for the final game of the season. The Eagles lost to Dallas Carter High in the regional playoffs on the last play of the game on a rainy Friday night. Jill and I made the trip to Dallas to see the game. The lead score changed three times in the fourth quarter. Talk about excitement! The Eagles were just twelve lousy seconds away from going to the semi-finals. We should have stayed in a motel, but she trusted me to drive her Jaguar back to Abilene in the pouring rain after the loss. I heard on Channel 9 news that Abilene is going to throw the team a parade on the nineteenth, the last day of classes before Christmas break, even though the team didn't win the state championship.

I don't want to talk about what losing the game meant to Reggie, our school, or the city of Abilene. Although it hurts us all to lose a game like this, it must feel 10 times worse to Reggie, having the hopes of the entire city on his shoulders. The winners take all, and there's little consolation for losers in this society. Those of us who've been on the losing end ease our pain by saying, "There's always next year." It's over now, and Reggie played as well as he could; our defense just wasn't good enough. Nothing more to say, no more football games this season.

Wednesday, December 31st, 1975

"Where were you at this time last year?" That's easy. I was on my knees praying to a god that doesn't exist. It's a year later, and my mother and the remaining members of her wayward congregation are still waiting for Armageddon. They're still going from house to house, promising to those who will listen that the end is at hand.

We didn't celebrate Christmas this year, but I did experience a Christmas celebration when I helped Joe open a few of his gifts. He was released from jail this month after serving nearly 13 months on reduced assault charges. He looks good, and it's nice to have him back. Joe said he saw Father O'Malley in jail, too.

Although Uncle Frank's family lives just down the street, we hardly ever see them anymore. I think it's strange how it all works out. Homeboy, here's another example of the pebble syndrome in our lives. The fire that killed my father's parents two years ago sparked my father's and Uncle Frank's reunion at their parents' funeral, which led to Frank's family moving to Abilene, which preceded Joe's assault on Laurie's father. I think it's strange, but the tree house hasn't been occupied since that infamous day.

Another example of the pebble syndrome is if I hadn't taken Jill's advice to install a phone line in my room, she wouldn't have been able to reach me the day she decided to get her abortion, leaving Reggie on the hook as a father to be. Her secret is safe with me. I even met her mother, Scarlett. We were at the parade for the football team on the 19th. It was getting late, and the adolescent crowd moved the celebration to the local Pizza Inn, known for its dark booths. Steady teen couples usually reserve them for their make-out rendezvous.

James and I were in the corner of the pizzeria playing an upright video game called "Phoenix." I was supposed to be the lookout man while Reggie and Jill were stashed in a booth making out. Then a hush fell over the crowded pizzeria.

"That's Jill's mother," I heard someone say as teenagers started pointing Scarlett toward Reggie and Jill. Quick on my feet, I stumbled across the room in the nick of time.

"Mrs. Andersen, you have a lovely daughter," I said loudly to the striking woman in Gucci.

"Why, thank you, young man. I don't think we've met," she said, extending her hand.

"I see where Jill gets her good looks from," I said louder, trying to signal the lovers in the booth behind me.

"Mama!" Jill said, wrestling herself away from Reggie's firm embrace while buttoning her shirt. "Tom, I'd like you to meet my mother, Scarlett," she said, blushing.

"Yo, dog, she is beautiful," James chimed in over my other shoulder, as he glimpsed Jill's half-exposed breast through her sheer blouse.

Then another sexily dressed young woman walked up in a mini skirt.

"Tom, this is my cousin, Kelly," Jill said as James and I leered. "Kelly is going to be an exchange student this semester. Kelly, why don't you tell Tom about the exchange program?" Jill said, trying to divert attention away from her compromising circumstances.

Before Kelly could speak up, Mrs. Andersen gently interrupted, "The fellows will have to learn about Kelly's new adventure later; it's time we headed for home. Kelly, you're still spending the night at our house, aren't you?"

"I'd like to spend the night with that!" James slyly remarked to me, stopping to stare at Jill, who was bent over gathering her things.

"I don't do white boys," Jill said, catching James off-guard and smiling slyly.

"They grow up so fast," Mrs. Andersen said, while placing her left hand over Jill's potty mouth.

"I'm not one to make any rash judgments, but I don't think Jill's father would approve of this situation, Reggie," Scarlett said, looking into his eyes. "But thanks for a wonderful season. Abilene really needed something to rest its hopes on. Like the old cliché says, there's always next season. James, I'm sorry if it makes you feel bad, but Jill always has been one to say exactly what she means. Tom, everyone these days grows up faster than ever; how did you get left behind?" she jested, noticing I was shorter than the others.

"I read somewhere in the newspaper that it's the preservatives in the foods we eat these days," I replied as we all headed toward our cars in the parking lot.

"If it's the preservatives in the foods that make us grow so much taller than our parents, then what happened to you, tiny Tom?" Kelly playfully said, rolling down the window on her black MG.

"Get in the car, James!" Reggie said as I started the engine.

"No thanks, I'll walk home. I'll catch you fellows later on," James said dejectedly as I revved my engine.

"Jill will say anything, homeboy," I said to James, who was moping along, shaking his head and kicking rocks. I pulled up beside him, but he kept his head turned away from us as we tried to coax him into the warm car, so we left him alone with his thoughts. There are times when you just have to let a person do what he's got to do.

Not everyone in America is prejudiced, but when I heard Jill say, "I don't do white boys," I didn't know how to react. Seeing James so tense, with no self-confidence left, after what some glamour girl he has the hots for said to him, I wonder just what's really going on with people in the 70s? But, like Bob Dylan said, "The times, they are a changin'."

Homeboy, times like these, when I'm up late at night writing and everyone else is asleep, questions start to run deep in my mind. Take James: James said the basketball camps in Philly were 90% black, and everyone there treated him like a black brother. Now that he's back in Texas, a white person takes issue with him. How can that be? At times like these, I don't feel like I have the foggiest idea about anything that matters. My mind bounces back and forth on my "pebble syndrome" theory, dissecting things I thought I had the answers to. I still don't have a clue where Jill's secret fits into the grand scheme of things. Is it all random chance? Is someone up in heaven playing dice? This might sound crazy, but sometimes I feel like we're just part of a game, with judges up there deciding who wins. I'm starting to think that a boulder has started its roll off the mountain to wipe me from the face of the planet.

Enough is enough. The clock tells me it's 4 a.m., and 1976 has officially arrived. Oklahoma plays Michigan in the Orange Bowl today, and Arkansas plays Georgia in the Cotton Bowl, but Reggie and I have our sights set on watching the Rose Bowl, where UCLA is playing Ohio State. He wants to see what kind of offense the Buckeyes run, since he just might be their quarterback in two years. Reggie said that, on his recruiting trip to Ohio last May, one of the coaches said, "At Ohio State, we make sure our star football players have a well-paying plush job, and our school booster makes sure they have the best cars on campus. All you have to do, Reggie, is sign on the dotted line, and everything will be just fine." Diary, it's our little secret, but Reggie said the Ohio State coaches also assured him that he wouldn't have to worry about academics at their university.

Catch you on the flip side of 1976.

Monday, January 26th, 1976

"Hypothetically, if there were a God and both football teams prayed for victory, which team's prayers would God grant?" I asked Miss Wiseman Monday after the Steelers defeated the Cowboys in the Super Bowl. It was a great game, and Reggie and I watched it in my room. Reggie learned how to rig up a bootleg cable, so we watched the game in vivid clarity. The bootleg cable also enables me to listen to Dallas radio stations, so now I'm able to hear the latest tunes. After the Cowboys lost, my father and the entire state went into mourning for days. The Cowboys are the unofficial religion of Texas.

I bought my first bag of pot. Jeff, Laurie's new boyfriend, sold me the "full lid" for $10, which seems a bit steep to me. A lid is a term for a bag of marijuana.

Sunday while we were watching the game, Reggie was sitting on my bed, talking on the phone to Jill. They were bitching and moaning because her parents haven't been out of town lately.

"Why don't you guys just use your mother's room on Friday nights?" I said. "She's always over at Billy Bob's."

"Tom, you're a fucking genius," Reggie said.

That simple suggestion spawned what we call the "sneak-out game." Here's how it works: I get off work at ten Friday night. Reggie calls me at Sambo's to let me know his mother has left for the evening, and then he puts his siblings to bed. I drive home and pretend to be in for the evening. About an hour after I arrive home, I wait to hear snoring from my parents' room. Jill calls me when her parents are asleep, and Reggie comes over to my house. Both of us push my car down the block and start the engine, so as not to awaken my parents. Then we pick up Jill and her girl friend at Jill's house, and we all go back to Reggie's. I entertain Jill's friend, keeping an eye on the clock, while Reggie and Jill make out in his mother's room. At about three, I give the two love birds the signal that it's time to go, and we drop the girls off at Jill's house. It worked to perfection last Friday.

"Tom, this is Demi, the exchange student from Japan. Kelly took Demi's place in Japan for a few weeks, and Demi is taking Kelly's place here. Demi is staying with me, and my only job is not to get her into trouble while she's here," Jill said, climbing into the car and giggling all the while.

I learned a lot from Demi in the three hours we talked Friday night.

"Do you smoke pot?" I asked, rolling a joint.

"Oh, no!" Demi said, blushing when I tried to pass her the joint.

So I stepped outside and puffed on the joint a few times before putting it out and going back inside. I was concentrating on Reggie's history homework when Demi interrupted me.

"Is that your homework?" Demi asked.

"No, it's Reggie's homework, but I love history, so I don't mind," I told her.

"Do you know anything about the history of Japan?" Demi asked.

"I know the people in Japan are almost evenly divided between Shinto and Buddhist," I said. "I lived on the Air Force base in Japan when I was a kid."

I put away Reggie's homework assignment, and Demi and I chatted like old friends.

"You know, the guy I bought this pot from—his girlfriend's mother is a Buddhist," I said.

"Although all Buddhism is based on the life and teachings of the Skamania Buddha, there are so many different teachings that it is impossible to fit them into a single, coherent system," Demi said as we sat on the couch sharing a bottle of Coke. "The teachings of the Buddha are called the dharma, and karma is the cycle of cause and effect caused by your actions. Tom, my intuition says you've got good karma, which means that you've done more good things than bad, so good things will happen to you."

Dharma, karma—the words coming out of Demi's lips blended in my head. I remembered bits and pieces later, but was too stoned at the time to put it all together. I don't know if it was the buzz or whether it was just a great conversation with a stranger, but I felt a real connection with Demi.

"Do teenagers sneak out at night in Japan?" I asked her.

"No way, Tom! In fact, that's why I became an exchange student. There are too many rules placed on girls in Japan, and I wanted a little taste of freedom, so I came here."

"Tom, I see you've got a new friend," Jill said from behind me, giving me an affectionate pop on the back of my head. "Tom, you're supposed to be our time keeper! It's ten after three; we were supposed to leave ten minutes ago."

It was an interesting evening—one that I never saw coming. All I did was make a little suggestion, and the sneak-out game was born. I'll look up dharma and karma when I get a chance. What I remember sounded pretty interesting. Everything changes so quickly these days. A month ago I had no social life at all, and now I'm the ring leader of the sneak-out game.

Sunday, February 29th, 1976

Two Fridays ago, I met Geetha. She's from India. The sneak-out game didn't go as planned, though, because Reggie's mother had an argument with her boyfriend at the last minute, and our whole plan had to be scrapped. Instead, we all went to see *Texas Chainsaw Massacre* at the drive-in theater in Jill's Jaguar. Afterward, I drove us all to McDonald's for burgers and fries. Geetha doesn't eat meat, but she did enjoy the French fries.

The next Friday, the sneak-out game worked to perfection. We were all at Reggie's way before midnight. Reggie and Jill disappeared into the bedroom, and Geetha and I were left in the living room, discussing what they were up to.

"You mean no one sneaks out like this in India?" I asked, rolling a joint from the nearly empty bag.

"Tom, teenagers in the United States are too loose," she said.

"What do you mean—just because we smoke a little grass?" I questioned.

"No, Tom, the women in the U.S. have so much freedom. Do you know that in my country most girls already know who they are going to marry? We have arranged weddings. I'm one of the lucky ones," Geetha said as I handed her the joint. "No, I don't smoke weed," she said, pushing the joint back my way.

"Suit yourself," I told her, and then went outside to smoke on the steps of the back porch.

"Birth control plan announced by government" was the headline of the newspaper lying on Shirley's kitchen counter. Curious, I started reading, "The government of India is providing incentives for parents to undergo sterilization after having two children," I read aloud. "Hey, this article is about your country," I said as she drew closer to take a look.

We both read in silence, and afterwards, Geetha said, "Tom, India is really over-crowded. Even here in Abilene, people know about it."

"Why don't they just use birth control pills instead of sterilizing people?" I asked.

"Tom, not everyone thinks like the people here. Eighty-five percent of India is Hindu, and Hindus don't believe in birth control, except by self-control," Geetha said. "I'm lucky—my parents have money, so I'm sure I'll be coming to the United States for college."

Geetha was impressed that I knew what the words dharma and karma meant and was shocked to hear that I knew that Muslims had taken over India long ago, because India was a society without weapons. Geetha taught me a lot about the Hindu culture and faith.

"Mental calmness is our goal. We try to achieve freedom from desire by holding our attention on one focal point," she said to me as we were relaxing on the floor after doing yoga.

"Tom, what are you doing down there on the floor, trying to get laid?" Reggie said, breaking our trance-like state.

"Damn, I must be stoned as hell," I said to Reggie, gathering myself up.

"You don't have to get stoned to achieve this state of mind," Geetha said as she stood up, too.

"Tom, you've fallen down on the job again!" Jill said, coming out of Shirley's room half clothed to give me a slap on the back of my head. "It's twenty after three! Boy, you've got to start paying attention," she said as we all scrambled into the car.

I'll never forget how I felt with Geetha that evening. As Reggie and I dropped the girls off, I wanted more than anything to kiss the little Indian girl good night.

Wednesday, March 31st, 1976

It's the last day of March, and I'm just now getting around to updating you on what's gone down this month.

We had another stupid bomb drill earlier this month. Some senator in Washington D.C. said something to the effect that Israel has revealed that they have atomic weapons, and everyone in Washington D.C. is freaking out, so everyone at school is paranoid. Who do they think they're fooling with that crouch under the desk business?

Everything on television is about the election. It's Jimmy Carter this and President Gerald Ford that on every channel. I should be more interested in it, but I'd rather watch *The Bionic Woman*. Boy, who's better looking, Lindsay Wagner or Farrah Fawcett? I've got Farrah's new poster hanging on my wall. Mama can't stand it, but it's my room, and there's nothing she can do about it.

Sahara from Turkey was here in March. She's Muslim and wasn't supposed to eat bacon, but she did anyway. I didn't really hit it off with her. I don't know what it was; we just didn't click. We went on a double date with Jill and Reggie to the Abilene High basketball tournament. James was totally the star of the game. He ended the tournament with an average 30 points, 20 rebounds, and 2 assists per game. Now the papers are filled with stories about him. Sahara didn't enjoy the game at all. She kept complaining about how short James' shorts were and how sex is everywhere in America from our billboards to our television commercials. Muslims must live in the Stone Age. She said Muslim men can have as many wives as they can support. Now that's a religion I'd like to join.

The game was the first time Jill and James had come face-to-face since her remark about not doing white boys. She shot him down again at the tournament when he tried to flirt with her. She turned to him and said, "You always want what you can't have."

Reggie scored with Jill behind the gym after the game. Somebody warned them that her father was in attendance and may have seen them holding hands. I'll keep you informed, Homeboy.

Monday, May 24th, 1976

Imagine there's no Heaven
It's easy if you try
No hell below us
Above us only sky
Imagine all the people
Living for today

Imagine there's no countries
It isn't hard to do
Nothing to kill or die for
And no religion too

Imagine all the people
Living life in peace
You may say I'm a dreamer
But I'm not the only one
I hope someday you'll join us
And the world will be as one

Imagine no possessions
I wonder if you can
No need for greed or hunger
A brotherhood of man
Imagine all the people
Sharing all the world
You may say I'm a dreamer
But I'm not the only one
I hope someday you'll join us
And the world will live as one

I've pondered these lyrics by John Lennon for many weeks. I took a look at the culture around me, and it feels like I'm starting to see with my ears and hear with my eyes. John Lennon may be wrong; life doesn't come down to class and religion. It's like Reggie says—it's them against us.

The "end of the age" finally did come, but it turned out to be the end of the "age of innocence." My brother and Joe left for Air Force basic training after enlisting last month, and my mother persuaded Dad to take her and my sisters to the JW convention this week, so I had the entire house to myself for a whole week. Reggie's birthday was Friday and my parents weren't due back until late Sunday night, so we had big plans.

The phone in my bedroom rang.

"Hello, Reggie's answering service," I said, only half jokingly.

The "end of the age" finally did come, but it turned out to be the end of the "age of innocence."

"Tom!" Jill shouted into the receiver. "Why don't we throw Reggie a surprise party Friday at your house, since your family is away?" Wow! There she was with another plan to share. "You've got to meet Petra. She's from Germany, and she's so much fun. Kelly will be in town, too, so I'll bring her along."

Friday night, between Reggie's house and mine, there had to be 30 or 40 half-drunk and stoned teenagers running around, and I was part of the crowd. The song "Tonight's the Night" by Rod Stewart was playing loudly from someone's radio, and a girl came towards me.

"Hi, I'm Petra, the exchange student from Germany," she said, handing me one of the two cold beers she was carrying. "You know, German beer is twice as strong as American beer."

"Oh, yeah?" I replied in my best jive voice.

"And we serve it warm," she cooed.

Petra and I were standing in my kitchen, when I noticed my bedroom door was closed. "Now, who has the nerve to be using my room without my permission?" I thought.

"Petra!" I said, "Let's go!" nodding my head toward the closed door.

I knocked on the door with sweaty palms.

"We're just about to finish up," a familiar voice called from behind the door.

"It's safe," my mind reassured me; it was my Pee's voice that cried out from behind my locked bedroom door, but something seemed suspicious; I'm not quite as dumb as I seem.

"Tom, this is between the three of us, right?" Kelly said, appearing in the door frame behind Reggie. I could see it coming, but I couldn't stop it. I lost a sort of innocence in that moment that could never be regained. Kelly, a sexy brunette, fixed her feathered hair in the mirror and turned to me with a sheepish wink. "Tom, we all keep secrets, and the older we get the more we all have."

Reggie and Kelly exited my bedroom, as Petra and I went in.

"Tom, get with it," Reggie said, jerking his head toward the bed.

"What's that?" Petra asked, as I grabbed for the open book on my desk.

"It's my diary," I said. "I wanted to jot down a couple of things for future reference while they're still fresh, because I sometimes feel an odd disconnect between my feelings and the events and people in my life."

"You mean like that Reggie fellow?" Petra said, in her German accent. "Who is he to you?"

"He's going to be a world-famous athlete one day, and I'm going to be his sports agent," I said without a second thought.

It came to me all of a sudden; the pebble syndrome had dropped a tiny stone in my mind about my relationship with Reggie. "His sports agent" echoed in my mind for the next several hours.

"Tom, did you hit that?" Reggie asked me on Saturday, opening my front door, as I was cleaning up after the party. But, by the look on my face, he could see that I hadn't. "Come on, brother man, you'd better get with the game. Tom, do you realize that if it wasn't for Jill's exchange-student friends, you would never have had a date? You'll be seventeen in less than two weeks, and I bet you're still chokin' the chicken, imagining what the real deal feels like."

I knew he didn't mean to hurt my feelings, but I still felt insulted. Still, he was right; I would never have been on a date if it wasn't for Jill. And he was also right about me spending my time imagining the real thing. But I could feel my time coming; I could see it now, and I couldn't stop it even if I'd wanted to.

Barbara Waters spoke from my television screen: "Faith in established institutions, like the nuclear family, religion and trust in one's government continues to wane. The sexual revolution, contraceptive pills, higher divorce rates, and a greater incidence of premarital sex have forever changed relations between the sexes."

"In other news, in Abilene, Texas, the Catholic Church has reached a settlement in the case against Father O'Malley. The families of the two victims will receive an undisclosed monetary settlement, and Father O'Malley will be removed from all duties involving contact with children, and will be placed in another parish."

It all came together at once; I could finally put my finger on it. "Susan!" I cried from within. I hadn't kissed a girl, or even made a move toward the opposite sex, since her suicide. It took the mention of Father O'Malley to drop all the pieces in place and help me understand.

Barbara Waters said that, by the end of the decade, the feminist movement will have changed everything. It was just like Reggie said—us against them, and the women are gaining on us. I could see clearly now, with Reggie's help, that I'd been wasting my time overanalyzing life, getting caught up in complex questions of race and religion, when all I had to do was learn the rules of the game. From now on I'll spend my time learning how to play the game.

Part V
AT SEVENTEEN
Valley of the Dolls

Saturday, June 19th, 1976

How many people can say that they
lost their virginity on their birthday?

My birthday horoscope read: Hope and faith in your-self and your abilities will be your best assets in being able to experience something you've never felt before. This is the year to use your smarts and talents more to your advantage. Put them to work for you.

How many people can say that they lost their virginity on their birthday? Homeboy, I am one of the select few who can. Bambi Lovelace was her name—an unusual name for an extraordinary girl. I met her at Sambo's. She and her sister were having lunch in my section.

"Who's the little girl with you, young lady?" I asked, pouring her a cup of coffee, as I looked her over appre-ciatively.

"Oh, Tom, is it?" she said, glancing at my name tag, "this is my sister, Lolita."

She was the foxiest girl I've ever waited on, and I knew from the moment I saw her that there was a spark between us. "We took my mom's car out for the after-noon. We live just around the corner, and my mother lets me take Lolita to the park once in a while. Today, we decided to stop for lunch before we hit the park." She extended her hand to me.

"Bambi—that's an unusual name," I said when I returned with their order.

"My name is unusual, too," Lolita said, trying to attract my attention.

"God, I'm bored. All I've done this summer is babysit my sister," Bambi said, pouting her lips and looking up at me from under her thick lashes.

"I get off in about an hour; I could meet you at the park," I said.

"My name is not so ordinary either," Lolita said again, still vying for my attention. "My father once told me that my name is famous because some guy wrote a novel about me."

"Yes, I've read that book, and you are just as much of a flirt as the main character. The only difference is that you're trying to steal attention away from your sister, instead of your mother," I said, chuckling and looking the whole time at Bambi.

It didn't take long for Bambi to spot me sitting behind the wheel of my Ford Fairlane, tampering with the 8 track tape player. Bambi and I walked around the park, hand in hand. It seemed like every song on the radio cried out to young lovers. We heard Marvin Gaye's "Let's Get It On" and Chicago's "If You Leave Me Now." My heart sang in tune with Bambi's—a harmony only young lovers can sing.

Reggie showed up and was kind enough to watch Lolita, while I lost my virginity in the back seat of her mother's car. But, like the song says, "Many a tear has to fall, but it's all in the game."

I waited nearly a week for Bambi's call before I realized it wasn't going to happen. Reggie and I were lying around watching *The Dating Game* when the phone rang. I grabbed for it, hoping it was Bambi, but, as usual, it was for Reggie.

"Pee, I know you thought that you and this Bambi girl had something special, but the only thing special about her is her name. Just think, if I hadn't showed up that day, you'd still be a virgin." Then Reggie noticed that I was scratching at my crotch and jumped up off the bed. "Boy, that ho must have given you the crabs. You've been scratching all afternoon."

"But she said she was a virgin, too," I said.

"Tom, every guy plays the fool at some point, but it's normally after he's known her for awhile. So, in a way, you're lucky you found out before it got too heavy. It's cruel," Reggie said with mock puppy dog eyes as we walked down to the drugstore for a bottle of black and white ointment. "Brother, man may have the muscle, but woman has the hustle."

I read the directions on the bottle of ointment, which was supposed to relieve the itch Bambi left me with, but it wouldn't do a thing about my disappointment.

"Tom, this won't be the last time a woman gets one over on you, either," Reggie said as I stood lost in thought.

"Reggie, this says I have to shave myself before I use it."

"Yeah, Pee. That's a riot," he said, laughing loudly enough to attract attention.

I guess I've led a sheltered life. I should have been more skeptical about Bambi's boredom. If I had, perhaps I wouldn't have the crabs.

Friday, July 2nd, 1976

Abortion was in the news today. Lois Lane, the news honey that does the evening radio broadcast, echoed from the car radio, "The Supreme Court ruling that women's spousal consent is not required, and single women over eighteen do not need parental consent before having an abortion is getting strong opposition from foes."

It was probably the most eerie time I've ever spent with Reggie and Jill. We were on a double date, driving to the movie theater in Jill's Jaguar to see *A Star is Born*. Jill smiled meaningfully my way as I pulled into the parking lot. The DJ said, "I'm going to play this request, because it's a fact that a smile doesn't mean what it used to."

Smiling faces sometimes pretend to be your friend
Smiling faces show no traces of the evil that lurks within
Smiling faces, smiling faces sometimes
They don't tell the truth uh
Smiling faces, smiling faces
Tell lies and I got proof

I turned the engine off.

"Hey, that song is banging, and we've got ten minutes before the movie starts. Let's finish listening to it,"

Reggie said, reaching from the back seat to turn the ignition on.

Reggie winked at me, and I winked back.
Smoothy immediately started in: "Tom, you're
sworn to keep Reggie's and Jill's darkest secrets,
but why should you be holding their fate
in your hands?"

The truth is in the eyes
Cause the eyes don't lie, amen
Remember a smile is just
A frown turned upside down
My friend let me tell you
Smiling faces, smiling faces sometimes
They don't tell the truth, uh.

"Shut it off. Let's go inside and get in line for popcorn," Jill said, annoyed.

Again, I turned the ignition switch to off.

"Like, hey, we've got time, and I want to hear it, too," said my date, Mindy.

Smiling faces sometimes pretend to be your friend
Smiling faces show no traces of the evil that lurks within
Smiling faces, smiling faces sometimes
They don't tell the truth uh
Smiling faces, smiling faces
Tell lies and I got proof.

Reggie winked at me, and I winked back. Smoothy immediately started in: "Tom, you're sworn to keep Reggie's and Jill's darkest secrets, but why should you be holding their fate in your hands?"

While I was standing in line for popcorn, Jill came up and tapped me on the shoulder. "Reggie knows nothing, right?!" Jill said to me mocking the wink that Reggie had given me earlier.

"I'm not so sure I've got the guts to play this game," I thought to myself.

Later, Reggie and I ran into each other in the men's room.

"Yo, man, be cool. You'd better be careful with that tongue. Jill's not as stupid as you think, and she kind of picks up on what you were alluding to in the car," I warned him.

"Tom, you worry too much. Do you still remember our bet?" he said as we went into the lobby.

"What bet?" I whispered, seeing the girls coming toward us, but he didn't answer.

After the movie, we made a late-night food run to McDonald's and dropped Mindy off.

"Tom, Mindy's pretty. Where did you meet her?" Jill asked from the back seat.

"We met at the mall last week in front of the Gap Store."

"Tom, let me refresh your memory; last week, I bet that you couldn't get a date for tonight," Reggie said in front of Jill.

"That's right. You said I was living my life vicariously

through you, and you bet me $5 that I couldn't get a date. Pay up, buddy."

"Boys will be boys," Jill said, giggling.

"I bet you can't score with Mindy," Reggie said.

"I bet I can," I said, extending my right hand to seal the bet. Reggie's remark bothered me, though. He shouldn't have said that I live vicariously through him in front of Jill.

When Reggie and I got into the Fairlane after he kissed Jill goodnight, Swagger reminded me that I had gotten the date with Mindy without a handsome jock as my wing man. All I did was talk to her. One topic led to another, and then the next thing I knew she was sitting next to me in the theater.

"Tom, you'll never be able to score with women like I can," Reggie said.

"Brother, don't bet on it," I said playfully.

"Ok, I'll keep track of every girl I sleep with, and you write down in your diary the girls you sleep with, and at the end of my last high-school football game, we'll see who wins," he said.

Sunday, August 1st, 1976

My horoscope for last week predicted finances and love being major factors in the week.

Sambo's is open 24 hours a day, so shifts are being worked around the clock. I got off at about 4 p.m. today, after working a double shift, which means I started work Saturday night at 10. I waited all week for fortune to shine on me, but I didn't see any extra money lining my pockets. But Reggie got laid, not once but twice. Still, working the night shift on the weekends has its advantages. Saturday night a popular band called America sat in my section, and I had the pleasure of waiting on them. Boy, did it ever pay off! It was after 2 a.m. when they came through the doors.

"Hey, dude, is this the only place in town for grub this time of night?" a scruffy white guy with long hair asked, poking his head in the door.

"Well, if you go up the road about a mile, there's another place that stays open late, too, but it closes at 2, so don't waste your gasoline," I said, as he turned to speak to the bus driver behind him.

"Hey, kid, we're from out of town. What kind of food do you serve here?" he asked.

"Sambo's is your run-of-the mill, 24-hour, get-whatever's-on-the-menu-at-anytime dive," I replied, noticing their tour bus. "Did y'all come down for the cross-town scrimmage game?"

"No, dude, my band just played a concert at the Taylor County Civic Center. Man, haven't you ever heard of a band called *America*?" he asked, pointing to the name on the bus.

"No shit?! Yeah, I've heard y'all on the radio. In fact, our new FM station plays you guys all the time," I said.

"Yeah, they sponsored our concert tonight," he said.

"How many people are in your band?" I asked.

"Eight of us are on the bus," he said.

"Sambo's has the best coffee in town, and I can seat you in the private party room. The food isn't bad, either," I told him.

"Bro, you got a deal," he said.

Not only did I wait on the band, but business was slow, so I also cooked their food while the regular cook slept off a hangover in the storage room.

"A hundred dollars?!" I shouted, when I found the hundred dollar bill under a coffee cup next to the bill. It was the first time I'd ever seen a real hundred dollar bill. I ran out and thanked them, and they let me check out their bus before they pulled out.

"Hello, new jean jacket. Hello, new Earth, Wind and Fire album!" I shouted as they drove out of sight. I usually don't make $100 in two weeks. The lead singer, Dewey Bunnell, and I got along very well. He told me that the group's hit song, "A Horse with No Name," has been banned from several stations because people think it's about heroin.

On Saturday, I went to the scrimmage. They say everything is bigger in Texas, and that couldn't be more true than in the case of high school football. Over 18,000 people showed up for the game, and, once again, I had sideline tickets courtesy of Reggie. As luck would have it, Roger Staubach, the Cowboys quarterback, was also on the sidelines. I didn't get to talk to him, but I noticed another guy with him as he strolled up and down the field.

"You must be Roger's agent," I said to the man, who had started walking toward the concession stands.

"Yes, I am," he said as I trailed after him.

"Hey, what kind of qualifications do you have to have to become a sports agent?"

"You just have to know how to negotiate with the penny-pinching owners," he responded, a slick smile painted over his face.

"I mean, sir, what kind of degree do you have to have?" I shouted as he moved away from me toward the restrooms.

"I don't have a degree, son. In this business, all you've got to know is how to talk to people, and I've always had a gift for that."

I went to work that evening after the game feeling a lot more confident about my future chances of becoming Reggie's agent. Reggie had scored during six of seven total possessions. He seems unable to do any wrong these days. On top of being a football hero, he got laid twice in a week, and now leads 2-0 in the hustle game. He left my house about an hour ago, after spending four and a half hours talking to Jill on my line. I showed him my hundred dollar bill.

"Tom, I'll bet you that bill in your hand that you won't get laid again for a month," he said before he went home, and I was fool enough to take him up on it before I really considered the stakes. Losing a hundred dollars on a bet would be stupid. I should never have started the hustle game. Reggie has all the moves, on and off the field, and I'm way out of my league. Now, I'm risking $100 with the odds stacked against me.

Reggie set the rules of the hustle game as follows: A score only counts if the girl's not related to you and you haven't scored with her before. He gave me credit for Bambi, even though that happened before we started the game. What a pal! So, now the score is Reggie Thomas 2, Tom Jones 1.

Sunday night television calls, and it's time for *All in the Family*, followed by *The Jeffersons*. Later!

Friday, August 13th, 1976

Jill and Reggie make me sick to my stomach—walking around the mall, holding hands. Jill was singing along to Mary Well's hit, "Nothing you can say can take me away from my guy." Then, Reggie started humming "My Girl." They make me want to puke.

"Are you Reggie Thomas, the best football player in Abilene?" a blonde in hot pants asked, giggling and blushing.

"Actually, he's the best player in Texas," Jill answered. If Jill only knew how her man screws around, she wouldn't be singing.

But Reggie is like the town savior. Everywhere we go, somebody comes up to him, saying things like, "Are you going to take us to state this year?" or "Reggie, when are you going to break another record?" It's like being with a celebrity. I've never heard such a fuss over a high-school quarterback.

"Yeah, sure, we'll win state this year. You can bet on it," Reggie told some old black lady, after she kissed his cheek for luck. You can bet on it? The only thing you can bet on is me losing a hundred dollars to him in less than a month.

I also took a date to the mall with us. Her name was Mary Anne, and believe me, I loved being seen with this fox. Tom definitely wanted to be Mary Anne's man.

"Can I buy you another ice cream?" she whispered in my right ear as my car sat idle in the parking lot of the Dairy Queen where she's employed. I got to first base with her in the parking lot before she had to punch in. She had the sweetest lips I'd ever tasted, but then everything went sour.

"Tom, I really enjoyed hanging out with you and your famous friend. When can we go out with Jill and Mr. Reggie again?"

Spooky immediately asked, "Tom, how can you be sure Mary Anne is going out with you because she likes being with you?"

Getting to know women is a real challenge for me, and now I don't know how I can be sure where I really stand with this Mary Anne chick. I'm so confused. Reggie says it's all a game, but when I kissed her sweet lips, all I wanted to be was whatever she wanted me to be. Home alone, I've had a few hours to cool off and think. I just hope someday I can outgrow this nerdy stage I'm in and be a pimp, like Reggie.

Tuesday, August 24th, 1976

"Homeboy," Laurie says, "hello." I saw her last week, when I was buying a lid from her boyfriend, Jeff. Laurie said that she thinks it's groovy that I'm still keeping a diary about the teenagers of the 1970s. I think its fab that Laurie and Jeff are still a couple. They've been together nearly seven months now. Laurie told me to write down that she says, "Hello," and that (just in case some narc happens to read my diary) I scored that bag from Jeff—she only smokes, she doesn't sell. Ha, ha.

My hundred dollar bill is on the line with less than a week to go. Now, that ain't funny. And Reggie scored again. Reggie 3, Tom 1!

Wednesday, September 1st, 1976

When I started toking nine months ago, Laurie always said, "Smoking pot cures boredom," as she passed me the joint. And she was right; after a few hits, my mind drifted in new and interesting directions.

"Hey, Tom, the Cowboys are playing their last pre-season game tonight. Do you want to watch it with me?" my father asked on Friday.

I had less than three days left to save my hundred dollars. I stepped out back to smoke a joint before the game started and let my mind roam for a while before going inside. Howard's stepfather called my father to chat about the Cowboys during halftime. I was stoned out of my mind and eavesdropping, as it became apparent that Leonard was bitching about the Mexican family that moved onto Bowie Street.

"The more things change around here, the more they stay the same," I thought to myself. Wasn't it just four short years ago that he was bitching about white flight?

The network returned to the game in time to show the Cowboys cheerleaders finish the half-time show. I thought about Jill. She had called earlier to brag that she'd been re-elected as head cheerleader. No change there, either. Then, during a public service announcement in the third quarter, a pretty school teacher on the hood of a sports car warned drivers to drive carefully in school zones now that school was in session again. She reminded me of Miss Wiseman. I'll have her for Modern History III. More of the same.

"Hey, Dad, would you help me finance a new car?" I asked after he hung up the phone.

"Tom, a new car is way out of your league," he said. "When you start making more money, then I'll consider it."

The following Saturday, Dave lost a waiter and gained a cook. I pick things up quickly; all I've got to do is watch someone once. So, when the morning cook didn't show up, instead of calling Dave, I just stepped behind the grill and made every order brought to me. Dave was shocked when he showed up, and the rest, as they say, is history.

"Tom, I can guess from your body language that I've got a new cook," he joked. "Same deal applies, though, even if you will be a senior and a cook, this year. You come in at four and work until ten and I'll pay you for the whole 8 hours."

"Consider it done," I said.

Homeboy, by five that Saturday evening I was the proud new owner of a black and white 1970 Chevelle Super Sport convertible, courtesy of our new Mexican neighbors. I met their eighteen-year-old son, Mario, at school. I'd seen him from time to time, but never had a reason to talk to him. He introduced me to his father, Mario Senior, and it turned out that he owns a small car dealership called Rodriguez Brothers. Before my father could tell what was up, I had him in the Fairlane on the way to the car lot, while I explained how I managed to get 80 cents more an hour in one day.

Mr. Rodriguez picked up his telephone receiver and started to dial.

"Mr. Jones, what's your social security number?" Mario Senior asked.

"Don't you need to talk to my bank before we sign these papers?" Dad asked.

"No," Mario said, as I exchanged my old keys for the keys to the Chevelle. "My brother is my business partner and lives in Mexico. He just checked your credit score, which, by the way, is excellent, Mr. Jones. So, we're all set. We'll send you a payment booklet in the mail within thirty days," Mr. Rodriguez continued, as my father shook his head in disbelief and co-signed the note for twenty-six hundred dollars. "Don't look so worried," Mr. Rodriguez said as I danced around the office. "Things just move more quickly nowadays. There's nothing to worry about."

If you want to be an instant hit with high school girls, just pull into school on a Monday in a Chevelle Super Sport. By Tuesday, the last day of the bet, guess who had a white cum stain on the black leather backseat of his new wheels? None other than yours truly. Reggie 3, Tom 2.

My father just poked his head into my room to ask me how I'm enjoying my new car. Then he started bitching about Uncle Frank, because he got another DWI last weekend right after having his driver's license reinstated a week ago. Like I said, the more things change the more they stay the same.

Dig it.

Saturday, September 4th, 1976

I double dated with Jill and Reggie tonight. We went to see *Silver Streak*, starring Gene Wilder, Jill Clayburgh and Richard Pryor. It was hilarious. Is there any man on the planet funnier than Richard Pryor? I don't think so! He's got a new album, *Bicentennial Nigger*, which I will own tomorrow after work. I'm also going to buy the 8-track tape, so that my friends can listen to it in my car.

Dave wants me to work a double shift again tomorrow, so I'm turning in early tonight, while Reggie and Jill are probably tangled and sweaty. They mentioned driving over to Kelly's crib, because Kelly's parents are in Austin on a business trip this weekend. Reggie's place won't work, because Shirley's upset with her boyfriend and has cut him off from sex. If our parents knew what goes on when they're not around, they'd never leave us home alone.

Catch u up later.

Monday, September 13th, 1976

"*Que Paso, amigo.* Hey, Tom, what's the skinny on finding a bag around here?" Mario Junior asked, after flagging me down as I was driving past his house.

"Homeboy, we have a dealer in the neighborhood, but I'll have to arrange it, because he's a friend of mine, and when you're a friend of mine, I don't tell your business in the streets," I said. "Get in. I'm on my way to Taco Bell, but we can try to catch him on the way home. How much are you looking for?"

"I've got a dime I can spend," Mario said.

"A dime is fine; that'll get you a full lid."

We went to eat, and then we stopped to pick up the bag. We were rolling a joint in the car, when someone knocked on my window. I hit the power button next to my arm to roll the window down.

"Cool! Power windows," Laurie said, as Mario tried to stuff the bag out of sight.

"Yes, isn't it neat? Hello, ladies," I said with a devilish smile, and then she smiled.

"Hey, is that Richard Pryor?" Laurie asked.

White folks got them some new nigger—they've brought them Vietnamese over here to America, and they didn't ask us shit!

The three of us—a Mexican, a white girl, and a black guy—all burst into laughter.

"Tom, why is it o.k. for black people to say 'nigger,' but not for white people?" Laurie asked. I had no answer; it had never occurred to me before. "Anyway, why don't y'all come inside and fire up that number? Jeff's parents are in Houston, and I know you bought that from him anyway. Grab the Richard Pryor tape, too," she said, trotting toward Jeff's house.

"I knew it had to be that flower-power hippie selling the grass on the block," Mario said, as if he had just solved a real mystery.

"Laurie and Jeff are cool, and she wouldn't have invited you to his house if she didn't think you were cool too, Mario," I said, as we got out of the car. "I like the black paint with white racing stripes; it makes your car look like a skunk," Mario said, nodding his head up and down.

"A skunk?!"

"That's a compliment, bro," he said. "And those 350 horses under the hood kept anybody from even getting close to you when we were racing earlier."

"The Skunk! That's what I'll call her from now on," I said in front of Jeff's door.

I looked back at the car, and it occurred to me that, with a 3-0 record, maybe I could make some money off of the Skunk.

The fine Colombian we smoked at Jeff's house turned a great day into a wonderful night. Now, Jeff, Laurie and I have all added Mario to our list of friends we can trust.

Thursday, September 30th, 1976

There is a famous song from the Sixties, "See You in September." Today is the last of September, and I can finally sit down long enough to tell you about one September day to remember. I'm playing catch-up for the entire month.

Looking back on the month, I see my life filled with games and scores. Whether it's football, drag racing, or the hustle game, there's always a score to tally. Well, I'm 5 and 0 at racing. Mario was right; that 350-horsepower engine is just what the doctor ordered. Girls, girls, and more girls flock to watch us in that racing machine. I was sure that I was finally even with Reggie in the hustle game, but that was short-lived. I didn't see him all weekend, and I really thought we were tied at three apiece after I laid Leah Thompson Friday after the game. It was the first time I snuck into a girl's bedroom, and it'll probably be the last.

"Hey, Tom, is that your new car?" Leah said, sauntering up to me as I was cruising around after the game. Leah's a blonde bimbo who's a junior at Cooper. She's almost as well-known for being as fast as my car.

"Yeah, baby, this is 'the Skunk,'" I said, stopping so that she could stare.

"Why do you call it 'the Skunk'?" she asked, looking amused.

"Because this baby beats all cars put up against it, when the fellows gather at the track behind the abandoned warehouses," I said, smirking.

"You mean you race this car?" she cooed, leaning in the passenger-side window.

"Yeah, and you can get a ride from me anytime," I said. "You want to get in?"

Leah got in and we rode around until she was so in love with my car that she felt the need to express that love to me. Leah doesn't do backseats, so we snuck into her room through her window. Unfortunately, her father woke up while we were in the mix, and I had to jump out of the window, leaving my Flagg Brothers shoes behind. I'll have to get them from her later. Those shoes cost me a whole $15.

Later, I noticed that slick pimp, Reggie, had another notch on his headboard, making the score Reggie 4, Tom 3. Reggie isn't doing too badly on the football field, either. We're 6 and 0, and playing a home game against the Cougars this Friday. They have a surprising 6 and 1 start to their season with their bye week still ahead of them. The entire city is anticipating this Friday's game.

September also leaves us with women dominating the news media.

"Ordination of women as priests and bishops approved by the Episcopal Church" was one newspaper headline

last week. Then, *Patty Hearst gets a seven-year sentence for her role in the bank robbery* was the lead story on NBC. My father said she got a light sentence because she's a rich, white girl. So, why the hell would a rich girl rob a bank? Then, Barbara Waters, who NBC recently stole from CBS, reminded the world about the third anniversary of the tennis match Billie Jean King won against Bobby Riggs. Now, girls like Laurie act as if girls can beat boys at sports for real. My father told me that Barbara Waters made the news because she got a lot of money when NBC hired her. The other networks are calling her "the first woman of television," and my mother, who never used to watch the news, now keeps a watchful eye on it. She says that the evening news is a man's job, and she'd rather watch Walter Cronkite. Barbara Waters' eyes sparkled as she reported the news that women can now be Episcopalian priests.

"A woman priest? What is this world coming to?" my mother exclaimed with disgust. "The man is the head of the house, just as Christ is head of the church," she mumbled.

After all of the stories about women in the news, Laurie goes around singing Helen Reddy's "I am woman—hear me roar." I'm confused about all this women's liberation stuff. My mother complained about it to my father at breakfast one day, and he responded by bragging that one day his daughters will have the opportunity to participate in sports just like boys. I don't really understand how there can be women who don't want to be allowed to be priests and men who celebrate the idea that women will compete in sports. But my dad seems thrilled about Title IX.

"Title Nine? Is that anything like cloud nine?" I joked to my father. It's the first time I'd ever heard anyone talk about the effects of the new legislation on society. I read the newspaper regularly, but Title IX was passed in 1972, and its ramifications are only now being noticed. When my father started talking about girls playing sports like boys, and his daughters one day playing football, I thought for sure my father must have smoked some of my weed. Everybody knows that girls are supposed to watch football, and not play football. Just imagine tackling a sweaty girl in P.E.! Wait a minute. On second thought, count me in.

Friday, October 8th, 1976

You know you've made it when your name is printed on the walls of the rival school. Reggie and I were at Cooper last Monday, having lunch with Jill after we destroyed the Cougars in last Friday's game 52-10. We strolled around the Cooper campus like we owned it before grabbing a quick bite to eat with Jill.

"Tom Jones left his shoes under my bed," was scrawled across a wall near the janitor's closet. I knew exactly who wrote it; I never did get those shoes back.

This Friday, the Cooper team had their bye week, so Jill didn't have cheerleading duties to prevent her from seeing Reggie play. He's been scoring bigtime on the field lately, and last Friday's game was his best ever, giving us a 7- 0 record. It's the age of video, and watching all the sportscasters surround Reggie after his record performance just made me shudder. Cameras flashed everywhere, blinding Jill and me as we watched from a bench nearby.

"Tom, I'm glad I could witness Reggie playing the part of the star," she said, her eyes reflecting the flash bulbs.

I'd bet that there were 10 reporters and 50 girls waiting for Reggie outside the locker room. I guess I'm lucky Jill was there or Reggie would be way ahead in the hustle game.

"Tom, my dad is taking us to Aspen tomorrow for three days," Jill said, as we stood up to leave. "So, take good care of my shining star while I'm away. I've got an early flight, so I won't get the chance to tell Reggie how wonderful he looked on camera," she said, closing her car door and waving goodbye.

"I've got to get up early myself and work a double shift," I said, walking into the darkness of the emptying parking lot, happy that Jill was too blinded by the camera lights to notice any look I may have had on my face. It's getting harder and harder for me to keep Reggie's infidelity from her—I just like her too much, and I know she's going to get hurt in the end, whether that end comes sooner or later.

Saturday, October 16th, 1976

Now, what's the name of the game? I'm not sure; all I know is that while the cat's away the mouse will play. I finally caught up to Reggie at the end of the week, and to my surprise, he had another notch on his headboard. He said some freshman girl told him she'd do anything for the quarterback of the team, and she was true to her word. This encounter between star and groupie happened the same Friday night Jill came to the game but had to leave early. So, Reggie 5, Tom 3.

Friday, October 22nd, 1976

Why do ABC, CBS, and NBC all have to show the debates between President Ford and Jimmy Carter? What a waste of the boob tube! It's Friday night, and our high school had its bye week this week, so I hung around the crib just to watch *Hawaii 5-0*, but all that was on was the debate. I got bored, so I strolled across the street to see what Reggie was up to.

"Hey, Tom, come on in. I'm just catching a few Zs, waiting on my girl to bring me some chow from Taco Bell. You know this brother's got no funds, so Jill said she'd hook me up after their game," Reggie said. Not five minutes later, Jill pulled up dressed in her cheerleading uniform, handed Reggie his food, and came over to greet me.

"We won tonight, so we're 8 and 2, and if we meet your team in the playoffs, it's going to be a different outcome than the pounding y'all gave us a few weeks ago," she said, mock choking me.

"I'll leave you two lovebirds alone," I said when I noticed Reggie winking at me to get lost.

Tonight, Laurie caught a glimpse of Jill. Abilene isn't exactly a small town, so you don't always know all your friends' friends.

"Who's that frat bitch with the Jaguar at Reggie's?" Laurie asked as we shared a roach outside of Jeff's house.

"Oh, that's Jill Andersen, Reggie's main squeeze," I replied.

"You mean 'Andersen,' as in the airport?" she asked.

"Yeah, that's right."

"I hate frats!" Laurie said, disgust displayed across her face as she walked off, leaving Mario and me to toke alone. Boys are so much different than girls. Girls seem to hate one another at first sight.

Right now, I'm just alone and bored.

Friday, October 29th, 1976

Jill's favorite words are, "You always want what you can't have." She couldn't be more right. I'm sitting here in study hall class, updating you, Diary. High school is a joke. Normally, I do all of Reggie's homework and mine too during study hall, but Reggie's teachers don't give him homework on game days, and I've turned in all of mine already.

I wanted so badly to be Reggie this morning, just to feel the excitement of being the star of the team at the pep rally in the gymnasium full of people chanting your name, as you lead them into battle-cry cheers to psych them up for tonight's game.

"Yo, what's up, blood?" Reggie said when I saw him after the pep rally. "Say, man, Jill is on my ass like white on rice, and between quarterbacking and keeping Jill in the dark about the hustle game, I'm beat. Why don't we change up the rules a little bit?"

"What kind of change?" I asked.

"Well, since I can't get away and play like I want to, let's say that if you sleep with the same girl—Jill, for example—that counts as a score," Reggie said.

"You're up 5 to 3 already, and you're a local hero. You're out of your mind if you think you can run that game on me," I said as we stumbled down the hall, laughing.

"Damn, Tom, that's why we're such a great pair; you're always thinking ahead. But I'm getting a bit nervous. I saw the chick you had in the Skunk yesterday during lunch. She was pretty hot!" he said, smiling. "Now, if I had your wheels, I'd be banging a new chick every night."

"Good luck tonight in Midland. When does the bus leave?"

"In an hour," Reggie said, before we ran our respective directions.

I'm doing better at the hustle game than Reggie thought I'd do, and it shows in his nervousness. Reggie's going to have to get up pretty early before he can run this kind of game on me. Change the rules? No way.

Well, I've got to wrap our update session. My older sister just slipped me a note via the girl in front of me that says Jill called last night while I was at work, and I need to call her back right away. I wonder what she wants. She's probably just checking up on Reggie again. Talk to you later.

Tuesday, November 2nd, 1976

The more things change around here, the more they stay the same.

"Tom, if you were stuck on a desert island and could only bring one 8-track, which one would you bring?"

It was like déjà vu as I looked at the road rushing under the grill of the car. The conversation was going almost exactly as before in virtually the same spot as we raced home from the same clinic we visited last year around this time. That note proved to be more of an adventure than I'd anticipated.

"Tom, you have to know somebody who can pull this off," Jill urgently pleaded.

"Damn it, Jill, it's Friday night. What do you mean you weren't sure before, but now you're absolutely positive?!" I yelled into the receiver.

"It's Sunday night, and you've got me breaking into the safe in my father's office to make a fake ID for some fucking white girl frat friend of yours. This is a serious crime that we could do serious time for."

Mario turned eighteen two months ago, and now he and I have committed forgery.

"Fucking A, Tom. It's Sunday night, and you've got me breaking into the safe in my father's office to make a fake ID for some fucking white girl frat friend of yours. This is a serious crime that we could do serious time for," Mario said, concerned.

"Dude, just give me the $90 you have and give me the rest later. Um, Tom, this looks like that chick, Jill—the one that Reggie goes out with," Mario said, starting to sound suspicious. "You and Jill are driving way up to Dallas to do this?"

"Yeah, bro, but don't worry. We've done this before," I said without thinking.

"Damn, Tom, you're quite the player. I would have never thought that about you," Mario said, giving me a high five.

"No, it's not like that!" I said quickly. Mario turned out the lights, and we headed out the door. I turned to Mario as he was locking the door, placed my hand on his shoulder and said, "For Jill's sake, this secret should remain just between us."

"Tom, there is no real secret if you're banging a

buddy's girlfriend and get caught. You'll just have to pay the price for it," he said. "But we're cool, Tom. Hey, bro, you're the man."

"Many thanks, amigo," I said.

The world will always remember today as the day that America elected Jimmy Carter, but I'll remember this as the day that Jill's eyes turned from a pale blue to twilight blue, while she heaped another heavy secret onto my growing pile.

"He took advantage of me," Jill said out of the blue as Christine McVie's voice echoed in the Chevelle: *You can take me to paradise. Then again, you can be cold as ice. I'm over my head, over my head.*

I pushed the stop button.

"Who took advantage of you?" I asked.

"My father did when I was little. He made it into a little game. I'd get what I wanted if he got what he wanted," Jill said, staring ahead into the descending darkness.

"Did you tell your mother?" I asked.

"It's a family secret, Tom. Nobody wants to listen, and everyone pretends not to see," Jill said. "My father always gets what he wants, but, for the rest of us, I'm certain we will always want what we can't have," Jill said, her voice trailing off.

For a moment I was overwhelmed by the weight of all of our secrets. If there is one thing I didn't need, it's another secret to carry around. I found myself unburdening myself to Jill about my religious upbringing and what my mother's beliefs had put me through, about the suicide attempt and my sessions with Dr. Scott, and how that led to him testing my IQ. She couldn't understand how someone with my smarts could be duped, and I was suddenly struck by the ironic truth that my "intelligence" has done nothing to protect me from being taken in by fairy tales and superstition.

"What modern invention changed your life the most, Jill?" I asked, trying to lighten the moment.

"Plastic surgery, definitely," she said to my astonishment. "In Mexico, you can get a nose job at just about any age, and J.R. gave me a new nose when I was fifteen," Jill said, proudly displaying the result.

Until that moment, I honestly didn't know that the words, "plastic" and "surgery," were ever used together. No wonder Jill is so attractive, if at 15 years old, she was already receiving touch-ups to her body.

"I think finding my brother's birth certificate changed my life the most," I said.

"What do you mean?" Jill asked.

"Well, one day, while I was looking for my vaccination records, I discovered that Mike and I are only half-brothers. The date on his birth certificate shows that my mother was pregnant when my parents got married—almost six months pregnant. My parents' claim to fame was the fact that they'd only known each other for four months before they got married, so my mother had to have been at least two months pregnant before she met my father," I said. "Mike was really upset by the revelation, and my sister, Carol, insinuated that he might have been adopted. That discovery started my pebble syndrome."

"Damn, Tom, you're like a freaking TV Detective Kojak," Jill said, looking bewildered. "I would never have figured all that out just by looking at a birth certificate and a marriage license. No wonder you're so smart."

Jill turned the stereo off as the Fleetwood Mac song faded into the distance. It was silent for a second. "Tom, what the hell is the pebble syndrome?" Jill asked. I chuckled and began to explain.

"The pebble syndrome is a theory that I developed after an event I read about in the newspaper. You see, there were these Japanese tourists in Colorado, and they had only been in the country for three hours, when a boulder rolled off a mountain and crushed their tour bus, killing them. Witnesses on top of the mountain said they saw a bird drop a pebble and cause the boulder to tumble, though experts say that something else must have caused it. So, whenever some minute event radically alters someone's life I call it 'the pebble syndrome,'" I said, taking a swig of Coca Cola and stepping on the gas.

"I'm searching my mind to see where Reggie's, and my, pebble syndrome began. I couldn't have imagined me pregnant with Reggie's baby twice in about a year's span of time. Gosh, Tom, it all seems to happen so fast these days," Jill said as she glanced at the instrument panel on the dashboard of my Chevy. "Tom, you'd better slow the fuck down before we get pulled over. You're going at least 25 miles per hour over the damn speed limit."

"Sometimes, you're too down to earth for me," she teased, pretending to slap my face. "I'm always looking in *People Magazine* for some clue in the celebrities' eyes as to how they became stars, and here you are so grounded." she said, relaxing in the passenger seat. Then suddenly she popped up and pointed. "Tom, slow the fuck down. The Man's sitting on the side of the highway; I'm sure he clocked you!"

We were probably ten miles down the road before we stopped searching the rearview mirrors for possible Texas highway patrol car lights. I had no idea I was driving over 90 miles an hour.

"Damn, that was close," Jill said, grinning. What she said next surprised me. "What are words for anymore, Tom?" she asked, digging in her handbag.

"Words are a communication tool," I said matter-of-factly."

"What I mean is that the world moves so fast that no one has time for words anymore. I don't even read my magazines; I just glance at the pictures as I turn the pages. I mean, why read a book when you can see it as the movie of the week?

"Here, baby, finish this doobie; I'm done with it," Jill said, passing me her joint.

"You've bogarted the joint again, Miss Pretty Lips," I teased as she leaned her head on my shoulder.

"By the way, I got the lip job in Argentina. It must have cost J.R. at least a grand. People fly in from all over the world to get work done in Argentina," Jill mumbled, beginning to doze off against my shoulder, and I realized that she was right; there I sat, wanting what I can't have. Guiding my Super Sport down Interstate 20 at 96 miles an hour in order to get back in time for curfew, I still felt that the girl next to me was out-pacing me. Then, Smoothy asked the $64,000 question: "Where did the pebble syndrome start with Jill and me, and where could it lead?"

Saturday, December 18th, 1976

I feel entirely too close to Jill after our third long road trip together to another high school football playoff game. The Cougars made the playoffs in November but they lost to our team in a game that made the headlines the next day—"Reggie's Day." Reggie scored nine times, resulting in a lopsided victory. So Jill and I traveled together, following Reggie to the district playoffs, then the regional playoffs, and, finally, the semi-finals—one day away from a state title game. The last game was the regional game in Midland, and, due to scheduling, it was played on a Saturday evening instead of a Friday. Jill and I decided to stay in Midland overnight instead of driving back, and it was there, in a motel room after the game, that I made a decision.

"Jill, we can't play this game any longer or one of us is going to get burned," I said, placing the room key in the lock.

"Tom, our casual flirtation is perfectly normal," Jill said nonchalantly. "Grow up. I've always known you want me, but you know you can't have me."

I immediately felt the tension lift. Then and there, I chose Reggie over Jill. I care about Jill, and had been very close to telling her about the hustle game, but Reggie is my Pee, so his secret is still safe, at least for now. When the teenage queen of your dreams looks you in the eye and says, "You'll never have me," it takes something out of you. I really thought Jill and I had something extraordinary between us that only lovers have, but I was dead wrong. And she's my best friend's girl. How far would I have gone to have her as mine? Would I have told her about Kelly and Reggie or Reggie and the others? Maybe! But, thank the stars above, I'll never have to wrestle with that question again because Jill's eyes revealed no romantic feeling for me. Besides, hadn't I learned my lesson about expressing my feelings to the opposite sex with Susan? Look at all the pain that caused me.

Reggie and the victorious Abilene team joined Jill and me at the motel restaurant after the game. Abilene fans ate from the buffet with new and ever growing Eagles fans from all over the state. There's nothing like being one victory away from the state title. One television reporter described it best when he said, "It's probably the closest thing to Heaven you'll ever get here on Earth, and the most fun you'll have with your clothes on."

As school regulations required, all of the players rode back on the team bus after the game, and Reggie Thomas, the star that he was, was no exception. But Jill and I stayed. She lied to her parents about her whereabouts, but I didn't bother lying to my parents. For some, it may be gradual, but for others it happens suddenly—that day when an adolescent decides to take control of his own life. For me, it was instantly. In the moment, when I decided to not call my parents, I became my own man.

Jill slept on one side of the king-sized bed, and I slept on the other, but I would have traded all five other scores just to score once with Jill. When she dropped me off at Sambo's the next morning, she said, "It's not a game, Tom. You and I are good friends, and we'll always be just good friends," and blew me a kiss goodbye.

"Well, things can't go on between us like before; it's too hard for me, so I'll see you around!" I shouted as she gazed into the rearview mirror, putting on fresh make-up.

"Uh huh, Tom? Well, the state finals game is in Austin next week, so what time are you picking me up?" Jill said coolly.

"I'll call you," I said, winking and knowing that I had just lied to her.

Sunday, January 2nd, 1977

Homey, let me tell you about Reggie. He could have given that extra ticket to the Rose Bowl to anyone, but he gave it to me. I sat next to him at the game in Pasadena on New Year's Day. The tickets were courtesy of the USC coaching staff. One of the USC Trojans' assistant coaches invited Reggie to watch USC play, after hearing about our heartbreaking loss in the semi-finals. Reggie left the Eagles tied and in position for a winning field goal with fifteen seconds on the clock, but, as fate would have it, the placekicker didn't cleanly receive the snap from the center, and seconds drained from the clock. It was an eerie feeling, watching the fluke play as the other team ran down the field celebrating their surprising win.

Some spectators called the game the "terrible towel game," because the kicker had signaled to the center that he needed a dry towel, but the center's towel was also soaking wet. With no time-outs left and the clock ticking, the slippery ball had to be snapped, and the kicker lost his grip on the ball. The absence of a dry towel made a difference in hundreds of lives, and the 13-0 season went down the drain on a soggy football field.

Airfare came with the tickets, and Reggie's mother assumed that Reggie would take her along, but as Reggie and I boarded the flight to Dallas to meet a connecting flight to California, all I could see back on the tarmac was a tipsy Shirley drowning in her own tears. Shirley had drunk way too much before taking us to the airport. She even had the nerve to curse me out in front of the ticket agent for Reggie not taking her. As Reggie would say, "The bros come before the hoes."

I could tell by the looks on their faces that the USC coaches had also expected to see Shirley. After all, the golden rule in college recruiting is: "Have the mother in the palm of your hand, and her son will follow shortly." But Reggie and I were making our own rules. Accompanying him on recruiting trips (even disguised as a sympathy gesture) is something I'd only imagined in the distant future. Without warning, the future is here.

There's a popular song on the radio these days with lyrics that go "I know a little bit about love, and baby, I can guess the rest." Well, with the pace of things these days, I've adopted that strategy in all areas of my life. Homey, I've become an excellent mimic, and mimicking a sports agent is just what I did out in California. The USC coaching staff billed their game against Michigan as "the game of the ages." The term, "black quarterback," was floating around everywhere, because, for the first time, USC had put a black quarterback at the helm. Vincent Evans was his name, and the coaches wanted Reggie to see what it felt like to be in such a highly-charged atmosphere. One coach explained to Reggie that being a black quarterback comes with heavy scrutiny from foes and peers alike.

"You don't just have to be as good as the white players; you have to be better, and you have to earn the respect of your team by working harder and playing better than anyone else on your team or any other team," he said as we watched the game.

Vincent Evans not only played well in the game, but was named MVP after leading his team to a 14-6 victory. The notion of a black quarterback not being able to handle scrutiny or pressure was dispelled in a single game after Vincent's performance.

It was a wet towel that caused our team to lose the state title, but also that got Reggie and me to California. That seemingly unimportant detail might just be the start of one of several pebble syndrome moments in the lives of Reggie and me.

Sweetness, Otis, Juice, Ali—all these nicknames have one thing in common. People instantly know who you're referring to.

"Reg, with your talent, you'll surpass all these guys in name recognition," OJ Simpson whispered as he autographed his USC jersey number 32 for Reggie. "You've broken all my high school rushing records, and you still have a year left to play at the high school level. Rumor has it that you've got a better throwing arm than most college quarterbacks, so there's nothing stopping you from possibly being the first guy to go straight from high school to the NFL."

"OJ, do you really think I could beat out starting college quarterbacks?" Reggie asked.

"Sure, Reg, you're the real deal. You're better than Vincent. And who says you have to go to college? Hell, you could probably join the NFL right now. Don't be afraid to push the envelope, Reg. You don't have to be a quarterback; with your talent, you could play any offensive position. With the right agent, you could make the NFL roster after your senior year of high school and get paid now," OJ said before he joined his adoring fans.

OJ Simpson called Reggie "Reg," so from here on, so will I. Every great athlete needs a catchy name, and my

first job as his agent is to disseminate Reg's new name.
Thanks, OJ.

Sunday, January 9th, 1977

Our world is moving at twice the speed of light. I'm sitting next to my Pee on another flight home from California. The headline of the *L.A. Times* reads: "Eleven-year-old starts college." If you had bet me last Monday that I'd be on another flight home from Southern California with Reggie, I'd have bet 100 to one against it. I'd have to buy one of those new Texas Instruments "calculators" to figure out what the odds really are. This free trip was courtesy of Ruben Patterson, a sports agent that Reg and I met at the Rose Bowl. He invited us to watch the Super Bowl between the Oakland Raiders and the Minnesota Vikings. Our seats weren't as good as we had for the Rose Bowl, but it was magical and surreal anyway.

Ruben Patterson called me directly on Tuesday, asking for Reg the day after we came home from the Rose Bowl. I thought it was a prank caller, but then Ruben started talking about sending an overnight package with tickets and hotel accommodations, and talking about Pasadena in a way that only a person who had been there could.

I keep pinching myself to make sure I'm not dreaming, but it's all for real. Reg and I missed school Thursday and Friday because we left Abilene as soon as the tickets arrived. The trip cost me my job, but to hell with it; I've got bigger fish to fry.

"Dave, I know I was a no-show last weekend, and I know you don't understand why I have to go away again this weekend, but it's Reg and me against the fucking world now, and I've gotta go," I told him on Wednesday.

He shot me the finger as I closed the door to his office, and I knew I was fired. I left him short-handed by leaving him without a morning cook over the holiday weekend, and doing it on back-to-back weekends made him even angrier.

I also missed my father's retirement party last weekend. My father had been looking forward to it for weeks, but if I'm going to be an agent, I've got to take advantage of every opportunity I get to establish myself. Carol called me long distance to say that my brother didn't make it to the party, either. Supposedly, his flight was delayed because of a freak snowstorm in Denver. He was supposed to fly home after finishing basic training on Thursday. I wonder what the odds were that neither of us would be at the party.

I'm updating my diary while Reg sleeps in the large leather seat next to me. Flying first class is definitely a step in the right direction. Reg has leg room, and I actually have a real table to write on. I wish I could describe every detail of our trip, but I've got to end our session for now. Reggie has homework due in the morning.

Monday, January 10th, 1977

Seriously, how does it all work? If I hadn't seen it myself, I would have sworn it was mathematically impossible. During our descent into Andersen Airport, I had just put away Reg's homework assignment on Cleopatra, when our stewardess' voice came over the PA: "Ladies and gentlemen, the captain has turned on the fasten-seat-belt sign and we're about to touch down. All passengers at this time must prepare for landing."

The plane taxied to the gate.

"Yo, bro, that's Jill's family's plane," Reg said, pointing to a small private plane with lit, red tail lights.

I handed him the lukewarm towel that the stewardess had left for him thirty minutes ago.

"I hope your mother is true to her word about picking us up," I said.

"Speaking of picking up, I'm leading you in the hustle game 8 to 5 since I managed to get laid this weekend," Reg said with the schoolboy grin he's famous for.

"I wish they all could be California girls," I sang, elbowing his ribs gently. *It was too easy for Reggie to get laid this weekend,* I thought.

"Hey, what did Ruben talk about when you guys had lunch on Friday?" I asked.

But before he could answer, the stewardess' voice came back over the PA: "Ladies and gentlemen, welcome to Abilene Andersen Regional Airport. The local time is 10:59."

Reg and I were standing next to the luggage carousel, waiting for our bags to arrive, when passengers from a St. Louis flight started to trickle in.

"Hey, brother, what the hell are you doing here?" I yelled when I saw Mike in the crowd.

"Hey, Tom, I just got in from St. Louis. I'm home on leave for a month," he said as we hugged.

"Reg and I went out to Southern California for the Super Bowl," I said as Mike shook his head in disbelief.

The carousel started moving, and baggage began to spill out toward the 50 or so waiting passengers. I couldn't believe my eyes when I saw Jill walking toward us.

"Just leave it here. I'll take care of it," she said, handing the baggage attendant $20 after he took her bag off his cart. "Hey, Tom, what are you doing here?"

"We just flew in from sunny California," I blurted out, pointing toward Reggie.

Kelly, JR, and Scarlet were approaching fast, followed by a baggage attendant. The trio noticed Reggie right away and stopped their caravan to come over and greet us.

"Nice to see you again," Jill said, turning to Reggie.

JR extended his hand towards Reggie. "Hello, son, we're just in from San Jose. Congratulations on your playoff victory over the Cougars."

The baggage kept going around and around as I stood contemplating the probabilities of this chance meeting. Then the combination got even more bizarre; Mario walked over and tapped me on the back. "Yo, Tom, I had to drive Shirley to the airport. She kept insisting she could handle it, but, Homey, she was slurring her speech and wobbling around," Mario said. He winked toward Jill. "Hey dude, how were the California girls; did you and Reggie get to meet some movie stars?"

"Yeah, Charlie's Angels," I said.

"No shit?!" Mario replied.

"Just kidding," I said.

There I was, holding everyone's bag of secrets. Was I the pebble that would start us on a course of destruction? If so, then why me?

"Why don't you ride with us?" Mike asked, pointing toward my parents standing near the exit.

We all went our separate ways, but I couldn't help feeling that a meeting like this had to be more than just a coincidence. The odds against all of us arriving at the airport at the same time were just too great, and I felt a little spooked, seeing the holders of so many dangerous secrets in such close proximity to one another—Jill and JR, Kelly and Reggie, Jill and me, and Mario sitting like a cherry on top.

Thursday, February 10th, 1977

It's been a month of calculations and miscalculations. Even with my 148 IQ, I didn't foresee that losing my job also meant losing my income. I just wasn't thinking ahead. How stupid of me! Dave refuses to give me a good reference, and the last two jobs I applied for held it against me that I quit on Dave the way I did. So, I only have $12 in my bank account, and with the price of gasoline at an all-time high of 62 cents a gallon, plus cafeteria lunches, I'm guessing I've got about two weeks before I'm really desperate.

Mike left yesterday for his assignment in Nevada. Sharing a bedroom with Mike again placed a total damper on my sex life, so Reg is even further ahead of me. Reg 10, Tom 6. By the way, my number six was Jackie, a senior in my modern history class. Miss Wiseman paired us up for an assignment on Title IX. I drove her home after school so that we could work on the assignment. Both of her parents were still at work. People at school think that Jackie's a dork wasting her life in her room. How wrong they are!

We had just put our study materials away when Jackie said, "Hey, wanna have sex in my parents' room?" I should have known she was more than what first meets the eye by the way she played footsie with me under the kitchen table while we did our assignment.

"Really? I always thought you were a prude," I said. "I mean, you dress like it's the Forties."

"Tom, the way I dress at school is all a sham. I'll take an inch, but I love to take a mile, if you know what I mean," she said, leading me upstairs by the hand.

Jackie made all of my fantasy dreams come true, and we actually fell asleep in her parents' bed afterwards. I wish I could have watched the sun come up in her indigo blue eyes, but I awoke just in time to dash out the back door just as her mother came in the front door. I certainly misjudged Jackie. I wonder how many times she's played her Miss Innocent game on some unsuspecting fellow, but I'm sure she's won more times than she's lost.

When Jill called me, looking for Reg for the fifth time in three nights, I told my "secretary," Carol, to take a message. Carol has been dutifully answering my phone when I'm not at home, and she left me a message: "Jill called again." Jill wants Reg back, but we're too busy hustling and screwing, and Jill doesn't count towards his score.

Also, my father is pissed off at me again, but what else is new?

"Tom, you're going to drive me to smoking again," he said, when he heard about my third speeding ticket. "And another thing, no more tutoring the school girls in your bedroom. Tom, you've invited at least three different girls home for studying, but locking yourself in your bedroom looks bad. What do you think your sisters are thinking when they see this behavior?"

My father is right about one thing: There isn't much studying going on in my bedroom, but that doesn't mean I'm not learning much. I must say that it's a brilliant scheme. I take a girl home with me, and we go to my room under the guise of doing homework. We lock ourselves in and presto! Tom gets laid without having to spend money on drinks, a meal, a movie, and a motel room. It's the only way that I'm able to make any headway against Reg. Now that my father has gotten wise to my scheme, I don't know what I'm going to do.

Scoreboard: Reg 11, Tom 8.

Tuesday, March 15th , 1977

Get your motor runnin'
Head out on the highway
Lookin' for adventure
And whatever comes our way
Yeah Darlin' gonna make it happen
Take the world in a love embrace
Fire all of your guns at once
And explode into space

I like smoke and lightning
Heavy metal thunder
Racin' with the wind
And the feelin' that I'm under
Yeah Darlin' go make it happen
Take the world in a love embrace
Fire all of your guns at once
And explode into space
Like a true nature's child
We were born, born to be wild
We can climb so high
I never wanna die
Born to be wild

These lyrics from this Steppenwolf song are the best way to describe what's going on these days in the '70s. Every night there is something freaky and new going on. For the fourth morning in a row, Reg and I met the milkman on our way home as he was making his morning deliveries.

"Hey, aren't you guys still in school?" he joked, seeing us walking home at four in the morning.

In spite of our two nights of chasing pussy, Reg is still leading me in the hustle game, and he's lucky that I'm down to my last $1.26 or I'd be ahead of him by now after what I've learned about playing the game with the girls at school.

Carol said Jill has been trying to reach me again. I know what Jill wants—it's always about where Reg is these days. By the way, I saw Jill's Jaguar parked in the wrong part of town three nights ago. She didn't see me, but I wonder what she was doing there at that time of night. More secrets? Only time will tell.

Tuesday, March 22nd, 1977

Oh yes, they call him the streak
He likes to show off his physique
If there's an audience to be found
He'll be streakin' around.

It was supposed to be the greatest night of James' life. Every newspaper and television reporter within a hundred miles turned out to cover the playoff game between the Eagles and Dallas' undefeated Carter High team. James had "the best season for any single player in America," according to most basketball fans. Reporters said it was even better than the season of some red-haired teenager from the West Coast, by the name of Bill Walton. James averaged 32 points, 11 rebounds, and 10 assists per game, and as the star of our team he put on a good showing against the Carter team in the playoff game, but was upstaged by a disturbance at half-time.

The Channel 9 reporter said, "Pardon me, sir, did you see what happened?"

"Yeah, I did. At half-time, I was going to get some popcorn, and some kid came right out of the bleachers, running through the gymnasium without any clothes on," the man said.

"It was a streaker, naked as a jaybird; nothing but his PF flyers on," his wife added.

James was upset that, instead of his great performance making the headlines, the streaker got all the publicity. Abilene lost the game, but James' record breaking season will live on forever.

Jill finally caught up with Reg and me at the game. Reg ducked out on her, but I stopped to talk for a minute. I told her I'd try to set her and Reg back up again after she lent me a few bucks to fill my gas tank.

Homeboy, it's a mixed-up, shook-up world. Boys want to be girls, and girls want to be boys. James Smith, still madly in love with Jill, wants be a black dude. The poor guy wants her more than Reg ever did, but she still wants Reg. Reg wants a white girl, but not Jill, and Jill's not into white dudes. Me? I just want to find a new gig.

Perhaps Jill's signature line is true, after all—we all want what we can't have. Being broke sucks.

Friday, March 25th, 1977

My third speeding ticket in two months—$15! A fronted bag of weed from Jeff—$12! Homey, I was down to my last 26 cents, and somehow I wound up scoring a new job; isn't life unpredictable? Mario's uncle hired me as a driver. I start this weekend over spring break. He said he'd fill me in on the details tomorrow. Tom Jones of all people, with my three speeding tickets, gets a job driving.

Catch U up later.

Thursday, April 14th, 1977

"Son, I'm not trying to be nosey, but I couldn't help noticing that your wallet is stuffed to the brim with cash. There must be over $400 in there," my father said, standing at the foot of my bed, looking concerned, waking me up in the middle of the afternoon.

"I haven't had the time to take it to the bank yet," I said as he ran his fingers over my wallet over and over again.

"Tom, I'm a driver, too, and I don't make anything like that kind of money. What kind of driving job pays like that?" my father asked.

"Dad, don't worry—it's all legitimate." I said, rolling over and pulling the covers over my head.

After his retirement in December, my father got a job working for the mobile library system, a pilot program set up by the city in conjunction with the school system to take books into neighborhoods that normally don't utilize all that the library has to offer.

I, on the other hand, landed a job smuggling wet-backs across the border. At $25 a head times eight trips to the Mexican border, this job is everything I could ever want in a gig. Once I start back to school tomorrow, I'll only be able to work weekends. And the job pays cash. I drive from Abilene to Del Rio, which is just across the Mexican border, and meet a man named Pancho at a small motel, where he loads Mexicans into the trunk of my car. After about an hour, I take off for Abilene. In Abilene, I pull into a small motel on the outskirts of town, where another man, Lefty, unloads the trunk and pays me $25 for each Mexican. The first time I drove down to the border, I thought it was some kind of setup, but when Lefty put $100 in my hand, I knew it was for real. How much easier can a job be?

We had 10 days off for spring break, and I drove down to the border eight times. It's funny how the pebble syndrome works. That one small bag I scored for Mario led me to this job. The worst part of the job came on my last run. My 8-track player broke, and all I could get on the radio from San Angelo to Del Rio was country music. Brother, you want to talk about Willie Nelson and Waylon Jennings? I now know all the latest country hicks. I listened to everything from Mary MacGregor's

"Torn Between Two Lovers" to Willie Nelson's "Blue Eyes Crying in the Rain." Country music isn't so bad once you get past the twang. I only wish the stations wouldn't play the same damn songs over and over.

I'll probably trade in my Chevelle for a car with a bigger trunk. The way I see it, a bigger trunk means more money. All this driving does have its drawbacks, though. I've been so busy on the road that Reg has pulled further ahead of me in the hustle game. Reg 12, Tom 8. While I was away, Reg didn't have any transportation, so he borrowed Jill's Jaguar to score with some bimbos, and rumor has it that he had a little fender bender. I'll get the details when I bump in to him, and will fill you in. I've got to run. My secretary says Jill is on the phone.

Catch U up later.

Thursday, April 21st, 1977

You find out a lot about people when the pressure is on. Tonight, Reg and I were dropping Jill and my date, Monica, off at Jill's house after they had snuck out to meet us at Reg's house, when we were ambushed.

"Watch out! That's Daddy in the bushes!" Jill screamed from the back seat of my car as we were kissing the girls goodnight.

Two shots rang out as J.R. attacked from the bushes. I don't know how I managed to miss the cars parked along the street, but we all escaped unscathed. I floored

the engine and managed to get us back to Bowie Street.
I parked in front of James' house, and the four of us ran
in a panic. Reg, that bastard, headed straight for his
house, leaving me with two terrified girls. I slipped them
into my room, where we now sit, waiting for the worst.
Jill is in the corner, pulling out a tie rag from her purse
and a bag of God knows what. Monica is staring at me
writing, and I'm scribbling as fast as I can, just in case I
never live to write another day. Holy shit! Jill's got a
syringe and she's fixing something. Now she's shooting
something into her arm. Wow, this is the first time I've
ever seen anyone voluntarily stick a needle in their arm.

"Tom, what the fuck are you doing writing? J.R. will
be here looking for us any minute now!" Jill urgently
screams in a loud whisper as I record every word coming
from her mouth. Homey, I'm scared, but all I know to
do to comfort myself is to write. Now, Monica is silently
sobbing. I just hope she doesn't get any louder; my parents are asleep not more than 30 feet away.

Jill just stood up and drew the curtain back to peek
outside.

"J.R.'s Cadillac is out there. I can see his rifle hanging
out of the car window. What are we going to do?!" she
whined.

"Tom, what is so important for you to be writing at a
time like this?" Jill shouted. "Get away from the desk and
put your damn diary away! My father could discover any
minute now that we're tucked away in this room!"

Where the fuck is Reg when you need him the most?

Friday, April 22nd, 1977

"Tom, there is a redhead crying at our front
door who says that her sister is here,"
my father said from the other side of my
door the morning after J.R. shot at us.

Parking my car in front of James' house turned out to be a stroke of genius. J.R. eventually left, unsure of which house we were in.

"Tom, there is a redhead crying at our front door who says that her sister is here," my father said from the other side of my door the morning after J.R. shot at us. To my father's surprise upon opening the door, Jill and Monica appeared behind me. "Tom, what's going on in here?"

"Dad, it's going to take a while to explain," I said. "A redhead at the door?"

"That must be Tracy," Jill said of her sister.

The last time I'd seen a picture of Tracy was two years ago on the I.D. Jill had used for her first abortion—and Tracy wasn't a redhead in that photo. My father first looked puzzled, then just stared blankly at me.

"It's my sister," Jill said with a sigh of relief. Tracy took Monica and Jill home, and I was left to struggle through a morning that seemed to last the whole day. By evening, though, things had cooled off a little, though coals still smoldered between my father and me.

It's that damn pebble syndrome again. The fender bender Reg had in Jill's car proved unlucky for us all. Tracy said the tow truck driver found Reg's wallet in her car and gave it to J.R. That wallet nearly cost four people their lives.

Reg finally showed up today, after all the action was long over. He was astounded that I wrote in my diary while J.R. was hunting us down, but I told him that writing is very therapeutic. Reg also couldn't believe he was idiot enough to leave his wallet in Jill's car. He said he never has any money in it, so he never missed having it.

Lived to tell!

Sunday, May 1st, 1977

In my wildest dreams, it never occurred to me that I wouldn't be living on the Bowie block. But here I sit, writing in my diary for the first time in my new place. I share this three-bedroom apartment with two other guys, Rick and Slick. My father suddenly and unexpectedly kicked me out of the house. I thought the whole bizarre situation with Jill and Monica had blown over, because it had been a week since the incident, and, as far as I was concerned, it was just another day in the life of a teenager. I was dead wrong!

I was sitting at our kitchen table on a Monday morning before heading to school. I hadn't seen my father all weekend because I had made another run to the border. When he came into the kitchen to start the coffee, I was so engaged in reading the newspaper that I hadn't realized he was standing over me.

The article that had caught my eye read: "Local Sambo's manager and three others suing Sambo's for breaching their retirement contracts." I scanned the article for my old boss' name, and there it was on line three. "Dave Cognomi is one of three managers still eligible for the retirement program suing Sambo's, Inc. for his promised pensions. 'It's a numbers game, and when only three of the 812 people who started with the company remain to the end, it says a lot about what's going on,' Cognomi said."

"Tom, you're not welcome here anymore," my father said quietly. "Your mother and I discussed the matter over the weekend when you were away on your so-called driving route. We considered changing the locks while you were away, but instead we're giving you until four this afternoon to get your stuff and go."

I took one look at him and knew he was serious. It was the end of the road for me at the Bowie residence. Spooky, Smoothy and Swagger convened for a quick conference. Spooky spoke first: "Tom, that's an impossible deadline; what are you going to do now?"

Smoothy said, "Life comes at you point blank. Try not to look so frightened."

Trying to buy some time, I said, "But, Dad, I'm a minor for another month. By law, you have to take care of me until I'm eighteen."

With his fist clenched and his eyes rolling back in his

head, he said, "Tom, it's today by four o'clock. Your shit needs to be gone!" Then he walked away.

The classified section was lying on the kitchen table, and I immediately turned to the "roommates wanted" heading. There were only four entries that fit my requirements, and, like any teenage boy with eight hours to find another place to live, I played eenie meenie minie moe and landed on an ad that read: "Two cool dudes, seeking a third to share expenses." I knew the vicinity of the address, so I ditched my classes and drove over. Cash is always king, and by high noon, I was the third resident in this three-bedroom apartment on Grape Street.

I was nervous when I came home to pack. I knocked at the door and my mother let me in. I thought nothing could feel stranger than knocking on my own door, but I was wrong. When I was looking in my parents' closet for my insurance card, I found a life-insurance policy that had been taken out in my name only a month ago. Are there more secrets, or do my parents know something that I don't?

Saturday, May 28th, 1977

At first I was a little disturbed by my parents' absence at my graduation, but then it dawned on me that I hadn't invited them. I had been so busy playing the hustle game that I hadn't sent out invitations. Miss Wiseman said that I could easily have been valedictorian if I had applied myself. Big freaking deal; what's that worth in the real world?

Laurie graduated, too. I ran into her after the ceremony.

"Hey, Tom. Where've you been?"

"Well, I guess you've heard by now that my parents kicked me out, so I haven't been in the neighborhood much," I said. "So, our 12-year prison term is finally over, huh?"

"I guess. I only have a few months' reprieve before I start a four-year term in the fall at Murray," she said, smiling.

"You're going to college? I thought only husband hunters did that, and you've already got Jeff. Or are you looking for someone else?" I joked.

"Come on. Things have really changed. Since Title IX, we can even get sports scholarships. I'm going to be a counselor. When I finish, I think I'd like to work with teens," she said. "What are you going to do with your future, now that you know that you have one?"

"I already told you; I'm going to be Reg's agent."

"You can't be serious! You're going to bet your entire life on that asshole quarterback? Do you at least have a plan B?"

"I won't need one. This is a sure thing. I mean, you've heard all of the predictions. Everyone's saying he's good enough to go pro right out of high school," I said defensively. "And I don't need four more years of being told what to think by a bunch of liars."

"Well, good luck. I guess I'll see you when you come around to see Reggie," she said, walking away toward Jeff.

Most all the boys from the Bowie block came to my graduation. I had to break the news to James about Jill being forced into a rehab in Dallas by her father. I guess I'm glad for Jill's sake that she's there. Like Curtis Mayfield said, "If you want to be a junkie, wow."

My new roommates, Rick and Slick, are pretty cool, and they both consider me like a baby brother. We have huge plans for my eighteenth birthday in two weeks. Having my own room and the freedom to pursue whatever honey the bee can catch has allowed me to inch closer to Reg in the hustle game. Reg 14, Tom 11.

Later!

Part VI
AT EIGHTEEN
Days of Our Lives

Saturday, June 11th, 1977

The people in the Stone Age were around three thousand years before they thought to invent the wheel, but it only took Reg and me an hour to get dressed and behind the wheel of the Skunk, and off to the disco club on my birthday. Reg read the yearly outlook for Gemini for June 10th while I raced my car between traffic lights:

> *You're almost there, so do what it takes to keep your focus. If you find your energy flagging, hand the baton to your partner and let him or her carry the weight for a while. Soon you'll be back in the game. Your secrets should stay secret for a long time.*
>
> *This is the year to keep your cool about whatever occurs; you will be challenged this year. You might learn something, whether or not you end up on the right side.*

You're almost there? My horoscope was wrong, baby; Reg and I were there. The lights, the sounds, and the ladies—my first experience at the discothèque was all I imagined it would be. The DJ played "Disco Lady" by Jonnie Taylor, "Disco Queen" by Hot Chocolate, and "Disco Inferno" by the Tramps. *Burn baby burn! Burn baby burn!*

Reg wore bell bottoms with a butterfly flower-collared shirt looking like Billy Dee Williams. I was decked out in my Flagg Brothers polyester pants with an imitation leather jacket and three-inch Cuban heels. A foxy sista sitting near our table even referred to me as "Kid Dynamite," as in JJ, the character on *Good Times*. My new roommates bought me drinks all night to celebrate my new legal status. Slick called me a virgin because it was my first time in an adult club. But, like Reg told him, "Tom hasn't been a virgin at anything since he found out that age is just a number."

The adults at the discothèque call the hustle game "the one-night stand," but Reg and I still like to call it "the hustle." "One-night stand," "the hustle"—what's in a name, as long as you're getting laid, right?

"Baby, can I buy you a drink? What's your sign?" Homey, I tell you it was literally that easy. "Baby, you've got a fat wallet; what do you do for a living?" the foxy mama said as I purchased us drinks.

Homey, I ended up picking up this 32-year-old woman, Desiree. I bought us breakfast at Sambo's at 3 a.m., and then we came back to my pad and danced under the sheets until nearly dawn. Desiree swore that I became a man in her arms, but what she doesn't know won't hurt her. Reg 14, Tom 12.

Thursday, June 30th, 1977

Who's the prize, and who's the game? Some of the females don't seem to have it right around here. I've recently bumped into a few ladies who are twisted enough to think that they're the prize and guys are the game. The girls in the United States could take a lesson from Geetha and the other Indian girls who know enough to see that they're lucky to have a man. "Let me have your phone number," I said to this 18-year-old bimbo, Vicky, at the discothèque the other night. Vicky and I had just boogied to five songs on the dance floor, and we were headed to the bar for another round.

"No, Tom, you give me your phone number, and I might call you," she said to my surprise.

"Are you jivin' me?" I responded.

I was the one buying drinks all night long, and she had the nerve to suggest that she might call me. As it turned out, last call for alcohol saw her with another vodka and tonic in her hand on my tab. You know the drill, Homey. Vicky didn't have to use my telephone number after all, because we ended up side by side in my bed before morning. With the morning came hints and comments from Vicky that I owed her a ride home for the good time that she had shown me the night before. Finally, I gave in and drove her to her apartment.

My 8-track tape player was still on the blink, so Vicky and I couldn't listen to her "Hotel California" tape.

"Tom, the damn 8-track player in this piece-of-shit car doesn't work," Vicky said, scowling.

To shut Vicky's annoying mouth up, I started scanning the FM stations in hopes of finding something she could jam to without bitching. I pulled the Skunk into the last-chance Texaco station.

"How much?" the attendant asked.

"Fill it up, and please check the oil. I have a long trip ahead," I said.

"Where the hell are you going?" Vicky asked, as if she had a right to know.

"If you have to know, I'm headed for Mexico as soon as I drop you off," I said.

"Who do you know in Mexico?" she asked.

"It's business, baby," I told her.

Vicky and I were listening to the Top 40 countdown while the attendant wiped the windows and messed around under the hood of my car.

"And the number one song in the land is 'Got to Give It Up' by Marvin Gaye," Casey Kasem announced.

"Last week the number one song was 'Dreams' by Fleetwood Mac," Vicky said, turning up the radio to hear the Marvin Gaye tune that was starting to play.

"The week before that, the number one song was 'Torn Between Two Lovers' by Mary MacGregor," I said, turning the volume down so I could hear the attendant.

"That will be $8.35, and your oil is fine, Mister," he said, poking his head in the car window.

One week, a disco song, the next a song by a rock group, and then a country song hits number one in America. The multiple styles blending in today's music is evident if you watch the music charts.

I pulled my car into Vicky's apartment complex. "Tom, I'd like to go to Mexico one day," she said, opening the car door.

I was in a hurry to leave her, so I scribbled my telephone number on a piece of paper from the floor of my car.

Handing it to her, I said, "Vicky, don't lose my number." Then I spun off, squealing my tires. Like Casey Kasem says, "Let's keep countin' 'em down." Vicky is lucky number 13.

Later, gator!

Friday, July 15th, 1977

I really thought the end of the world had come and gone without my noticing. I had just gotten back to Abilene when Rick tossed the newspaper on my bed. The headline read: "New York City Blackout!" The article reported that the blackouts were the lowest point in New York City's history. If you ask me, with New York City's financial crisis, a killer on the loose, over 1700 stores looted, and over 1100 fires still burning, the city might as well stay black.

Two other articles grabbed my attention. An article in the sports section read: "Tracy Austin becomes the youngest tennis player to ever win a professional tournament capturing the title in Portland, Oregon at 14 years, 28 days old." The second article read:

He started talking and reading when he was just 9 months old. He finished elementary school at 6 years old. He made the jump to college at age 10. And, by age 15, Wayne Dyer was earning a bachelor's degree in applied mathematics from Cal Berkley—the youngest in U.S. history to do so. Dyer, with an unlimited future ahead of him, is four days short of his 18th birthday and has been hired as the newest professor at the University of California.

If Tracy Austin and Wayne Dyer can make names for themselves as teenagers, I can be Reg's agent at the ripe old age of 18. Teens are getting the job done younger and younger all the time. Homey, let the world end tomorrow; we're going for what we want today.

Homey, this is the diary of the lost teenage.

Thursday, July 28th, 1977

The yearly horoscope Reg read to me on my birthday did warn me about challenges and not necessarily being on the right side.

"Collateral damage!" I heard Uncle Frank use this term to describe causalties in Vietnam. I overheard him once talking to Laurie's dad.

"Fred, carpet bombing produced lots of collateral damage, and I hope your son wasn't part of it," he said just before the tree house fiasco.

Homey, they were collateral damage, and I did shed a tear for them, but real life doesn't always turn out fine. It started out innocently enough—just another trip to the Mexican border like so many before. I had traded in my Super Sport for a late model Buick Electra 225 with a larger trunk, and Pam, a nice caramel-colored girl, decided she wanted to see Mexico during her summer break.

"What will your parents think if you're gone for an entire weekend?" I asked over the telephone as we made plans for our trip to Mexico.

"Both of my parents are in jail for drug related charges. They got busted two years ago. Now I live with my grandmother," she replied.

So, off we went to Mexico for the weekend. From the day we met a week ago, we got along as well as I've ever gotten along with any woman since Jill Andersen.

"Tom, let's just relax and be glad for this time together," Pam reminded me. I was so into her that I felt like I was losing myself.

We went a day early and stayed in the motel where I normally pick up my cargo so that we could have a little one-on-one fun. We did things to each other in that motel room that we would never confess to. Pam did more than I expected from a seventeen-year-old. It was my first blow job, but I didn't admit that to her; I just pretended I knew what to expect.

Homey, I could honestly talk to Pam, just like I'm writing in this diary, without reservation. The first night in Mexico, we sat outside sipping warm Mexican beer and watching people cross over into the United States.

"Why don't Mexicans like living in their own country?" Pam asked as I sipped my sixth beer.

"I hear it's the crooked Mexican government that drives them across the border," I said, and then I walked up and started kissing her as if I'd known her all my life. A Mexican boy with two little girls trailing behind him brought us the meal from the motel restaurant.

"Why do they keep having so many babies, though?" Pam asked.

I had to think for quite a while before answering. "Well, it's got to be because of the Catholic Church. They don't understand about birth control."

"What do you mean they don't understand birth control?" Pam questioned.

"Well, I've been down here several times. Most Mexicans are Catholic, and the Catholic Church has banned the use of birth control. If they weren't having so damn many babies, they wouldn't have to cross the border to take care of them. They don't even realize that the Pope isn't mentioned in the Bible, but they obey whatever he says."

I never thought about it until she asked the question, and the answer that came out of my mouth made more sense than any explanation I'd ever heard from an adult.

I didn't tell Pam about the scheme until the wetbacks got in the trunk.

"Tom, you're kidding. These people are going to ride all the way back to Abilene in the trunk of your car?" she demanded.

They say you're only as sick as your secrets, so, Homey, I'm leaving you the sickest secret I've ever written on the pages of my diary.

"Breaker 1-9, do you copy? That's a big 10-4, good buddy," I heard from my CB radio, as we re-entered the United States. I remember this distinctly, because the static made the wetbacks jerk around in my trunk. Three hours later, I walked back from checking on their condition at Pam's request. I have no idea how I pretended that everything was o.k. as I climbed back in next to Pam. I discovered the bodies just after we crossed into the Brownwood city limits. How long can this secret hold? It was an accident. I have no idea how they suffocated, but Pam and I had the music playing so loudly that we never heard their cries for help. I just keep telling myself that they were collateral damage.

"Sometimes I think it's a sin, when I feel like I'm winning when I'm losing again."

Sunday, August 14th, 1977

My insurance agent called to tell me that the Texas Highway Patrol found my burned out Buick on County Line Road 31 outside of Brownwood. The charred bodies of five people were found in the trunk of my "stolen" vehicle. My agent said a check would not be issued until next week, after a complete investigation. He apologized for my loss. My father called me right after I hung up the telephone. He's not buying my stolen-car alibi, but, hey, he'll have to remain suspicious. Diary, you and I will take this secret to our graves.

I made over $2600 in two and a half months, but I'd consider it a victory if I never see Mexico again, and if the highway patrolman doesn't ask me any more questions.

Homey, I should burn this diary right now, but my horoscope for the year assured me that though there would be challenges, my secrets would be kept for a long time to come. Without this writing outlet, I would have nowhere to go. I can't tell Reg about this, and Pam would die if she caught one whiff of what she was involved in.

Slick pounded at my bedroom door.

"Tom, that song has been playing on your turntable all day. Is everything o.k.?" he asked.

Same old song
Just a drop of water in an endless sea
All we do
Crumbles to the ground, though we refuse to see
Dust in the wind
All we are is dust in the wind.

"Dust in the Wind" by Kansas had been playing since Slick left for work, and it was still playing when he came home a few minutes ago. He also said Pam had called twice.

Although I haven't been behind the wheel of that Buick Electra 225 for over two weeks, I can still see their faces as I lifted the trunk lid, but then my mind instantly turns away. The heavy smell of gasoline fills my bedroom, and just as the match strikes to light the Buick on fire, the image fades away like dust in the wind. Sometimes this scenario plays in my mind 300 times a day. Swagger, the only voice left in my head these days, just keeps repeating, "Collateral damage." I now know why Uncle Frank drinks.

Wednesday, September 14th, 1977

"You've gone from driving a bomb-ass Super Sport to a Buick deuce and a quarter, and now this rice rocket?" Jeff said when we bumped into one another in the parking lot of the new liquor store. "Tom, how long have you had this?" he asked, examining my Toyota Corona.

"Not too long," I said.

"Laurie said she saw you studying at the Murray Library the other day."

"Yeah, I spend quite a few of my days there, studying up on how to be a sports agent," I told him.

"Laurie likes it there, I guess. She said she hopes to be the first woman to earn a bachelors in counseling from there. So, you still plan on being Reggie's agent?" he said, offering me a cold Lone Star from his six-pack. I opened my beer and clinked his bottle neck in salute. "You know, Tom, the Bowie block just isn't the same since you left. Another Mexican family moved in down the street." He set his cold bottle on the hot hood of my car. "So, what convinced you to buy this Jap Trap?"

"The salesman told me it gets over 20 miles per gallon," I said, shrugging.

"With gas prices going up, I guess you probably made a good decision," Jeff agreed.

"I don't drive as much as I used to, and spend most of my time at the library doing research. With Reggie off to another spectacular season, it won't be long before my hard work pays off."

Offering me another beer, Jeff said, "By the way, Mario thinks you're trying to avoid him. He also said to tell you that Lefty wants to see you."

The mention of Lefty sent my mind into a tailspin. Spooky said, "They've found out." Smoothy said, "Play it cool here. They know nothing; Jeff is just a messenger." Then, the heavy smell of gasoline filled my senses, and my mind went blank.

"I'm almost certain that Reg will make the jump from high school quarterback straight to the NFL draft in June," I said to Jeff, who was looking at me strangely.

"Are you all right?" he asked.

"Collateral damage is all. I'll take another beer for the road," I mumbled, reaching for the last one.

"Damn, Tom, you've had four beers to my one," Jeff said, surprised. "Maybe you ought to slow down," he said, surrendering it.

Whether you carpet bombed Vietnam or accidentally killed five Mexicans, alcohol becomes a good friend.

Wednesday, September 28th, 1977

Today is the day of the emergent man. Reg called my new private line at the apartment.

"Yo, Tom, where the fuck have you been?" Reg demanded.

"I've been lying low—just hanging around the crib," I mumbled.

"Well, are you getting any? Don't forget our bet," he joked. "I haven't seen your ass in two weeks. Why don't you come out to the pep rally Friday morning?" he suggested.

"Yeah, I'll try," I said. "Catch you later."

"O.k., Pee. Don't forget Friday," he said, hanging up.

It took that call from Reg for me to realize that I hadn't taken a sober breath in weeks.

I looked around at the dirty clothes tossed about my bedroom floor, and in that moment decided to clean up my life. By day's end, I had neatly stacked my clothes in the corner. On Friday morning, I washed away the vodka smell on my breath with Slick's Listerine, and set off for the pep rally. Reg met me in the parking lot.

"Take a look at that, Bro," Reg greeted me, pointing to a brand new, red Pontiac Firebird Trans Am. "Ruben Patterson—that sports agent from California—gave my mama the keys last night."

Seeing the new Firebird, I knew I needed to act. Ruben Patterson was trying to steal my dream, but I was ready. Some might call me a fool and say my dream is just another crazy teenage fantasy, but this one is for real. I've invested my whole future in this dream, and I'll make it come true no matter what lines I've got to cross.

Tuesday, October 18th, 1977

In a noisy discothèque, I spotted her tight mini-skirt hugging her thighs. I beckoned her off the dance floor with my index finger.

"That mini-skirt would look great crumpled up on my bedroom floor," I whispered in her ear.

That was all it took. The morning after found us sorting out our clothes from a pile on the floor. She brought me heaven, and although I should be sorry she'll only be remembered as my number 14, I'm not. Tom is back in the game, and only one chick behind Reg in the hustle game.

Later, Diary!

Friday, November 11th, 1977

When I think back on all the crap
I learned in high school
It's a wonder I can think at all.

Reg had a brilliant idea, so we drove the Firebird to Billy Bob's house to show off his new wheels. Shirley was there hanging out, and the four of us played a few friendly rounds of Blackjack. Now, Abilene has a reputation for having so-called gangsters, but Big Billy Bob Williams is well-known as the town's card hustler. As lady luck would have it, I won the first six hands. Shirley dealt the seventh, and right away I got the ace-10 combination, giving me the win. As the song says, "You've got to know when to hold 'em, know when to fold 'em, know when to walk away, and know when to run."

Pow! Pow! was all that I heard behind me as I rolled through the screen door onto the back porch, as two bullets from Billy Bob's 38 snub-nose rang out behind me.

You don't realize that you've been shot at until you're running at top speed down an open stretch of road with only the wind chasing you. It was about more than just losing to an 18-year-old kid. With each losing hand, Shirley egged Billy Bob on, further agitating an already intoxicated man. That makes four shots fired at me—two by J.R. and two by Billy Bob. There's only one way to read the situation positively: At least neither of them is a good shot, or I'd be dead by now.

Friday, November 18th, 1977

She was a fast machine
She kept her motor clean
She was the best damn woman I had ever seen
She had the sightless eyes

Telling me no lies
Knockin' me out with those American thighs
Taking more than her share
Had me fighting for air
She told me to come but I was already there

Diary, my #15 shook me all night long!
Later.

Friday, November 25th, 1977

And the band sang, "If you believe in forever, then life is just a one-night stand."

There was a keg party in celebration of the Eagles' 41 – 10 victory over the Odessa Permian team out in the sticks, with a local band playing cover songs from the Sixties and Seventies. The band was rocking, and Reg and I were singing along to the Righteous Brothers song, *Rock and Roll Heaven.*

Cindy and Mindy Sooner, a pair of famously promiscuous 19-year-old twins, found themselves stuck in the middle of the dirt floor, dancing with Reg and me at the end of the night. Homey, I don't know how they found out about this party, which was 30 miles from town in a wooded hideaway. There were at least 50 vehicles gathered around the huge bonfire. In the end, Reg wound up with Cindy in the front, and I ended up with Mindy in the back seat of the Firebird. About an hour later, I went to the front seat with Cindy and Reg got in the back with her sister. It was a first for all of us, and boy what fun we all had! Reggie scored his 17 and 18, and I scored my 16 and 17. Oh, what a night to remember in November!

"Thanks, Mr. and Mrs. Sooner! You've got two lovely daughters."

Later!

Monday, December 12th, 1977

Like sands through the hour glass, so are the days of our lives.

"Hello, this is Mrs. Shirley Thomas—Reggie's mother. Reggie's a little sore after last weekend's game, so please excuse him from classes today," I said, mimicking Shirley's voice.

"Will he be well enough for afternoon practice?" the secretary asked. "You know, Mrs. Thomas, a hot bath with some Epsom salts works wonders."

Reg and I were giggling silently at the other end of the phone.

I collected myself enough to say: "Thanks for that wonderful advice. I'll make sure he follows it, and we'll have him suited up by the end of the day."

"There are only three more games until we're the state champions. We're so proud of that boy. Tell him I hope he feels better," the secretary said before the line went dead.

I looked at Reggie beside me at the kitchen table, pouring himself an enormous bowl of cereal.

"Remember the time I deliberately cut school classes for about forty days? I was a practicing Jehovah's Witness waiting for the end to come. Thanks, Pee; I owe you one for saving me from that god awful cult. If I had known it would be so easy to cut classes, I would have cut more school classes years ago," I told him.

Monday morning brought a variety of firsts for Reg and me. Reg had never missed a game, and he had certainly never played hooky from Monday morning practice. Monday morning quarterbacking is a Texas tradition. Showing up for the analysis of Friday's game is just as important as winning. But there he was, watching me roll a joint while he ate his cereal.

"Thanks for covering my ass today. We must have been out until past four this morning," he said, looking at the clock. "Damn, is that clock right? 10:05? I guess I slept longer than I thought." Taking a toke for the first time in his life, Reg said, "I've never understood what the big deal is about smoking this stuff."

"Hey, brother, be careful. That's fine Columbian you're smoking," I told him, chuckling as he coughed.

"After that victory over Permian, a brother should be able to enjoy some time off. Tom, to tell the truth, I'm glad there're only three more games," he said, smiling and starting to relax. "I believe in my heart of hearts we'll win this time. If I could just bring Abilene a state title this year, the weight of the world would be lifted off my shoulders. No one knows what it's like to have the knee-buckling pressure of being the starting quarterback of the team picked to win every year." Slumping further into his chair, he said, "*Days of Our Lives* is on Channel 9 at eleven. Change the channel, so I can catch up on my soap."

The telephone in the kitchen rang while we were still sitting at the table. Paranoia is hell. Reg and I looked at one another to see which of us had the balls to answer the ringing phone.

"Joe's Pool Hall, may I help you?" I said after finally picking it up.

"Joe's Pool Hall! I must have dialed the wrong number," a familiar voice said.

"Hey, don't hang up, Slick!" I yelled.

"Why the hell did you answer the telephone like that?" he asked.

"We thought it might be the high school calling back to check on Reg," I said.

"You guys are over there getting stoned, aren't you?"

"How could you tell?" I asked.

"Because if you weren't stoned, you'd realize that the school would call Reggie's house to check on him," he said, laughing. He started singing: "*They'll stone you when you're at the breakfast table. They'll stone you when you're young and able. I would not feel so all alone. Everybody must get stoned.*"

The box of cereal was empty, and Reg was searching the cabinets for more, but all I could think about was whether or not the school would call Shirley. Reg grabbed the new box of Frosted Flakes.

"Damn, I'm suddenly hungry as hell!" he said.

Placing the receiver against Reg's ear, I said, "Listen to this nigger," letting him listen to Slick's singing. I sparked the half-smoked joint back up and took a toke before handing it to Reg.

"Like sands through the hour glass, so are the days of our lives," said the voice on the television as the soap opera began.

Thursday, December 22nd, 1977

Oh, very young what will you leave us this time?
You're only dancing on this earth for a short while

Everything changes so fast these days. I was at the pep rally, and at intermission I decided to roam the old halls. I wandered toward my old restroom and found myself in my old favorite stall. Four years ago, the walls were covered with things like, "niggers stink" and "I hate peckerwoods." Now, the walls read: "For a great blow job call Jenny at 867-5309," "For a good time, Leach Leggett leaves her bedroom window open all the time," and "Mary Ann fucks on the first date." It seems like our generation has gone from focusing on race to focusing on sex overnight. I guess I've been too busy on the sexual end of the spectrum to notice. It suddenly dawned on me that there haven't been any race riots

---

The makeup and the grown-up clothes—it
seems they start younger every day.
Even Wendy seems to be pretty young to
be looking for that kind of fun. But, just
like all the liberal young misses, she wanted
a boy with a bad reputation.

---

since my freshman year. Somehow, all of that anger has been redirected to more enjoyable activities.

Oh very young, what will you leave us this time?

If Reg thinks that he's feeling the pressure to win the state championship, just wait until he hears that we're tied in the hustle game. At the pep rally, I bumped into Teri Hunt's sister, Wendy. Remember the sheriff's daughter with the red Mustang who Reggie dated? Remember the time Teri and I drove up just as Reggie was pulling Wendy's pants down? That's her! She's sixteen now, but who can tell just how old they are these days? The makeup and the grown-up clothes—it seems they start younger every day. Even Wendy seems to be pretty young to be looking for that kind of fun. But, just like all the liberal young misses, she wanted a boy with a bad reputation.

"Hey, big boy, don't I know you from somewhere?" she said, pouting with her red glossy lips as I passed her in the hall.

"Hey! Little Wendy, is that you?" I responded.

"No one calls me 'Little Wendy' anymore," she said, rolling her eyes.

She and her prep girl friend were loitering in the hall, commenting on what the other girls were wearing.

"You got a car?" Wendy asked, as if she didn't really care. "I can skip homeroom, and we can split," she said, adjusting her mini-skirt. Wendy just happened to be looking for a little adult education, and Professor Tom obliged her with a private tutoring session back at the apartment.

Believe it or not, this is now life in high school. In the old days, Reggie's motto was, "Eight to eighty, blind, crippled, or crazy." These days the motto should be, "Find 'em, finger 'em, fuck 'em, and forget 'em." I can't wait to tell Reg that I scored a piece of something he never had.

Scoreboard: Tom 18, Reggie 18.

Saturday, December 31st, 1977

Camera one closed in on CBS's Barbara Waters, and the CBS news soundtrack began to play in the background. Barbara Waters spoke:

We begin tonight's newscast with a story out of Abilene, Texas. Nineteen-year-old football phenomenon, Reggie Thomas, was arrested 24 hours ago, just before the Texas State high school championship game. Before what was supposed to be his final high school game, Thomas was arrested on a child-molestation charge. The charges were filed when deputies discovered blood-stained panties in the Firebird Thomas was driving. A fourteen-year-old girl claimed she'd been picked up by Thomas and forced to have sex with him. Reggie Thomas' life of young fame and fortune is in serious jeopardy as police and authorities struggle to determine what other charges will be pursued against the star quarter-back. NFL scouts were already talking about Thomas. He may be the only high school quarterback ever considered for the NFL draft. In other news ....

Wow! Reggie's number 19 may end up costing him 20 years, and me, my dream of becoming the youngest sports agent in history.

Sunday, January 15th, 1978

The week that was!

Saturday January 7th

"Hi, I'm Mr. Right. Someone said you were looking for me," I told the stranger leaving the dance floor. "'Love So Right' by the Bee Gee's—a nice slow jam. May I have this dance?" I begged as she tried to claim her seat at the crowded bar.

"Tom!" replied a familiar voice. "I'm Mr. Right? That's original."

"Miss Wiseman, I've never seen you here," I said as we stood stunned to see each other outside of our normal venue.

"It's Fanny, Tom, now that you've graduated," she said, extending her hand towards me.

"Fanny, I would be honored if I could have this dance," I said, leading her onto the dark dance floor.

"'Hi, I'm Mr. Right? Someone said you were looking for me?' You must have stolen that line from *Looking for Mr. Goodbar*," she whispered, laughing.

She held me tight as we danced in the dark in a room full of strangers. Later, I thought I'd found heaven in her arms. But in the morning when I woke up, she was gone.

Sunday, January 8th

Come out Regina, don't let me wait, you Catholic girls start much too late. But sooner or later, it'll come down to debate, and a Protestant girl might as well be the one.

Regina, they showed you a statue and told you to pray—they built you a temple so you could keep me away, but they never told you about the price you would pay, for the things that we might as well have done.

She had on a nice white dress at a party on her confirmation. Regina counted on me when she was chanting on her rosary. Regina showed me the sign and I send her the signal later in the evening and Regina bought the entire line.

Some say there's a hell for those who won't wait and others say its better at heaven's gate, Regina and I both re-

alize we'd rather laugh with the sinners than cry with the saints, because the sinners are much more fun.

<u>Monday, January 9th</u>

It's late in the evening, and Lola's wondering what clothes to wear. She puts on her make-up and brushes her long blonde hair. And then she asks me, "Do I look alright?" And I say, "Yes, you look wonderful tonight."

I tried to give her consolation when my friend, her ex-husband let her down. But like a fool I think I may be in love with her too soon.

What do you do when your mind starts to tell you that you're truly getting lonely and an ex-friend's old lady is going to be waiting by your side? Have I been running and hiding much too long, or is this empty feeling just my foolish pride? We made the best of the situation just before Lola drove me insane. That Lola, she had me on my knees, she suddenly had me begging her please.

There was nothing wrong with me wanting Lola to just stay in with me, but if you want to hang out you've got to take her out.

We go to a mutual friend's party and everyone stops to stare at this unexpected couple walking around the air. Too many drinks and I've got an aching head. It's time for me to go home now, so Lola takes away my car keys and helps a friend of mine send me off to bed. As she turned out my lights, I can faintly hear her say, "My darling, you were wonderful tonight."

Tuesday, January 10th

Although I've patronized the same Safeway near my apartment several times, this Tuesday was the first time I've seen Ruby. She was standing in front of me in the express lane, lost on how to use the new scanners. "Nothing ventured, nothing gained," they say, so I decided to help her. In return, she made me dinner at my house and offered herself as desert, but as quickly as I learned her name, it was "Goodbye, Ruby Tuesday."

> *Don't question why she needed to be so free*
> *She'll tell you it's the only way to be*
> *She just can't be chained*
> *To a life where nothing's gained*
> *And nothing's lost*
> *At such a cost.*

Wednesday, January 11th

She was a little too tall and could have used a few more pounds; the black-haired beauty with wide, dark eyes was famous around town for the firm points on her chest. Betty Lou was an open book to most of the local fellows, but she was a mystery to me. She hadn't been out of the county jail three hours when I picked her up on Main Street. We were both restless and bored, so we went to the drive-in where we spent ourselves in the back seat of my car. We used each other, but we both got our share. I woke up alone with frosted windows. I sat upright and started humming a Bob Seger tune. I looked for her in the pool halls downtown, but she was nowhere to be found.

Thursday, January 12th

Lights, camera, action!
Dear Peg,

I have the Polaroid of you hanging above the headboard. I'll always keep the nude photo of you, but I'm leaving you this letter. Last night was a dream come true—you and me starring in our first foreign film. Your big debut had real potential. Too bad your real job interrupted us. Baby, I would have loved to pick up where we left off, but, as they say in the business, have your people call my people.

Tom

Friday, January 13th

There's a new disco in the west part of town, where a girl named Brandy works, laying whiskey down and listening to the lonely hustlers at the bar pass their time talking about their previous scores. A lonely hustler at the bar says, "Brandy, fetch another round," so she promptly pours more whiskey down. Another lonely hustler at the bar says "Brandy, you're a fine girl, what a good wife you would be— yeah, your eyes could steal a true hustler from the game."

But at night after the bar closes down Brandy walks with me through a silent town. In his eyes, Brandy could see the moon fall and rise and she loved to hear the way he told her his faded stories. But the morning comes and she's

still in love with a player who's no longer around, and
Brandy does her best to understand why she likes to hear
him say, "Brandy you're a fine girl, what a good wife you'll
be."

Saturday, January 14th

"My name is Tom. Remember it; you'll be screaming it later."

We pulled in just behind the bridge. Tom, the smooth operator lays her down, and Ling, my China girl says quietly, frowning, "Gee, life's a funny thing. I'm from China and drive a Chrysler, and you drive a Toyota."

"I love to try new things, and I've never been with a Chinese girl," I said, smirking as I looked her over.

"Like what you see?" Ling whispered.

She took my jewelry and my last dollar. I'd have given her anything just to hear her scream, "I want the young American!"

Tuesday, January 31st, 1978

TAYLOR COUNTY HEALTH DEPARTMENT

City of Abilene Health Division   January 27th, 1978
1030 South Sayles Blvd
Abilene, Texas 79607

Thomas Jones
610 Grape St.
Abilene, Texas 79603

Dear Mr. Thomas Jones:

Thank you for your visit to the Taylor County Health Clinic on January 25th. Our office has tried unsuccessfully to reach you several times by phone.

We regret to inform you that you tested positive for a venereal disease. Please contact the clinic as soon as possible. It is also imperative that you contact people with whom you have been intimate, because they, also need to be tested.

Penicillin shots are administered at the city health department Monday – Friday from 8 a.m. to 5 p.m.

The Taylor County Health Department holds our clients' privacy in the highest regard, but the health and welfare of others is also a top priority. If the seven people listed on your form haven't contacted our office by February 15th, then certified letters will be mailed to them.

Names listed: Fanny Wiseman, January 7th; Regina, January 8th; Lola, January 9th; Ruby, January 10th; Betty Lou, January 11th; Peg Steely, January 12th; Brandy, January 13th; and Ling, January 14th.

Dr. Marcus Welby M.D.

Monday, February 6th, 1978

Finch, Hutz, & Mason, Attorneys at Law

Thomas Jones   February 4th, 1978
610 Grape St.
Abilene, Texas 79603

Case: 07854

Dear Mr. Jones,

This letter is to inform you that our client, Jackie Blue, demands that you take a test to determine the paternity of her son, Eric Wayne Blue, born on October 31st, 1977.

The State of Texas has arranged a hearing on the matter in Judge McMichael's courtroom for February 14th in courtroom B-1 of Family Court. You must appear at the K1 service window and submit to a paternity test or surrender your rights under article R-12. If you surrender your rights, Miss Blue will file for child support payments to begin immediately.

Miss Blue is open to discussing custody and visitation arrangements for Eric.

Sincerely,
Perry Mason
Attorney at Law

Wednesday, February 15th, 1978

Dear Son:

Since Reggie's arrest, it's as if you've disappeared. It seems that no one from the Bowie block has seen or heard from you. I'm writing in hopes of reaching you through the mail. I hope you're still living at this address, or that one of your roommates will forward this letter to you.

Losing a football game shouldn't be the most important thing in your life, but your long absence tells a different story.

Uncle Frank was diagnosed with cirrhosis of the liver and is at Hendricks Memorial Hospital. The doctors don't give him much time, so you should visit him soon.

A girl named Pam has called several times looking for you. She says the two of you went to Mexico several months ago, and now she's having your baby. She seems to think that having your baby is a lovely way of showing how much she loves you.

The Watchtower constantly mentions that worldly associations are ruining the youth of our day. The worldly behavior Carol witnessed between you and

Reggie seems to have rubbed off; she has run off to Las Vegas with an airman from the local base.

When you moved out of our house you left behind several issues of *Popular Science*. I happened to glance through an old issue and stumbled across an article about a new invention called a "telephone answering machine." If such a device is invented before Jesus comes back, you should invest in one. Your father and I have both tried to reach you by phone without success many times.

The youth today lives much too fast, but it won't be long now before Jesus returns to save you from imminent ruin. But, Son, could you slow down long enough to call your parents and let them know that you're still alive? Pam would like to speak to you, as well.

By the way, Reggie's mother wants me to ask if you can help come up with the $10,000 bond needed to spring Reggie from jail.

Your mother,

Louise

OBITUARIES

Abilene Reporter   Monday, February 20th, 1978

Frank J. Jones, 44, died on Friday. Services will be at 2:00 p.m. Wednesday at the Kingdom Hall of Jehovah's Witnesses with Pastor Slowley officiating. Burial will be in Bethel Cemetery.

Born May 30, 1933 in Greenville, South Carolina,

Frank was the son of the late Theresa and William Jones. He was a retired U.S. Army veteran of the Vietnam War.

Frank was preceded in death by his parents; a brother, Walter; and a sister, Linda.

Survivors include: his wife, Trudy, and five children: Joe, Derrick, Mallory, Sheila, and Ann.

Family visitation will be from 6:00 p.m. to 7:30 p.m. Tuesday at Elliott Funeral Home.

Tuesday, April 4th, 1978

Dear Tom,

It's been a week since I've laid eyes on you, and I still don't understand why you asked me to move in with you six weeks ago only to disappear so suddenly.

There is no easy way to hear you say, "I'm sorry, but I don't really love you like I thought I did." I long for your company, but I'm always alone, and your apologies won't make it right.

In spite of the fact that our union was marked by a funeral instead of a wedding, I felt as if our happy family had only just begun. The two of us standing as a couple at Frank's funeral made me feel so close to you, and the next two weeks of living with you brought me more joy than I ever dreamed. I was filled with fantasies that we would be just like the Cleavers, but something changed in you in the third week. I'm not really sure, but I think it happened after we left the doctor's office with the ultrasound results. The lines of communication between us seemed to change. Still, as the fourth and fifth weeks passed, I had hoped that we would find a place of our own and grow old together.

The trip to Mexico last July will always be a fond memory, and our little girl will serve as a constant reminder of the consequences for trusting my heart and ignoring the warnings of my mind.

Why and sorry won't make it right this time.

Tom, for the last several weeks, the only company I've had is the television. Just knowing that the time we spend together has become a chore for you makes me see how wrong I was to believe that having your child would be enough to keep us together. You're missing for a reason, and no amount of wishful thinking can convince me this live-in situation is a permanent result of a weak moment in Mexico.

This "Dear-Tom letter" is to tell you that I'm moving back in with my grandmother. She was right; I'm a baby having a baby, and you haven't taken a sober breath since I've known you. I don't have a clue where all this anger in you is coming from. The men on TV are always happy when a girl says that she's having their baby. No one could ever love you more. Is it just that I'm the one? With both of my parents in jail, perhaps I just wanted somebody to hold onto. Now all I want is to end this pain.

It's still so hard to believe that you're not in love with me.

I hope you read this letter and won't toss it in your dresser drawer with all the unopened letters from Reggie.

From the one who loves you,
Pam

P.S.-Who is Jackie Blue, and why does she think you're her baby's father?

BIRTH ANNOUNCEMENTS

Abilene Reporter Monday, April 17th, 1978

ABILENE – Belinda Joyce Scott, 6 lbs. 8 oz. & 22", was born Friday at Hendricks Memorial Hospital to Pamela Greer. Visitation is 9:00 a.m. to 7:30 p.m. at Hendricks Memorial Hospital.

Abilene Reporter Wednesday, April 19th, 1978

POLICE BULLETIN

Abilene police were called to the 2900 block of North Bowie Street yesterday after neighbors reported an engine running for a lengthy time in a closed garage. When police arrived they found an intoxicated 18-year-old behind the wheel. When officers questioned him about the incident, he said it was just a prank gone awry.

Officers noted rags beneath the car and a garden hose in the passenger seat. No further information was available at the time of reporting.

Friday, April 21st, 1978

Hey, Tom,

I am leaving you this note, because yesterday I saw an article in the paper that really caught my interest. Seeing a hose on the passenger seat of your car only added to my suspicions.

Rumor has it that you're living back at your parent's house, but I haven't seen you. Carol says you've been bitching and moaning about your child support situation, but you should have known better. She also mentioned that you had to notify Miss Wiseman to get tested at the clinic. You know, women are not your problem. Nine months ago it was Jackie; this month it's Pam; six years ago it was your mother. For a smart guy, you're still as dumb as the day I met you.

Tom, it's time to grow up. We both know you tried to commit suicide again. It pains me to imagine you're still looking for the easy way out. It's lucky that you didn't know enough to secure the rags around the hose in the tailpipe before you started the engine.

You were raised on the Good Book, but you still can't understand its warning: you reap what you sow. Your perception is still so skewed. You live your life as if you were the last teenager. From one old friend to another: stop making excuses for what you've done with your life and, worse, stop blaming the women in your life for your mistakes. God helps those who help themselves. Tom, grow up, get a job, and start paying your child support!

The world didn't end in 1975, nor when Reggie was arrested. The times are changing; you've still got time to pursue other options. College would be a great start. Also, rumor has it that you haven't been sober in quite awhile. My father went to Alcoholics Anonymous, and it's working for him. Get some help! Whatever happened to that Dr. Scott dude you were seeing when we first met?

Peace.

Your friend,

Laurie

Family Psychiatry
3500 South First Avenue Circle – Suite 200
Abilene, Texas 79607

May 1st, 1978

Thomas Jones
2099 North Bowie St.
Abilene, Texas 79603

Re: Your visit on April 29th, 1978
Client File No: DCO1959

Dear Tom,

It was painful to hear about your botched suicide attempt. As you sat in my office last Tuesday, I couldn't help but reflect on the five years I've known you. It seems there's always been some kind of pain in your life. We've talked about the foolishness of your mother's religion and the bigotry and hypocrisy of teachers, ministers and other authority figures, but now you have the choice to ignore the teachings that disgust you so much. Still, I get the feeling that there is something else under your anger.

I've come to believe you are one of the most intelligent people on the planet, so there is little that I can tell you that you don't already know. My main recommendations are that you give up your drinking and the one-night stands, and stop living as if each day may be the last. People will always be caught up in the myths of the day, but looking for goodness in life doesn't make a person cloudy in his judgment. The sun still shines on man's journey through time. Perhaps it's time for you to let the sun shine in on your life and make that new start. Remember that even the longest journey begins with a single step.

Don't let Spooky scare you to death, tell Swagger to shut up when his advice can only lead to trouble, and let Smoothy take the lead. In my experience, the answer often lies somewhere in the middle. Tom, you're the only person who can stop your pain.

Respectfully yours,
Phil Scott, Ph.D.

Saturday, May 27th, 1978

Dear Pee,

As I rot away in this cell on my 20th birthday, I finally realize what freedom really means. I sit here listening to a worn out song playing on the radio, hardly believing that I can't remember the name of the song, and, in a few years, nobody will remember my name either.

It worries me that I haven't heard from you since my arrest. Lately, I've even resorted to praying that you're not dead or even worse, tucked away in the French Foreign Legion, blaming yourself for my incarceration, but none of the letters I sent have been returned. I keep wondering if I have the wrong address, so this time I decided to send the letter to your parents' house.

Just tell a bitch she's got pretty eyes, compliment her on her hairstyle, promise her you'll marry her, or put Barry White on the stereo, and the next thing you know her pants are below her ankles. Those were the days my friend, and who'd have ever thought I'd end up here? Women are suckers for a compliment, and we sure gave them what they wanted in order to get what we wanted.

Sitting here in this cell with all the time in the world to rest my bones has given me plenty of time to think. I don't blame you at all; the way I see it, our hustle game just got way out of hand, and it's a damn shame that my fate rests in the hands of 12 people who must decide whether Lolita Lovelace or Reggie Thomas is lying. The truth, from what I remember about that night, is that Lolita was just like every other girl who wanted a ride in my car—practically begging for it.

I was only one victory away from fulfilling the hopes and dreams of an entire city, and I'm still one victory away. Some guys here have assumed that I'm guilty before I've even been to court. Others are certain of my innocence, but mostly they wonder if I could have won us the title game. Would the city of Abilene finally have had that elusive championship banner hanging over City Hall?

Tom, there is something to be said about the lack of pressure I feel behind these bars. Just between you and me, I feel less stress about facing my slutty accuser than I felt with the weight of the city's hopes sitting on my shoulders. I'm not the hero the town labeled me as for the last four years; I was a high school kid trying to live up to their expectations.

The hustle game wasn't as easy on me as it looked, either; you just kept coming up with ways to score, pushing me to go even further to win. But it seems so unimportant now that all of my plans revolve around how to get out of jail.

I'm sorry that it didn't turn out like we planned, but at least we had fun while it lasted. Now, like the wine and the songs, the seasons have all gone.

Later,
Reggie

Part VII
AT NINETEEN
One Life to Live

Tuesday, June 13th, 1978

Dear Partner,

> *Our teenage years are a total blast, live them*
> *long because they go so fast.*
> — Thomas L. Jones, Author

Even with communication technology rapidly changing, it took reading your letter to show me how quickly time is slipping away. There was so much I wanted to say to you right after your arrest, but, frankly, I couldn't even pick up the telephone, let alone write a letter. Your arrest left me completely unable to communicate. Seeing it covered on the CBS evening news evoked turmoil in me that I never knew existed. I began 1978 by running from one woman to another, seeking comfort they couldn't give. In the process, I set some new records in the hustle game, only to realize that you weren't around to admire my prowess.

In March, we buried Uncle Frank. The old cliché, "Here today, gone tomorrow," played itself out right before my eyes. I spoke with him in the hospital on Thursday, and the following Monday we were at his graveside. Another death in such a short period of time sent shock waves through my brain; I completely shut down, and lost all positive emotion. Reggie, I was left with only one emotion—anger; my mind turned inside out, and I just lost it. My live-in girlfriend at the time, Pam, couldn't put up with me, so she left with our un-born baby in her belly.

Partner, I was so lost without you. And every other day I found bad news in my mailbox. I had gotten two girls pregnant and was looking to hide my dick in every new woman I met, in order to cover up my fear of in-timacy, but like the song says, "Mercy, mercy me! Things aren't what they used to be."

I am proud to say that I am miles ahead of where I was emotionally just yesterday. Still, I can't testify as to where my mind might take me tomorrow. All I can do is tell you a little bit about what has gone down since you've been behind bars.

Partner, the drinking I did on my last birthday nearly cost me another DWI. Since your incarceration, I've gotten two DWIs. On my last birthday, a cop pulled me over just past 10 a.m. while I was driving the city's mobile-library van. The officer that flagged me down looked me over and said, "Son, you reek of alcohol, and it's not even noon yet. Don't tell me you just had a few beers, because I know intoxication when I see it. I should take your ass straight to jail." But he just handed me back my license and said, "Not many people get pulled over on their birthday, and the unlucky few that do are pretty much just like you—celebrating a little too much, a little too early. It says here you're nineteen today, but you look all of forty-five. Looks like you could use a break. If you'll hand me the keys, I'll drive you home." The police officer looked me in the eye and said, "Tom, congratulations on your last teenage birthday. You teenagers don't realize how fast your twenties will fly by and the responsibilities ahead of you." Then he rambled on about how before the 1850s there was no such thing as "teenagers" as we define the word. Kids either went to work in factories or on family farms, usually before their tenth birthdays, and more often than not they had children of their own by their teens. Most people died before they turned thirty-five; boys often died in horrible wars, and girls died in childbirth.

Like the pebble syndrome, you never know where that small, trivial bit of knowledge planted in your brain will lead you. Well, I slept off the booze and nerve pills that I had taken that morning and woke up two days later, when my mother handed me your letter. Once I became coherent, I sat on the side of my bed reading your letter, and things came properly into focus. That police officer set the pebble syndrome into play in my life. He had unknowingly handed me a piece of history that is still stuck in the back of my mind. I had failed to realize all that has occurred in our generation. The teenagers of our generation have learned more in five years than our parents learned in their whole lives.

As I was reading your letter, it dawned on me that something special is occurring in our time. It's the teenagers in our generation that will forever change the landscape of history. It's more than the sex, drugs, and rock and roll going on in our day. I don't have the foresight of Nostradamus, but I can see the girls burning their bras down in Austin and the boys growing into men faster, big enough to replace the men in the Los Angeles Coliseum sporting arena.

History has always been my favorite subject and I read a lot about how history casts its shadow on modern times. For instance, if the Chinese had never built the Great Wall, Rome might be still standing. When the Mongols discovered that they could not conquer China, they turned their attention westward. I look around at the Bowie block, and suddenly, I see how Mexicans have changed the Texas landscape.

In a million years, if anyone ever reads my diary, he will discover it was all on the tip of my tongue—trying to bring light to the no-longer young, as time laughs in our faces. Which of our African forefathers could have foreseen that you would be one high school football game away from becoming the richest teenager in history? You were primed to become the next football superstar, but somehow we were too busy playing other games to recognize what we had. But all might not be lost; after your trial in November, you're sure to be a free man by Christmas. I think we should sit down and write a book about what transpired. Unbeknownst to our forefathers, all the breeding done to produce the perfect slave ended up producing you, Reggie—a stud with lightning fast reflexes and uncanny speed. With all the stuff you and I went through, it is amazing we weathered the storm. Why didn't the cops arrest Lolita for seducing you? We know how she is, and hopefully the jury will see through her lies so you can be a free man again.

When future generations watch what went on in the 70s on TV, they will see that our only crime was living out the truth of our youth. With all the new worries and freedoms of our time and the threat of nuclear annihilation, we did what anyone would have done—lived our lives to the fullest every single moment.

"Enlightenment" is the new term being thrown around these days by scholars, and the philosophy books teach about theories that our souls may continue to live on in different bodies, paying for mistakes made in previous lifetimes. If this is true, then the real crime is that we have spent so much time unburdening ourselves from the irrational fears of our forefathers and all their scriptural nonsense.

In a thousand years, when another country is built on top of the United States, and the new society seeks to discover what happened to adolescence, they won't need to look any further than our generation. When they read about the rapid changes—everything from the women's movement to the escalating divorce rate to the exportation of the teenager—they'll have to conclude that this was the age of the lost teen age. Hopefully, future societies will still know how to read and will discover my diary buried in the rubble. I hope I've captured what it was like to have lived through this lost teen age.

Only two years have passed since I moved out of my parents' house. Now that I'm temporarily living back there, I'm witnessing just how quickly technology has changed things. An entire society now caters to the desires of teenagers. My sisters have telephones in their bedrooms already, and the motto of today's teenagers seems to be "everything all the time." This may come as a shock, since you know how old fashioned and strict my parents used to be, but the television has become the household God here. There are televisions in Carol's room, my parents' room, and the living room, and my two sisters are glued to the screen all day long. Strangest of all, my mother watches the new 24-hour cable news network. I teased her about gazing into the screen, waiting for news that Jesus is coming back soon.

Even I am having trouble keeping up with the brisk pace and constant change. Sometimes, I get a crazy urge to get in my car and drive away from it all. But then I realize that I could travel 10,000 miles and still be lost in my own mind if I don't keep up.

Brother man, since you've been locked up, it's given me time to think, and lately I've been thinking that I should just stop drinking and maybe give...

Oh, well, enough for now.

Holler back, bro.

Wednesday, June 28th, 1978

Dear Pee,

Here behind bars they say, "A letter from home is a sign you're not alone."

Thanks, Tom. I'm eternally grateful to you for keeping me informed about what's happening on the outside. You once said, "In the future, one's friends will become one's family." How true those words are for me now. You're the closest thing I have to a family. It's been over three months since my mother has written or visited me. And that sports agent, Ruben Patterson, stopped communicating with me the day after the judge set my bond.

I heard a song on the radio that went:

I was thinking about what a
Friend had said and I was hoping it was a lie.

Your last letter caught me off guard. It was amazing to read about the changes at your house. I hated to hear it, though, because lately all I've done is read my Bible, and I'm starting to build an unshakeable faith in Jesus. Some of your letter confused me, though. What were you talking about when you wrote that we might be paying for mistakes made in another lifetime?

The radio remains the most influential thing behind the jailhouse walls. Everyone wishes we had a television to watch. It would sure make the time pass faster. The guards bring a television into the jail for the night shift, and we fight like dogs over whether to watch *Sanford and Son, All in the Family,* or *Charlie's Angels.* In your last letter, you mentioned that there's a new 24-hour news channel. What in the world will they think of next? Maybe, if we'd had all-night television, we wouldn't have stayed out all night so much.

The other night I saw the NBA finals playoff game between the L.A. Lakers and the Philadelphia 76ers. Magic Johnson is something special—he single-handedly won the game for the Lakers. By the way, if you see James, tell him to holla at a brother.

It is so hard to describe what it feels like behind bars. The City of Abilene provides us with a copy of the Sunday paper, but I miss watching sports on TV. Rumor has it that a prisoner is suing for full-time access to television. Hopefully, Jesus will rescue me from this jail, and I won't be in here much longer, so that suit won't affect me. My attorney, Jason Cochran, assures me I'll be a free man after my trial.

Your letters remind me of when we used to hang out at my house, and all you had to complain about was the people who spat in your face as you sold your magazines door to door. When I sit on my bunk reading your letters, I find it amusing how quickly things change. It's ironic to see how our roles have reversed—me finding Jesus in jail and you losing your way on the outside. It also makes me giggle to read about your struggles to find enough money for the two child support payments hanging over your head. So many times I thought about what my life might have been like, if only Jesus had blessed me and Jill with a child. Perhaps I was shooting blanks while we were together. I was always surprised that she never got pregnant. If you ever run into her, please, tell her that my love for her still remains, and perhaps the Lord will bring us together again. I now realize that she may have been the best thing that I ever had.

In your last letter you wrote, "Another death in such a short period of time sent shock waves through my brain." Did I miss something? Who else died?

Is your diary still keeping all of our secrets?

Partners for life,

Reggie

Friday, July 7th, 1978

Dear Partner,

It's always great to hear from you. Your last letter reminded me of a song playing on the radio these days, which goes:

> *You saved your own special friends*
> *'Cause here you need something to hide them in*
> *And you stay inside that foolish grin*
> *When everyday now secrets end*
> *Oh and then again*
> *Years may go by*

Mario recently told me that he ran into you when he was arrested for possession of marijuana. You and Jill will always remain my own special friends, and your secrets are locked up tight in my diary, but someday we should sit down and talk about some things. Until then, please, don't ask. Things happened so fast, and life-changing decisions had to be made on a moment's notice. None of us knew the costs and consequences of our actions. Now that I'm older and a lot wiser, I know you had a right to know some of Jill's secrets, because they were your secrets, too, but as Jill always said, "We always want what we can't have." After all, her decision involved your child, too. Let's leave it at that, and one day soon we'll set aside a moment to talk.

By the way, Jill was sent to a fancy drug rehab center in Dallas by her father, and your one-night stand with Kelly is still safe from Jill's ears.

Let he that is without sin cast the first stone.

Your pee,
Tom

SPORTS SECTION

Abilene Reporter   Friday, July 14th, 1978

Portland, Ore. – James Smith from Abilene, Texas was the 29th pick in the NBA draft and signed with the Dallas Mavericks. At eighteen, Smith is the youngest player ever chosen in the NBA draft.

Dallas Mavericks President of Operations, Frank Cuban said, "James has plenty of talent and potential, but he won't be a starter for the Mavericks anytime soon."

Converse, Cuban's athletic shoe company, plans to market a new shoe around Smith. Cuban said attracting younger customers to his brand is essential in a market climate where everything is geared towards the growing younger market.

Walter Cronkite College of Journalism
Housing, Dining & Employment Services
75 Hallett St.
Dallas, Texas 73003   July 18th, 1978

Thomas Jones
2099 North Bowie St.
Abilene, Texas 79603

Dear Mr. Jones,

Congratulations on your acceptance to the Walter Cronkite College, School of Journalism, for the fall semester of 1978. Enclosed in this letter is information to help you reserve accommodations in the residence hall on campus.

All freshmen are required to live on campus for two academic semesters. Additional information on the college's Freshmen Rules book may be obtained by contacting the Freshmen Center on campus.

Your application for the librarian assistant position has been approved. Your start date at the Walter Cronkite College Library is August 21st.

If you have any questions about enrollment, please contact the Freshmen Center at (617) 735- 9191 for assistance.

Sincerely,
George Sparks
Housing, Dining, & Employment Services

Finch, Hutz & Mason, Attorneys at Law

Thomas Jones   July 24th, 1978
2099 North Bowie Street
Abilene, Texas 79603

Case: 07854

Dear Mr. Jones,

Your paternity results for Eric Wayne Blue were negative, and Jackie Blue hereby absolves you of any and all parental responsibility for her child.

The State of Texas has also officially released you from all parental obligations as of July 21st. Any further questions on this matter should be in writing and addressed to the Division of Child Support.

We sincerely apologize for any inconvenience this matter may have caused.

Sincerely,
Perry Mason
Attorney at Law

Saturday, August 19th, 1978

Dear Reggie,

I feel born again in the summer of my twentieth year. I finally feel at home in my head like never before. I've left my past behind me, and you might say I've found the keys to open every door.

July kept my head and heart spinning with each new letter, but we live in a world where everything is possible. In a single month, I've seen James go from school-yard legend to having his own signature shoe. And you're now reading a letter from the newest member of the Walter Cronkite College, School of Journalism. Yes, my friend, in two days I'll be living in Dallas and studying my way to a future filled with possibilities. And check this out! Modern technology cleared me of my child support obligation for Jackie Blue's baby by proving I'm not the father, thereby cutting my child-support payments in half.

Pam, my baby's mama, dropped Belinda off at my parents' house for them to babysit two weeks ago. It was the first time I'd ever laid eyes on my baby girl. Abruptly, Laurie's words—"The women in your life aren't your problem"—rang true. Belinda's tiny hand in mine melted my heart, and I suddenly saw my life before everything got so crazy—the way it used to be, and I realized that I had begun a relationship with my daughter long ago. Suddenly, there is so much time to make up everywhere I turn—time that I wasted away I now realize I only stole from myself.

Love,
Tom

Tuesday, October 10th, 1978

Dear Tom,

I can't wait to see your baby girl as soon as I get out. It gave me goosebumps to read about the joy you describe and your feelings for the new bundle of joy in your life. Sadness mixed with my joy, knowing Jill and I could have had that same joy, if not for an on-the-spot decision; but never blame yourself, and never let anyone tell you that secrets are enough to keep true friends from being true friends.

I know all you ever dreamed of was being a famous sports agent. But now I imagine you writing at your desk, looking so grown-up and impressive. One day, you'll write a poem for your daughter that will take her breath away.

Everyone knows I dreamed of being a famous quarterback, a real superstar with dream girls at my beck and call. But I guess my dream is on hold until I win this trial. With my trial date looming, I spend a lot of time with my attorney these days. He assures me that the case will come down to the word of a star quarterback or a promiscuous white girl. The closer my trial date comes, the more fear I feel, especially after all the times we lucked out in our teens. Just the other day, I was reading from the Gospels: "The people in those days chased a brand new star, ever towards the west. They crossed the mountains far and wide, but when they came to rest they could hardly believe their eyes. The miracle they sought was nothing but a child."

Tom, where do those broken dreams go, and why can't we all just be children again for awhile?

God bless,
Reggie

Monday, November 27th, 1978

Dear Reggie,

Life, they say, is like playing baseball: Be sure to round the bases and whenever possible steal home plate.

The road ahead shows that we've only just begun, and the secrets of the universe whisper in our ears, teaching us, with each new day, to leave the world outside the apartment door. Gina and I walk hand in hand around campus, openly displaying our affection for one another. Others seem to envy us. I overheard one woman say, "They have a lovers' glow," as she pointed toward us. Suddenly, Reggie, I find myself planning the rest of my life around this young woman with a Spanish surname, and I'm not concerned in the least about what society says. I wish I could tell you exactly where it all started, but I can't really remember; one day Gina was just there. She's a 23-year-old senior with a seductive foreign accent, and she refers to me as her "sweet pea."

When I was seventeen, I dreamed of having a queen, a woman composed of every admirable quality. My dream has come true, and I gave my queen a diamond ring.

I heard my mother bragging to Gina on the phone that she and my father had only known one another for three or four months before they got married, and they're celebrating their 20th anniversary. She also remarked about the 50% divorce rate and said she was surprised that I would ask any woman to marry me. I've been surreptitiously living off campus at Gina's place since the second week of classes. What began as two people sitting next to each other in World Religion class discussing the origins of man has turned into a life-long conversation. Living off campus has also enabled me to see Belinda on weekends and this past Thanksgiving.

Gina asked to read my old diaries, so she can learn more about me. You know as much about me as anyone. I'm asking you, fellow Gemini, should I let my future wife read about my teenage years?

It's funny how life works out. Gina has been heart-broken all her life because doctors say she can't have children. Having Belinda utter her first words in front of Gina was one of the most magical moments we ever shared.

Two months ago, if someone would have told me that my life would include electric bills, diapers, and the woman of my dreams, I would have said, "No way." But the times, they are a changin'.

Remember Thomas Medlock? We both know he was gay from the beginning, but remember my ex-room-mate, Slick? He could have had (and did) any woman he wanted, so why did he choose Thomas Medlock? That's right; you read it here first. I saw Slick and Thomas in a lovers' embrace not long ago when I was in Abilene. Reggie, I swear there's a third sex emerging. Take Boy George—a make-up wearing, limp-wristed singer, but he's the hottest thing on television these days, and the truth is, at first glance, I couldn't tell if he was a boy or a girl. It's as if no one knows who they want to be now that society has given them a choice.

On another note, you aren't missing a thing; the more things change, the more they stay the same. I noticed when I was reading one of my old diaries that, in 1973, Howard Medlock's step-father's chief complaint was that so many white people were moving away to escape the black families that had moved in. Well, nothing's changed but the skin color of the complainants. I was back home the other weekend, and Leonard had put his house up for sale, because, and I quote, "One-too-many Mexican families have moved into the neighborhood."

Partner, with you stuck in jail, I hate to drop this bombshell on you, but I don't want you to hear it from someone else. The other night, Gina and I double dated with Jill Andersen and James Smith here in Dallas. We went to a Maverick's game where James is a bench warmer on the team. Isn't it ironic how the pebble syndrome came into play in our lives to land us all in the same city? J.R.'s decision to send Jill to a rehabilitation center in Dallas two years ago resulted in her taking up permanent residence here. Then, James was drafted to the Mavericks, and my dream of becoming a writer landed me at Walter Cronkite College. Who would have ever thought that our fragmented paths would bring us all together under the big-city lights of Dallas? Then, James, who tried so hard to be black, ends up with Jill, who swore she'd never date a white guy. Jill is working part time as a guidance counselor at a local Planned Parenthood clinic on the upper west side. She's also studying to be an X-ray technician. James said the team pays him $12,000 a week just to sit on the bench. Guess who picked up the tab!

With the world so mixed-up, I've begun asking myself, "What in the hell am I supposed to teach my daughter about these changing times?" I must sound like my parents so many years ago, when they were trying to keep up in our ever-changing world. Fortunately, I have this warm 24-year-old woman to help me through the murkiness of a world that gets cloudier with each new channel on cable.

I have to go, but don't worry. On December 6th, Gina and I will be in court to support you. We both hope and pray that things go your way.

Later,
Tom

Monday, December 4th, 1978

Dear Tom,

It was great to hear about the folks back home. I'm glad somebody still enjoys weekends at home. It sounds like Gina is quite a find. You asked me if I thought it was a good idea to let her read your old diaries, and I have to say that I don't think it's a good idea. Trust me on this one, Pee.

It's great to hear about you having a kid in the house and a family on your mind. When you wrote that Belinda had spoken her first words at only six months I wasn't surprised. You were born with the gift of gab, and like father, like daughter.

In spite of my history with Jill, I was happy to hear that she is happy with James and focusing on her future. You tell that brother, James, that I always knew he'd get her if he persisted. And tell Jill her philosophy was wrong: Sometimes you can have what you want.

I'm extremely nervous about my trial. The prosecution is talking about DNA evidence. What the hell is DNA?! My attorney says for me not to worry, but frankly, I'm scared to death. Technology changes so fast. Damn, Tom, I miss being a free man. Sometimes, I close my eyes and pretend I hear your car pulling up in the driveway as I'm in bed at home. I remember how we set our sights on the evening and didn't come home until dawn. Then a guard taps on my cell door, and the moment's gone. We had it made, and we didn't even realize it. I'll never forget those days.

Later,
Reggie

December 6th, 1978

HEADLINES

Abilene Reporter-News

The long awaited trial of former Eagles quarterback Reggie Thomas is set to begin today after several weeks of delay. But this event has turned into a trial of the justice system, which some say is biased against women and others say is unfair to men.

Thomas is accused of sexually molesting 14-year-old Lolita Lovelace on December 31st, 1977. Lovelace, now fifteen, is set to testify in a trial of black versus white and male versus female. This will also be the first trial in Abilene to utilize DNA evidence. Many of the town's residents blame Lovelace for the Abilene High School's loss in the state football finals.

The scrutiny she has been under since Thomas' arrest is enormous. There are reports that her father was fired from his meatpacking job at Swift's plant days after the arrest after serving there for 22 years. A spokesman from Swift said the quarterback's arrest had nothing to do with Mr. Lovelace's firing, but other long-time employees think otherwise. Candi Lovelace, Lolita's mother, will also testify. She claims her car has been vandalized on several occasions since Thomas' arrest.

Flamboyant local attorney, Jason Cochran, will attempt to persuade jurors that Lovelace seduced Thomas and that there was no forced sex between them.

Assistant District Attorney Marsh Lark plans to introduce DNA evidence, which is a new method of identifying criminals. Like fingerprints, DNA is unique to each individual, and it can be found in blood, other bodily fluids, and body tissues. DNA was analyzed from Lovelace's underwear, which was found in the back seat of the Trans Am Thomas was driving when he was arrested.

Lark told reporters, "Reggie Thomas fumbled the ball on this one. This key piece of evidence could be the difference between first and ten and fourth and long for him."

December 11th, 1978

Abilene Reporter-News

Abilene, Texas — Reggie Thomas was found guilty of child molestation and has been sentenced to eight years in the Texas State Penitentiary. His prison term begins January 11th, 1979, and will be served in the medium-security correctional facility at Huntsville, Texas. Upon completion of his sentence, Thomas must undergo a treatment program dealing with sex offenders.

Judge Eli W. Walker of the 8th Judicial District Court awarded Thomas 18 months of time served.

Thomas will be 28 at the time of his release, almost certainly eliminating any chances of a professional football career.

Saturday, January 6th, 1979

CITY BEAT SECTION
POLICE & FIRE BLOTTER

Abilene Reporter-News

Burglary – 1300 block of North Pioneer Drive,
Thursday:

Unknown persons made entry into a local church by breaking a rear window. Once inside, the suspects took candy and an undisclosed amount of cash before attempting to make entry into an area with an alarm. The suspects then fled the scene before police arrived.

Theft – 800 block of Ogden Place, Thursday:

A trimmer was stolen from the bed of a man's pickup. Later, the Abilene Police received a call reporting an illegal electricity connection in the 1300 block of Andy Street. The suspects had apparently connected directly into the power line and, in doing so, they bypassed the meter and diverted the power directly to their own residence. While in the home, officers found a woman who was allegedly in possession of a marijuana plant. She was arrested and transported to Taylor County Jail.

Assault – 1400 block of Tumbleweed Road, Tuesday:

A woman reported that a young, intoxicated, teenage girl bumped into her car in the parking lot of Mel's Diner. The young female ripped the victim's glasses off and slapped her face. When the woman threatened to call the police, the suspect drove off in a white Pontiac Grand Prix. The victim said the teenager looked familiar, but couldn't quite remember where she had seen her before.

Saturday, January 6th, 1979

Abilene Reporter-News

WEDDINGS AND ENGAGEMENTS

LANE-GORDON

Fred and Lynn Lane of Abilene, Texas are pleased to announce the engagement of their daughter, Laurie Marie Lane to Jeff Clark Kent, son of Richard and Sue Kent of Abilene, Texas. Miss Lane is a 1977 graduate of Abilene High School and presently attends Abilene Christian University, where she majors in counseling and minors in elementary education. Jeff Kent graduated from Abilene High School in 1976 and is presently employed at Goodyear Automotive as a machinist. Family and friends are invited to an outdoor wedding at Rose Park on Sunday, June 10th, 1979.

Monday, January 8th, 1979

GINA'S FIRST LETTER TO TOM

Dear Sweet Pea,

By now you must have found that I've had the locks changed. I've spent the past three weekes at my parents' house in San Antonio trying to figure out how I could have ever fallen in love with you. After I began reading your diaries, it became clear that either I've been blind or you've been deliberately deceiving me.

Collateral damage?! Tom, those people, as poor as they were, had souls just like you and I do. It's clear that you have neither a conscience nor a heart, or you could never have referred to those poor, desperate people as if they were flies, casually splattered on your windshield. Even Frank was wrong to carpet bomb during the war, no matter whose side he was fighting for.

You must be a monster, and I never want to see you again.

Gina

Monday, January 22nd, 1979

TOM'S FIRST LETTER BACK TO GINA

Dear Gina,

Hello, it's me, Tom, the monster.

Gina, those trips to the border were years ago, and it

all started out innocently enough. What happened to those five men was totally an accident. I see now that by using "collateral damage" to describe a human being was a bit cold. But our government uses those words to explain away war disasters all the time, and I didn't know any better.

I was wrong. It was wrong. But believe me, I've learned from my mistakes. Gina, please, look at the whole picture! I'm not a monster. I was just a boy caught up in the craziness of the world around me. I had been disillusioned in my spiritual life, and I didn't believe in anything anymore. I've changed. Believe me.

Yours eternally,
Tom

Thursday, February 15th, 1979

GINA'S SECOND LETTER TO TOM

To Tom, my former sweet pea:

It seems to me that the more I read about you the more horrified I become. I read as far as January 1978 but could not bring myself to read any further. How could you and Reggie have believed that tricking women into one-night stands was an acceptable way to treat women? And worse, you describe that disgusting game as love.

I know, the times are changing and neither the boys nor girls quite understand their roles anymore, but the man I want to marry knows how to treat a lady. Sex is not a game leading to a grand prize; it's a gift between people in love. I know that the advertising motto is, "Sex sells," but I never believed you bought into that rap. Now I wish I didn't know. My heart tells me that you're not really like that. After all, you even asked for my hand in marriage in an old-fashioned way. But, in these changing times, a girl can't completely trust her intuition, because we're quickly learning that boys play games that we aren't hip to yet, that players only love you when they're playing.

I enjoyed reading about your "pebble syndrome" theory. You're certainly a bright guy with a bright future. At times, I wonder why that small pebble started our relationship rolling eight months ago. Please, tell Laurie and Jeff that I wish them the best in life. I used to think that we were as lucky as they are, but I now see that I should have gotten to know you better before I lost my heart. It seems I didn't know you at all.

I hope you've noticed that women are neither the game nor the prize.

Sincerely,

Gina

Saturday, March 10th, 1979

TOM'S SECOND LETTER TO GINA

Dear Gina,

In the Old Testament, Abraham said God told him to kill his son, Isaac, but none of the people around Abraham heard this voice from God. You asked how Reggie and I could have had such ridiculous beliefs? In today's society, if Abraham had said God told him to cut Isaac's throat, I guarantee he would not be the father of three great religions.

How does anyone come to a certain belief? I don't know. What I do know is that, not seeing you for the past two months, I realize just how much you mean to me and just what effect a person's history has. But, Gina, I can't change my past. I've only got the future to look forward to, and I'd give anything to have you in it. I know the devil didn't make me do the things that I did, and God certainly didn't, either. I know I'm to blame, but I can't help feeling sorry for myself because you're no longer beside me.

Our friends ask me about you every day. I say you're doing fine, and I expect to hear from you soon, but they know that I'm dying inside without you. I'm sorry for what you read about me. I'm sure it was hard for you, but nothing can be more painful than my life without you.

You have taught me so much. You showed me that re-ligion and rituals are not the only way mankind expresses their love for the Gods. I only wish you had kept reading, so that you could see how I've changed. With you, I learned to read between the lines in the Bible and how to forgive my mother and her church for their ignorance and the pain it caused me. I now see that a person is made up of a collection of life's events, and she did the best she could. The same beliefs that hurt me help her.

Gina, please, keep reading. I know I don't deserve it, but I'm begging for another chance. You were the one who taught me that different beliefs work for different people, and that understanding and forgiveness are the only real answers in this life.

Still yours,
Tom

Tuesday, April 10th, 1979

TOM'S THIRD LETTER TO GINA

Dear Gina,

I found an old 1976 football photo of Reggie holding his MVP trophy after our victory over the Cooper Cougars. Before meeting you, Gina, I thought that those Friday-night games were the most glorious days of my life. The pep rallies and bathing in school spirit all day led to a wonderful night. But, Gina, those Friday-night heroics couldn't compare to the joy you brought me over the three months we lived together.

It's devastating what happened to my pee and me in such a short time. I think to myself, "If Ruben Patterson hadn't given Reggie a Trans Am, perhaps he wouldn't have thought that scoring in our game was worth losing eight years of his life."

But, Honey, that's neither here nor there. I miss you and I keep asking the same questions time after time: "What's it all about? Is it only for the moment that we live? Are we meant to take more than we give? Does life belong only to the strong?"

I visited my parents this past weekend, and thought about how much things have changed there. Four years ago, our parents were taking care of us, and now I see Laurie dropping her father off at AA. My father quit smoking, and my mother is studying to be a nurse at the local community college.

Pam kept our daughter Saturday night, so I cruised the old clubs where Reggie and I used to hang out. The DJ in one club was playing a new sound called Rap and Punk music. This new stuff is all the rage, and one club is now alcohol-free and caters to a younger crowd. They call it a teen club, but I didn't see anyone there who resembled the teenagers I grew up with. Too much make-up and not enough clothes on those bodies reminded me that the age of innocence is over everywhere. Hell, you couldn't tell if the girls were 12 or 20. And I hate the new music, too; you can't tell what the artists are singing about. Wow, listen to me sounding so much like my father. Strangest of all, I couldn't get in because I'm only two months shy of being 20, and this club only caters to the teen set.

In the three months without you, I've had time to reflect on some stuff I wrote in my diary. One particular event that shaped my world was the night Cousin Joe hit Laurie's father with that whiskey bottle. I remember the police officer telling me that Joe was being arrested on assault charges and that Joe's violent behavior was probably caused by smoking marijuana. I convinced myself that I would never smoke marijuana. Years later, when I finally tried it, I distinctly remember thinking that I had been lied to—marijuana made me feel calmer than I'd ever felt. But my disillusionment with authority didn't really begin there. I had already been lied to by my church, my parents, and a priest. I'd seen James' cousin married off to a pervert. I had so much anger in me.

I realize now that all that anger just evaporated when I met you. Just gazing up at the stars with you was enough to make me forget this whole messed up world. Remember the first time someone called you "my old lady" as we passed a joint around? I ask you, how long are you going to stay away? What about all our dreams? Are they just distant memories for you now? The days seem so long without you, and my nights are eternities. Wanting it all was one of the reasons I went for it all at a young age—the car, the money, the crib. There was no tomorrow; today was the only thing that counted. And today, I want to be with you, no matter what it takes. Just tell me what I have to do.

Love,
Tom

Thursday, May 17th, 1979

Fax that Tom sends Gina:

"Return to sender. No such person at this address," was the worst news that the mail carrier could have delivered to me. Communication is the key to every relationship, so this is a last ditch attempt to keep our relationship alive. I hope this reaches you at Manpower. People are starting to talk about new technology replacing human beings. I beg to disagree; technology is just a tool, and I hope this fax will convince you to change your mind about me. Without you, I feel incomplete. I was really lucky to find the one person who heals my soul. Gina, please, read on. After you finish reading, if I'm still not the person you want to spend the rest of your life with, I will respect your wishes.

Love Always,
Tom

GINA'S EMAIL TO TOM

From: Gina Sanchez (GinaSanchez@manpower.com)

Sent: Thurs 05/24/79 11:17 PM

To: Thomas Jones (ThomasJones@waltercronkitecollege.com)

Tom, I've been so busy studying for final exams that I could barely breathe. I was so disturbed by reading your diary that I moved away from our apartment without leaving a forwarding address, but now I see you in a different light. I took your advice and read the rest of your diary. Reading the last half, I found that you learned a lot in a very short period of time. Growing up with your mother's extreme beliefs must have been quite disturbing. But you learned a lot from your friends and the exchange students you met. If you're a Buddhist, you may believe that your pebble syndrome began in another lifetime. Christians believe the pebble syndrome starts at conception. I understand the phrase, "What God has brought together let no one tear apart." The universe brought us together for a reason. For better or worse, Tom, I'm yours. I've wasted too much time away from you, and we have a long future together to talk about the poems, prayers, and promises.

Tom, I hope this brand new way of communicating finds its way to you. They call it email, and I've sent it to your in-box at the Walter Cronkite library system emailing address, because I know you, like everyone else I know, can't afford a computer yet. I sent this correspondence to you by way of email at your place of employment because emailing is supposed to be technology's fastest way of communicating. The communication world is moving at light speed. As the song goes, "Video killed the radio star." Cassettes will replace 8-track players in new cars. I wonder if that will change society as much as FM radio changed things in our adolescence. FM really brought cultures closer together and made music a key ingredient in social change. Look ahead and you will see that video is changing the scene as well, and there are more changes to come. There are already rumors that television and video will eventually put print media out of business.

Tom, I'll be most happy to attend Laurie's and Jeff's wedding with you on June 10th. There'll be so much cause for celebration, knowing that June 10th is also your 20th birthday, and the first official day after your teen years. I can't wait to see Belinda again, and maybe I'll be lucky enough to catch the bouquet, so you and I can start planning our life together.

See you soon,
Gina

Thursday, June 7th, 1979

Dear Tom,

It's been almost seven years since your family dropped me off at the airport. Everything comes full circle, after all. I hear you've got a child of your own, and Louise tells me you're enrolled in a journalism school in Dallas. I guess your first diary was the right gift, and journalism school sounds like a perfect fit for you. When you combine your penchant for writing with your curiosity about events around you, it makes perfect sense for you to be a journalist.

Your grandfather always used to say, "The eyes are always searching for something they've never seen." Now that you've got a few years under your belt and you're a father, I hope you see your mother wasn't so terrible after all. I know it must have been hard for you and your siblings growing up without holidays under such a strict code of dogma, but, as time goes on, we see that what works for some folks doesn't necessarily work for others; no one can live another man's life. And since your mother became a Jehovah's Witness she hasn't been in a straight jacket again.

Your brother, Mike, and I recently had dinner at my house in New York. Who would have ever thought that radical Mike would be a Sergeant in the Air Force? He told me that you really struggled when the doomsday prediction didn't come true. Tom, I hope you've gotten past it and put it all behind you. As we look back, there are things we all wish we could have changed, but hindsight is always 20/20, and forgiveness for ourselves and for others is the only way to walk away clean. Don't bother your mind with the trivial numbers game that Christians and scientists like to argue about, because there's not a soul on earth who really knows.

Anyway, my flight from New York will be arriving at Andersen Airport at 2 p.m. June 10th, and you'd best not be late picking me up. I know that's your birthday, but you can party with the girls after you've dropped me off at your mother's house. One day, your mother tells me about a girl named Pam, and the next time I talk to her it's Gina. I'm still an old-fashioned gal, but you modern kids can do whatever turns you on. I can't wait to meet my grandniece.

Love,

Aunt Frances

Monday, June 11th, 1979

LOCAL EVENTS

Abilene Reporter-News

Two teens dead after two-car crash on State Road 66

Two people died after a head-on collision on Airport Road 66 yesterday afternoon. Lolita Lovelace, 15, was taken into custody at the scene. She was apparently out joyriding in a Pontiac Grand Prix near an abandoned air strip known as a frequent teen drinking hangout. The girl had a learner's permit from Abilene High School, a spokesman for the Texas Department of Safety said.

Witnesses said the girl was traveling northbound on 66 and crossed the center line, striking a southbound Toyota, killing Thomas Jones, 20, instantly. Later, his passenger, Pam Greer, 17, was pronounced dead at a local trauma center.

DPS spokesman, E.F. Hutton, said there is suspicion that Lovelace was intoxicated. Bottles were found in the Pontiac and she smelled of alcohol. Lovelace was the complainant in the case of former star high school quarterback Reggie Thomas, who was convicted on child molestation charges last November.

Another witness said Lovelace may also have had a connection to Thomas Jones. The witness said Lovelace repeatedly apologized to Jones by name before police led her away.

No charges have been filed pending blood tests, which are required by state law for all automobile accidents that involve a fatality.

According to public record, this was Lovelace's second driving offense. No speed estimates were available on Sunday, but the road was dry and the weather was clear according to DPS.

The incident remains under investigation.

Tuesday, June 12th, 1979

OBITUARIES

Abilene Reporter-News

Thomas L. Jones, born on June 10, 1959, in Boston Massachusetts, died on Sunday several hours before his to be 20th birthday. Services will be held at 2 p.m. Wednesday at the Kingdom Hall of Jehovah's Witnesses with Pastor Slowley or Pastor Duncan officiating. Burial will be in Bethel Cemetery. Thomas was the son of Larry and Louise Jones. The family moved to Abilene from Okinawa, Japan in 1970. Jones was attending Walter Cronkite College of Journalism in Dallas, Texas. Survivors include his siblings, Mike, Carol, Gayle, and Kim; and his daughter, Belinda. Family visitation will be from 5 p.m. to 7:30 p.m. Saturday at Elliott Funeral Home.

Pam Greer, 17, died on Sunday at a local trauma center. Funeral services will be held at 3 p.m. Sunday at Hamlin Baptist Chapel of Faith, with Reverend Howard Medlock officiating. The family will receive friends at a visitation from 3 to 5 p.m. Saturday at the funeral home. Born August 28, 1961, in Brownwood, Texas to Wayne and Cora Greer, Pam attended Abilene High School. Greer lived in Breckenridge for a short time before moving to Abilene in 1968. Survivors include her parents, Wayne and Cora; her grandmother, Etta Mae; and her daughter, Belinda.

Tuesday, June 26, 1979

PUBLIC RECORDS

Abilene Reporter-News

Adoption papers filed by Gina Sanchez for custody of Belinda J. Greer.

Monday, December 31st, 1979

Gemini, June 10
The highway of life provides many roads to choose from. If you choose to joyride, look before you leap; one false move could prove devastating. On the other hand, when one road ends, another road begins.

I picked up Tom's diary, which had been given to me after his tragic death. Reluctantly, after six months, I have decided to close it out for him. Tom's horoscope for his birthday echoes hauntingly in my mind. I will take my cue from the universe by opening up another avenue for the child that Tom and Pam left behind.

June 10th, 1979, should have been a day of celebrations and reunions. Instead, we buried Tom a few days later, on a small plot not far from Pam. Lolita Lovelace goes on trial next month for murder. Her attorney has filed a motion to reduce the charges to vehicular manslaughter instead of murder. I think murder is more fitting, as she took the man I loved away from me when she chose to drink and drive. But I know that is just my pain and anger speaking. All of our plans, the life Tom and I were so proud to embark upon, vanished that sunny afternoon, and, even after six months, I can hardly hear his name mentioned without breaking down into tears.

Since Tom's death I've had a chance to reflect on my life, Tom's life, Pam's life—everything, trying to make sense of the events and what it could mean, and how this could possibly be part of the universal plan, but I'm still confused. "It's life's illusion I recall; I really don't know life at all." The day we met, Tom told me I was the first person he had met who believed in God but didn't have a religion. Now, I'm not sure what I believe.

Still, I'm grateful for Belinda, so I haven't lost all faith. Tom's pebble syndrome has come to fruition in my life. Belinda will be my daughter as soon as the Taylor County

Courthouse clears the adoption papers. I couldn't bear to see Belinda stuck in a foster home or living with Pam's elderly grandmother.

Young people didn't used to live a life of privilege, fun and frivolity, like Tom and I did in our teens. Who can say which is better? If teens today weren't so reckless and carefree, maybe Tom would still be alive. On the other hand, he might not have become the man I fell in love with, and I wouldn't have this beautiful little girl to love and be loved by.

All ages are defined by what they leave behind. History allows us to figure out for ourselves what the universe is trying to teach us. This age leaves in its wake a bevy of communication tools—transistor radios, telephones, fax machines, calculators, computers and letters. But, if history teaches us anything, it's that often it's the slaves who become the masters, so don't say we haven't been warned.

It's only human to wonder where our pebble syndrome starts with every relationship. Even as I see the way I must go now, I still wish I had known then what I know now—perhaps I would have spent more time with Tom. I sit here on the last day of this decade with Belinda sleeping beside me. I can hear the fireworks celebrating the beginning of a new era.

Gina Sanchez

WHERE ARE THEY NOW?

Jill Andersen married a black blues musician. They have a daughter.

James Smith played in the NBA for three years and later became a high school coach.

Reggie Thomas was released in 1982 and is now serving a second prison term for child molestation.

Laurie Lane Clark is a guidance counselor at Abilene High School.

Jeff Clark owns a local junk yard.

Larry Jones took early retirement from his second job and enjoys his third grandbaby.

Louise Jones is a part-time nurse and a full-time pioneer for the JWs.

Mike Jones was kicked out of the Air Force and now works in the music industry.

Carol Jones Carter is divorced from an Airman and has married a second time to another Airman. They live in Las Vegas with their two kids.

Lolita Lovelace was convicted of manslaughter and released after three years in a juvenile facility.

Mario Rodriquez is married with six kids and owns his own body-shop business.

Fred Lane is celebrating his 12th year of sobriety.